The Continent Of St. Louis
The Search For Answers

J. L. Reynolds

authorHOUSE®

AuthorHouse™
1663 Liberty Drive, Suite 200
Bloomington, IN 47403
www.authorhouse.com
Phone: 1-800-839-8640

© *2009 J. L. Reynolds. All rights reserved.*

No part of this book may be reproduced, stored in a retrieval system, or transmitted by any means without the written permission of the author.

First published by AuthorHouse 7/10/2009

ISBN: 978-1-4389-5625-1 (sc)
ISBN: 978-1-4389-5626-8 (hc)

Library of Congress Control Number: 2009903610

Printed in the United States of America
Bloomington, Indiana

This book is printed on acid-free paper.

DISCLAIMER

With the exceptions of public figures, all characters
and events in this book are fictitious.
Any resemblance of fictitious characters
to persons living or dead is purely coincidental.

All fictitious characters in this book
are the sole properties of, J. L. Reynolds.
No reproduction or publishing of this book in any form
will be allowed without the express written
permission of, J. L. Reynolds.

DEDICATION

This, my second novel, is dedicated to my beautiful wife Donna.
I thank her for her help, support and encouragement,
as I continue with this story.

ACKNOWLEDGEMENT

I wish to again thank Kelly Carter for her creative artwork
in designing the dust jacket for this and previous books.

Kelly's other work can be seen at www.madspiderstudio.com

FORWARD

SEPTEMBER 22, 2009

VINCE DAVIS HAD COME a long way since he had taken over as Director of Seismology at the UCSD offices in San Diego. His job had gone smoothly and without incident, until the fateful morning of August 18th, 2009.

First, had come the destruction of San Diego, then California, the West Coast, then the world. For most, there had been no escape, but Vince had been rescued by the military and was chosen to lead a secret group of seismologist looking for a way to get a handle on the escalating disaster.

He had failed to find a way to cope with the disaster, but in trying, had discovered a plot by sinister military and government officials to hide the truth of the impending disaster from the world.

Escaping the government treachery, he and a few allies were forced to find their own way. In the end, he and his group had survived the disaster and were attempting to start a new life on an outcropping of land, which had once been the City of St. Louis.

Vince claimed all of that had happened in 2009, but in reality, had it?

AUGUST 28, 2005

VINCE HAD BEEN CONFINED to the Gifford Mental Health Center in San Diego, for claiming he had lived through a disaster that had destroyed California and the world in 2009. What happened next would be a test of his sanity, in a world where no one would believe his story, and where nothing was going to be the same for him, or anyone else.

That was now his situation, and his reality.

PROLOGUE

GIFFORD MENTAL HOSPITAL...AUGUST 25, 2005

THE SUN ROSE BRIGHTLY through the window of room 1122 at the Gifford Mental Health Center in San Diego. It was another beautiful Southern California morning in late August and another uncertain day for the patient in room 1122 to face. The patient was Dr. Vince Davis. He was the Assistant Director of the Seismology Center at UCSD, in San Diego.

Before being committed, Vince had appeared to be a dedicated, hard working young man of thirty years, and had been very involved in his work at the Seismic Center. All that changed for Vince, in the early morning hours of August 18th, 2005, when his phone rang at three a.m. that morning and awakened him from sleep. The call was from his boss, Dr. Wilson Leyland, the Director of the Seismic Center.

Dr. Leyland's call, was a request for Vince's help, studying and analyzing, newly discovered seismic activity that was taking place in the Salton Sea area of California.

After speaking to Vince briefly, Dr. Leyland had been astonished and confused by, Vince's behavior and responses. The man he had spoken with, had not seemed to be the, Vince Davis, he knew and worked with. Instead, he was argumentative, and seemed disconnected from his usual, inquisitive personality. His odd and unusual behavior had led Dr.

Leyland, to believe he was not speaking with, Vince Davis, at all. After hanging up, Dr. Leyland had thought over what the person, who had identified himself as Vince, had said and asked. None of it had made any sense. Vince, would have normally jumped at the chance, to be involved in a new project and would have never argued with him, nor have made the unbelievable assertion, that he and others, were already aware of the activity in the Salton Sea area. Dr. Leyland knew the outrageous assertion was impossible. After a few minutes of uncertain anxiety, he placed a call to 911, and asked the police to check into the situation.

San Diego County Sheriff's Deputies, arrived at Vince's house, and knocked on the door. Getting no response, they entered the unlocked house and found a partially dressed man, without identification, lying unconscious and unresponsive on the bathroom floor. The man had a large, swollen, blood soaked abrasion on the back of his head, leading the deputies to believe the man had been the victim of foul play. They made a quick search of the house, finding no signs of a struggle or forced entry, and no indications that other residents lived in the home. After initial treatment by paramedics, the unresponsive victim was taken by ambulance, to the UCSD Hospital emergency room.

Police summoned Dr. Leyland to the hospital, where he identified the unconscious man as Vince Davis. Vince was thinner, his hair was longer and he was unshaven, all of which was disconcerting to Dr. Leyland, but there was no mistaking who the man was. Police questioned Dr. Leyland about the phone call he had made to Vince, and asked if Vince had any enemies. Dr. Leyland assured police, Vince had no enemies, and the injury was ruled accidental.

Dr. Leyland remained at the hospital, hoping to speak with Vince, and ask what had happened to him from the time he had left work earlier that day. That man had been well dressed and well groomed. The man he had indentified bore little resemblance to the neat appearing, Vince Davis, whom had left the lab a few hours earlier.

A short time later, the Neurologist assigned to Vince's case, spoke with Dr. Leyland, and asked if he was aware of any previous blackouts or similar injuries in, Vince's past. Dr. Leyland knew of none, but was able to furnish the name of Vince's personal physician, for information in that regard and then asked the Neurologist if Vince was going to die. The Neurologist told him Vince's condition was stable, and it would be unlikely he would die. He went on to say, that preliminary blood work showed no signs of alcohol or drugs, and MRI results had shown no signs of brain hemorrhage or swelling. He said in most cases, an injury such as Vince had sustained, left the victim with nothing more than large headache. The following day, he turned Vince's care over to his personal physician, Dr. Jason Stuart.

Vince woke from his coma at the end of a week. From the time he was well enough to make himself understood, he told and retold an unbelievable story to Dr. Stuart, his co-workers, and anyone else that came in his room.

The story was the same to all. He had experienced a world ending disaster that had begun in California in August of 2009 and had spread around the world in a harrowing 35 days. He said he had been the leader of a courageous group of people that had joined forces in the struggle to survive and that they had narrowly escaped death many times, living to be the sole survivors, in a completely destroyed St. Louis. To anyone that had listened long enough to hear him complete the story, he finished by insisting the disaster was actually going to occur in 2009 and that it was his obligation to warn authorities and help make plans to prepare for the cataclysmic event. When no one had believed him and instead tried to calm him, he exhibited ever-accelerating anger, resulting in his removal to the psychiatric wing, not allowed visitors, given mild sedatives and sometimes restrained, in an effort to control his outbursts.

Dr. Stuart had no experience in mental disorders, but he realized Vince was in serious trouble, and could possibly be experiencing a mental breakdown. Unable to cope with Vince's outburst of anger and hostility, he consulted with a staff psychiatrist, seeking his advice. The psychiatrist recommended, Vince should voluntarily admit himself into Gifford Mental Hospital, for a complete evaluation and diagnosis of his problem, under the care of experienced professionals.

Vince refused to admit himself, leaving Dr. Stuart with no recourse other than to obtain a court order that would confine Vince, to a mental hospital, for evaluation and treatment. Dr. Stuart felt the move was necessary and also in, Vince's best interest.

Vince became enraged when paramedics came to move him. He fought with staff members until he was subdued, given stronger sedatives, and placed in restraints for his trip to Gifford Mental Hospital.

CHAPTER ONE

EARLY MORNING...AUGUST 28, 2005...REALITY

VINCE STOOD STARING BLANKLY out through the bars that covered his window, not seeing what was before him, instead seeing what was in his mind. He had gone over the events, time after time, and had always come to the same conclusion. *I'm not crazy, but they think I am! It wasn't something I imagined or invented!*

He now realized, that no one believed he was in 2009 one minute, and then back in 2005 the next. The isolation and hopelessness of his situation, were now his constant companions and ruthless enemies, of his mind.

From the beginning of his confinement, he had resisted the efforts of the hospital staff to comfort and reassure him. His irrational, and at times, almost violent behavior, had forced the hospital staff to sedate and restrain him on several occasions. During those induced sleeps, he had experienced countless dreams about the disaster. During his most recent dream, he had seen Donna's face leaning over him, as if she was in a fog. It had seemed as if her lips were moving, forming words, that his ears could not hear. He tried to answer, but for some reason, no matter how hard he tried, he couldn't speak. Then a shadowy figure of a man in a white coat leaned over and looked at him. The man had a syringe in his hand, and said. "He's becoming excited, Miss Stevens. This will calm him down."

Vince thought he felt the sting of the needle going in. He tried to speak, but couldn't. *Who the hell are you? What's happening to me?* Were the questions he thought and wanted to ask, but his lips wouldn't move. Then Donna, the shadowy figure and the fog, began to disappear. As the images slipped away, he thought he had began calling out to her, feeling sure she had found him somehow, and could still be there, but she didn't answer. What he did hear was a man's voice, which was yelling at him.

"Goddamnit, you're crazy, you bastard! Shut up! There's no one in this room, and you're never getting out of here! Get that through your thick head, you numbskull! This will shut your ass up!"

He had struggled uselessly against the straps that held his arms firmly in place, but this time he actually felt the sting of the needle, held in crude hands that showed no mercy. Tears of desperation and fear had streamed down his face, as he felt the certainty of defeat and isolation that overwhelmed him. Becoming exhausted, he had fallen back against his pillow, barely hearing the man snarl out his last words, as he slipped into the darkness.

"Goddamn, it's about time you calmed down, you crazy son-of-a-bitch! Let's go, he'll be out for hours."

COMING OUT OF THE FOG

AS TIME PASSED, VINCE'S mind began clearing up. With a clearer mind, he thought constantly of the two men who had came to his room, that dark and troubling night. One had been dressed in a white coat and had seemed pleasant and caring, but the second man who came to his room was boisterous and uncaring. He had no idea who either were, but he clearly remembered the second man's loud voice, yelling at him, saying he was crazy and that he was never getting out. Those words had penetrated beyond the fog of his delirium. Those words had stung him deeply, and remained, as if they had been burned into his memory. He hadn't known where he was then, or why he was being held against his will, but he knew now, and realized that he had only two choices. He would have to begin cooperating with his captures, no matter what it took, and bide his time. Doing otherwise would mean he would remain a prisoner of their whims and restraints, until he actually went crazy.

The realization he came to that morning, changed everything for him. From that point on, he vowed never to talk about 2009, Donna or the shadowy figure in the white coat. That time and those persons existed and appeared only, in his dreams. The room he was being held captive in, was his real world. The surly orderlies that came, calling him crazy and cussing him, were the real persons in his life. He had hated every second of his confinement, and the bad treatment he had been subjected to, but he wasn't going to complain or feel sorry for himself any longer. He was going to accept his situation, for what it was, and begin looking for a way to escape. He was going stop telling the story, no matter how many times he dreamed about it, or was asked to tell about it, and make the best of his confinement.

Although he didn't realize it at the time, his resolve and determination had restored his self-confidence and brought him back from the edge of insanity. An achievement, no doctor or hospital stay would have ever accomplished.

FREE OF RESTRAINTS

AS HE STOOD BEFORE the window of his room, he instinctively tested the bars and found them firmly secured. He had no idea of how long he had been confined, it all seemed like a bad dream. He had lost weight, looked haggard, and at times, was withdrawn. As he looked out the window, his mind unconsciously reflected back to his last dream. He had been unable to put a face on the shadowy figure in the white coat, and wondered. *Who was he? Was he actually in my room? Did he give me an injection when Donna was trying to talk to me? Why couldn't I answer her?* Desperation filled his mind. *I've got to find a way to escape! I have to get out of here!* That thought ended and another took its place. *Even if I find a way to escape, how can I warn anyone? They'll think I'm crazy, just like everyone here does.*

Each night, he found himself hoping for a new dream that would show him the way to escape. That dream never came.

Dr. Gunderich Woitasczyk, M.D., PhD., the head of psychiatry at Gifford, had jumped at the opportunity to take over Vince's treatment and study what appeared to be an entirely new mental psychosis, which had no precedent in psychiatric medicine.

Although respected by his associates, Dr. Woitasczyk was known to be an opinionated egotist, and for the most part, an unlikeable, authoritative man, who was balding, wore thick glasses, and appeared to be in his late sixty's. He was from the 'old country' as he called it, and spoke with a guttural German accent. He was never lost for words, when bragging about European Doctors, and especially those from Germany. In his opinion, they were much more intelligent, and far greater in their skills, than those he had encountered in the United States. He never went so far as to say he was the best, although it was obvious from his demeanor that he presumed as much.

Dr. Woitasczyk had an irritating habit of taking his thick, rimless glasses off and squinting, while reading Vince's chart, and at times speaking aloud to himself in German, while noting items on the chart.

Vince had disliked Dr. Woitasczyk's demeanor, his guttural accent and irritating habits from the start. He found Dr. Woitasczyk to be an unlikely candidate for a psychiatrist and didn't care for the attitude he displayed, which was more like a military commander, rather than a doctor. Vince, had related his dislike of, Dr. Woitasczyk, to his nurse, while at the same time asking if another psychiatrist, who spoke better English was available. The nurse had told him that, Dr. Woitasczyk, was considered the best psychiatrist on the West Coast and there would be no change of psychiatrists, in his case, suggesting he cooperate with Dr. Woitasczyk, rather than criticize him.

Vince had thought about asking Dr. Woitasczyk why he didn't go back to Europe, since he felt the 'old country' was so much better than the United States, but he thought better of it and accepted the nurse's suggestion. He had been cooperating when Dr. Woitasczyk saw him, but soon learned, that Dr. Woitasczyk was not an understanding man, and had very little patience. Every time Dr. Woitasczyk encouraged Vince to tell his story, Dr. Woitasczyk would interrupt him in his arrogant manner and tone, seizing every opportunity that came along, to point out how ridiculous and unbelievable his story was. He soon realized he was wasting his time and words on Dr. Woitasczyk and decided to quit telling him or anyone else the story, even when encouraged to do so. Instead, he would laugh when it was brought up and say he must have been rendered delusional, by the blow to his head when he fell. He adopted a new and friendlier attitude when visited by the nurse or Dr. Woitasczyk, but not toward the uncaring and callous orderlies.

Dr. Woitasczyk had considered Vince's change in attitude and better behavior as a possible sign of improvement. He had told Vince, that his calmer state and admission of his delusion, showed signs that he was on the road to recovery. In reality, Dr. Woitasczyk suspected it was all an act, and was prepared for the relapse, he felt certain would come. When it didn't happen, Woitasczyk started praising Vince's change in attitude and behavior, although still not convinced.

"I'm very pleased to see your improvement, Mr. Davis. Perhaps, if you continue to show improvement, as you have, you will get to go home in a few months and possibly go back to work with Dr. Leyland, at the seismic center. But not until you're recovered fully and are capable of dealing with day-to-day reality. It's good to see that your mind is stabilizing and beginning to clear itself of the delusion you were suffering under." Woitasczyk had said.

Vince knew he hadn't been suffering under any delusions and knew there wasn't anything wrong with his brain, other than what it had been subjected to since he had been locked up. He remembered everything very clearly, especially the 2009 date on the shiny, Lincoln Penny, which he no longer had. The penny had not been found, when they had gone to search his house.

"They found no penny, Mr. Davis. It's all in your mind, and is simply part of the delusion you are suffering." Woitasczyk had told him.

He knew he hadn't developed, or was suffering from a mental disorder that, Dr. Woitasczyk, referred to as, Mental Post-Forming.

He sat there and listened to my story, and then came up with his brilliant diagnosis of, Mental Post-Forming. A mental disease unheard of, until the know it all bastard, dreamed it up! The asshole's writing a scientific paper about his, so called new discovery, and he said I'm going to be in it as his case study. He said he's going to submit the article on his newfound disease and diagnoses for treatment to the International Psychiatric Journal and the bastard's using me as the Guinea Pig! What a cocky, unlikeable, stuff shirt,

Prussian bastard he is! He has his own answers for everything I say, and he's too stupid and arrogant to know the difference or even try to understand me, let alone believe me.* The more Vince thought about Woitasczyk's diagnosis of him, the angrier he became. He could hear Woitasczyk's clinical, callous, and uncaring words in his head, just as if Woitasczyk was still standing there, with his smug and all knowing look, on his face.

Young man, what you're suffering from is a desire to see the ordinary events you work with on a daily basis, that are by and large routine and not particularly challenging, to turn into something catastrophic. The fact that you alone could confront the disaster and therefore become a driving force and national hero in dealing with the events is a grandiose projection of your mind to compensate for the routine and boring job of being a seismologist. That projection in itself wasn't enough though. Your mind had to go further and make sure that everyone else in your capacity had either retired or gotten killed, leaving only such an important person, as you must have imagined yourself as being, to be conscripted by the government to deal with the disaster. The fact that you see yourself at the highest level of importance, in your mind, signifies the level and depth of your delusion. To you, it means that the United States Government has recognized that, you and only you, would be able to do the job and therefore with no other person of your ability in the World, appoint you as the Director Of Homeland Disasters, which of course doesn't exist, except in your mind. Regardless of the fact that the office of Director of Homeland Disasters doesn't exist, you say the office was created specifically for you and offered to you alone, which you humbly accepted, making you the highest and most important person in your field. The fact you say you were superior to the Director Of Homeland Security and the Director Of FEMA, points this out even more clearly, and all of this is prima fascia evidence of the length your mind and your imagination has gone to, in justifying your escape from your mediocre, hum-drum profession. After considerable thought and research, I have found that this type of disorder can be best described and named, Mental Post-Forming. In other words, your mind has taken your normal job and responsibilities and has molded or formed them into the fantasy that you say you experienced, which in reality was only a figment of your imagination, which you have come to believe is true. I know you think all of what you said is true. I also know that no one believes you, and that is what has led to your erratic behavior in recent days and forced your admission, as a patient, into this facility. You are the first example of this kind of behavior or disorder, which the psychiatric profession and I have ever encountered. The Psychiatric Board has examined my diagnosis of your symptoms and treatment for your disorder. Given the fact that no other cases of your disorder have ever been encountered, in Psychiatric Medicine, the board has found my diagnosis to be accurate and well researched. The board has agreed with my diagnosis, and has endorsed the name, I suggested, for your disorder. Both of our names and a brief description of the disorder, as well as my suggestions for treatment, will be in the International Psychiatric Journal soon.

Vince, remembered how proud and sure of himself, Dr. Woitasczyk, had looked the day he had spewed out his degrading diagnosis of him in his harsh accent, but at the same time bragging himself up as if he were a genius. *The bastard stood there grinning like a possum eating shit, after telling me how crazy and diseased I am, while bragging about his great discovery and diagnosis. He hasn't discovered anything! He'll lose that shit faced grin, when 2009 rolls around!*

Vince was now spending all his time and thoughts, looking for a way to escape his confinement. He had learned he was being confined in the psychiatric section of the hospital, located on the 11th floor of the building. The barred windows and locked door had given him a feeling of imprisonment, rather than hospital care. He wasn't allowed visitors and had no sense of what the surrounds were, outside his door. He was sure there was only one floor above the 11th. He had heard and seen the Medi-vac's arriving. From their altitude, as they approached, he knew they couldn't be more than one floor above him.

Although he had been told his personal physician had checked up on him for the first few days after his commitment, he had no memory of the visits, or anything else, other than the surly treatment, he had received from the orderlies, which had lessened in recent days. His clearest memory was fighting with staff members and paramedics, when he was taken from the hospital and moved to Gifford, against will. Everything that had happened to him since he had been committed, was blurry until recently. He had a clear head now and noticed that anytime Woitasczyk or the nurse came to his room, two orderlies always escorted them. He ran over possible escape scenarios in his mind while pacing the floor. *I can't overpower the two orderlies. I'm not in good enough shape.*

The thought of escape became his sole focus, but looking at his face and body in his mirror made him realize he had lost his edge, and the strength he had felt in the previous months. He had begun daily exercise in an attempt to regain muscle tone and strength, as the desire to escape, became the only thing he thought of. He planned to be in better shape and be better prepared, when the time came for his escape, and the only way out he could see, was through the window. He would have to somehow remove the bars, and then find some way to climb to the roof, where he could commandeer the chopper when it landed. *Going down will be impossible.* He had thought.

He had no identification or for that matter, any kind of personal affects whatsoever. He knew it would be hard finding his way on the outside with nothing but his wits and daring. He had examined the bars on the window. They were anchored to the wall with bolts that were torqued tight and couldn't possibly be loosened, with anything, but a good wrench. To make matters worse, the windows couldn't be opened. He would have to break the glass when it was time to go, and would somehow, have to make it back to his house, get his personal things and get lost, until he could find a way to contact the others who had been with him, and went through the ordeal. *What if they don't remember anything.* He wondered. *They'll think I'm crazy too.*

The thought of no one else having any memory of the events left him feeling down, but still defiant. *I'm not going to consider that possibility! I have to get out of here and I can't wait until Woitasczyk says I'm okay. That may take months, maybe longer.*

He searched for anything he could improvise to use as a wrench, and found nothing. He was like a caged animal, pacing the floor, and going over the items in his room. There was a chair-table unit and a bed. Both were attached to the wall. He went in the bathroom and looked around. Everything was stainless. The stool, the sink and the shower were all motion activated and had no knobs. Even the mirror was polished stainless. All of the bathroom fixtures were plumbed through and attached to the wall. His toothbrush was flexible and couldn't be used for a weapon and he didn't have a razor. Every other day the orderlies stood and watched him, shave with the razor they brought, and then took back, when they left.

He looked up at the bathroom ceiling searching for anything, but found nothing. He reached up and pressed on the ceiling with his hand testing the resistance. The painted surface was hard and made of concrete. Then he saw something he hadn't noticed before. The bathroom ceiling was lower than the ceiling in his room.

He went back into his room, stood on his bed, pressed on the ceiling, and found it was constructed of concrete as well. Other than a small grille that covered a speaker that played canned, soothing music all day, the fire sprinklers, the vents and the overhead light were the only things that came through the ceiling. As he got down, he heard the door opening and the two orderlies came bursting in.

"What in the hell do you think you're doing, Davis?" One asked.

Vince then realized there was a camera in the room. They were watching his every move, they wouldn't have come to his room otherwise. Thinking fast, he feigned a relapse.

"I'm going nuts! I need to get out of here now! I'm locked up in here like a prisoner twenty-four hours a day! I haven't done anything to anyone, or done anything against the law. I can't stand it in here anymore! There's nothing but the ceiling and walls. They're closing in on me! You've got to stop the ceiling from coming down on me!"

"Well, you're not getting out through the ceiling! It's concrete you stupid bastard!" One orderly chastised him. The other laughed and said. "You're in here for your own good, Davis. Settle down for Christ's sake! The ceiling isn't coming down on you. It's just your imagination. Do you want something to calm your nerves?"

"I don't want anything for my nerves! I want out of here!" Vince shot back.

"Well, you're damn sure not getting out of here! I can promise you that! You had better calm down. Get down off that bed and lay down or I'm calling Dr. Woitasczyk!"

"Call him! I don't care! I don't get any newspapers or magazines. I can't smoke. I don't get any visitors and I can't call anybody. There's no TV in here and nothing to do except listen to that canned music all day. You'd go crazy too! Anybody would!"

"All right, goddamnit! That's enough! Settle down right now or we'll put you back in restraints. Is that what you want?" The orderly threatened.

"No! Get the doctor!" Vince screamed

"Okay! Calm down, Davis! I'll go call him, but you had better not give him the same bullshit you've been giving us. He'll tell us to put you back in restraints if you do! Are we clear on that?"

"Yes! I'm getting down! Call Woitasczyk!"

Vince lay down on his bed and heard one orderly talking to the other as they left his room. "The bastard's gone off the deep end again, Dawdry! Woitasczyk isn't going to like this. He'll probably blame it on us! He's already down on Crawford and Blake's asses for all the shit they pull."

"They're both screw-ups and they deserve it, but this isn't our fault, Crischell." Dawdry said and then went on. "I'm putting in for a transfer. Did you see the look in Davis's eyes? The bastard looked like he would have killed us, if he got a chance. Screw working in this loony bin. I've had it! Come on, it's time to go home."

Vince was relieved as they left, but he hoped he hadn't overplayed his act. He knew all them were his enemies, including the nurse. He felt sure any of them would turn him for the slightest provocation. *I've got to be careful. The sons-of-bitch's are watching me and probably taping everything I do.*

He scanned the room looking for the hidden camera, but couldn't see it. *It must be in the light housing or the speaker vent. There must be one in the bathroom too.*

He'd been given a lucky break discovering he was being watched. The thought hadn't crossed his mind, but now that he knew, he was sure they'd be monitoring and taping his room 24 hours a day, seeing every move he made. Even if he found a way to escape, he knew the camera was going to be a problem. *They'd be on me in seconds. I wouldn't make it fifty feet.*

He lay down on his bed and tried to relax. Dr. Woitasczyk arrived an hour later, accompanied by Crawford and Blake, the two day shift orderlies.

"What is this all about, Mr. Davis? What's wrong? Are the thoughts about the disaster coming back?" Woitasczyk asked.

"No! It's not that! I don't think about the disaster at all anymore. It's this room and being locked up. It's getting to me and I know I'm not crazy, but I'm going crazy! I feel like a prisoner, only it's worse. Prisoners have rights, they get visitors, they get to read and have things to do, but

I don't. I get nothing to read, no TV, I can't smoke and I get nothing but that canned music all day. I can't call anybody and I don't get any visitors. I haven't broken any laws, but you're treating me as if I have. I have parents back in Missouri, they probably don't even know I'm locked up here. If you were in here, you'd be crawling the walls, just like I am."

"Perhaps, Mr. Davis, but I am not having the problems that you are. I thought you knew your parents had been notified. It indicates here on the chart that you were informed of that."

"Nobody said, anything to me!" Vince responded.

"You were told, Mr. Davis. Look here, the chart has been initialed by the nurse. They know you're here, they want to see you, but it's too soon. You need to relax and just think about getting better and getting out of this room and mixing in with the general population. We will have to see how you interact with the other patients before you can have visitors, or even begin to be considered for release, and that will take some time. This little relapse you were having today, is proof you're not ready yet. Do you want me to give you something, so you can relax, and get some rest?"

"No! I'm fine, and I'm not crazy! Getting out of here is what I am thinking about." Vince replied.

"We do not refer to patients as being crazy, Mr. Davis. Crazy is not a word we use here. We are professionals and we conduct ourselves as professionals. You won't hear that word used here." Woitasczyk said.

"Oh really?" Vince replied.

"Ya, really." Woitasczyk replied.

"Try listening to the tapes of the conversations in this room. They call me crazy all the time!" Vince said, pointing to Crawford and Blake.

"Do you?" Woitasczyk asked.

"No! That's a lie, Doctor! We may have said he was acting crazy, but we didn't call him crazy." Crawford said.

"That's right, Dr. Woitasczyk! Davis is lying!" Blake said.

"Do not use the word at all!" Woitasczyk said to them.

"They're the ones that are lying! Listen to the tapes, you'll find out I'm the one that's telling the truth!" Vince said.

"What makes you think we have tapes of your room, Mr. Davis?" Woitasczyk asked.

"Every time I fart, they come running in my room with their batons. Just listen to the tapes. You'll see I'm not lying." Vince asserted.

"You're a very perceptive man, Mr. Davis. I'll check the tapes as you suggested." Woitasczyk said as he looked at the two orderlies.

"Why can't I have some reading material? I'd like to have a newspaper or something to read." Vince said.

"Come to think of it, that might be a good, therapeutic idea. If you were given newspapers to read on a daily basis, it might help to bring you back to reality. The world is a fairly, normal place, Mr. Davis. Ya, I think that will help." Woitasczyk turned to the orderlies and said. "See that he gets the Union Tribune every morning with breakfast."

"What about a TV?" Vince asked.

"None of the patients have a television in their rooms. For now, I think the newspaper will be fine. In a couple of weeks, we can see if you're ready to mix in with the other patients. We have a television in the activity room."

"Thanks, Doc." Vince said.

"Don't ever refer to me as, Doc!" Woitasczyk shot back in an insulted tone. "I am a psychiatrist, not some old west Doc, Mr. Davis. I have a PhD. in Psychiatric Medicine!"

"I've got a PhD. in Geology, Doctor. I think I'm past the, Mister Davis category myself, wouldn't you say?"

Woitasczyk's angry facial expression softened as he regained his composure. "By all means, Dr. Davis. Ya, I knew that! My, I do think you're getting better. That will be all for today, get Dr. Davis today's newspaper." Woitasczyk said to Crawford and Blake.

Touchy bastard! Vince thought, as the three left the room.

He got up, went to the bathroom to look for a camera, pulling up his gown, and sitting down on the stool. *Let them think I'm taking a dump, if they're watching.* He thought, as he looked the bathroom over for the concealed camera. He couldn't see any place where a camera might have been hidden, however, he did see an approximately two-foot square opening, above the shower with some kind of keyed locking mechanism.

An access door! He thought and wondered. *What can I do about it with them watching every move I make?*

Just then, he heard the door open again. A moment later Crawford stuck his head in the bathroom opening and said. "Here's your paper, Davis. What are you doing?"

"I'm taking a dump! You should know that, with your goddamn cameras! Come on in and take a whiff!" Vince replied sarcastically.

Crawford stepped back and said. "No thanks! I'll take your word for it."

"Looks like he's wised up about the cameras." Blake said.

"I guess so, but he doesn't have to worry about it, does he Blake?" Crawford asked.

"Hell no! You're in the women's section right now, Davis. There aren't any cameras in the women's shitters. They were removed because the women bitched about their privacy and all that shit. Until we get an opening in the men's section, you'll be in this room. You can do anything you want to in the bathroom, we can't see you!" Blake cackled, bursting into laughter, joined by Crawford.

"Very funny! You're both assholes! Get the hell out of here!" Vince snarled.

The two continued laughing as they shut and locked the door. He picked the newspaper up off the bathroom floor and headed back to his bed to lie down. The stool flushed behind him.

Screw, those bastards. He thought, as he looked at the date on the paper. It was August, 28th. He had lost a lot of time. *I'm going to have to get busy. I'll check the access panel after lights out.*

Just then the canned music stopped. The music was replaced by the Crawford's voice. "Dr. Woitasczyk said you can have four smokes a day, starting tomorrow. One with each meal and one at bedtime. If there is anything else, your majesty would like, just press the bed button and give us a call."

He could hear Blake laughing with Crawford, and then the canned music started again.

I'd like to kick their asses! He thought, and then started reading the paper. The music totally faded from his mind as he scanned the newspaper. He read it from front to back. Finished, he lay back and without knowing it, he fell asleep.

"What's he doing?" Blake asked Crawford.

"He's asleep. He's probably dreaming about saving the world." Crawford replied, and laughed.

13

"Do you think any of that shit he's been putting out could happen? You heard him tell Dr. Woitasczyk he has a PhD. in Geology. Woitasczyk knew he did." Blake said.

"Hell no, I don't! You're an idiot, Blake! The bastard's crazy!" Crawford replied.

"Hey, lay off of me, Crawford! You never know what's possible. Dr. Frankenstein made that monster that killed a lot of people. Frankenstein was a doctor."

"You're nothing but a moron, Blake! That was fiction. There never was a Frankenstein monster." Crawford rolled his eyes at the stupidity of his partner.

"Then why did they make a movie about it? Tell me that smart ass!" Blake retorted.

"Would you two shut up?" The nurse barked. "I don't know why they assign imbeciles, like the both of you, to the mental ward. You're both qualified to be a patient here, and quit calling Dr. Davis crazy. If I hear you say it again, I'll report you!"

"I didn't say it, Crawford did!" Blake protested.

"You're both guilty!" She replied and then said. "Go check on Rudolph Watkins and take a mop and cleaning bucket. Look, he's used his feces to draw Swastika's all over his walls again."

"I'm not a janitor!" Blake complained as he looked at the monitor.

"Move!" The nurse barked.

As the two trudged off down the hall toward Watkins room, Blake asked Crawford. "Why in the hell don't they give Watkins some chalk? It'd be a damn site easier to clean up than that crap!"

"Woitasczyk offered him chalk! The crazy, Nazi bastard, wanted paint. He must be protesting. Let's get the bastard." Crawford replied as they went in Watkins room.

"Get out of my bunker, you swinehundt's!" Watkins shrieked as he fought with Crawford and Blake, while they dragged him out the door. He continued to scream as they dragged him down the hall towards the showers.

"Notify the Gestapo! Call, Herr Woitasczyk! The enemy has stormed my bunker! Call in the firing squad! Kill them!" Watkins shrieked as he fought with the two.

Several inmates heard Watkins screams for help and came running up, shaking their fists and jeering Crawford and Blake as they passed. Soon all order was lost as the inmates protesting Watkins rough treatment began rioting. In an instant, all control was lost and the men's side turned into a full-fledged melee, with chairs and other furnishings being thrown from the rooms into the hallway as inmates who knew nothing of Watkins plight, joined in and ran rampant up and down the halls, destroying anything they could lay their hands on. Crawford hit one of the rioters with his baton, which was a mistake. The inmates then turned on Crawford and Blake and began pelting them with a barrage of books and anything else they could find to throw.

"Turn the bastard loose! They're trying to kill us!" Crawford yelled as he turned and ran for the nurses' station, followed by Blake. Crawford hurriedly led the nurse toward the metal security door as Blake beat the inmates off with his baton and radioed hospital security for back-up. Safely outside, they watched as the inmates pounded on the steel door, cracking the wire mesh, reinforced windows, while others continued destroying anything they could find. As they watched the entire wing being demolished, the nurse looked at them and said.

"All I asked you to do was clean up the mess! Now see what you've caused."

Blake and Crawford said nothing in reply. They both knew they were going to feel the full fury of Dr. Woitasczyk's wrath.

CHAPTER TWO

UNCERTAINTY

VINCE HAD HEARD NOTHING of what had gone on over in the men's side. He woke up several hours later with the newspaper scattered across the bed and on the floor. He had seen a small article on the inside pages that related to small aftershock disturbances still coming from the Salton Sea area. He picked up the page and read it again.

Filler news. He thought after re-reading the article. *No one in California takes earthquakes seriously. The article might not have been there at all if they'd had an ad to fill the space.*

His room light went out as he finished the thought. He got up and went in the bathroom, which was illuminated by a small night light. He propped a washcloth under the spigot's electric eye so the water would keep running and went to the shower and examined the access panel opening closer. The door was fitted tightly into the opening. There was no way he was going to get a grip on it without a screwdriver or a pry bar. The plastic knives and forks the hospital furnished for eating would be useless. He was going to need a paper clip or a bobby pin to try to pick the lock, as Dana had done at the camp on Taum Sauk.

Everything reminds me of something that happened in 2009. He thought as he looked at the lock. *Dana would have had that open in seconds, but where in the hell will I get a bobby pin or a paper clip?* He questioned himself.

He removed the washcloth and returned to his bed, thinking. *They can see me, and they can hear me. I have to be careful, when and if, I get a chance at the access panel. One strange sound and they'd be in here to see what was going on, just as they did today.*

He sat down on his bed, propped his pillows up and leaned back against the headboard. His eyes focused on the far away stars in the night sky outside his window, and thought. *I'm about as close to getting to those stars, as I am to getting out of this room.*

He couldn't get the thought of escaping out if his mind as other thoughts came. *I'm not going to get much sleep tonight. I know that access panel leads somewhere. It has to be a plumbing or electrical access area. If the plumbing sprung a leak, maintenance would have to have a way to get to it and fix it. I'm betting the access panel leads to crawl space above, and the crawl space leads to a wet wall somewhere in the interior of the building that runs adjacent to all the rooms. Somewhere in the building there has to be a door to bring the tools and supplies in to work on things. It has to be in some hallway or maintenance area outside of the mental ward. The architect who designed this building wouldn't have made that mistake. If I can find that door, I can find my way out of this hospital.*

Freedom filled his mind, but he was a long way from it, and he knew it. Rather than dwelling on the thought of escape, he instead started thinking about what he would do, once he was out. *If I can get to the roof when one of the Medi-vac's land I might be able to catch the pilot off guard.*

He knew he could fly the chopper, he also knew he could disable the transponder. George had taught him both. He thought of George and the others he'd spent the short time with, four years in the future.

Where are they? He wondered. *Do any of them know or remember anything that I do, or was it all a dream?*

He felt the scar on his arm and he knew none of it was a dream, but he still remembered his last dream. It now seemed more like a nightmare. He had tried to talk to the person he had thought was Donna, and had tried to call her name, but the shadowy figure in the white coat, had stopped him. When he woke up and found himself alone in the darkness of his room, he had wondered if he was actually crazy. *Am I actually doing what Woitasczyk says I'm doing? Is it all a figment of my imagination?*

"Hell no!" He shouted aloud. Seconds later the light came on in his room as the voice of Crischell, one of the night shift orderlies, called out. "What's wrong, Davis? Push your button if something's wrong!"

They can hear every sound I make! He thought. He pushed the button and answered. "I guess I was dreaming. I woke myself up."

"Well lay down in the bed like you should be at this hour. We've had enough trouble here today, so lay down and go to sleep!" Crischell barked.

"What trouble?" Vince asked.

"Nothing that concerns you! Do you need me to get you something to help you sleep?" Crischell asked.

"No. I'll be okay. Just turn off that damn light! Jesus Christ! Do you people work twenty-four hours a day? Don't you ever go home? What the hell time is it anyway?" Vince asked.

"It's nighttime, now get to sleep!" Crischell barked.

"I know it's nighttime!" Vince shot back. "Tell Dr. Woitasczyk I want a clock. I'm tired of not knowing what time of day or night it is."

"All right, pipe down! I'll leave him a note." Crischell said.

"Why don't you just tell him?" Vince asked.

"He's gone for the day. The nurse will give the note to him in the morning, so lie down and shut up. I don't want to hear anymore out of you. Your voice is carrying all the way down the hall!" The light went out and Vince realized they couldn't see him unless the lights were on. *That's good to know.* He thought, as he saw a shooting star streak through the sky in the black moonless night outside. It brought back to mind the warm August nights when he was a kid and had slept outside on the lawn of his parents' farm in St. Louis. Those were good times and good memories.

I wish I were back there right now. He thought. *I could start all over again. I'd change some things. I'd be anything other than a seismologist.*

With the multitude of unanswered questions rolling around in his mind, he laid his head down. Sometime later that night, without knowing it, he fell asleep, began dreaming about the disaster and woke with a start. Disoriented, he jumped up out of his bed and yelled. "Look out it's falling!"

He had been dreaming that he, Jim and Donna, were standing under the ruined Gateway Arch. The broken top portion had come loose, and was falling down on them, as they stood posing for their victory' photo.

The light in his room came on suddenly and Crischell called out. "What's wrong now, Davis?"

The overhead light's sudden brilliance hit his eyes as he looked up for the falling Arch. He shielded his eyes, covered his head with his arms and yelled. "Get out of the way!" Expecting the impending blow any second.

"Davis! What's wrong, goddamnit?" Crischell shouted.

Vince was caught up in the dream. The voice he heard, sounded like Gen. Lawson. It had the same authoritative, demanding tone.

"Answer me you son-of-a-bitch! What's wrong, goddamnit?" Crischell demanded.

Getting no response from Vince, he jumped up, and said. "Come on, Dawdry! The bastard's out of his mind again!"

Vince felt threatened by Crischell's demanding voice, thinking the voice that was yelling at him was, Gen. Lawson. He was so caught up in his dream, he thought he was responding to Lawson's angry tone, and yelled. "You're dead you bastard! I saw you die!"

Still thinking the Arch was falling, he jumped out of bed, pulled his blanket over his head for imagined protection, and ran blindly into the wall, bouncing off and falling to the floor. Crischell and Dawdry came in his room, and found him laying there.

"Get up you crazy bastard!" Dawdry yelled, "Nothing's falling on you! Goddamn! You're the worst nut case we've ever had here!"

Unhurt, Vince looked up at the two faces staring down at him, and realized where he was. "What are you talking about?" He asked.

"You were screaming your ass off! You said the ceiling was falling on you!"

Vince then remembered the dream, he felt foolish, and said. "Oh, that?"

"Yeah, that! Get your ass up off the floor! It isn't daylight yet." Dawdry said.

"I was doing some exercises." He lied.

"Get your ass back to bed! Woitasczyk's going to hear about this little episode." Crischell threatened.

Vince laughed, and said. "Okay, I lied! I just wanted to see if you two assholes were awake. I couldn't sleep."

"You better find some other way to amuse yourself, Davis! We don't think it's funny!" Cussing under their breaths, the two left.

"Don't forget the clock!" Vince yelled to them as the door closed. The light went out seconds later.

Vince went to his window, and looked outside at the world that was passing him by. He saw cars coming into the parking lot as he looked down, and thought. *Probably employees coming in to work and hating it. They don't know how lucky they are. I'd trade places with them in a heartbeat.* He then recalled the dream he'd just had. *If they really knew what happened, they'd put me back in shackles!* He shook his head rapidly as if trying to shake the image from his mind. *If I don't get out of here soon, I'll lose it!*

His thoughts went back to escaping. He had never felt so out of control and helpless, in his life. Even when things were going wrong, as he and the others had fought to survive, not so long ago, he had still felt like he could make a difference and could find a way, and did. The helpless feeling reminded him of his arm when it had been wounded, and had been infected. He hadn't wanted to lose his arm, and he didn't want to die. He'd found a way then and he would now. He rubbed the scar feeling it with his hand and thought. *It's real! It was all real! No matter how long I stay in this hospital, or what anyone says, it was real! Woitasczyk thinks I'm a lunatic, so do the orderlies. Maybe I'd have been better off if I had died of the infection. I wouldn't be here now.*

Another strange thought crossed his mind. *If I had died of the infection, would I have died in 2009, or would I have materialized back in 2005 and died in my bed?*

"Shit! I've got to take a shower." He said aloud. "I feel like I'm going nuts!"

"What was that, Davis?" Dawdry asked, hearing him speak.

"I'm going to take a shower, is that all right with you?" He asked.

"Get it over with, and get your ass ready for breakfast!" Dawdry ordered.

Vince started to give them the finger, and decided not to. He went into the shower feeling safe from prying eyes and examined the access panel more closely. The locking mechanism looked like it would be easy enough to pick if he could get his hands on a paper clip, or some other slender, metal object. He remembered seeing Dana pick the office door lock on Taum Sauk with two small pieces of metal.

Where am I going to find something? He wondered.

He finished his shower, and put on a clean gown. He went back in his room and started looking again.

There has to be something. He thought, as he looked at every object in the room again. He went to the window and saw the sun was up. *Must be around eight.* He guessed.

He heard a noise at the door, and then it opened. Dawdry and Crischell came in with his breakfast, followed by the nurse, who had his medication.

"Well, how's mister fun and games?" Dawdry asked. "Did you get back to sleep?"

"I told you I couldn't sleep. Do you guys watch me twenty four hours a day?" Vince asked disgustedly.

Dawdry laughed and asked. "What's the matter? Didn't you get your beauty rest?"

"It looks like you did, you asshole!" Vince said, looking into the bleary, blood shot eyes of Dawdry, who was standing there in his wrinkled, dirty whites. "What's your problem? Did I wake you two assholes up?" Vince asked, glaring at Dawdry.

"Watch your mouth, you bastard! Crazy or not, I'm not taking any shit from you!" Dawdry hissed.

The nurse intervened, and asked. "Dawdry, what did you just say?"

"I told him I wasn't taking any shit from him, and I'm not!" He replied.

"Before that." She said.

"I don't remember." Dawdry replied.

"You said he was crazy, Dawdry." His partner Crischell said.

"I did not!" Dawdry replied.

"Yes you did." The nurse said. "That's the last time I want hear that! Do you understand?"

Dawdry apologized and the nurse went on, answering Vince's question. "Yes, you're watched twenty-four hours a day, Dr. Davis. It's for your own safety and protection." She said.

"And what we don't see is recorded." Dawdry added. "Have you been doing something nasty, you don't want us to see?" He asked and started laughing.

"Screw you, you peeping tom!" Vince said. "You're all alike! You're a bunch of smart asses! I'll kick all of your asses, if I get the chance!"

"Dawdry! Shut your filthy mouth! That's enough out of both of you!" The nurse scolded. "Here's your medication, Dr. Davis. You'll have to take it before I leave."

"What about the clock I asked for?"

"The doctor hasn't come in yet. I have the request attached to your records. Dr. Woitasczyk will see it, when he comes in. Now take your medication." The nurse replied.

"Don't be a problem, Davis!" Dawdry said. "You're not the only patient here. Take your pills. You'll get a clock if Dr. Woitasczyk okay's it. Hurry up, you're breakfast is getting cold."

Vince looked at Dawdry, he smiled and stuck out his hand.

"That's better." The nurse said, coming forward and handing Vince the small paper cup of water and pills.

"Down the hatch, I want to see you swallow." She said.

"What are these pills?" Vince asked.

Dawdry became impatient. He started moving toward Vince, and said. "Davis, I'm not going to tell you again! Take the goddamned pills!"

As he moved toward Vince, the nurse turned to get out of Dawdry's way. Vince saw the nurse's cap was held in place by two bobby pins in the back. Making the best of the confusion, he feigned tripping, fell into the nurse, and grasped at her upper torso for support. He took her down with him as he fell, spilling the water and pills across the floor.

"You clumsy, ox! What a stupid thing to do! Get your ass up right now!" Dawdry yelled as he placed the food tray on the table. Vince rolled over the nurse's cap as he got up and removed one of the bobby pins and palmed it.

The nurse, still lying on the floor, was holding her hip and moaning in pain. Dawdry's face was livid with anger as he bent down to assist her.

"Get on the bed, Davis, and I mean now!" Dawdry ordered.

Vince got up and sat on the edge of his bed, sliding the bobby pin under the cover.

"You're going to get it now!" Dawdry threatened. "You're going to be back in restraints, if I have anything to say about it!"

"You're damned right he is!" Crischell barked.

"It was an accident! I tripped! I didn't mean to hurt her." Vince replied.

"Shut up! Lie down on that bed and don't move till I tell you to." Dawdry keyed his radio and called for assistance as the nurse continued to moan in distress on the floor.

"Try not to move." Dawdry told the nurse. "You may have broken something. Help is on the way."

Crischell glared at Vince, showing his anger, and said. "You make one false move and you'll need a doctor too."

A few minutes later, a doctor and two assistants burst into the room. The doctor bent down and said. "Take it easy, miss. I'm Dr. Perkins. Where are you injured?"

The nurse, who was now in tears, said. "It's my hip."

Dr. Perkins felt the area the nurse indicated was injured, he turned to his assistants, and said. "She may have a broken hip. Get a gurney and a lifting board, hurry!"

As the two assistants left hurriedly with Crischell, Perkins asked Dawdry, how it had happened.

Vince started to speak, but was interrupted by Dawdry. "Shut up, Davis! You've caused enough problems!" Dawdry yelled.

"Well get on with it." Perkins said to Dawdry.

"The clumsy bastard tripped. He knocked her down and fell on her."

"What's your name?" Perkins asked Dawdry.

"Willard Dawdry. Clint Crischell and me pull the overnight shift in this ward."

"Was he trying to attack the nurse, Dawdry?" Perkins asked.

"No, the nurse was handing him his medication and water. The clumsy bastard tripped over his own feet, when he reached out to get them."

"Watch your language, Dawdry!" Perkins cautioned him as he looked down at the nurse and asked. "Is what Dawdry said, true?"

She nodded in agreement.

"All right. You'll have to submit a report of the accident before you leave your shift." Perkins said to Dawdry.

Dawdry looked at his watch, gave Vince another glaring look, and said. "If you'd taken those pills the first time I asked you, this wouldn't have happened. I'll guarantee you it won't happen again!" He was tapping his baton in his hand again.

Vince looked at Dr. Perkins for some sort of support or defense against Dawdry's threat and said. "It was an accident, Doctor. I got my feet tangled and tripped! Dawdry's just trying to take his anger out on me. Crischell and him are both jerks, they treat me like this all the time. I'm not a prisoner, there's no reason for their jailhouse guard attitude and tactics."

Dawdry's face turned red as he felt the sting of Vince's words.

"I told you to shut up, Davis!" He shouted.

"That's enough!" Perkins said to Dawdry, then he turned to Vince and said."Dr. Woitasczyk will be here soon. I'm sure he'll want to talk to you as soon as he arrives. I'll tell him what you said."

Vince nodded his head and smiled at Dawdry as the two assistants returned and lifted the nurse onto the gurney.

"Take her to x-ray, I'll call in a request." Perkins told his assistants, and then said to Dawdry. "Clean up this mess and get that report filled out!"

"Yes, sir." Dawdry said as he sheathed his baton. While picking up the nurse's cap, and spilled pills, he asked. "Do you want Davis to take these pills, Doctor?"

"Not after they've been on the floor, you idiot! I'll make a note for Dr. Woitasczyk. He'll send replacements or bring them when he sees Davis."

"What about his food? He hasn't eaten yet." Dawdry asked.

"Get him another tray, take that one back." Perkins ordered.

Dawdry looked at his watch and said. "I'm officially off duty. Can someone else bring his food while I fill out the report?"

"No! Get the food first, and then fill out the report." Perkins replied. "I'll stay here till you get back with the food."

Dawdry looked back as he left. He was glaring at Vince as he shut the door.

"Are you okay? Did you get hurt in the fall?" Perkins asked Vince.

"I'm okay, Doctor. I'm sorry about all of this. I hope the nurse isn't hurt very badly. Will she be okay?"

"She'll be okay." Perkins said. "I'm not sure her hip is broken. It might be just a bad bruise. I'll know for sure when I see her x-ray. She won't be working for a while though."

Dawdry returned with the new tray of food, and he and Dr. Perkins left. Vince sat looking at his food, regretting hurting the nurse, but was elated at the same time. He had the tool he needed. *I hope it works.* He thought a he got up slowly off the bed, rubbing his arm as if in pain. He sat down at his table, and ate his breakfast. For the first time, the food tasted good. He now had a tool and a plan for getting out of there. He felt like celebrating, but instead kept a serious look on his face. He wasn't going to smile and give the orderlies any reason to come back to his room. He knew they were watching him, but he didn't know Dr. Woitasczyk was right beside them.

"Does he know about the riot you idiots caused?" Woitasczyk asked Crawford.

"It wasn't our fault, Dr. Woitasczyk! You should have kept Watkins in a padded cell!" Crawford protested.

"When the day comes that I need patient advice from either of you I'll let you know! Does Davis know about the riot?" Woitasczyk asked again.

"I don't think so. He didn't mention it." Crawford replied.

"Good, come with me, I want to hear his side of what happened in his room this morning." Woitasczyk said.

CHAPTER THREE

LEARNING THE GAME

DR. WOITASCZYK KNOCKED ON the door and came in. Crawford, was at his side.

"Had a little excitement here this morning, did we?" Woitasczyk asked.

"Yes, I'm sorry. Is the nurse okay?" Vice asked.

"It's just a hairline fracture, she'll be sore, but she'll be okay in six weeks or so. I read Dr. Perkins and Dawdry's report. How did you trip on your slippers?" Woitasczyk asked, with a questioning look on his face.

"I got one foot tangled in the other. I guess I must have been standing on the edge of the other when I tried to reach for my pills."

"I'll make sure that doesn't happen again. I'm signing an order to get you some tennis shoes, socks and some pajamas instead of the gowns. How does that sound?"

"That's great! What about a clock?" Vince asked.

"I've ordered you a battery operated clock. There are no electrical outlets in this room. That's the best I can do." Woitasczyk replied.

"Any clock is okay. How about a battery operated TV or radio? I'll pay for it." Vince said.

"One step at a time, Dr. Davis." Woitasczyk replied.

"Okay, the clock will be fine for now. At least I'll know what time it is." Vince replied.

"I have arranged for you to be moved to the men's section tomorrow afternoon. We finally have an opening there." Woitasczyk said.

"What happened, did someone escape?" Vince asked and laughed.

"Of course no one escaped and that is not humorous!" Woitasczyk retorted. "We have an opening due to a patient being moved to isolation. I want to start daily therapy with you as soon as we get you moved."

"Sounds good to me." Vince lied.

"Excellent. If your condition continues to improve as it has, perhaps you can have more freedom and we wouldn't have to lock your door, except at night." Woitasczyk said.

"That would be great! I'm looking forward to more freedom." Vince said and smiled.

"You'll be allowed to mix in with the other patients in the men's section. We have a community room, with a television and magazines. I think that will help further your rehabilitation. The patients play cards, dominos, chess and other games that help stimulate the mind. In time, you will be good as new." Woitasczyk said.

"I'm feeling pretty good right now, Dr. Woitasczyk. I'm ready to get out of here." Vince replied, thinking of the bobby pin.

"In time and with further improvement, you will be getting out of here. However, you won't be able to go back to your profession, not at first anyway, but perhaps later, if you don't have any regression. You would be required to attend weekly outpatient therapy as a condition of your release, when that time comes."

"Thank you, Dr. Woitasczyk. I appreciate your help and understanding." Vince lied.

"Thank you, Dr. Davis. I always do my best for the patients put in my care. I am very pleased to see your improvement in attitude. Crawford has your newspaper and medication. We won't have a replacement nurse until tomorrow." Woitasczyk replied.

"What are the three pills I'm taking, Doctor?" Vince asked.

"One is an anti-depressant, one is for hypertension and the other is a blood thinner." Woitasczyk replied. "Your heart rate was extremely elevated when you were first taken to the hospital. Your pressure was through the roof, you could have had a seizure at any time. I've been watching your chart since you've been here, after today, you will be taking just the anti-depressant. You may even be able to get off those, if you continue your improvement."

Dr. Woitasczyk stuck out his hand, shook with Vince, and said. "I hope to see continued improvement from you. If so, you may be a candidate for an early release. Things will get better for you when you get to mix in with the other patients."

"I'll be out of here sooner than you think." Vince replied, thinking of the access panel.

"Let's hope so." Woitasczyk, unknowingly replied. "I'll send Crawford back with some pajamas, tennis shoes and socks. What size shoe do you wear?"

"A ten. I'd prefer plain pajamas, if that's okay." Vince said.

"I'll have Crawford bring you some scrubs for today. We will have to order the plain pajamas."

"Thanks, Dr. Woitasczyk."

Crawford handed Vince his pills. Vince slid them under his tongue, took a drink, and swallowed. Crawford handed him his paper, as he and Woitasczyk left. Vince immediately went to the bathroom, spit the pills in the stool, sat down and got up, activating the flushing mechanism. He watched as the water swirled, taking the pills down the drain. *It's a hell of a note when a man has to sit down and pee like a woman, to get the toilet to flush.* He thought as he went back in his room.

Dr. Woitasczyk had arrived back at the nurses' station, just as Vince sat down on his bed and picked up the paper. "Davis is up to something, I know he is." He said to Crawford.

"What makes you think so?" Crawford asked.

"All of the sudden he's become too damned accommodating. Both of you keep your eyes on him. Let me know if he does anything unusual." Woitasczyk said.

"He doesn't act like that when you're not in the room. He can be a real prick sometimes." Crawford said.

"With the help we have around here, it's no wonder! Pay attention to what I am saying, Crawford!" Woitasczyk snapped back.

"Yes, Doctor. What would we be looking for?" Crawford asked.

"If he starts whistling, singing, talking to himself or anything unusual." Woitasczyk replied. "I have never had a patient with his particular problem before and I have never seen any mental patient suffering from a psychosis recover as fast as he seems to be. Lately, he hasn't mentioned one word of his story that got him committed here. Either he's keeping it suppressed somehow on his own or it was all just a foolish lie to get attention. If that's the case, he's paying a big price for his foolishness." Woitasczyk said.

"You mean you think he's faking?" Crawford asked.

"No, he wasn't faking, as you call it. His previous behavior was genuine, and I know that he has Mental Post Forming, but he seems to be masking those symptoms at present. He'll have a relapse, you can count on it." Woitasczyk replied.

"How soon?" Crawford asked.

"I haven't studied his case long enough to make that prediction. It could happen today or a week from now. I'll have to keep a close watch on him to see if his improvement is a calculated plan on his part to look improved, or if his improvement is just a temporary remission. Let me know the minute anything changes in his behavior." Woitasczyk said.

"Dawdry said he was acting like a prick, before the nurse got hurt. He said Davis was up raising hell during the night." Crischell said, with a look of justification on his face, thinking his revelation would put him in favor with Dr. Woitasczyk. Instead, it angered Woitasczyk.

"That wasn't in Davis's records this morning! Why wasn't it?" Woitasczyk snapped back at Crischell.

"I don't know. I guess Dawdry forgot to write it down after the nurse got hurt." Crawford replied.

"All of you are worthless!" Woitasczyk screamed. "How am I supposed to keep up with what's going on, if it's not written down on his record? That's your job, not mine, goddamnit!"

"It's not my fault." Crawford countered.

"You could have mentioned it before Dawdry went home, for Christ's sake! But, oh no! That is too logical for you dumkoph's! Why did you wait to tell me until after he had gone home?" Woitasczyk bellowed.

"In all the excitement, I forgot to tell you." Crawford replied sheepishly.

"I'm placing you and Dawdry on report and I'm putting a disciplinary letter in both your of files! This is your last warning! If either of you, let something like this happen again, I'll fire you both and you'll both be walking down the street talking to yourselves!" Woitasczyk hissed.

"Dawdry's the one that talks to himself. I don't do that!" Crawford rebutted.

"Shut up you idiot! Walking down the street talking to yourself, is a goddamned cliché." Woitasczyk screamed.

"I don't know what a cliché is, Dr. Woitasczyk." Crawford replied.

"Ach der lieber!" Woitasczyk said crossing himself. "Look up Dawdry's phone number for me. Can you at least accomplish that?"

"He just moved. I don't know what his new number is." Crawford replied.

"That's just great! Now I'll have to wait and talk to him in the morning!" Woitasczyk screamed.

A group of patients heard Woitasczyk's loud outburst and started walking toward the nurses' station. Woitasczyk saw them coming, fearing another outburst from the recently agitated inmates, he said in a calm voice. "There's nothing to see here. Go back to whatever you were doing."

"Where's Adolph?" One asked.

"Do you mean, Rudolph Watkins?" Woitasczyk asked.

"Yeah, where is he? We can't play dominoes without him." The man said.

"Don't worry, there'll be a new patient in his room tomorrow. He's very intelligent, he can take Rudolph's place tomorrow. Go back to what you were doing." Woitasczyk said in a childish tone.

As the inmates walked away, Crawford seized the opportunity of the break in Woitasczyk's angry mood and asked. "About, Davis, Doctor? Is there anything in particular, other than what you've already mentioned, that you want us to be looking for?"

Woitasczyk turned to Crawford and asked. "What was that you said?"

Crawford repeated the question and Woitasczyk realized his loud outburst in earshot of the patients had been unprofessional. He regained his composure and said. "Thank you Crawford. Let me look at my notes on Davis."

He leafed through the notes and then said. "I interviewed most of his colleagues. None had ever seen him act in any way other than a

The Continent Of St. Louis - The Search For Answers

normal person. They said he had no ego and no bad habits. They all saw him as a good fellow worker and dedicated seismologist. The one thing in his recent behavior that doesn't fit their profile of him, is asking for cigarettes. I checked back with his boss, Dr. Leyland. He informed me that to his knowledge, he and the other employees at the seismic center had ever seen him smoke."

"What could that mean?" Crawford asked.

"I'm not certain yet, however, it's not unusual for mental patients to have split personalities. The Davis we are seeing now makes no mention of the disaster. In fact he seems to be avoiding the subject altogether. That very well could mean that a secondary personality has taken over as a defense mechanism and it is that personality that smokes cigarettes."

"Do you mean Davis could be insane in one of the personalities and sane in the other?" Crawford asked.

"My, you surprise me, Crawford. That is an excellent question, but the answer is no. The person we may be seeing now could appear sane, and I admit after talking to Davis this morning, one would think so. However, the other personality will be stronger as well as dominant, and will resurface." Woitasczyk said.

"Why is the current personality asking for cigarettes?" Crawford asked.

"From past cases I have treated, I have learned that it is a suppressed part of the usual or normal personality, which this alter-ego personality, is not obligated to suppress. Davis may exhibit other personalities, over time, but one thing's for sure. The personality that got him committed here, had Mental Post-Forming. The one we are seeing now doesn't appear to have that problem and that's why he appears normal and rational, but deep inside the other personality is still lurking." Woitasczyk said.

"Will you have to cure all of his personalities?" Crawford asked.

"A cure is impossible, Crawford." Woitasczyk replied.

"But didn't you tell him he would be getting out of here sometime in the future?" Crawford asked.

"Ya, I did, however, he won't be getting out. A psychiatrist always tells their mental patients they will be getting out some day. Most patients don't understand why they were committed in the first place. They need something to cling to, and hope of release is the strongest medicine a mental patient can have, but for most, the day never comes." Woitasczyk replied.

"Then you don't think Davis is recovering?" Crawford asked.

"No, I don't. Although, he seems to be more normal, I think it's just a projection of his calculating mind and I'm sure he's already anticipated a favorable response in return, by exhibiting the better behavior. Other than the Mental Post-Forming, it's too soon to make any kind of permanent diagnosis regarding what may be signs of multiple personalities. Nevertheless, I can tell you this for sure. He won't be getting out of here soon, if ever." Woitasczyk said.

"If he was insane, could he have become normal again?" Crawford asked.

"There is not even a chance of it." Woitasczyk replied. "One doesn't get over insanity like a cold or the flu. Davis definitely has the type of psychosis I diagnosed him as having, I'm certain of that, and his symptoms could re-occur and present a more violent personality at any time. Be very careful when you're in his room, and don't turn your back on him for a second. He'll become violent again, when he discovers his more pleasing personality isn't going to get him released. "

"What if it doesn't exhibit violent behavior? What will that mean?" Crawford asked.

"I'm sure he will become violent again. I've treated too many patients during my career to think otherwise. However, if he doesn't become violent again, there would be only four reasons to explain his non-violent behavior." Woitasczyk replied.

"What are they?" Crawford asked.

"The first would be that he was telling the truth, which of course, I don't believe at all. What he claims happened to him is impossible. The second alternative would be that he doesn't have Mental Post-Forming and made the story up to get attention. If that were the case, it has obviously backfired on him, and he's now found himself in a situation he couldn't have imagined would happen to him, and is looking for a way out. I don't think that's the case either. Third, I truly believe he does have Mental Post-Forming, and he believes everything he has claimed happened, but is still looking for a way out, since he insisted he has the obligation to warn the world. I'm sure the change in his behavior is just a ploy to get on our good side, which of course isn't going to work and

The Continent Of St. Louis - The Search For Answers

when it doesn't his original personality will reappear." Woitasczyk said with an air of confidence.

"What's the fourth reason?" Crawford asked.

"There is no fourth reason! Where did you get that ridiculous idea?" Woitasczyk asked.

"You said there were four reasons, just a minute ago." Crawford said.

"You must be hearing things! I clearly remember saying three, and that's because there are only three reasons!" Woitasczyk replied, getting an angry look on his face.

Crawford could see where the conversation was going. He changed the subject back to Vince, and said."Then Davis won't be getting out of here."

"No, he won't." Woitasczyk replied.

"Then he is crazy after all?" Crawford said.

Woitasczyk went off the deep end when Crawford used the word crazy. "Mein Gott, Crawford! How many times do I have to tell you dumkoph's that the inmates are patients with mental illnesses. Most of them are insane and insanity is a mental illness treated by professionals like myself. I don't want to hear any of you referring to them as crazy! Do you understand?"

Crawford apologized and Woitasczyk went on, in his doctor in charge tone. "Davis is insane, Crawford, and I want you to remember that. He's been telling the same lie so long that he believes it is fact, and has painted himself into the lie as the only hope and savior for the future of humanity. He has no idea he's insane, his erratic behavior is the result of no one believing him, and being committed to this institution. What he claims is going to happen in 2009, will not happen then, or ever. When 2009 rolls around he will still be in here and when it does and nothing happens, he will most likely get worse. He may end up in a straight jacket in a padded cell, but in any case, I'm sure he will never be released. Patients I have treated during my practice that have had similar psychoses only worsened as time went by. Davis will not be any different, so watch him close and watch what you say to him and never call him crazy."

"I will, but everybody knows that no one has been to the future and came back. Can't you give him a lie detector test, and prove to him that he's lying?" Crawford asked.

"Polygraphs are not a tool usually considered viable by psychiatrists. We know that mental patients have lied so long they believe what they're saying." Woitasczyk replied.

"I'd ask to take one if I was in here!" Crawford said.

"Dr. Davis hasn't mentioned taking a polygraph and I better not find out any of you dumkoph's are telling him to do so." Woitasczyk snapped.

"The less I'm around him the better I like it. I'm not looking for any conversations with him, but what if he asks me about it?" Crawford asked.

"Then you would tell him he'll have to speak to me about it, but even then I'd be reluctant to do so. He is not a criminal, he hasn't committed any crimes and he isn't a prisoner. He's a patient that simply needs to be confined, and I want you to remember that, Crawford. I don't want any of you antagonizing him, ridiculing him, or mentioning a polygraph to him. At this stage of the game and in view of his apparent improvement, I think taking a polygraph might set him back. We would have to ask him questions regarding his story. If we prove he's lying he wouldn't believe it, and I'm sure it would most likely set him off again. I don't want to see that happen." Woitasczyk replied.

"But if he passed it wouldn't that show he was telling the truth and not insane or making it up?" Crawford asked.

"Not necessarily. You don't believe him, do you?" Woitasczyk asked.

"No, at least I don't think so." Crawford replied.

"Well, you better not start believing him! Take Rudolph Watkins as an example. You saw what he did to his room. He claims he's Hitler and has the stupid mustache and plastered down, dyed hair to go along with it. Other than the fact he insists and believes he's Hitler, hates all Jews, and wants to exterminate them, he appeared to be sane, but he's not and he proved that yesterday. He most certainly would have passed a polygraph before yesterday, so keep that in mind and keep a close eye on Davis." Woitasczyk said.

Blake had walked up and heard the tail end of the conversation about Vince, and said. "Jeez, if I was locked up in here telling a crazy story nobody believed, I'd damn sure be asking to take a lie detector test just to show I wasn't lying and wasn't crazy."

"Stop using that word Blake! I just told Crawford to quit using crazy, in regard to the patients. I don't want to hear any of you saying it again!" Woitasczyk snapped.

Crawford had a slight smile on his face as Woitasczyk dressed Blake down. "What are you smiling about, Crawford?" Woitasczyk asked. "Do you think something amusing is going on here?"

"No, Doctor." Crawford replied feeling the sting of Woitasczyk's words again.

"Well, get serious! And you!" Woitasczyk said to Blake. "Think about what you're saying, you idiot! Even if Davis passed a polygraph and did not appear to be lying, would you believe he lived a different life in the future?"

Blake said nothing and Woitasczyk went on. "You couldn't possibly believe that anymore than you could believe he has come back from the future to save the world, and got put in a mental institution for his trouble. You don't believe him do you?"

"Well… I don't think so." Blake replied hesitatingly.

"Don't think so? What in the hell is the matter with you? No one believes him, that's why he was committed here for Christ's sake! You'd have to be an idiot to believe that! Some of what the patients have, must be rubbing off on you!" Woitasczyk snarled.

Blake said nothing and Woitasczyk went on. "Don't just stand there! One of you go and make the rounds, the other can keep his eyes on the monitor and watch Davis."

"Yes sir." Crawford replied, thinking Woitasczyk was through, but he wasn't. "I'm warning the both of you! If you cause anymore problems like yesterday, I will fire you both. You're lucky the news media didn't learn about the riot you caused yesterday, that's the only reason you two still have your jobs. Now get to work!"

As Woitasczyk left, the two relaxed. When he was out of earshot, Blake started complaining. "What happened yesterday wasn't our fault and he didn't have to call me an idiot!"

"Well, you sounded like one!" Crawford said.

35

"Screw you, Crawford!" Blake retorted.

"Screw you, you stupid bastard! You heard him, get going! Take this clock, and these clothes and shoes to Davis." Crawford said.

"Do it yourself, you prick!" Blake replied. "I hope he kicks your ass good, when you go in his room!"

"Come on, I'll go with you, if you're afraid." Crawford said patronizingly.

"I'm not afraid, goddamnit!" Blake replied defensively

"You're just too much of a chickenshit to go by yourself, Blake! Admit it, and I'll go with you!" Crawford retorted.

"I am not! The camera is recording everything anyway. We can check the tape when we come back and see if he was doing anything while we were gone." Blake countered.

Crawford knew Woitasczyk might be back any minute and find the errand not done. Realizing Blake wasn't going to go by himself, he said. "Okay, I'll go with you, Blake."

On the way down the hall, Blake said. "Hey, you remember those Terminator movies, don't you?"

"Yeah, so what?" Crawford replied.

"They sent Terminator's back from the future three different times." Blake said.

"They were movies, for Christ's sake! You're full of shit, Blake! The future is tomorrow, goddamnit! It ain't here yet. He didn't go to the future and then come back. Woitasczyk's right! You're an idiot! How did I get stuck with you, as a shift partner?" Crawford snarled.

They reached Vince's door and knocked. "Davis we're coming in." Crawford said. "We've got your clock and clothes. Get back against the wall, opposite of the door."

"Who's the big chickenshit now, Crawford?" Blake demanded. "When did you start asking him to get back against the wall? He's not a criminal. He ain't no axe murderer or something."

"Screw you, Blake! You know damn well you're afraid of him!" Crawford retorted.

"Come on little boy!" Blake said, offering Crawford his hand, as if he was leading a child into the room.

Crawford pushed his hand away, unlocked the door, and yelled. "We're coming in, Davis!"

Vince was against the opposite wall, as Crawford opened the door and both walked cautiously in the room.

"What's wrong?" Vince asked.

"Nothing. Here's your stuff." Blake said, tossing the articles down on the bed, while watching Vince closely.

"Let's go!" Crawford said to Blake, in an apprehensive tone. They both looked straight at Vince, saying nothing, as they backed out of the room, locking the door behind them.

"Davis could tell you were afraid of him." Blake said as they walked down the hall.

"Oh, bullshit! You were afraid of him too!" Crawford retorted. "You sure as hell wasn't going in his room by yourself, were you?"

Vince could hear them saying, screw you, to each other and arguing as they walked down the hall. He laughed and sat down on the bed and picked up the clock with one hand while he palmed the bobby pin with the other. He got up and placed the clock on his table, went in the bathroom and slid the bobby pin under the edge of the stainless shower stall.

Something's going on. He thought, as he came back and sat on his bed. *They were acting strange, as if they were afraid of me.* He removed his gown and slippers and put the scrubs and shoes on. *I have to try to get out tonight. I can't be here tomorrow and be moved to another room.*

He had wolfed down his lunch when the two orderlies had brought it and now it was time for supper. His appetite was soaring, he had a plan, he had a goal and he was making sure he got out with a full stomach. He didn't know when he might eat again, but he had to get away tonight and somehow get to his house before they missed him.

Crawford and Blake had watched Vince on the monitor all day. Vince had done an Academy Award job of acting for their benefit. He knew they were watching.

"Woitasczyk's getting paranoid." Crawford said to Blake. "Davis has acted normal all day. He doesn't seem dangerous to me."

"You better not let Woitasczyk hear you calling him paranoid, even though the bastard is. I think he's just as crazy as the rest of the lunatics' in here." Blake said, and looked in the direction of Woitasczyk's office. Woitasczyk was watching them, through his window.

"Shit! Blake said.

"What's wrong?" Crawford asked.

"He's watching us. Do you think he heard us?" Blake asked.

"Who's watching us?" Crawford asked.

"Woitasczyk! Don't look! He'll know we were talking about him." Blake said.

"Jesus Christ, Blake! You're the one that's paranoid! He can't hear us!" Crawford replied.

"For all I know, he might be able to read lips. We better get busy, what were we doing?" Blake asked.

"Talking about Davis. Woitasczyk didn't say he was dangerous. He just said to keep an eye on him and watch out for any strange behavior. Woitasczyk would lock you up if he saw how you're acting."

"Get off my ass, Crawford! You're the one that looked like you were going to shit your pants, when we took Davis's clothes in!" Blake retorted.

"Woitasczyk said he could become violent!" Crawford said, defending himself.

"Do you want me to get your mommy?" Blake asked, and then ducked Crawford's retaliatory swing.

As they scuffled and voiced derogatory remarks to each other, Dawdry and Crischell walked down the hall and punched in. As they reached the nurses' station Dawdry asked. "What's up men?"

"Woitasczyk's going to be up your ass! That's what's up!" Crawford said.

"What for?" Dawdry asked.

"You didn't write Davis's behavior from last night on his chart. Woitasczyk reamed my ass for it this morning, you idiot! You better lube your pucker ring up good. Here he comes!" Crawford said.

Dawdry looked up and saw Woitasczyk walking their way, and said. "That's bullshit! I had to stay over for an hour on my own time! Where's the transfer papers? I'm getting out of this nut house."

"Too late! He's already seen you!" Crawford said, as he and Blake started laughing.

"Dawdry!" Woitasczyk called out.

"Yes Doctor?" Dawdry replied meekly.

"I want to see you in my office, now!" Woitasczyk said emphatically.

"Ask him for a kiss before he bends you over, Dawdry." Crawford said.

"Go to hell, Crawford!" Dawdry replied.

"You better get a hemorrhoid pillow to sit on tonight! You're going to be sore down there!" Crawford said to Dawdry, and then said. "Come on, Blake! I don't like to hear a grown man cry."

CHAPTER FOUR

ESCAPE

VINCE LAY ON HIS bed after eating supper. He had saved the paper to go over again while waiting for lights out. He re-read some of the articles for a while and then started going over his escape plans in his mind. He knew they were watching and he wasn't going to do anything that would get their attention and spoil his chances.

He finished the paper and looked at the clock. It was nine-thirty, the lights would go off in a half hour. He got up from the bed, got out of his clothes, went in the bathroom, stepped in the shower and the water began to flow. *Always the perfect temperature.* He thought, and wondered how it was done.

There were no controls inside the shower. The water began to flow when the electric eye detected his motion entering, and went off when he stepped out. He removed the bobby pin and straightened it out. He bent it back and forth several times until it broke into two pieces in the middle. He bent a small hook on one end of both pieces and inserted both in the lock using one to push the tumblers down and the other to turn the lock. After two attempts, the access panel dropped open slightly. Vince stopped it with his hand and eased it open slowly until it hung down vertically, supported by its hinges. He grabbed the outer edges of the opening and put his weight on it, wanting to make sure the opening wouldn't give way, when he pulled himself up. Finding it sturdy, he pulled himself up and looked toward the wall where the stool and lavatory were located. Other than the small amount of light that shown directly above the opening, the interior was pitch black. He held himself in place hoping his eyes would adjust to the darkness, but it was hopeless. He couldn't see anything, and his heart sank as thoughts of failure began to enter his mind. *What the hell can I do now? I can't crawl around up there in the dark.*

He started letting himself down, when something slid down the side of his face. It was a light cord. He reached up with one hand, pulled the cord, and the area above lighted up. He pulled himself back up and saw a crawling platform, which led to an opening in the wall, above the toilet and lavatory. He was elated. He switched off the light, let himself down, let the water cover him, came out, dried himself off, walked back into his room and looked at the clock, only ten minutes had passed. He was getting anxious and knew it. He pulled back his covers and lay down. He picked up the newspaper again and started looking at the pages. He wasn't reading. His eyes didn't even register on the newspaper. He was seeing the access panel. His mind was on escape.

Twenty minutes later, the lights went off. He got up quickly, grabbed his spare towels, gowns, his pillow and the newspaper, stuffing and arranging all of it under his cover, making, what he hoped they would mistake for his sleeping body. Satisfied with the ruse, he went quickly to his bathroom, turned his scrubs inside out, put them on, and slipped into his socks and tennis shoes. He wet a washrag in the lavatory, squirted some soap on it, and tucked it inside his last towel and slid it under his belt line to use in case he got dirty climbing out through the wet wall. He stepped over the electric eye of the shower, pulled himself up through the hole and sat on the platform. He reached down and pulled the access panel shut with the hooked bobby pin. The spring-loaded lock clicked into place, almost noiselessly. He switched on the overhead light and made his way to the wet wall opening. Sliding the latch, he opened the panel door. There was another light cord inside the opening, he switched it on, went back and switched off the first light, then returned to the opening.

He looked down and saw a small metal ladder, attached to the wall, leading down to the floor. The small area contained enough room for a maintenance persons use, while servicing the plumbing and electrical. He stepped onto the ladder, closed the panel door, and climbed down to the floor. He looked to his left, and saw a lighted access shaft that ran vertically, in the center of the building. The steady hum of machinery could be heard, as he walked to the edge of the shaft. He looked up and down and saw that the shaft extended from the basement to the roof, with all of the utility lines for the building attached to one wall. He saw that each floor, on both sides, had a small platform identical to one he was standing on that was connected by ladders. He also saw a small lift used for bringing the tools a maintenance man would need to service the lines. He looked up and saw what looked like larger platform at the top. Light was shining in through vent slots in the sides of the walls that protruded above the roof. He went back and switched off the light in the service area, then returned, stepped out onto the ladder and climbed to the platform. There he found a door that lead out onto the roof. The light streaming through ventilation panels illuminated the small room he was in. Cigarette butts littered the floor next to a stool that he could see no purpose for. He looked out through the slits in the ventilation panels and saw the chopper pad, lighted brightly in the darkness. He was ecstatic, and thought. *Freedom's just a chopper ride away.* His hands shook from the exertion of his climb. *I'm really out of shape.* He thought as he pushed the doors quick release handle, opened it slightly, and peered out.

There was no one in sight. He looked for the cameras he knew would be there and spotted them. He also knew the hospital would have a security staff. Someone would be monitoring the cameras from an office inside. He undressed and turned his scrubs right side out and put them back on. He washed his hands and face with the washrag, insuring he had no dirt or grease on him to make him more noticeable once he reached freedom. He toweled himself off and dropped the towel and washrag down the shaft. Now all he had to do, was wait for the chopper he knew would come sooner or later and hope nobody discovered he was gone from his room. He was rolling his plan around in his head when he heard the beat of chopper blades in the distance. He waited anxiously as the beat of the blades came closer. He held his breath, hoping it wasn't some other chopper, headed elsewhere. It drew closer and started slowing down.

It's a Medi-vac! Come on, come on. Come to me baby. He thought and sighed with relief as he watched the Medi-vac slowly setting down on the pad.

The pilot shut the engines off and the rotors began slowing down. The paramedics jumped down, pulling the patient out as two hospital orderlies rolled a gurney up. The paramedics transferred the IV bags and monitoring equipment to the gurney and the four left, hurrying toward the emergency room. As Vince watched, the pilot got out, closed the patient access door on the Medi-vac and headed inside the hospital as the Medi-vac's blades came to a standstill.

It's now or never. He thought as he opened the door, stepped out, and found no one in sight. He looked up and saw the camera swing around on its turret, it was now pointing directly at him. He felt like a Deer caught in the headlights of an oncoming car. He knew he couldn't make a break for the Medi-vac without making it known, he was escaping. He waved at the camera, shut the door and walked slowly toward the hospital entrance, with his heart pounding in his chest. He was hoping whoever was watching would mistake him for a hospital worker and not sound an alarm. He was holding his breath while he walked, and thought. *If that camera follows me all the way to the entrance, I'm sunk!*

He heard the unmistakable sound of the camera moving on its turret. He stole a look, and saw it had swung back to its original position. Without a seconds hesitation he turned, ran to the chopper's door, and got in the pilot's seat. He looked the instruments and controls over and hit the switch. The engines came to life and the blades started rotating. He revved the engine higher and lifted off, just as the pilot came running out the door. He swung the chopper around and headed for El Cajon, as the pilot stood there in disbelief, yelling unheard obscenities at him. *It won't be long before they have a police chopper, up looking for me.* Vince thought, opening the throttle to maximum. He headed east as the engines roared, above him.

After watching the Medi-vac disappear into the darkness, the Medi-vac pilot had ran back inside to call the police. The two flight paramedics were coming down the hall as he ran toward them, yelling. "Call the cops!"

"What for?" One asked.

"Some son-of-a-bitch stole the Medi-vac!" Workman whined.

"Are you bullshitting us?" He asked.

"Hell no! The bastard just flew away in it!" Workman replied.

"Who was it, Workman?" He asked.

"I don't have any idea! I came in to take a piss and when I went back out, the Medi-vac was flying away. We've got to call the cops!" Workman insisted.

"Well, call them, Workman!" The paramedic said.

"I can't! I don't have my cell phone! It was in my bag in the chopper." Workman moaned.

"Well, we've got to notify somebody." The paramedic said.

They reached a nurses' station and called security, who in turn, called the police and the Medi-vac office. Twenty minutes later, as police looked on, a second Medi-vac chopper landed on the roof, dropped off the office manager of the Medi-vac company and lifted off again.

The office manager came storming up and started unofficially blaming the whole event on Workman.

"It wasn't my fault!" Workman protested. "I just went in to take a piss. I wasn't gone five minutes and the Medi-vac was leaving. The bastard has my billfold, all my money, my credit cards, and cell phone, goddamnit!"

"Take it easy." A police sergeant said. "My name's Rowland. I'm in charge here, don't worry, we'll get him. What's your cell phone number?"

"555-4302." Workman answered.

"Is that in the 619 area code?" Rowland asked.

"Yes, what difference does that make?" Workman asked.

"If he uses the phone, we can trace him to the location he's calling from. Which way was he headed?" Rowland asked.

"He was headed east when he left. He's miles from here now. He could have gone in any direction, once he cleared the area. He could be anywhere by now." Workman said.

"Burton." Rowland said.

"Yes, sir." A fellow police officer answered.

"Radio this cell phone number into dispatch and tell them to call the number and see if the bastard answers. Tell them to get a trace set up first."

As Burton left, Rowland turned to Workman and asked. "Did you get a good look at the individual who stole the Medi-vac?"

"No, it was already heading away when I came back out on the roof." Workman replied.

"Then you don't know if it's a man or woman we're looking for?" Rowland asked.

"No." Workman answered.

"Okay, we're going down to security. I guess that's all I need from you for now." Rowland turned to the Medi-vac officer and asked. "Did you bring the Medi-vac's I.D. number and other information for me?"

"Yes, here it is." He said handing it to Rowland.

"Okay, sign this complaint. After that, you can all go for now. Someone will get back to you if we need you further." Rowland said.

Workman's boss signed the complaint and Rowland walked off with two other police officers, heading for security.

"Goddamnit, Workman! This is going to be your ass!" His boss shouted. "You can damn well bet you're going to get some time off for this! I'll damn sure guarantee you that! Do you know what that unit cost?"

"No, sir." Workman answered.

"Well, you will when it comes out of your pay! You'll be working for free for the rest of your goddamned life!" His boss hissed.

"It wasn't my fault!" Workman protested.

"Who's fault is it, then?" His boss bellowed.

"Yours and the goddamned companies!" Workman shot back.

"How do you figure that?" His boss demanded.

"You sent me out on four straight runs without a piss break! I needed to piss so bad, I would've pissed my pants before we could have gotten back to the office." Workman said.

"Take a piss bottle with you next time, if there is a next time!" His boss barked.

"Union rules specify that we get a piss break after two flights! You sent me on four!" Workman countered.

"Not in the case of emergencies! That paragraph pertains only to pissing after routine flights!" His boss shot back.

Workman was beginning to see the uselessness of his argument and said. "Fine! I'll piss on the chopper floor next time!"

"There won't be any next time if I have anything to say about it! The home office will go ballistic, when they find out about this, in the morning. My ass is going to be on the line and your ass is going to be there right with me! Son-of-a-bitch! What a mess you've made of things!" His boss complained.

"I didn't do a damn thing wrong! How in the hell could I have known some asshole was going to steal the Medi-vac!" Workman protested.

"I don't have time to stand here and argue with you, Workman! I've got to get back to the office." His boss retorted.

"How are we getting back to the office?" Workman asked.

"You aren't going back to the office. You're suspended without pay until your hearing comes up!" His boss bellowed. "Come on." He said to the paramedics. "There's an ambulance waiting downstairs to take us to the office."

"How am I going to get home?" Workman whined. "My wallet was in my bag in the Medi-vac."

"Walk, for all I care." His boss said, as he left.

"Can't you give me a ride? I live right off the 54. It's right on the way." Workman yelled.

"The walk will give you a lot of time to think about your screw-up! You're looking at a month off without pay, at the minimum. Don't call us, we'll call you!"

Rowland was in the security office with a security clerk, reviewing the recordings taken from the roof camera, at the time of the hi-jacking.

"Right there! See him? The man that's coming out of the door." The clerk said.

Rowland watched as Vince waved at the camera.

"Freeze it right there." Rowland said. "Bring it in close. Let's see what this bastard looks like."

Vince's face zoomed in. His image distorted slightly as it pixilated, making it impossible for anyone to identify him positively.

The Continent Of St. Louis - The Search For Answers

"That didn't help." Rowland said and asked. "Do you know who he is?"

"No, I don't know him." The clerk answered. "I'll have to copy his image and run it through our employee database."

"Are you sure he works here?" Rowland asked.

"No, sir, but he has scrubs on." The clerk said. "Most of the employees wear scrubs."

"Does he have an I.D. badge on?" Rowland asked.

"I can't see any, sir." The clerk answered.

"What would he have been doing in that access room? Were you on duty when he came out the door? Did you see him?" Rowland asked.

"Yes, sir, I was. I saw him when he waved at the camera. Several employees use that room for a quick smoke. The hospital and the grounds are a no smoking environment. Smoking isn't allowed anywhere inside or outside on the grounds. I assumed he was smoking, knew he was caught on camera and waved."

"Burton, get up there and seal off the area, then call the detective unit. Tell them send a team over here to bag any evidence." Rowland said and turned back to the security clerk and asked. "Have you identified him yet?"

"Not so far. The photo I.D. database, didn't find any matches. I'm running it again to make sure. That's not a good image of him. It's distorted and it might not digitize good enough to make a perfect match."

"Can you do feature characterization comparison on his face?" Rowland asked.

"Yes, I'm going to do that next."

"Get me the identity, address and phone number of anyone in the database, whose facial features are close." Rowland said.

"It's coming up now, sir. I'll have it in a minute."

"Can you print me a few copies of the suspects' photo for downtown?" Rowland asked.

"No problem, Sergeant."

Thirty minutes later, two detectives arrived. It was Billy Edwards and Don Harper, known to be a couple of wise guys and not Rowland's first choice, if he had been given a say so.

"What's up, Sergeant Rowland?" Edwards asked.

"Someone hi-jacked a Medi-vac off the roof. I have some boys up on the roof guarding the room the suspect was in. See if you can find any evidence he might have left behind."

"What are we looking for?" Harper asked.

"Jesus Christ, Harper! Are you a detective or not?" Rowland exclaimed.

"You know damn well I am! Quit being a prick and tell me what you want us to look for!" Harper shot back.

"He may have been smoking in there. Collect any butts, otherwise, the usual. Have forensics do a rush on it." Rowland said.

"Right, Sarge." Edwards said as they left.

"Screw him!" Harper said when they got out of earshot. "I should have told the bastard to check the shit out himself."

"Why didn't you? Were you afraid of him?" Edwards asked.

"Screw you, Edwards! I noticed you were kissing his ass with that 'right, Sarge' shit! At least I had balls enough to call him a prick, while you stood there waiting for a thank you!" Harper retorted.

"There you go again, letting your Alligator mouth overload your Hummingbird ass! You're going to get your ass suspended some day, and you'll have your diarrhea mouth to thank for it, when it happens." Edwards said.

"I'll still be on the job when you're pushing a broom in some bar, you alcoholic bastard!" Harper snapped back.

Edwards threw a perfectly extended left hook, hammering Harper directly in the center of his chest. Harper's legs immediately collapsed from under him as his breath belched out in a ragged gasp. He fell face forward to the floor, smashing his lips into his teeth. As he lay their gasping for breath, Edwards leaned over him and snarled.

"You say one more word about me drinking again, and I'll beat another lung out of you! You know I haven't touched a drop in over a year!"

"I think you broke my goddamned ribs…" Harper wheezed, rolling over, while clutching his chest.

"You can thank your lucky stars I pulled up on that punch at the last second, otherwise, I might have caved your ribs completely in! Quit your bellyaching and get your ass up!" Edwards spat back.

"I can't move you son-of-a-bitch! My goddamned ribs feel like they've been separated, and a couple of my teeth are loose." Harper grumbled as blood trickled down the corner of his mouth.

"That's your own damn fault, smart mouth! Get your ass up!" Edwards hissed.

"Give me a hand, you asshole! You knew I was only kidding! You almost killed me, you bastard!" Harper complained.

"You're lucky that's all I did! Wipe that blood off your smart ass mouth before Rowland comes looking for us!" Edwards said, looking back over his shoulder.

"You're afraid of Rowland, aren't you?" Harper said, as he staggered to his feet.

"Don't go there, Harper!" Edwards threatened.

HOSPITAL SECURITY OFFICE

THE SECURITY CLERK CAME back in the room and said. "Here's the list, Sergeant. There are three possible matches."

Rowland compared their photos to Vince's image. "None of these are him." Rowland said.

"No, sir. I didn't think so. They're all day shift employees. They wouldn't have been on duty."

"How often do you notice someone using the access room for a smoke when you're on duty?" Rowland asked.

"Once or twice each shift."

"Do you turn those people in for smoking on the premises?" Rowland asked.

"No, sir, I haven't, in the past."

"I'll bet you will now, when your boss finds out what went on here tonight." Rowland said.

"Yes, sir, I'm sure I will."

"Thank you, you've been a big help. What's your name?" Rowland asked.

"Ben Allen. Could you put the part about me being a big help to you, in your report so my boss can see it, sir?" The clerk asked.

"No problem, Ben."

Rowland went back to the roof and met the two detectives.

"What's wrong with your mouth?" He asked Harper.

"I ran into a door." Harper replied.

Rowland shook his head and asked. "What have you got for me?"

"Not much." Edwards answered. "A few different brands of cigarette butts, a few hairs and some smeared prints. I don't think forensics is going to be able to do much with this. Did you do any good with security?"

"No. They've got the suspect on video coming out of this room, but his face is too distorted to identify when it's blown up. He doesn't show up on the employee database either." Rowland answered.

"What made security think he was an employee?" Harper asked. "Was he wearing an I.D. badge?"

"No. He was wearing scrubs, but he wasn't wearing an I.D. badge. The clerk saw him coming out of the door. He waved at the camera, so the clerk thought he was an employee taking a smoke break." Rowland answered.

"Well that won't help much. They sell scrubs at Wal-Mart. It could have been anyone." Edwards said.

"What about a terrorist disguised in scrubs?" Burton asked. "What if he planted the bomb, intending to use the Medi-vac to make his getaway."

"Christ! I didn't think of that!" Rowland exclaimed. "Call it in, Burton, tell the Bomb Squad I said to keep it quiet or the media will be all over the place!"

Burton keyed his lapel radio and started to call headquarters.

"I said call it in, Burton! Go use the telephone! You know damn well the news media listens to our radio calls!" Rowland barked.

"Sorry, Sarge." Burton replied and left to find a phone.

"What's inside that room?" Rowland asked Harper.

"It's really just a platform. It's a service entrance for maintenance employees. There's a ladder and a lift that goes down inside the hospital." Harper replied.

"Did you go down and check the interior?" Rowland asked.

"Hell no! It's dark in there! I shined my flashlight down, and couldn't see the bottom. I wasn't going down that goddamned ladder! I'm afraid of heights." Harper replied.

"Look, you stupid bastard! If he planted a bomb, it's probably somewhere down there. Get your asses back in there and see what you can find!" Rowland barked.

"Screw you, Sarge! That's the bomb squad's job. I'm not getting my ass blown up! This is your show, not ours. Come on Edwards. Let's get the hell out of here before the place blows sky high."

"I thought you said you're a detective, Harper!" Rowland barked.

"I am and I'll still have my ass intact when yours is blown sky high!" Harper spat back.

"I'm putting all of this in my report! The Chief will have both of your asses on the carpet in the morning!" Rowland threatened.

"Screw you and screw the Chief!" Harper yelled back over his shoulder as they walked away.

"Rowland will turn your ass into the Chief for saying that. You know they're buddies." Edwards said.

"Screw the Chief! I've got to go see a doctor. I think you caved my ribs into my lungs, I can't breathe." Harper wheezed.

An hour later, the Bomb Squad arrived. One group began sweeping the hospital floors with dogs. Another started a search of the shaft from the rooftop. Since there had been no actual bomb threat called in, the hospital was put on ready alert. Security personnel were standing by, while the sweep was made.

The two night shift Mental Ward orderlies were leaning back in their chairs reading magazines, not paying any attention to the alert.

"Another bomb scare." Dawdry said to Crischell.

"They won't find one." Crischell replied. "They never do."

"I'm going in the back room and take a nap." Dawdry said. "Wake me up if we have to get out of here."

"Piss on you! The bomb can blow your ass up for all I care." Crischell retorted.

"Screw you, Crischell!" Dawdry retorted. He gave him the finger and left.

CHAPTER FIVE

ON BOARD THE MEDI-VAC

VINCE WAS NEARING EL Cajon, when he heard a phone ringing. He reached in a bag in the seat beside him and pulled out a cell phone. He laid it down and ran his hand around in the bag, and pulled out a wallet. He flipped it open and saw a pilot's license in the centerfold. He looked at the photo and recognized the pilot as the man who had been shaking his fist at him as he flew away.

He'd probably like to get his hands on me. Vince thought, putting the wallet and phone back in the bag as he tried to think of places he could land. *I have to find someplace close to my house to set down.*

Not wanting to be spotted, he avoided Gillespie Field, flying south of the airport. He remembered the Marine Corporal telling him they couldn't land at Gillespie Field when the Marine chopper had rescued Jim, he, and two co-workers from the Seismic Center at UCSD. They had dropped the co-workers off in Santee to be with their families, and had then taken Jim and he to Area 51. He thought of those two men, he could see them trying desperately, to run across the shaking ground of the Santee High School Football Field, and thought. *For now, they're still alive and well.*

Warning them of the disaster crossed his mind for a second, he then realized, he couldn't remember their names. He was having difficulty sorting things out. He was mixing things that happened in the future, in with the present. *Neither of them would be working at the center yet. They might not even live in the San Diego area.* He thought.

It seemed like years ago to him, that all of that had happened. For him and everyone else, it would be four years before it happened again. He thought about how no one had believed him and thought he was crazy when he had tried to warn them. He came out of his memories realizing he was now on the run. He snapped back to reality, realizing he hadn't escaped yet. He scanned the skies around him looking for any signs of pursuit and found none. So far, he had been lucky, no one was following him. He flew on and spotted the Granite Hills High School football field below.

Perfect! He thought as he slowly descended, setting the chopper down as light as a feather and switching the engines off. He knew someone would have heard the chopper as it was landing in the residential area and would report it. He started to get out and then caught himself at the last second, and thought. *I've got to get rid of my prints.* He wiped the controls down, then the phone and billfold. Satisfied, he stepped down to the ground knowing he needed to get away from the area as fast as he could. He saw household lights coming on in the neighborhood as he took off at a jog for his house, which was at least, a mile away. He ran until he was out of breath, slowing down to a walk, as his breath came in ragged gasps and his sides ached.

Ten minutes later, he reached his house, went around back, and went in through the back door of the garage. It felt strange, yet familiar. It was like when he had gone back to his grandmother's house after graduating from college. It was the same house, with the same furniture, but everything seemed smaller than he had remembered it to be. He went into the kitchen from the garage and made his way to his bedroom. He opened all the blinds and let the moonlight shine in to illuminate the room. He got out of the scrubs and changed to jeans and a t-shirt, got a suitcase out and started packing the things he would need. Then a thought struck him. *I don't have my wallet. It's in our room at the motel in 2009. What am I going to do without it?*

Then he saw his wallet, a package of Winston cigarettes and a lighter laying on the nightstand beside his bed. He picked up his wallet and thought. *How in the hell can this be here?*

He went through the wallet and found his driver license, pilot license, his UCSD I.D., and all of his credit cards.

"Shit, I am crazy!" He said aloud after finding the contents intact. "I have to be crazy! There isn't any other explanation."

A neighbor dog started barking, startling him back to reality. He went to the window and shut the blinds. *I've got to get out of here now!* He thought.

As his eyes adjusted to the semi-darkness, he went to his fireproof box and got out the five hundred dollars he kept for emergency money and put it in his pocket. He found his address and phone book next to his cell phone that was sitting in the charger.

Goddamn! He thought. *How could that still be here, when I had it with me when we were rescued by the Marine chopper.*

He couldn't remember what had happened to it. He hadn't tried to use it since the night he'd tried to call his parents on the flight from D.C. to Springfield.

Then another thought struck him. He went back to the garage and saw his car. He had walked right past the car without seeing it in his hurry to get in the house.

Oh, damn! He thought and began to realize why no one had believed him. *I told them I drove my car to the lab the night San Diego was destroyed and here it is in the garage. No, wonder they think I'm crazy! They must have seen my cell phone and wallet laying on the nightstand when they took me to the hospital!*

He felt foolish and his face began to flush. He put his hand to his head and thought. *Maybe I am crazy.*

He went back to his bedroom and started gathering his things, thinking. *They'll lock me back up in that room if they catch me and I'll never get out.* He put the cell phone in his pocket and threw the rest of the things he was taking in his suitcase. His mind was racing. He began feeling panic setting in. He sat down on the bed, tried to relax, and started sorting out what he would need to start a new life somewhere else. All he knew was that he couldn't get caught. He knew he would be finished, if he got pulled over by the police. He felt certain they already knew he had escaped and thought. *They'll be looking for me everywhere and the first place they'll come is here after they figure out it was me that stole the Medi-vac. When they find the car gone, they'll know I was here and what I'm driving.*

He knew they could easily find out what kind of car he drove and what the license number was. He put the title to his car in the suitcase with the rest. He knew he was going to have to sell the car and buy another, when he got out of California. He turned on his laptop and checked his bank account. He had over twenty thousand dollars in his checking account and noticed that UCSD was still paying him. He had another thirty thousand in his savings, and thought. *Fifty thousand dollars will get me a long way away from here. I can take a cab to the airport, catch a flight to South America and disappear.*

As quickly as he had thought of the idea, the foolishness of it became apparent. *I don't know anybody in South America! I can't go there!*

He tried to think of other more suitable destinations and realized he couldn't be seen at the airport, and thought. *I'm screwed! I don't have any other choice! I'm going to have to use my car. I'll just have to get lost until it's safe to come back here.*

It seemed like a million other thoughts were rushing through his mind as he considered what to take and what to leave behind. He knew he couldn't return to the house and didn't want to forget anything. He became jittery and pressed for time as thoughts of his situation and the feeling of being a hunted criminal, with a dragnet out for his capture, came to mind. *I'm not a criminal, except for stealing the Medi-vac and without any prints, that will be hard to prove, besides, no one knows I can fly a helicopter.*

He was ready to leave and looked around the room one last time. He saw his diplomas on the wall and thought. *I might need them.*

He took them down and threw them in the suitcase along with his laptop and the picture of his mom and dad. He knew his parents must be worried about him. They had talked on a regular basis since he had been in California.

Maybe that's where I should go. He thought, but his mind started playing tricks on him. From his surroundings, it seemed like he was back in 2005, but his mind was still in 2009. He remembered that he and his parents were at Camp Davis the last time he'd talked to them, and wondered if they were at the farm. Then he remembered Woitasczyk said they knew he had been confined to Gifford. *They must be worried to death*. He thought.

He considered calling them and telling them he was all right. He then remembered the time difference between San Diego and St. Louis and realized it was too late.

He went to his nightstand, got his .357 Magnum, the box of shells and his permit. He couldn't imagine why he would need a gun, but a gun had been had been his constant companion in 2009. Without a second thought, he threw it in the suitcase.

What else? He wondered as he looked around the room and remembered his toiletries. Before closing the suitcase, he went to the bathroom to collect the items. The instant he entered the room, his mind flashed back to the night Dr. Leyland had called and woke him in the darkness of that early morning in August. He remembered being confused and thinking, he was dreaming. He had walked into the bathroom, turned on the light and had looked at himself in the bathroom mirror. He had seen a reflection he had barely recognized, wanted a cigarette, reached for the lighter in his fatigue pocket, and the penny had fallen to the floor. He remembered picking the penny up, being shocked and panicked when he saw the date and thinking a cold shower would wake him up, but he never took the shower. The next thing he remembered was hearing the Sheriffs' Department announcing themselves, knocking on his door and calling out his name. The last thing he remembered was tripping on his pant legs and falling backwards.

All of that now, seemed like it was years ago as he looked at himself in the same mirror and remembered Woitasczyk telling him they never found the penny. Woitasczyk had told him the penny and everything else was part of his psychosis, but he had felt certain, it wasn't. He was sure the penny had to be there, if not, then they found it and were lying to him. *It's got to be here! Why would they lie*. He wondered.

He was sure he had dropped the penny and the discs, but he didn't see any sign of either and thought. *Maybe it is all in my mind. Maybe I imagined all of it like Woitasczyk said I did.*

He thought of his car in the garage and the other things that were in his house, that shouldn't be there. He knew there was no way to explain it and began thinking of the Twilight Zone, where anything was possible.

He dismissed the idea and thought of Woitasczyk's boastful speech. *I wonder if his men found the penny and the discs, and he's keeping the fact from me.* Then he reconsidered the thought. *Why would he do that? What would he have to gain? I don't like Woitasczyk, but I don't think he would have kept me in the mental ward if they had found the penny and the discs.*

He got down on his hands and knees and looked behind the stool. He didn't see anything at first, and almost got up to look elsewhere. He poked his head further alongside the shower and the stool base till his head touched the wall and saw the penny. *There it is!* He thought in his excitement.

The penny was on edge leaning against the back of the toilet base, still as shiny as ever. He reached around, grabbed it, stood up and looked at the face. 2009 gleamed brightly back into his eyes.

"I knew I wasn't crazy!" He said aloud, staring at the penny. "None of it was a dream. None it was a figment of my imagination, or the so called Mental Post-Forming, as that know it all Woitasczyk, so proudly announced it was."

He realized he'd been talking out loud to himself and laughed. He continued staring at the penny recalling finding it at Lambert Field and remembered the carnage he'd seen walking around the destroyed terminal. and thought. *If I hadn't escaped from Gifford, Woitasczyk would have screwed up everything. Is he in for a surprise when he comes in tomorrow morning. I'll be in Arizona by then.*

He packed his toiletries in his suitcase, went to the kitchen, got a baggie, put the penny in the baggie, and put it in his pocket. *My proof.* He thought, and smiled to himself.

He flipped on the TV and shut the rest of the blinds. KQTV was reporting breaking news. The reporter was reporting live from in front of the hospital he had escaped from. Police and dogs could be seen in the background, as the woman spoke. *Here it comes.* He thought.

"Ladies and gentlemen, it looks like the bomb scare was a hoax. Police aren't giving out much information at this point, but we have learned from informed sources, that police were called in about an hour ago to do a floor-by-floor search of the hospital. As far as we know, there was no bomb threat called in to the police or the media. We hope to get Sergeant Rowland, who is heading up this investigation, to fill us in later. So far, the hospital has had no comment regarding the bomb scare.

The only thing we do know for sure is that a Medi-vac helicopter was hi-jacked from the rooftop of the hospital about two hours ago, by as yet, unknown persons. We have no idea at this time if the two incidents are related."

The reporter held her hand to her ear listening to her director at the station. Vince was sitting on the edge of his chair, waiting for the reporter to mention his name, as an escapee and the hi-jacker of the Medi-vac.

"Excuse me for that." She said. "I have further developments in the Medi-vac hi-jacking case." *This is it!* Vince thought.

"We have just learned that the Medi-vac helicopter has been found in El Cajon at the Granite Hills High School football field. Neighbors had called 911 earlier, reporting the low flying helicopter and its landing at the football field. Although speculated by some sources, we don't know yet if this whole thing may have been some prank, carried out by students. One source, who asked not to be identified, has suggested the bomb scare may have been a diversion tactic used by the hi-jacker of the Medi-vac, to confuse the police. School officials that have been contacted, have no comment at this time. We have learned however, that police are now checking to see if there are any students in the El Cajon area that have a pilots licenses and in particular, a helicopter certification. Stayed tuned in, I'll keep you posted and be back live as this story develops. Reporting live, I'm, Jean Simmons."

The station went back to the scheduled programming. Vince turned off his TV, smiled to himself, and thought. *They're chasing the wrong person. No one knows I'm gone, and they won't till tomorrow morning.* He was relieved.

FLIGHT

VINCE, THREW HIS SCRUBS and tennis shoes in a plastic bag to dispose of later. He grabbed the suitcase, and took both to the garage and put them in the trunk of his car. He reached up, unscrewed the light bulb, then pulled the quick release chain on his garage door, and rolled it up as quietly as he could. He released the parking brake, put the car in neutral, pushed it out the door, and coasted down the driveway to the street. He went back inside, rolled down the garage door, attached the lifting mechanism, screwed in the light bulb and locked the back door behind himself as he went out. He got back in his car and coasted to the corner before starting his engine. He looked back up the street and saw no lights on in any of the houses. Confident no one had seen him, he put the car in gear and turned the corner.

He looked at his dash clock, it was one a.m. He stopped at a convenience store, filled the gas tank, bought some snacks, cold drinks, a cup of coffee, a carton of cigarettes and some lighters.

He stopped next at the Bank Of America and withdrew an additional five hundred dollars from the ATM. He looked in all directions as he walked back to his car. There was no one was in sight. Certain he hadn't been seen by anyone that knew him or had forgotten anything, he headed for Interstate 8, and Arizona.

He turned on his radio and sipped his coffee as he drove. He listened as they continued the report from the hospital. He laughed out loud and almost spilled his coffee when he thought of Dawdry and Crischell sitting in the nurse's station thinking all was well.

They'll get chewed out good in the morning. He thought and wondered how long it would take them to figure out how he had escaped and then realize it was he who had hi-jacked the Medi-vac. He smiled as he drove, proud of the ingenuity and resourcefulness he had used in his escape from Gifford. His escape reminded him of one of his favorite movies, 'The Shawshank Redemption.' He imagined he must have been feeling the same sensation, Andy Dufresne had felt, when he escaped from Shawshank.

It was only a movie. He thought. *But Andy wasn't guilty of anything, and neither am I.* Then he remembered the Medi-vac.

They're calling it a hi-jacking as if there were passengers on board. When they put two and two together, I'll be a hi-jacker, as well as, being an escaped lunatic, when they find me gone.

The thought troubled him, but was soon gone as he drove on through the night, heading east, with hundreds of other thoughts running through his mind. *Where am I going?* He didn't know for sure. *What will I do when I get where I end up? I'll have to work that out.*

He thought of his parents again. *When they find out I escaped, it will add to their worries.* He reconsidered his thought of calling them and decided not to call. *The less they know about me, and where I am, the better it is for me and them.*

He remembered how his parents had coped with the disaster in 2009, and had made it through, mostly on their own. *They'll be all right. It will be better if I go see them in person, when I can.*

He saw a Highway Patrol Cruiser going in the opposite direction, which brought him out of his thoughts. He pulled off at the next rest area and checked his taillights and headlights. He didn't want to get stopped for any reason. After checking, and finding all working perfectly, he got back on the interstate and resumed his journey east, thinking. *I'll stop in Yuma and gas up and get a motel.*

He didn't feel sleepy, but his body ached from the rigors he'd put it through, while escaping and running to his house. *A soak in a hot tub will feel good, compared to the monotonous shower in my room at Gifford.*

His mind wandered back to his house. *My yard looked overgrown in the moonlight. I'll have to find a lawn maintenance service that accepts credit cards.* He wasn't worried that his house would sit empty while he was gone. It was paid for and the monthly utility bills were debited from his bank account. One thought lead to another as he drove on. *When they find out I'm gone, the first place they're going to look for me is my house.*

He tried to think if he had left any clues behind that would tell them he'd been there. He could think of nothing that would indicate in any way that he had recently been there. *A few missing clothes and toiletries won't be noticed.* He thought. Then he remembered his car. *They'll notice it's missing. I'm going to have to get rid of it soon!*

The thought of selling his house entered his mind. *How can I do that when I'm on the run?* He wondered.

He lost the San Diego radio station signal and switched to a station playing music. He tried to relax, but he still had the feeling of an escaped prisoner that everyone was searching for.

He saw a few cars heading in both directions as he drove, looking at each suspiciously, as they passed. Lost in his thoughts of what he was going to do, the miles slipped quickly away.

He came back to reality as he passed through the giant sand dunes and crossed over the Colorado River. Yuma's lights shinned brightly ahead, he was feeling better, he was out of California and felt safer knowing he was out of the grasp of California law enforcement. He pulled off Interstate 8 at the first exit with a motel and checked into a room. He was sound asleep fifteen minutes later with his .357 Magnum on his nightstand.

CHAPTER SIX

THE COVER-UP

DR. WOITASCZYK WAS UP early. He had turned his TV on at five a.m., watching the unfolding bomb scare and Medi-vac hi-jacking stories at the hospital. He called the nurses' station and talked to Crischell, who sounded half-asleep.

"Everything is running smoothly." Crischell said.

"What has Davis been up to?" Woitasczyk asked. "Did you switch on the lights and check on him occasionally, like I told you to?"

Checking on Vince had completely slipped Crischell's mind. He, and Dawdry, had slept most of the night.

"Yes." He lied, without fear of being caught. Nothing ever went on at night.

"What was he doing when you checked?" Woitasczyk asked.

"Sleeping." Crischell replied. He switched on the lights in Vince's room and saw what he thought was Vince, lying in his bed, and said. "We had a bomb scare here tonight, but everyone slept through the floor check. There hasn't been a peep out of anyone all night."

"I will be in early. I want to see Davis as soon as I get there." Woitasczyk said.

"Okay, anything else?" Crischell asked.

"Has Watkins room been cleaned up?" Woitasczyk asked.

"Yeah, everything's back to normal." Crischell replied.

"Good, I'm going to move Davis to Watkins room today. I want to go over a few things with him before I move him. Make sure he's up by seven and have the paperwork ready. I'll be there by then." Woitasczyk said.

"Yes, sir. I'll take care of it." Crischell hung the phone up, tapped his baton loudly on the inner office window, and yelled. "Wake up, Dawdry! Woitasczyk's going to be in early today."

Dawdry came out of the office rubbing his eyes. "What time is it?" He asked.

"Five-fifteen, we forgot to check on Davis last night. I told Woitasczyk we did, so don't forget it." Crischell said.

"You better write it in the log. Woitasczyk checks it the first thing." Dawdry said.

"Why do I have to do everything?" Crischell asked.

"You told him you checked up on Davis, I didn't. It should be in your handwriting. What time is Woitasczyk going to be in?" Dawdry asked.

"He'll be here at seven. He's moving Davis to Watkins room today." Crischell said.

"Why don't you wake Davis up now?" Dawdry asked. "That will piss him off."

"No way! I'm not doing that. I don't want the bastard all stirred up when Woitasczyk gets here. We'll wake him up at six-thirty."

"I've got to take a piss." Dawdry said.

"You smell like you already have! Look at the front of your pants." Crischell said, needling Dawdry.

"Screw you, Crischell! Why are you always such a prick?"

"So I can jack with you, Dawdry! Get going, clean yourself up, and get on some clean whites. You stink!"

Dawdry was a medium built, Neanderthal looking man, with red, wiry hair that was matted down over his beetle brow. His blue eyes were bleary and bloodshot. His wrinkled, white trousers were stained with what looked like dried urine on the crotch, and his shirt had food stains on the front, left over from his sloppy eating habits. He looked more like a drunk than an orderly. He walked toward the restroom, mumbling to himself and grabbing some clean whites on the way. "Worthless buck toothed asshole!" He said under his breath, thinking of Crischell.

"I heard that!" Crischell yelled at him, unconsciously feeling of his prominent front teeth.

At six-thirty, Crischell turned on the lights in Vince's room and called over the speaker. "Wake up, Davis! Dr. Woitasczyk wants to see you in a half hour. You're moving today! Rise and shine!"

There was no movement from under the covers and Crischell got angry.

"Wake up Davis! Get your ass out of bed, right now!" He shouted.

Again, there was no movement in response to his voice.

"All right smart ass! Have it your way! We're coming down there right now! If you're not out of bed when we get there, you're going to damn well wish you were! We'll drag your lazy ass out of bed and dump you on the floor! I'm not messing with you, get up!"

There was still no movement.

"Let's go." He said to Dawdry. "I'm going to teach that lazy bastard a lesson, he won't forget."

They arrived at Vince's door and pounded on it with their batons.

"Last warning Davis! Be up, or you'll be wishing you were!" Crischell shouted.

Getting no answer, he unlocked the door. With batons ready, they went in and saw what they assumed was Vince.

"You asked for it!" Crischell yelled, raising his baton in the air.

"Don't hit the bastard!" Dawdry yelled. "You start beating him, and he's going to claim brutality."

Crischell lowered his baton and pulled the cover back, ready to drag Vince out of bed, and discovered the ruse.

"What the hell? Where are you Davis?" Crischell shouted. "Go look in the bathroom, Dawdry."

"Not by myself! Screw you, Crischell! You go!"

"You're a big pussy!" He said to Dawdry, and then yelled. "All right Davis! Your fun and games are over! Get your ass out of the bathroom now, or we're coming in and get you!"

Crischell fully expected to hear Vince say okay and come out laughing at them for making a fool out of them. There was no reply.

"Let's get him." Crischell said to Dawdry. "I don't want Woitasczyk up my ass when he gets here. He already sounded pissed on the telephone."

The Continent Of St. Louis - The Search For Answers

They went in the bathroom, there was no sign of Vince.

"What the hell? He's not here!" Crischell said to Dawdry. "You didn't leave the door open when we came in, did you?"

"Hell no! Do you think I'm stupid?" Dawdry asked.

"Hell yes, you're stupid! Look under the bed, you asshole! He's probably hiding there. Bend all the way down, he's probably trying to hide back against the wall." Crischell ordered.

Dawdry didn't bend down all the way and Crischell shoved his baton in the crack of Dawdry's ass, goosing him.

"Stop it you homo! Get your baton out of my ass!" Dawdry yelled.

"Is he under there?" Crischell asked.

"No! He isn't here! I can see all the way to the goddamned wall! I'm tired of your shit, Crischell! Look for yourself if you don't believe me!"

"I believe you! Get up!"

As Dawdry got up, Crischell said. "We're in some deep shit here. There's no way, Davis could have gotten out of this room, without help. What the hell are we going to tell Woitasczyk?"

"Hell, I don't know! You figure it out smart-ass! You're the one who talked to Woitasczyk and said everything was okay."

"You've got to give me some help here, Dawdry! We've got to cover our asses somehow. Have you got any ideas?" Crischell asked in desperation.

"Blake said he thinks Davis is like those Terminators. He thinks Davis is a time traveler. Maybe he went back to where he came from in the future." Dawdry replied.

"Shut that bullshit up! This is serious, goddamnit!" Crischell yelled. "He's escaped somehow, that's all. You're a moron, just like Blake!"

"All right, smart-ass! You know it all! You tell me how he escaped." Dawdry replied.

"The door was locked. Davis isn't a time traveler and he wasn't Houdini, so someone had to have helped him escape." Crischell replied.

"No one had the keys, but us. I think what Blake is saying makes sense." Dawdry said.

"You would, you dumb shit! Damn! I'm tired of hearing about Blake's science fiction bullshit! Let's go, we've got to check the tapes before Woitasczyk gets here. Maybe we can find out how he got out of here before Woitasczyk comes in."

They went back to the nurses' station and reviewed the recordings of Vince's room, starting just before lights out."

"There he is!" Crischell said. The screen went blank for a few seconds when the lights went out.

"Son-of-a-bitch! Where is he?" Crischell yelled.

The video camera had not been able to adjust immediately to the darkness. All they could see was indistinguishable movement for a few seconds, and then it was gone. After the camera adjusted, the rest of the tape showed the fuzzy form of a person, under the covers, in the bed. They watched the blurry recording for a few minutes and then fast-forwarded the tape up to the time when Woitasczyk had called and Crischell had turned on the lights. They clearly saw the same form, that they had seen, when they had entered the room.

"You should have turned the lights on like Woitasczyk said." Dawdry complained.

"What good would that have done? I would have thought he was in bed. You would have too, if you had stayed out here like you should have!" Crischell retorted.

"Don't try and blame this on me!" Dawdry barked.

"You're just as guilty as I am!" Crischell retorted.

"What are we going to do?" Dawdry asked.

"Check the corridor tape! Someone helped him, that's for damn sure!" Crischell replied.

The corridor tape revealed nothing. No one, other than the police and dogs, had been in the corridor all night, until they had gone to wake Vince.

"What the hell are we going to tell Woitasczyk?" Dawdry asked.

"That, Davis isn't in his room." Crischell replied.

"Oh, that's brilliant! He's going to know we were asleep!" Dawdry whined.

"You were asleep, Dawdry. I wasn't." Crischell lied.

"You aren't going to tell him are you?" Dawdry asked.

"If it means saving my job, I will." Crischell replied.

They both shut up as Dr. Woitasczyk walked in the corridor entrance.

"Is, Davis ready for me to see him?" Woitasczyk asked as he walked up.

"No, Doctor. He's not in his room." Crischell answered.

"Not in his room? Where the hell is he then?" Woitasczyk asked.

"We don't know, but he's not in his room." Crischell replied.

"Did he break out?" Woitasczyk asked in an alarmed voice.

"No, sir, the door was locked. There wasn't a sound from his room all night." Crischell replied.

"That's impossible! Check the tapes!" Woitasczyk roared.

"We've already checked the tapes, no one but the police was in the corridor all night, until we went to wake Davis up." Crischell replied.

"You mean to tell me you two were here all night and never had a notion that he was breaking out? Neither of you heard a damn thing?" Woitasczyk demanded.

"No, sir we didn't." They both replied.

"Then how the hell did he get out of his room?" Woitasczyk asked angrily.

"We don't know, sir." They answered.

"You were both asleep, weren't you?" Woitasczyk demanded.

"No, sir. He was, I wasn't." Crischell replied.

"Why, you ass kissing squealer!" Dawdry said making a move toward Crischell.

"That's enough out of both of you!" Woitasczyk snapped. "You're both responsible, and I'm placing both of you on report! Call security, Crischell. Get them up here. You come with me, Dawdry. I want to check his room."

Dawdry unlocked the door of Vince's room and they went in. Woitasczyk looked the room over. He checked the window, the bathroom, under the bed and found nothing, and said. "He couldn't have gotten out of here, by himself!"

"Do you think he's a time traveler? Did he go back to the future?" Dawdry asked Woitasczyk.

"You must be an idiot! Where did you get that ridiculous idea, for Christ's sake? Hell no, he's not a time traveler you, dumkoph!" Woitasczyk snarled.

"Well, he isn't here! We told you that!" Dawdry said.

"I can see that! I am not blind or an idiot like you! There's a logical explanation, and I'll find out how he got out of here! If you two had anything to do with his escape, you'll both be walking down the street talking to yourselves."

"Walking down the street talking to ourselves? I don't know what you mean." Dawdry said.

"You'll both be fired! Is that plain enough English?" Woitasczyk bellowed.

"It's not my fault, Doctor! I didn't help him. I was asleep! Crischell had to be the one that helped Davis." Dawdry replied.

"One thing is for damn sure, Dawdry! Someone helped Davis, he couldn't have escaped from this room otherwise! I'll find out which one of you worthless morons is lying, and when I do, you'll both be facing charges!" Woitasczyk hissed.

"I didn't do it, and I'm not lying! We both looked at the recordings before you got here. Davis didn't come out the door and no one was in the corridor, other than the police all night." Dawdry said.

"Do you expect me to believe no one helped him and he just disappeared into thin air?" Woitasczyk asked.

"I admit I was asleep, but Davis was in this room when we checked right before lights out and now he's gone. Has anyone ever disappeared or escaped from here before?" Dawdry asked

"Absolutely, not! No one has ever disappeared and no one has ever escaped!" Woitasczyk yelled, as the hospital Security Chief, David Norton, walked in the room with two guards.

"What's happened, Doctor?" Norton asked.

"A patient has escaped, Norton." Woitasczyk answered.

"Who was it?" Norton asked.

"His name is Vince Davis, Dr. Vince Davis." Woitasczyk replied.

"How did he escape?" Norton asked.

"How the hell would I know?" Woitasczyk spat back. "If I knew how he escaped I wouldn't have called you! Call the police! Tell them Davis has escaped and get them over here!"

"Is, Davis dangerous? Is he criminally insane?" Norton asked.

"No. Davis is not any danger to anyone, but himself. He's not a criminal. He suffered a break down, he's delusional, or at least he was." Woitasczyk replied.

"Well, this is all we need! First, some of your orderlies caused a riot in the mental ward, then some prankster called in a bomb threat and

The Continent Of St. Louis - The Search For Answers

probably hi-jacked a Medi-vac last night, and now this! The hospital's security reputation is going down the tube. Can't we wait and see if he shows up at home or work?" Norton asked.

"I don't think that would be advisable." Woitasczyk replied.

"For Christ's sake, why not? You said he isn't dangerous. If we let this out who's going to believe he's not dangerous? The media will have a field day with this one. It's going to look like a bunch of fools are in charge here!" Norton exclaimed.

"No one knows about the riot and the other incidents you're referring to are not my responsibility, Norton! I think we should get the police involved." Woitasczyk said.

"My ass is in a sling now! I had to send four of my men to the mental ward to quell the riot and two of them got the shit beat out of them by your lunatics! They're off on industrial injury leave and we'll be lucky if they don't sue the hospital. If they sue, everyone in San Diego will know we had a riot here and then every reporter in town will be crawling all over my ass and the hospital again, like they were last night! Is that what you want?" Norton asked.

Woitasczyk didn't answer and Norton went on. "Look, you know goddamned well if we report the escape someone will find out about the riot. I'll call the police if you insist, but you better think it over." Norton said.

Woitasczyk had thought it over, but there wasn't a good choice. He didn't want the media to find out about the riot, knowing it would be a negative mark on his perfect record and reputation. He was teetering toward reporting the escape anyway, but then he saw Dawdry standing there, with a blank look on his face, as a stream of drool ran out of the corner of his mouth. The thought of the media snooping around and talking to Dawdry or any of the other orderlies crossed his mind, and he made his decision.

"All right, we'll keep the police out of this for now if you say so, but we have to find Davis and get him back here, before anyone finds out he's missing."

"Where do you think he might go?" Norton asked in a relieved tone.

"His office is just a few blocks away. I'll call his office and find out if he showed up there." Woitasczyk said.

69

"Good, but don't tell them he's escaped." Norton said.

"What the hell am I going to tell them?" Woitasczyk asked.

"Tell them he's been provisionally released, but he's still under your care and you're checking up to see if he reported for work." Norton said.

"Ya, that's a good idea. I'll do that." Woitasczyk replied.

"What exactly is wrong with, Davis?" Norton asked

"He was committed here because of a delusion he had in regard to his work." Woitasczyk replied.

"You said he's a doctor, what field of medicine is he in?" Norton asked.

"He's not an M.D. for Christ's sake! He has a PhD. in Geology. He's a seismologist, at UCSD. He studies cracks in the damned Earth and that's what's wrong with the bastard. He has some foolish notion the world is coming to an end." Woitasczyk replied.

"No shit? He said the world's coming to an end?" Norton asked.

"Ya, but he's the one that's full of shit!" Woitasczyk spat back.

"Well that doesn't seem dangerous to me. A lot of people have said the world's coming to an end, and we're still here. Thank you for your cooperation, Dr. Woitasczyk, but remember, we've got to keep this quiet." Norton turned to Dawdry and asked. "Do you understand? Not a word."

"Yes, sir." Dawdry answered, as he wiped the drool on his shirt sleeve.

Woitasczyk had doubts and second thoughts as he looked at Dawdry and said. "Maybe we're making a mistake, Norton. Maybe we should go ahead and report the escape."

"If you do, I'm out of it! It's not my fault one of your lunatics escaped. You'll take the heat for it, not me! It will be in all the papers and on TV. They'll smear your name from hell to breakfast and make you look like some kind of mad scientist whose creature has escaped. You know that!" Norton snarled.

Woitasczyk knew Norton was right. He could see the headlines and envisioned the maniacal reporters having their way with their slanted stories, which would most certainly smear his name and reputation. He spoke up."Okay, we're doing this your way, but I'll guarantee you, it'll be out on the street in an hour! This fellow thinks Davis is a time traveler!" Woitasczyk said looking at Dawdry.

"You've been working in the mental ward too long young man. I'll see if we can get you transferred to another floor." Norton said, to Dawdry.

"Thanks, I wanted out of here anyway." Dawdry replied.

"You better get rid of his partner too! Neither one of them are worth a damn!" Woitasczyk remarked, as he left the room.

"Where did you get the idea Dr. Davis is a time traveler?" Norton asked Dawdry.

"Davis said he was from 2009. Now he's gone and there isn't any way he could have gotten out of here. I think he's like one of those Terminators. How would you explain it, sir?"

"You heard, Dr. Woitasczyk. Davis worked at UCSD. He was in here because of problems relating to his work. This is 2005, where did you get the ridiculous idea that he was from 2009?" Norton asked.

"I told you! Davis said he was from 2009! You should have heard the stories he was telling. Blake thinks he came from the future." Dawdry said.

"Who's Blake? Is he one of the doctors, that are treating, Davis?" Norton asked.

"No, he's a day shift orderly." Dawdry replied.

"An orderly?" Norton questioned Dawdry in disbelief.

"Yeah! Blake's up on all that futuristic stuff. He reads all the magazines and books about time travel and going to the future." Dawdry replied.

Norton was about to respond to Dawdry in a negative manner. He opened his mouth ready to tell Dawdry how stupid he was for believing such a ridiculous idea. Then he recognized Dawdry's Neanderthal heritage in his facial features and build. There was an almost childlike, quizzical look in Dawdry's bleary eyes as he stood there with his mouth hanging open, revealing his yellowed crooked teeth. Norton thought about what Woitasczyk had said about getting rid of him, and thought. *He's a dumb bastard, all right! No wonder Woitasczyk wants to get rid of him. I'd be wasting my words on him.* "Thank you, young man." Norton said. "Remember, not a word of this can get out." Norton left the room thinking. *He's the one that should be a patient here.*

Dawdry looked at his watch, it was time for him to go home. The day shift had arrived to replace him and Crischell. He passed Crawford on his way down the hall, who said. "I hear you and Crischell messed up bad last night."

"Go to hell!" Dawdry replied and kept on walking. He looked for Blake and didn't see him, and thought. *I'd like to talk to him. Davis has to be a time traveler. Where else could he have gone?*

Dr. Woitasczyk had returned to his office, waiting anxiously till 8 a.m., to call, Dr. Leyland. When Dr. Leyland, answered his call, he asked. "Has Dr. Davis reported for work today, Dr. Leyland?"

"Why no, Dr. Woitasczyk. Should I expect him? Has he been released?" Leyland asked.

"He has been released provisionally." Woitasczyk lied. "It's my responsibility under the provisional release to make sure he follows through with the terms of his release."

"I understand. Do you feel he's fit enough to be doing his usual job?" Leyland asked.

"That's why I called. Dr. Davis is better, but he is still required to check in with my office each day. I haven't heard from him this morning. That's the reason why I called." Woitasczyk lied again.

"I'll remind Vince, to call you the minute he comes in." Leyland replied.

"I would prefer that, Dr. Davis, didn't think I was spying on him. It would be better if you called and let me know when he comes in, without letting him know. Would that be possible?" Woitasczyk asked.

"Yes, I can do that. I could use him here to help me, if he's better." Leyland replied.

"He is better, but he's under obligation to continue taking the medication I have prescribed to treat his psychosis. In the event he doesn't come in, it may be a sign that he's not taking his medication." Woitasczyk said.

"Do you want me to call you if he doesn't come in?" Leyland asked.

"By all means. Do you know if he has any close friends or associates here in town? I know his family lives out of state." Woitasczyk said.

"Jim Lewis and he are very good friends." Leyland replied.

"How may I reach, Mr. Lewis, Dr. Leyland?"

"He works right here at the lab. Do you want to speak to him?" Leyland asked.

"No, not at this time. Do you know of anyone else that Dr. Davis might have known, other than at the lab?" Woitasczyk asked.

"No. Vince kept pretty much to himself and his work here." Leyland replied.

"Ya, that's what I thought. Thank you, Dr. Leyland." Woitasczyk said.

"I see you had a little trouble over at your place last night." Leyland said.

"Ya, but it's all under control now. Thank you Dr. Leyland, goodbye." Woitasczyk said, and leaned back in his chair, wondering. *Why do they call fools who look at cracks in the Earth a doctor? They can't fix the cracks. All they can do is look at them.* Then his thoughts turned to Vince. *Where can he be? I'm going to look like a goddamned fool when that article comes out in the journal and I've lost my prize patient.*

POLICE HEADQUARTERS...SAN DIEGO

SAN DIEGO POLICE CHIEF, Wayne Brewer, had Sergeant Rowland in his office in regard to the bomb scare, the evening before, and was questioning Rowland.

"Where the hell did you get the idea there might have been a bomb in the hospital, Rowland?"

"We came to that conclusion as a possibility, when hospital security couldn't I.D. the suspect, as an employee." Rowland answered.

"Why did they think he might be an employee?" Brewer asked.

"He had scrubs on, Chief."

"Scrubs? They can be bought anywhere." Brewer said.

"I know. Harper told me that." Rowland replied.

"Did you have any reason to think the man was a terrorist? What did he look like?" Brewer asked.

Rowland showed Brewer the photo of Vince on the roof. "He doesn't look like a terrorist to me." Brewer said, and then asked. "Who is he?"

"We don't know." Rowland replied.

"Let me get this straight, Rowland. You said the person on the roof had scrubs on and he hi-jacked the Medi-vac." Brewer said.

"That's right, Chief. He had scrubs on." Rowland replied.

"I'm not putting two and two together here, Rowland. Maybe you can straighten me out. What did the hi-jacking have to do with calling the Bomb Squad?" Brewer asked.

"The hospital security clerk said employees used the service access room to smoke in, so he assumed it was an employee." Rowland replied.

"And when you found out he wasn't?" Brewer asked.

"Well, Corporal Burton brought that up, sir. He thought it might have been one of the terrorists, they've warned us about. You know, the ones that have been blowing up buildings like the hospital and such. It sounded logical at the time." Rowland answered.

"Logical? Goddamnit, Rowland! Are you out of your mind?" Brewer roared.

Rowland started to speak, but Brewer cut in. "Here's what it sounds like to me, Rowland! It was a screw up! Do you understand?" Brewer asked.

"Yes, Chief." Rowland replied.

"Because of you and that stupid, Burton, I've had to lie my ass off this morning. The media is on this like stink on shit. If they find out you instigated that call to the Bomb Squad, you won't have any stripes, and I won't be sitting in this office. Do I make myself clear?" Brewer roared.

"Yes, sir. That's why I had Burton call dispatch instead of using the radio." Rowland replied.

"That's the only smart thing you did and the only thing that's saving both of our asses right now. Send Corporal Burton in, you're dismissed." Brewer barked.

"Yes, sir. Thank you, Chief." Rowland said leaving the office.

CHAPTER SEVEN

NOTHING ON THE NEWS

VINCE HAD JUST WOKE up and was still lying in his bed at the motel. He turned the TV on, lighted a cigarette, and began watching the news. There was no mention of his name throughout the broadcast. The bomb scare and the hi-jacked Medi-vac was the big news. Police Chief, Wayne Brewer, had no comment on the bomb scare, except to say the hospital was safe and that no bomb had been found. He directed any questions to the hospital's Chief Security Officer, David Norton, who was on hand also. The news media was in a furor for details and threw one question after another at Norton, who just repeated what Brewer had said.

Jean Simmons was on hand and asked Chief Brewer if the details of the bomb scare were classified.

"At this time, I have said all I'm allowed to say, in regard to the bomb scare." Brewer replied. "But, I can tell you this. We're closing in fast on the individual who hi-jacked the Medi-vac. We'll know very soon who he is and it won't go lightly on him."

"It's been suggested that the hi-jacker called in the bomb scare, so that the police focus would be on that, while he made his getaway. Is that true?" Jean asked.

"We're looking into every angle of what happened last night at the hospital and we haven't ruled that out, Miss Simmons. Thank you, no more questions." Brewer said.

Reporters were yelling question after question, while Brewer and Norton left the podium. Jean was the loudest and most persistent. "Wait Chief! I'm not finished yet! Is there some kind of cover-up going on?" She yelled.

She was ignored, as were all the other, media representatives.

Vince got up, turned off the TV, then took a shower and dressed. He went to restaurant adjacent to the motel, scanned the local paper for his name, and found nothing.

This is strange. He thought. *They had to find out I was missing this morning. If there's a cover-up going on, it's my escape.*

He wondered why they weren't reporting his escape, but was happy they weren't. They were giving him more time to get away, without worrying about getting caught. *That's another lucky break.* He thought as he finished his breakfast, and headed back to his room to pack up and leave. A couple next-door, who were leaving at the same time, noticed Vince's California plates, and asked where he was from.

"I work in San Diego, but I live in El Cajon." Vince replied.

"Are you on your way back? We're going there also." The man said.

Vince thought for a second and then said. "No. My job has been relocated to the Midwest. I'm taking a little vacation on my way there."

"I'll bet you're going to miss California. We've heard it's wonderful in the San Diego area." The man said.

"It is, but for now, I have to go where my job takes me." Vince replied.

"Property is cheaper in the Midwest." The woman said. "We sold our home, but it's not enough money to buy a home in California. We just simply can't afford the cost of buying a home in the San Diego area. Unless I go to work, we may have to rent a house or buy a mobile home."

"I know. Prices have skyrocketed since I bought my home. I'll probably put it up for sale, if I can't come back." Vince replied.

"You say it's in El Cajon?" The man asked.

"Yes." Vince replied.

"That's where we want to find a place. I'm taking over as Principal at the Granite Hills High School." The man said.

"The school was in the paper and on TV, this morning." Vince said.

"We saw that. I don't think it was one of the high school students that hi-jacked the helicopter. That's quite a way above a high school prank." The man said.

"I agree. I'm sure it wasn't." Vince said.

"Here's my card. I'm Bob Epperson, this is my wife, Margaret."

"Glad to meet you both." Vince said, shaking both of their hands.

"If you can't come back and decide to sell or rent your home, give me a call at the high school. The numbers written on the card." Bob said.

Vince took the card, thought for a second, and then said. "I'll tell you what. My house is sitting there going to waste while I'm gone. I know I won't be back for a while, maybe months, so you might as well take my keys and the garage door opener, and check the place out." Vince said.

The Epperson's didn't know what to say. They hesitated and Vince went on. "I'll write down the address and the phone number. I've got an El Cajon map in my car, It's easy to find. If you like it, just unload your stuff, and move in. I'll call you in a few days and we can talk over any arrangements that would suit you. It's paid for, I can carry a mortgage on it if necessary."

"Why, I don't know what to say, Mr. ...?"

"Davis, Vince Davis." He said.

"You've got yourself a deal, Mr. Davis." Bob said.

"Your truck's not very big. It doesn't look like you have much with you." Vince said.

"No, we got rid of most of our stuff. We were going to buy new when we found a place." Margaret said.

"I tell you what, my place is furnished. Maybe we can make a deal on the house and contents." Vince said.

"All right, Mr. Davis. That sounds good." Bob said, and asked his wife. "What do you think, Margaret?"

"Well, I don't know. We've just met Mr. Davis. This is all so rushed."

"Margaret, it solves our dilemma. I wasn't relishing the thought of living in a motel, neither were you." Bob said.

"Well, all right, if you say so. But you know I like time to think things over. What if we don't like it? What will we do then?" She asked with a worried look on her face.

"If you don't like the place, you can give the keys to my neighbor on the south. His name is Larry Williams." Vince said.

"Margaret, what do we have to lose?" Bob asked.

"Nothing I suppose. I guess I'm just nervous." She replied.

Bob looked at his wife and wondered if she had taken her medicine, but didn't think it appropriate to ask her, and said. "Come on Margaret. This will make it easier all around. You know I have to be in my office at the high school, Monday. We won't have time to look for a place and at least we won't have to stay in a motel. If you don't like Mr. Davis's house, we can look for another place, providing Mr. Davis would let us rent if for a month or two."

"That, would be fine also." Vince said.

"What do you say, Margaret, is it a deal?" Bob wanted her to agree, but he knew he shouldn't force her to say yes. He waited while she thought it over.

"If you think it will be all right, I agree." She said.

"Looks like we're all in agreement." Bob said to Vince. "What about the utilities? Will it be okay to leave them in your name until Margaret decides for sure that she likes the place. If she doesn't like the place, we can pay for what we use."

"That will be fine. The phone and all are on debit payment. I meant to arrange for a gardener while I was gone, and forgot. The yard needs some attention, would you arrange to have a gardener take care of it for me?"

"Do you have a lawnmower and other tools?" Bob asked.

"Yes, they're in a shed out back?"

"I enjoy yard work. I'll take care of the lawn. You won't have to be concerned about that." Bob said.

"Okay, we've got a deal. I'll write a note to my neighbor, Larry. You won't be able to miss his house. He has a Chargers helmet for a mail box."

"No shit?" Bob asked.

"Bob!" His wife exclaimed. "You know I don't like that kind of language."

"Sorry dear." Bob said and laughed afterward. "A Chargers helmet? I've got to see that."

"Larry's a good guy, Bob. But he does hit the suds on the weekends. Tell him I said hi when you get there."

Vince gave them the note and they exchanged a little more small talk and then parted company. He had no intention of heading for the Midwest. Not at the present, time anyway. He was heading north. He was going to Las Vegas. He got out his road atlas and saw that US 95 was just a few miles east on Interstate 8. He packed the rest of his things, got in his car and headed east. As he drove, he was feeling good about things. He didn't have to be concerned about the house anymore. He knew they would like it. It had solved a big problem for them and him. As he drove, a curious thought came to mind. *It's a strange coincidence. We met in passing and had two things in common. El Cajon and Granite Hills High School. What's the odds?* He wondered.

He began thinking about the person the police were chasing. *They'll never find out who it is, if I have anything to do with it.*

He saw the sign indicating US 95 was one mile ahead. He slowed down, took the exit ramp and then headed north. He set the cruise control for just under the speed limit, turned his radio on and scanned the stations. There still wasn't any news of his escape, on any stations.

KQTV OFFICES...SAN DIEGO

JEAN SIMMONS HAD GOTTEN a tip from her inside source at the Police Department, early that morning. The informant had told her the Chief was covering up the bomb scare, but didn't know why. After receiving the tip, she had called Police Headquarters and asked for an exclusive interview with Chief Brewer. She wanted to pin the Chief down on the issue and put him in a corner he couldn't get out of, but her request was respectfully declined by the department spokesperson.

Although disappointed and angry, by the department's unwillingness to cooperate, she was not a person who gave up easily. The refusal had simply fueled her determination to get to the bottom of the matter. She then called the hospital and asked for an interview with their Security Chief, David Norton. Norton's office told her he was unavailable for comment, since the matter was still under investigation by the police.

Infuriated by the refusals of both offices, she decided to try a different avenue of approach. She called the station and asked her director to set up an interview with the Mayor's office to discuss current issues facing the city. The Mayor's office agreed to the interview and scheduled it for later in the day. The interview with the Mayor was now her top priority. She sat everything else aside and grab her yellow note pad. She wrote her first question for the Mayor in bold red ink.

'Your Honor. Informed sources have confirmed that a cover-up is going on in the Police Department and the hospital, in regard to the bomb threat. Are you prepared to respond to that allegation?'

She knew it was likely that the Mayor would know nothing about the cover-up and figured the Mayor would say his office would have to look into the matter, but she intended to put Chief Brewer in a bad light by telling the Mayor of the department's unwillingness to grant her an interview. She continued her notes with a follow up statement, which was in truth, conjecture on her part, with an air of criticism, and accusation toward the Police Department and hospital administration, thrown in.

'Your Honor, I believe we both know what I said is true. My source said that it's true and he's never been wrong before. I have no idea why the Police Department and hospital administration are covering this up. When you discover that it is true, then perhaps you can get back to me and explain the reasoning behind that decision. Chief Brewer and Mr. Norton have both been avoiding questions in regard to a cover-up. I hope, for the sake of the city and your office, the decision wasn't made with the intent to hide the truth from the public.'

She smiled as she completed the note, imagining the scene with the Mayor being blindsided and pinned in a corner by a reporter, in his own office. She reveled in the thought of how pissed off the Mayor was going to be, and knew he would get on the phone the second she left his office, and start chewing some asses. *This will really get the shit stirred up! The Mayor will be all over Brewer and Norton's asses, and then I'll get some answers. I wish I could be there and see the assholes squirm, when he reams their asses!*

She smiled broader, at the thought of the toughest Mayor, San Diegans had ever elected, going to work on Chief Brewer and Norton's asses. *I'd better get ready!* She thought, as she smiled to herself in her bathroom mirror, and began preening for the appointment. She had

The Continent Of St. Louis - The Search For Answers

no idea the Mayor was already pissed off, and was already dialing his phone.

Immediately after her appointment was scheduled, the Mayor called, Chief Brewer, and said. "KQTV just called and asked for an interview with that bitch, Simmons. She's up to something! You know goddamned well, she always is. Have you got any idea what she wants?"

"Did you agree to the interview, your Honor?" Brewer asked.

"Yes. What else could I do? What in the hell is she up to, anyway?"

"She called here earlier, your Honor. She wanted me to agree to an exclusive interview with her in regard to the bomb threat." Brewer replied.

"You're not giving her the interview, are you?" The Mayor blurted out.

"Hell no! We're still investigating the connection between it and the Medi-vac hi-jacking. I can't give her any information." Brewer replied.

"Why in the hell is she calling me then?" The Mayor barked.

"You know her. She's probably going to try and get you to put some heat on me and Norton." Brewer said.

The Mayor became infuriated. "Who does that bitch think she is?" Before Brewer could answer, the Mayor went on. "I'm going to cancel the interview with her. Screw the bitch!" He said, and slammed his phone down.

As the Mayor hung up, Brewer let out a sigh of relief, and thought. *That bitch isn't going to let this go.* His thoughts were interrupted by his secretary buzzing him on the intercom. "What is it." He asked.

"David Norton called while you were talking to the Mayor. He said Jean Simmons wants an interview with him about the bomb threat."

"Did he agree?" Brewer asked.

"No. He wanted your approval first. So far his office has only referred her to your office."

Brewer relaxed again, and said. "Call him back and tell him, if he or his office releases anything in regard to the bomb threat, he'll be arrested for interfering with a police investigation."

"Yes, sir."

81

J. L. Reynolds

A CALL TO THE SEISMIC CENTER OFFICE

VINCE WAS LOST IN thought. He was in the middle of a desert that went aimlessly on. He rolled the circumstances of this, his second experience in the year 2005, over in his mind. Nothing was the same. *This is a paradox, or more like a crazy dream. My life is going on for a second time in 2005, but everything is different. I'm not going in the same direction as I did the first time, because I know things I didn't know the first time. I've been exposed to different people and different situations that didn't happen to me the first time.*

He tried to remember what he was doing on the same day, the first time around and couldn't remember. *Probably working in the lab just like always and probably going over the details of the Salton Sea quakes.*

He remembered doing that and remembered shelving the study when nothing further developed. They had just simply went on with their day-to-day work. That thought brought back more memories. *Dr. Leyland hadn't retired yet and Jim had just been working there a few months. I didn't know Donna at all and I didn't know any of the people I met in 2009 except for, Jim and, Dr. Leyland. I don't know if any of the others I met really exist, but I'm going to find out. I'm going to have to call the office soon and talk to Jim. He may be the only one I can count on now. I hope he doesn't think I'm crazy like everyone else does.*

The miles rolled on as he was lost in thought. He had passed under Interstate 10 and was nearing Parker, where he stopped, ate lunch and gassed up. He picked up an L.A. Times and scanned the articles. There was very little coverage of the San Diego events. The main story was that the police had not yet found the hi-jacker. *Nothing at all on me.* He thought. *Something's not right. Why wouldn't they have my escape in the paper or on the radio and TV?* He pulled out his cell phone and started to hit speed dial. He closed the phone and went to a pay phone and called the lab, and asked for Jim.

"This is, Lewis."

"Hi, Jim. It's Vince. Don't say my name!"

"Damn! Where are you? What the hell's going on?" Jim asked.

"I can't tell you where I am right now, but I'm okay. Has anyone been looking for me?"

"Dr. Leyland said your doctor called looking for you. He told Dr. Leyland, you were temporarily released and asked Dr. Leyland, let him know if you showed up for work, but not tell you. Are you okay now? Are you back to normal? Dr. Leyland, said you were coming in to work." Jim said.

"I'm fine, Jim. I always was. Coming back to work isn't an option I have right now. I want you listen close, to what I have to say."

"Okay, I'm listening?"

"I wasn't released, I escaped."

"Escaped! What the hell?" Jim gasped.

"Hold your voice down, Jim and listen. I know what I told you and everybody else, sounded crazy. I don't blame anyone for thinking I was crazy. If I was in your place, I would have thought what I said was crazy also."

"You weren't the same person from one day to the next. You didn't even look the same when I came to see you in the hospital, before they put you away."

"I know, I saw myself in the mirror. I know what I looked like."

"But, the things you were saying, that's what no one understood. That wasn't you. You never mentioned any of that until you came out of the coma. You were talking about things that were going to happen in the future, some kind of disaster."

"I know, Jim. I remember it all. I should have kept my mouth shut. I would be in there working with you if I had. What I need is your help."

"If you escaped, why isn't on the news, and why did your doctor say you were temporarily released?" Jim asked.

"I haven't figured that out yet. I thought it would be in all the papers and on the news. The doctor that called, is Gunderich Woitasczyk. He's a big shot psychiatrist. He wrote a paper on his diagnosis of my condition. He was publishing it in the International Psychiatric Journal. Maybe it has something to do with that, I don't know and I don't care. I'm not a criminal, Jim, although they treated me like one. I didn't break any laws and the police didn't arrest me. Will you help me or not?"

"What do you want me to do? I'll help if I can." Jim replied.

"Thanks, Jim. I want you to get all of the records Dr. Leyland, has compiled on the Salton Sea quakes. Put them on a disc and bring it to me." Vince said.

"Where will you be? When should I meet you? Are you here in town?" Jim asked.

"No, I'm not in San Diego." Vince replied.

"Where are you, then?" Jim asked.

"I'll call you at home tonight and let you know. Has Dr. Leyland, completed his Model?" Vince asked.

"He completed it yesterday." Jim replied.

"Can you get that information for me also?" Vince asked.

"I don't know. You were the only one Dr. Leyland asked for help. He hasn't released his findings yet. It would be like stealing, if I copied his information. I'll get fired if I get caught." Jim replied.

"I know I'm asking you to go out on a limb and I know you're not sure of me. I'll send you an email tonight with proof I was there, when it all happened, in 2009. So were you and, Donna."

"Me and who?" Jim asked.

"Donna Stevens, the blonde who works in the support office."

"That's crazy, Vince. I don't think I can help you, I've got to go."

"Wait, Jim! Don't hang up! Listen! I can prove what I'm saying. I can prove it right now." Vince said.

"How can you prove it over the phone, Vince?"

"By something you told me in 2009."

"Something I told you? I don't know, Vince. This sounds crazy to me."

"Decide that after I tell you."

"Okay, but it better be good! Go on."

"You were away at camp when your parents and brother were killed in the North Ridge quake in 1974. That's why you got into Seismology."

The phone went silent.

"Jim! Are you there?" Vince asked.

"No one knows that, Vince! How did you find out?"

"You told me and the others at our camp in 2009, when we were facing the end of the world."

"Did you check my background when I was hired here?" Jim asked.

"No, I didn't hire you, Dr. Leyland did, and he or I, wouldn't have had access to your personal information records. All personal records are kept in human resources."

"Knowing about me doesn't really prove anything, Vince. I could have told you that and don't remember doing it." Jim said.

"I'll tell you something else then. Donna is going to quit and join the Air Force soon." Vince said.

"She may have told you she's planning to do that." Jim replied.

"Ask her if she knows me or told me she's planning to join the Air Force." Vince said.

All right, I will. Is there anything else?" Jim asked.

"There's a lot more, and there's no way I could have known any of it, Jim." Vince replied.

"Go on." Jim said.

"Dr. Leyland is going to release the findings from his Model predicting the signs of the disaster that I got sent to the funny farm for talking about. He's going to be ostracized in the Seismology field, and retire. No one will believe him except the government."

"Jesus, Vince. Dr. Leyland, hasn't mentioned retiring." Jim said.

"He's not really going to retire, Jim. He'll go to work for the government in 2008 and set up a brand new, secret lab at Area 51."

"That sounds crazy, Vince!" Jim said.

"I know it does, but hear me out. Don't hang up until I've told you everything!" Vince pleaded.

"Okay, I'm listening."

"Dr. Leyland is going to design new Seismology equipment after he retires. All of it will work with a satellite the government is going to send up from Cape Kennedy. We were there, Jim. You, Donna and I." Vince said.

"Wait a minute! You said Dr. Leyland is going to design new equipment. Do you mean he's going to work with the companies that manufacture the equipment?" Jim asked.

"No, Jim. He'll design it himself." Vince replied.

"How can he do that? He's a seismologist the same as we are." Jim said.

"Dr. Leyland has a PhD. In Electrical Engineering as well as his degree in Geology."

"How do you know that? He's never mentioned it." Jim said.

"He told me in 2009." Vince replied.

"Aw shit, Vince! This is getting deep!" Jim said.

85

"I know, but it's true. Ask Dr. Leyland, if he has the degree in Electrical Engineering."

"Okay, I will, but you said, Miss Stevens is going to join the Air Force. How does she end up at Area 51?" Jim asked.

"Dr. Leyland will get to choose the people that will work on the project. He'll have her reassigned to Area 51 when his lab is set up." Vince said.

"Jesus! This is going to be a stupid question, but how do you and I end up there?" Jim asked.

"We were taken there by helicopter, when the earthquakes destroyed San Diego and the West Coast." Vince replied.

"Jesus, Vince! Area 51? That's not even supposed to exist. Is this what you've been telling everybody?" Jim asked.

"Yes, Jim. I told anyone who would listen to me about it. That's why they put me away." Vince replied.

"You know all of this, sounds like something out of a comic book." Jim said.

"I know it does, but I want you to believe me, Jim. If you don't, you and everyone else are going to die." Vince said.

"You're serious aren't you?" Jim asked.

"Yes, I'm serious! We went to Area 51! Governor Sullivan was there along with Dr. Leyland, Donna, and a bunch of Military brass. Please don't write me off as a lunatic, like everyone else has." Vince begged.

"Do you mean, Lieutenant Governor Sullivan?" Jim asked.

"No, Jim. He's the Governor of California in 2009." Vince replied.

"Do you know how crazy this sounds? No wonder, they locked you up!" Jim said.

"I know it sounds crazy and I know it's hard to believe, but I went back to my house when I escaped and I found the 2009 penny I said I brought back with me. I'm attaching a photo of it to an email I'm going to send you tonight. All I'm asking you to do is talk to Donna first, then look at the penny. I'm holding it right now, it's real, Jim!" Vince replied.

"I don't know her, Vince!" Jim replied.

"Just ask her. That's all I'm asking you to do!" Vince said.

"If I approach her out of the blue and ask her if she's joining the Air Force, she'll think I'm crazy." Jim replied.

"Not if she's planning to join the Air Force, and I know she is and I also know she hasn't mentioned it to anyone yet." Vince said.

"That still won't prove anything. She could have told you that." Jim replied.

Vince could tell that Jim wasn't convinced and was trying desperately to think of a conclusive way to prove what he was saying, and couldn't, except for saying. "You'll just have to take my word for what I've told you, Jim."

"Let's back up a minute. How did you escape and get to your house without getting caught?" Jim asked.

"Through an access panel in the shower ceiling. I climbed a ladder to the roof and hi-jacked the Medi-vac and landed it in Granite Hills." Vince replied.

"The Medi-vac? That's a helicopter. You've never flown a helicopter that I know of. Are you making this up because you saw the hi-jacking story on TV?" Jim asked.

"No, Jim. An Air Force Captain taught me how to fly a chopper in 2009. Everything I've told you is the truth, so help me, God." Vince said.

"Vince, you're not religious! You don't believe in God." Jim replied.

"I know, but how else can I convince you? Everyone says that." Vince said.

"I have to admit you sound like yourself, but all of this is really hard to swallow. The future? 2009? That's four years from now." Jim replied.

"In four years, Carter Lemming will be President, John Clemmons will be his Vice President and everything I told you is going to happen." Vince said.

"If you know it's going to happen, what can you or anyone do to prevent it?" Jim asked.

"The disaster can't be prevented, Jim." Vince replied.

"Why do want, Dr. Leyland's records, if it can't be prevented?" Jim asked.

"I need them to see what Dr. Leyland has learned so far, and then I can fill him in on the rest of the details, before he goes to Caltech with his findings." Vince replied.

"How will that help? You said he would be turned down." Jim said.

"He will be turned down, unless I can do something about it. Lemming is the one that hires Dr. Leyland, and Clemmons, is the one that covers up the findings from Dr. Leyland's lab, which leads to the world not being prepared, when the disaster hits."

"You said we can't stop the disaster! What kind of preparations can be made if it's still going to happen?" Jim asked.

"The Salton Sea cluster quakes were the warning for the disaster, Jim. Dr. Leyland already suspects that they were the beginning of something bigger, but he has no idea how big it's going to get. The final disaster started with no warning, and enveloped the world in thirty-five days. All I can hope to do, is warn the world. Everyone is going to have to get out the way, or they're going to die."

"This all sounds like it comes out of some disaster movie or book." Jim said.

"I know it does, and that's an improvement over a comic book, Jim. I admit it sounds unbelievable, but it's not fiction. It's all going to happen just like I said. I need your help, can you get what I need?" Vince asked.

"I can't say I believe all the things you told me, but I'll get the files and Model statistics copied while everyone's at lunch, and bring them to you. Where do want me to meet you?" Jim asked.

"I don't know yet. I'll phone you at home after I've sent the picture of the penny. Thanks, Jim. I was hoping I could count on you."

Feeling relieved, Vince hung up, got in his car, and headed for Vegas.

Jim sat there thinking, after Vince hung up. He'd always been a cautious person, but if he did what Vince asked him to do and got caught, he knew he'd be fired. *What am I getting myself into?* He wondered, not knowing whether to do what, Vince had asked, or simply tell Dr. Leyland, Vince had called. He thought about it a few minutes longer and made up his mind. *No one knew about me being at camp. I've never told anyone, so he isn't lying or making that up. But Dr. Leyland, could have told him about his Model when he visited him at the hospital and Miss Stevens, could have told him she was planning to join the Air Force.* He thought it over for a few more seconds and made up his mind. *Aw, shit! I'm doing it!*

Jim got up and left his work station, fully intending to copy Dr. Leyland's Model for Vince. As he walked toward Dr. Leyland's office, doubts began to run through his mind again. He looked around to see if anyone was watching him. *I damn sure don't want to get caught.* He thought, as he looked around.

He continued to question what he was doing as he walked into Dr. Leyland's office. *If I could be sure, he was telling the truth, it would make this easier, but how can I be? His whole story is crazy. If he wasn't released and really escaped from the mental facility, someone is going to be looking for him, if not already.*

Thinking that, he realized that was the reason why Dr. Woitasczyk had called. *Why didn't he say Vince had escaped?* He wondered.

That part didn't add up, but he knew Vince wasn't one to make up stories. He wasn't someone who told jokes or made fun of people, and was always serious about his work. He decided that no matter what kind of mental state Vince was in, he at least owed him the courtesy of the doubt, in trying to help him. *If he is in fact crazy, I'll know soon enough.*

He went to Dr. Leyland's computer, and quickly found the file for his Model. He opened it and studied the results, making sure he had the right one. Satisfied, he slipped a disc in and started copying the file, all the while feeling like a thief and looking around to see if anyone had come back from lunch. He didn't want to get caught and got more nervous, by the second, as the file slowly copied to the disc. His doubts returned as he anxiously waited for the file to complete. *I'll lose my job if I get caught. Why in the hell am I doing this?* He wondered and began to panic, as the fear of being caught, set in. His mind began to race. *Friend or no friend, I've got my own career to think about. Vince isn't acting or sounding like the person, I've come to know and respect. He's a totally different person. I'm getting out of here!*

The file completed copying just as he reached to stop it. He ejected the CD with a shaking hand and put it in his pocket. He looked around and saw that no one had returned to the office. He opened the file he'd copied and studied the results more closely. He saw, Dr. Leyland's specification and presentation sheet, marked to the attention of, Sandra Beatty at Caltech and was astonished. The things Vince had said, were all there. *What the hell am I thinking? As crazy as, Vince's story is, it's all here in, Dr. Leyland's spec sheet and Model.*

He knew that Dr. Leyland, had just completed the Model the day before, and the specification sheet had the same date. *There's no way Vince could have known that, or had a way of reading it. Jesus Christ! He must be telling the truth.*

He was now anxious to talk to Vince, later that night. He started feeling regret and embarrassment for his selfish thoughts. As he left, Dr. Leyland's office, he saw, Miss Stevens, waiting outside the door. He wondered if she had seen him.

CHAPTER EIGHT

THE EPPERSON'S TRIP

As Vince headed north for Las Vegas, the Epperson's were talking as their truck climbed the steep grade through the rock covered mountains.

"Mr. Davis seemed nice." Margaret said.

"Yes, he did. I'll bet his house is just as nice too." Bob answered.

"How do things like this happen, Bob? We had no idea where we were going to live and this just fell in our lap."

"Luck, or providence, Margaret, I don't know. But whatever it was, it couldn't have happened at a better time. We'll be there in a couple hours, I can hardly wait. Here, don't lose this note to his neighbor."

They drove on as their truck sluggishly climbed the steep, winding road. Car after car sped past them as their rental truck lumbered on. Their conversation had lapsed in to silence as they drove. Bob finally noticed the silence and looked at his wife wondering why she had become quiet. She hadn't said a word in the past five minutes. Suddenly, she spoke up. "Bob, I just got to thinking and I'm worried." She said.

"About what?" He asked.

"Why would a man turn over his house key to a complete stranger and ask them to move in?"

"Come to think of it, you're right. I guess I'm just too excited to think there might be a downside. I doubt if there is though." Bob replied.

"What if he's a criminal? What if he killed the people that owned the house and took the key and garage door opener?" Margaret asked, showing signs of becoming agitated.

"He didn't look like a criminal. That was a nice car he was driving." Bob answered seeing the beginning of his wife's distress signals.

"The car could have belonged to the people he killed. What if they're still in the house laying there dead? I couldn't stand to go in there and see dead bodies with blood everywhere!" Margaret exclaimed, beginning to lose control.

Bob turned his head and looked at his wife's face. It was a mask of terror. He could see she was envisioning the worst type scenario when they arrived at Vince's house, and said. "Settle down, Margaret."

"Don't tell me to settle down, Bob Epperson. I'm throwing this note out the window! Give me those keys and the opener, they're going too!" She screamed.

"Whoa! Slow down a minute." Bob yelled.

"Don't yell at me!" She screamed.

"Well, goddamn! What am I supposed to say?" He asked knowing his wife was experiencing another episode.

"Don't use that foul language when you're speaking to me!" She screamed.

"I'll say anything I want to!" He bellowed. "Give me that note. What do you want to do? Throw away the best opportunity we could have been offered?"

"I'm not giving you the note and we're not going to that house! Not ever! I'm not getting involved in a murder! We can get a motel tonight!" She was almost hysterical.

"Jesus Christ!" Bob said. "Would you listen to yourself? Give me that note, goddamnit! Don't you dare throw it out the window. What the hell is the matter with you?"

"Nothing, leave me alone! Stop yelling at me!" She screamed.

"I wasn't yelling! What's come over you? A minute ago, you said he was a nice guy, now he's a murderer! Get a hold of yourself, for Christ's sake!"

She started crying and said. "How could you possibly talk to me like that? You don't know! This kind of thing happens all the time and some poor, innocent person gets blamed. I'm not getting blamed for any murders! I'm not going to jail!"

She started rolling down her window.

"Stop it, Goddamnit! Don't you throw that note out!" Bob yelled. "We can show the note to the neighbor before we go in for Christ's sake! Give it to me!"

He lunged for the note and grabbed it before she threw it out the window. He momentarily lost control of the truck in his effort, causing the vehicles behind him to slam on their brakes and honk their horns. He regained control and continued driving uphill.

"What the hell is wrong with you?" Bob hissed. "We almost wrecked, we could have gotten killed!"

She sat in her seat and sobbed as honking cars passed them, with the driver's flipping them off and cussing them.

Bob returned the gestures, and asked."Have you been taking your Prozac?"

"Why do you care?" She answered.

"Because you're acting paranoid! I wish I had a tape of the shit you were just putting out! You've been reading too many of those cheap, murder mysteries. We're stopping at the next rest area. My hands are shaking and I almost pissed my pants."

"Are you going to make me go in that house?" She asked timidly.

"You can wait outside while I check it out. How's that?" He asked.

"Can't we get a motel first? I don't want to be anywhere near the house when you find the bodies." She replied. "I think you should call the police and have them meet you there before you go in."

"Aw shit, Margaret! Why do you have to do things like this to me? I'm not calling the police, and you'd better not either. I'll get a motel for one night if that will make you happy, but if you call the police, and start a bunch of shit like you did last summer, I'm getting a divorce. I'm not taking any more of your crazy outbursts. They almost put you in a mental hospital, remember? All of our neighbors thought you were crazy. Why in the hell do you think I gave up my superintendent job there and took a principals job here? We lost our asses, selling our house and I'm taking a hell of a pay cut."

"What do you want me to say? I didn't make any of that up. It's going to happen just like I said it is." She wailed.

"Look Margaret. We've been over this a thousand times. The world isn't coming to an end. Settle down, Dr. Benjamin has referred you to the best psychiatrist in California. His name is Dr. Woitasczyk. He told Dr. Benjamin he has a patient with a similar disorder, he's treating."

"I don't have a disorder and I don't want to see any more psychiatrists!" She retorted.

"You're going to see him, if I have anything to say about it." Bob proclaimed.

"Why are you treating me like this? I didn't want to move in the first place. It was all your idea!" She replied.

"We had to move! You know that! Dr. Benjamin was going to have you committed to an insane asylum if I hadn't agreed to seek treatment for you with Dr. Woitasczyk, and you're going to see him, that's for damn sure!" Bob declared.

"I'm not crazy, it's going to happen just like I said!" She insisted.

"You've told me that so many times, I could shit! Now you can tell it to Woitasczyk!" Bob said.

"He'll think I'm crazy! Everyone else does and now you do!" She sobbed.

"Dry up those tears and get your shit together! Do you want to mess this whole thing up? The house is the best thing that's happened to us in months. I'm not going to let you screw it up!"

Bob saw a sign for a rest area that was just ahead. He needed to use the restroom and asked. "Do you need to take a piss?"

"No! And you don't need to use vulgar language like that. I'm not some street slut! I've never heard you use such language!" She complained.

"You didn't take your medicine today, did you?" He asked.

"I haven't taken it for three days, and I'm not going too." She replied.

"You know damn well you're supposed to take it on a regular basis! I think you need to take it." He said.

"You're not a doctor! I don't need your advice and I don't need you telling me what to do!" She stormed back.

"Hey! I'm not the one who's losing it and I'm not trying to tell you what to do!" He retorted.

"Yes you are and you're being terrible and rude about it!" She complained.

"Oh, that's it huh? I'm a bad guy and I'm being a bully! Is that it?"

"Yes you are! You don't care about me at all!" She wailed.

"If I didn't care about you, I would have let Dr. Benjamin lock you up, but I didn't! Why in hell would Dr. Benjamin prescribe the medicine for you, if he didn't think you needed to take it?" He demanded.

"He's my doctor, not yours. Mind your own business!" She hissed.

"He won't be for long, that's for damn sure! You better take something right now, you're going off the deep end! A person doesn't need to be a doctor to see that!" He countered.

"Stop lecturing me! I'm not taking it now! It makes me sleepy and I don't want you falling asleep and running off the road and killing us both. I'll take it when we get to the motel!"

"Jesus, are you hearing yourself? You said we're all going to get killed in 2009! Why are you worrying about getting killed now, if you know you're going to die in 2009?" Bob asked.

"Someone will do something about it and some of us won't be killed." She replied defiantly.

"Oh for Christ's sake! Who is this super-hero? Tell me that?" Bob asked.

"I don't know, but we shouldn't have sold our house in Missouri and moved out here to this, god forsaken place!" She said and started crying again.

"I've heard enough of your shit! You damn well better take your medicine while I'm in taking a leak. If you don't, then I don't want to hear another word of your bullshit out of you, for the rest of this trip. Do you understand?" He asked.

She didn't answer and Bob pulled into a rest area in Pine Valley and ran for the men's room cussing all the way and mumbling. "Dead bodies? End of the goddamned world? The woman is crazy!"

VINCE CONTINUES HIS TRIP

VINCE WAS BACK IN California. He planned to stop in Needles for the night and pick up a digital camera to photograph the penny and email the photograph to Jim, later that night. He was hoping Jim could meet him in Las Vegas with the information, he had asked for. As mile after boring mile went by, he formed a plan, to rent a helicopter when he got to Vegas, hoping to get a close look at Area 51, knowing it was the only way he could verify that he had actually been there in 2009.

The plan came to an abrupt halt when he remembered he wasn't certified to fly a helicopter. *No one will rent me a helicopter without the certification.* He thought and went to plan B. *I can rent a small plane. That shouldn't be a problem.*

With that resolved in his mind, he continued the trip, until he saw a sign indicating Needles was the next exit. He pulled into Needles as the sun was setting and went into Wal-Mart and bought the camera and then checked into a motel. There was nothing on the news about him or San Diego. That story was getting cold and new things happened every day. He read the manual on operating the camera and snapped several close ups of the penny before getting a good one. He uploaded the picture to his laptop and sent an email to Jim with the photograph attached. Finished, he went out, got something to eat and gassed up the car, so it would be ready for the last leg to Vegas, the next day. When he got back to his room, he checked his email and found a reply from Jim. It stated simply. *I believe you, call me. I've got the files.*

"He believes me." Vince said aloud and sighed. Although he was tired, he felt revitalized and called, Jim on his cell phone.

"Where are you?" Jim asked.

"I'm in Needles. I'm driving to Vegas in the morning. Can you meet me there tomorrow afternoon?"

"Sure. Tomorrow's Saturday." Jim replied.

"Let me know your flight number and I'll pick you up at the airport." Vince said and realized he didn't even know what day it was. He hadn't paid attention. A habit he had picked up in 2009. *Who cared what day it was, with the world coming to an end.*

"I'll call you back and give you the flight number." Jim said.

"Thanks, Jim. I really appreciate your help. You have no idea how relieved I am. If you had turned me down, I had no one to turn to." Vince said.

"No problem." Jim said and hung up.

Vince laid down on the bed and drifted off. In what had seemed like only seconds to him, his cell phone rang and he jumped up not knowing

The Continent Of St. Louis - The Search For Answers

where he was. He'd been dreaming he was back at the hospital. He saw Jim's number in the view screen and said. "Yes, Jim."

"I can be there at two. Is that all right?"

"Fine, what airline and flight number?"

Vince wrote down the details and Jim went on. "Someone else is coming."

"Who?" Vince asked in a puzzled voice.

"Miss Stevens." Jim said.

"Donna? Why?" Vince asked.

"She caught me when I was getting your information and asked me what I was doing." Jim replied.

"Damn! What did you tell her?" Vince asked hesitantly.

"Just what you told me."

"Everything?" Vince asked.

"Everything, Vince. You were right about her joining the Air Force, she hadn't done it yet, but she had already talked to the recruiter."

"Who else knows?" Vince asked.

"No one. She's here with me now. I showed her the photo of the penny. She wants to talk to you. Hold on, I'm giving her the phone." Jim said.

Vince's heart started pounding and his breathing became irregular.

"Dr. Davis?" Donna asked.

"Yes." Vince managed to choke out.

"Mr. Lewis explained your strange story to me. You seem to know things about us and Dr. Leyland, which no one else knows or could know. I'm not sure that I believe the world is coming to an end, but I have to find out more. Do you mind if I come along with, Mr. Lewis?" She asked.

"Not at all, Don…Miss Stevens." Vince said. Hearing her voice had begun to calm him down.

"The penny, do you have it?" She asked.

"Yes, I've got it and it's real." Vince said taking it from his pocket and looking at it.

"And you got it in 2009." She asked.

"Yes, at Lambert Field, in St. Louis. The Terminal had caved in after a massive earthquake and killed most of the people there. I found it on the floor."

"I had heard that you were telling that story after you came out of the coma. I guess we all thought the concussion had affected your mind. Dr. Leyland said they went back to your house and never found the penny."

"They didn't look hard enough, Miss Stevens. It was standing on edge, leaning against the base of the stool, next to the wall."

"Dr. Leyland said that you had been temporarily released and he's looking forward to you coming back and working with him." She said.

"I wasn't released, I escaped." Vince replied.

"Jim told me that. He said you were the one that hi-jacked the Medi-vac." She said.

"Yeah, it was me, but I didn't call in the bomb scare." Vince said.

"Why hasn't the hospital reported your escape?" She asked.

"I don't know. It doesn't make any sense. The hospital must be covering it up for some reason or another." Vince said.

"The police have released the surveillance photo of the suspect who stole the Medi-vac. It was on TV and in the papers today. Mr. Lewis said it's you, but the police haven't identified the suspect as you."

"Then it has to be a cover up and I can't imagine why." Vince replied.

"Jim said the doctor that was treating you has been calling and looking for you."

"His name is Woitasczyk and he's got a huge ego. It wouldn't surprise me if it was him that's covering it up, although it's better for me if no one is looking for me."

"Are you okay? Do you need any money or anything else?" She asked.

"I'm fine. I don't need anything but some help and Jim took care of that. I'm glad you're coming, Miss Stevens. I'll meet both of you at the gate." He replied.

"We'll see you tomorrow then?" Donna said.

"Tomorrow it is. Thank you, Miss Stevens. Please put Jim back on the phone, I need to ask another favor."

"Yes, Vince." Jim said.

"I may need your help for more than just this weekend. Can you take some time off?"

"We're both taking two week vacations. We've got one-way tickets, we'll see you tomorrow."

The Continent Of St. Louis - The Search For Answers

"Thanks, Jim. The real proof lies inside that data and the Model. Thank you again for sticking your neck out and getting it for me. I'll see you tomorrow."

Vince lay back on his bed. He felt exhausted, but wasn't sleepy. He called the front desk for a six a.m. wake up call. He didn't want to oversleep.

JIM'S APARTMENT

JIM AND DONNA WERE discussing the situation and looking at the photo of the penny on Jim's laptop.

"He doesn't sound crazy." Donna said.

"That's what's wrong or puzzling at best." Jim replied. "He sounded crazy when I visited him in the hospital. I didn't believe him, no one did. When they didn't find the penny, he got worse. I didn't get another chance to speak to him after they confined him to Gifford."

"How else could he have known what he told you regarding me and Dr. Leyland, Jim? He was right in both instances and nobody could have known."

"It's eerie, Donna. He sounds like a fortuneteller or medium, but in any case, I really don't have any choice but to go and see what happens. I thought about not helping him, but I would have never told his doctor or anyone, that I had talked to him. Even if I had gotten caught at the lab copying, Dr. Leyland's documents, by someone other than you, I would have taken the consequences before telling my reasons." Jim said.

"You know you would have gotten fired, don't you?" Donna asked.

"Or maybe worse. I think what I did is called espionage. UCSD could have pressed charges."

"What made you do it, considering the risks?" She asked.

"Vince is my best friend. He's never lied to me or taken advantage of me, but after talking to him in the hospital, I started having stupid dreams about what he had said."

"I've never talked to him until just now, but I heard what he had said, and to tell the truth, I've been having strange dreams for a while." Donna said.

"How long?" Jim asked.

"Since, Dr. Davis was put in the Hospital. They're crazy dreams. It's been worrying me. They're the same almost every night." She said.

"What kind of dreams?" Jim asked.

"The world's coming to an end and I and a group of people, I don't even know, are trying to find a way to survive. They're so real, I wake up sweating and scared. I thought maybe if I did something else and got away from the lab, I might quit having them. That's why I was joining the Air Force and that's why I'm going with you. Dr. Davis and you were in the dreams also."

"Damn! I've been having the same kind of dreams. I thought I was just taking the story Vince had told me when he was in the hospital and building it up in my imagination and dreams. I wasn't about to tell anyone about it. They would have locked me up too." Jim said and laughed.

"Here's the worst, or maybe best part of my dreams. It's embarrassing, but I'm telling you anyway. Vinc…er, Dr. Davis and I are lovers and that's the crazy part. I don't even know him and I don't think he's ever noticed me. I've never spoken to him at the lab, although I would have liked to. He was always so busy and engrossed in his work, I came and went, and he never looked up."

"That's, Vince." Jim said.

"I know and I was too backward to make advances toward him for fear of being rejected." Donna said.

"I'm the same way. I've never been able to make the first move." Jim said, as Donna began to squirm and then said. "Let me finish while I still have the guts."

"I'm all ears." Jim said and laughed.

"We were lovers in my dreams! We were going to get married. I couldn't have begun to tell anyone about that and I knew I couldn't look at him or be around him every day if he returned to work with those thoughts in my mind. I was going to quit before he came back." Her face turned slightly red as she felt embarrassment come over her after telling the story.

"I know what you mean." Jim said. "I was too embarrassed to tell Vince that I had been dreaming about the stuff he told me. I even acted surprised like I didn't believe him. I was thinking of myself and my career, but underneath it all I knew what he was talking about. I wasn't going to admit it, but when he told me about my parents getting killed when I was at camp, I was convinced, but I still had reservations about helping him and possibly losing my job. Then I saw, Dr. Leyland's Model. Vince couldn't have known about that or me. When I told you what he said about you and you confirmed it, I knew I was doing the right thing."

"Okay, but why would I be dreaming about, Dr. Davis? I don't even know him! It's embarrassing!" Donna said.

"Vince was in my dreams too and I was in places I'd never been before. If you think yours was bizarre, listen to this, you won't believe it! I was underground at Area 51!"

"Area 51? That's where I was, and I was already in the Air Force. That's why I was going to join. How do you suppose Vince knew about that?" She asked.

"It doesn't seem possible, but he does." Jim replied.

"Do you think he knows about the rest of our dreams? You know the part about me sleeping with him?" She asked turning red again.

"I guess you'll find out, Donna." Jim said. Donna laughed trying to hide her embarrassment. After talking a while longer, Donna left for the night, went home, packed some things and called the cab company to pick her up the next day.

CHAPTER NINE

THE SECOND DAY AFTER ESCAPE

VINCE HAD BEEN DREAMING all night and had fought countless battles as he slept, woke up, and then went back to sleep. The illuminated clock numerals had indicated it was three-thirty the last time he'd woke up. Now he was dreaming he was restrained, as he had dreamed several times before. The same figure in the white coat was leaning over him, just as he had been in previous dreams. The figure had said something about the Arch and he had suddenly found himself laying on the ground, looking up at the Arch, in Riverfront Park. Donna, was there with him, and she was now leaning over him and talking to him. Although he couldn't understand what she was saying, he was trying to reach up to her, but his arms wouldn't move. He heard a loud ringing in his ears and woke with a start. His wake-up call had come and the ringing had brought him back to reality, just as it had on August 18th when Dr. Leyland, had called. He cussed and slammed the phone back down after learning it was his wake up call, and tried to shake the cobwebs from his head.

"This has got to stop!" He said aloud, realizing again, that all of it had been a dream. He couldn't imagine why he kept dreaming about the person in the white coat leaning over him. It wasn't the surgeon in the dream that he'd had flying back to camp Davis and he couldn't recall ever laying in a bed or being on gurney with what appeared to be a doctor leaning over him. All of his other dreams had mostly been about what he'd gone through in 2009, but the person in the white coat leaning over him had never actually happened to him.

He got up, took a shower, put on clean clothes, packed his bag and left, stopping for coffee and breakfast at Burger King. He pulled the penny from his pocket, looking at it through the plastic bag, and then compared it to a shiny 2005 penny he had gotten in change. They were exact duplicates except for the date. He put the 2005 penny in the bag with the 2009 and put the bag in his pocket. He scanned the L.A. Times for any mention of him or the Medi-vac hi-jacking while he ate his breakfast. There was nothing regarding any of it on any page. Finished, he got up, threw away his trash, returned to his car and got back on US 95 for the final leg of his trip. As he headed north, he saw a highway sign indicating the distance to Las Vegas was ninety-five miles. *An hour and a half.* He thought.

He turned his radio on and scanned the stations for news, apparently, nothing was going on. He found an oldies radio station, set the cruise control, relaxed and enjoyed the music. Thirty minutes later, he had left California for the second time in two days. Las Vegas was just an hour away.

Oh, Donna, by Ritchie Valens, came on the radio. His thoughts immediately returned to Donna. *Her voice sounded just like I remembered. But there was no sound of familiarity in it. She was businesslike and called me Dr. Davis. She doesn't even know me. I don't remember ever seeing her or speaking to her at UCSD. It's going to be difficult seeing her and remembering her as I do without showing it.*

He felt knots tightening up in his stomach, then he felt a fluttering feeling take over. *I'm in love with her and she doesn't even know me. I don't know how I'm going to act or what I'm going to say to her when I see her."*

The thought of seeing her again put a smile on his face and he began singing loudly, along with the song.

"Oh Donna, Oh Donna! I had a girl Donna was her name!"

A car passed him and the driver looked at him like he was nuts. He smiled, waved, and kept on singing as he drove on.

J. L. Reynolds

DONNA'S HOUSE

DONNA HADN'T SLEPT WELL. Her night had been filled with dreams of a surly general dressing her down and blaming her for the disaster that had started. No matter how hard she tried, she couldn't convince him that she had not made the mistakes. He and none of the others in her dreams had familiar faces. Everywhere she looked, she saw only sinister faces, staring and pointing at her. She had desperately appealed to those around her, asking for their support and corroboration of her explanation. Instead, those who surrounded her were shouting angry threats and shaking their fists, demanding she be put to death. In what had seemed like seconds, she had been charged with treason, found guilty in a court martial and was standing in front of a firing squad. As the squad raised their rifles to shoot, she heard the squad leader give the command. In terror, she had closed her eyes and heard a loud buzzing noise. In a subconscious reflex, she had instinctively jumped out of bed, clutching at her chest, screaming she wasn't guilty. She had bolted out of the bed, running blindly, trying to escape the hail of bullets that she knew was on the way and meant to kill her. She tripped on a throw rug and went head over heels, landing in a heap on her living room floor. Still thinking she had been shot, she lay there with her heart pounding, gasping for breath, feeling for the blood, she knew had to be spilling out. The loud buzzing continued from her bedroom and it finally dawned on her that it was her alarm clock going off. "Shit!" She said aloud.

Feeling like a fool, she got up on shaky legs and went back in her bedroom, turned off the alarm and thought. *This is a hell of a way to start my day. I'm not telling anyone about this!*

Finally awake, she turned on the light and made her way to the bathroom and looked in the mirror, and thought. *I'm getting old.*

Dissatisfied with her reflection, she smoothed out the skin on her face, and then thought. *He never complained about anything in my dreams.*

She laughed when she realized she was worrying about how she would look to someone she had only made love to in her dreams. *He doesn't even know me. What am I worrying about? He probably won't give a damn about how I look anyway and he damn sure doesn't know about my dreams.* Then another thought hit her. *I wonder if Jim told him. Damn! I hope not!*

She thought about the dreams with Vince and she smiled and reconsidered her previous thought. *I hope he did, but with my luck, he didn't!*

She released the skin on her face and said. "Come on old maid. It's time to take a shower."

NEARING LAS VEGAS

VINCE WAS CROSSING HOOVER Dam, remembering what it had looked like from the air, when it was destroyed by the massive quake. *No matter what I do, it's going to happen again when 2009 rolls around.*

He shook his head as he looked at the miles, of now placid water, stretching back from the dam as he crossed. He knew for certain where it was all going to end up and thought. *How can I make them believe me?*

He reached Boulder City and turned onto Interstate 515 for the last, short leg to the Strip. He had decided to get rooms at the MGM Grand because of its close proximity to McCarran. He pulled into the parking garage, went inside and paid for three rooms. He took his bag to his room and threw it on the bed. It was eleven a.m., he had three hours to wait. He went back down and entered the casino. It was alive with patrons, hoping to win the jackpot, dumping their money into slot machines as fast as the slots would take them. The familiar noise of the drums turning inside could be heard with an occasional jingle as one paid off and the coins fell. Win or lose everyone seemed happy. This was Las Vegas, this was their chance to strike it rich. He thought again about Hoover Dam. *None of this will be here in 2009. It will be different people except for the employees who live here. But even if they move and no matter where the tourists are from, the end will come all the same.*

He went into the dining room, sat down, ordered lunch as the thoughts of the future came, and went.

THE PROOF AND EXPLANATION

JIM AND DONNA MET at the Airport at noon and boarded their flight for Vegas. The flight departed Lindbergh Field at one p.m. It was a forty-five minute flight. They would be in the Vegas terminal by two. On the way, they were both nervous and made small talk, until the plane landed at McCarran. They gathered their carry-on bags, made their way up the jet-way into the terminal and looked around. Vince was not in sight, so they sat down and waited. Ten minutes passed without any sight of him and Donna asked a Customer Service Agent at the gate if there were any messages for her or Jim. She explained they were to be met when they deplaned.

"Oh! Your party is probably waiting just past the security screening area." She said. "Unless you have a boarding pass or ticket, you can no longer gain access to the gates."

Donna thanked her and she and Jim headed for the exit. Vince was waiting, with a smile on his face just outside the door as they walked out. Earlier, when he had entered the terminal, he hadn't been smiling. The terminal had reminded him of Lambert Field in St. Louis, where hundreds of dead people were pinned and buried beneath the collapsed roof. He shook hands with Jim and looked hesitantly toward Donna. She offered her hand and said. "Nice to see you again, Dr. Davis."

"It's nice to see you. Please call me Vince. May I call you Donna?" He asked.

"Yes, please." She answered.

Vince held on to her hand for a few seconds. It was not the hand of a stranger. He felt the familiarity instantly and thought she had also, although she showed no indication of it, in her eyes or on her face.

"Come on." Vince said. "We can catch the shuttle bus outside. I have rooms for both of you at the Grand."

The shuttle bus trip was short. They entered the lobby and Vince directed them to the elevators and then thought of the time, and asked. "Would you like to get something to eat before we go to our rooms?"

"Yes, I would." Jim said. "How about you, Donna?"

"Yes, that would be nice. We can eat and I can get better acquainted with Dr. Dav…Vince."

Vince called a bellhop and had him take their bags to their rooms. They sat down in the dining room and the same server, that had served him earlier, came to the table, looked at Vince, and said. "A little hungry today, sir?" She asked.

"I'll just have a salad." Vince said, and smiled.

Jim and Donna ordered, then, Jim started the conversation. "I hate to say it Vince, but you look a little worse for the wear. Where did you get that scar on your arm? Did it happen at the hospital?"

"No. It's part of my story."

"What's with those cigarettes in your pocket? When did you start smoking?" Jim asked.

"That's part of the story too, Jim."

He reached in his pocket and pulled out the plastic bag containing the two pennies. He opened it and laid the two, face up on the table, and said. "I got the 2005 this morning in change at, Needles." He slid them both across the table so Jim and Donna could see them.

"Damn!" Jim said, looking at the 2009 penny.

Donna pulled a small magnifying glass from her purse, bent down and looked closely at both of them. She raised her head, looked Vince in the eyes, and said. "Vince, I'm not an expert and I don't want to sound like I'm questioning you or don't believe you. Would you get mad or object if I asked if we can take this to a coin dealer and get a professional opinion?"

Vince looked at her and saw the seriousness showing in her eyes, and said. "Not at all, Donna. I think that's a good idea. After we eat, we can ask the desk clerk where we can find a coin dealer."

They finished their meal and asked the clerk, who pointed the way down a side corridor. "It's right next to the Jewelry Shop." He said.

They entered the store and a rather robust man, appearing to be in his, fifty's with an eye loop attached to his glasses, greeted them. "What can I do for you folks? Are you interested in some Silver Dollars in mint condition? I've got an 1889 CC, it's a gem." The dealer said.

"No." Vince answered. "We'd like to get your opinion on a penny I have."

"You mean an appraisal?" The dealer asked.

"No. I'm not interested in its value." Vince replied.

"What other reason would you have?" The dealer asked.

"We'd like to get your opinion in regard to its authenticity." Donna said.

"I don't usually do that unless I'm buying a coin, but what the hell. It will cost you twenty five bucks for me to take a look at it."

Vince laid the money on the counter, the dealer picked it up and asked. "What have you got? Let me take a look at it."

Vince handed him the penny.

"Hell, this isn't worth anything except a penny. It's brand new." The dealer said.

"Look at the date." Vince replied.

The dealer looked down at the penny in his hand, then quickly brought it closer to his eye.

"Goddamn! It's a 2009. Where did you get this?" He asked, dropping his eye loop down, examining the penny under ten-power magnification, and saying. "Jesus! It's real! It's a mint error, or a die error, or something. They must have been trying to make a 2006 and got the six upside down. Hold on, I want to check this out on the internet."

He handed the penny back to Vince and went to the backroom. He was back in less than a minute, and said. "I'll give you a thousand bucks cash for the penny. What do you say, mister? Is that a deal?"

"It's not for sale." Vince replied, and started to walk away.

"Oh, you can't mean that! Wait a minute, I'll give you five thousand bucks for it. I've got the cash in crisp hundred dollar bills. Look!"

He took a large roll of bills from his pocket and looked at Vince, hoping the large amount of money would sway him.

"No, thank you. That's a very generous offer, but it's not for sale." Vince said.

"Jesus Christ! What do you mean, it's not for sale? Everything can be bought at a price. Tell me how much, name your price. I can have the cash here in twenty minutes." The dealer said.

Vince thanked him, turned him down again, and said. "let's go." He put the penny back in the bag, with the 2005.

"You've got two of them for, Christ's sake! Why can't you sell me one of them?" The dealer asked.

"You can have this one." Vince said, handling him the 2005.

The dealer's eyes lighted up. "For free? Goddamn! Thanks mister."

As they walked to the door, the dealer yelled at Vince. "This is a 2005, you son-of-a-bitch! It's worthless!"

They heard the penny hit the floor, as he threw it down, and yelled. "Do you think you can come in here and try to make a fool of me in my own store? I want that penny mister, and I'm going to get it one way or another!"

His face was flushed with anger as he came from behind the counter. Jim stepped between Vince and the storeowner as he approached.

"He said he doesn't want to sell it, mister! Now back off!" Jim said.

A few people had gathered and were standing outside the coin shop listening to the coin dealer ranting as the three left his shop. As they walked away, a Hotel Security Guard looked at them as they passed and went in the coin shop to see what had happened. "Do you need some help. Did they steal something?" He asked.

"No. He's got a coin I want to buy. He wouldn't sell it to me."

The dealer watched as the three walked toward the lobby. "That's him." He said. "Follow him and find out if he's staying at the hotel. There's a few bucks in it for you if you get the information for me."

He slipped the guard a hundred dollar bill and said. "He's got a penny I want. There'll be a lot more for you when you find out who he is and where he's staying."

The guard took the hundred and asked. "How much are we talking about? What's the penny worth to you?"

"I offered him five grand for it and he turned me down. The five grand is yours if you get the penny." The dealer replied.

"I might need some help. I might have to cut the desk clerk in." The guard said.

"I don't want to know who helps you or anything about it. Just get me the penny." The dealer replied.

"What kind of penny is it?" The guard asked.

The dealer picked the 2005 penny up off the floor, showed it to the guard, and said. "It looks exactly like this one, except it's a 2009. Make sure you look at the date when you get it."

"A 2009? They aren't out yet! This is 2005." The guard replied.

"The one I want is a mint error. They were probably getting ready to make the 2006's and got the six upside down. They mess up like that all the time. Mint errors are always worth more than the other coins. Now get going."

The guard went in search of Vince. He didn't have far to go. He saw them in the hotel lobby and stood back keeping them in sight.

As they reached the hotel lobby, Donna said. "Boy, was he mad. Maybe you better put the penny in a lock box, Vince."

Vince looked back down the corridor. The dealer was pointing at them. He didn't see the guard watching them or shake his head in acknowledgement.

"Maybe you're right, but maybe not. Do you have another shiny penny?" He asked Donna.

She went through her change purse and handed Vince another penny while they stood with their backs to the guard. They approached the desk clerk and Vince asked for an envelope. He put Donna's penny inside, sealed it and asked the clerk if he could get a lock box. The clerk brought a form over and Vince put his name, the item, and his room number on it. The clerk gave him a receipt and they headed for the elevator.

"That Security Guard is watching us." Jim said.

"I, know." Vince replied.

They got on the elevator and went to Vince's room. Vince hesitated at the door and watched the security guard step out of the second elevator.

"We've got some trouble." He said as he closed the door.

"What's wrong?" Donna asked.

"That security guard followed us."

"I'm sorry, Vince. I had no idea the coin dealer would behave like that. Maybe you should sell him the penny." Donna said.

"It's not your fault." Vince replied. "You had every right to be suspicious of the penny, but I can't sell it to him. It's the only physical evidence that what I say is true."

"What about the discs you told me about when you were in the hospital? Wouldn't they be proof also?" Jim asked.

"Yes, they would have been if I still had them and had been able to open the files. I don't know where they are and I don't know what was on the discs. I suspect it was evidence relating to a cover-up that went on at Area 51. I didn't know the password required to open the files, and couldn't open them." Vince replied.

"I've got password decrypting software installed on my laptop, Vince." Jim replied. "I can change the password and gain access to anything. Then you can open the files."

"That would be great, Jim. But they weren't at my house when I found the penny. I have no idea where they are. I guess you're both going to have to take my word on that."

"I don't need any more convincing. The penny is proof enough for me." Donna said.

"Then, let's get down to business." Vince said. He told the whole story from the beginning to end, leaving out no detail. Two hours had passed while telling the story. Donna and Jim had sat, listening without interruption, the entire time. When he was finished, Jim told Vince about the dreams he and Donna had been having for the past few weeks. After telling about the dreams, he said. "Mine have been going on since you entered the hospital. I thought I'd been studying too much data. I was ready for a vacation."

He had purposely left out the part about Donna sleeping with Vince and asked. "Is there anything else you want to add, Donna?"

"No, that's enough for now." Donna replied.

Vince didn't know what she or Jim were referring to and went on.

"I'm not sure what this all means. I'm not even sure if what Dr. Leyland predicted, and happened to me in my experience, will actually come to pass. It all seems like a dream, but I believe it will. I'll have to study his Model before I can answer that for sure."

"I've got the disc in my laptop. Do you want to take a look at it?" Jim asked.

"I'd love to, but I need to explain further." Vince said.

"Go on." Jim said.

"Dr. Leyland, really didn't know how bad it was going to get. It wasn't until much later that he realized the extent of destruction the world was going to face. In the end, even he was flabbergasted, but his later findings may not be on the Model or specification sheet you copied. I don't think he's reached that stage of discovery yet."

"That doesn't make any difference, Vince. You're here and you have the penny to prove what you've said. Even if, Dr. Leyland's Model, doesn't include the later information, you already know the rest and it will prove Dr. Leyland was on the right track." Jim said.

Before Vince could respond, Donna asked a question. "Would you call what happened to you a paradox, since you were in 2009 and now you're back in 2005?"

"I don't know what to call it. I guess it could be called a paradox or an out of body experience, but it wasn't a dream, I know that. What it's called isn't what's bothering me." Vince said.

"What's bothering you?" Jim asked.

"It was all true and nobody believed me. I felt like I'd taken a trip to The Twilight Zone and couldn't get out." Vince said.

"It does sound like something Rod Serling could have dreamed up. Even now, with your proof and explanation, it still sounds like unbelievable fiction." Jim said.

"Even I don't know how the three of us could have been in 2009 one minute, then I'm thrown back to 2005, without the two of you. It happened in the blink of an eye. One second we were together and the next thing I knew, I woke up in my bed at home."

"It does sound like a dream." Donna said.

"I know it does." Vince replied, and went on. "Think about the dreams you've both been having. They couldn't have manifested themselves without an underlying factor or reason. I believe the reason you were both having the dreams is that both of you are still there and trying to reconnect with me." Vince said.

"Jesus! That would be some serious shit, wouldn't it?" Jim asked, all three laughed, and Vince went on.

"We were standing under the Arch, just like I explained. The next thing I knew, Dr. Leyland called and woke me up at my house in, El Cajon. Now here's where it gets deep." Vince said.

Jim lifted his feet up off the floor and said. "Go on."

"When Dr. Leyland called and woke me, I had on the same fatigues and blouse I was wearing in 2009."

"Do you still have them?" Donna asked.

"No, I guess they're still at the hospital or, Gifford." Vince replied.

"Go on. I'm sorry I interrupted you." Donna said.

"Take a look at the scar on my arm. I got cut during one of the earthquakes in 2009. Jim, knows I didn't have the scar before and obviously, it's healed to such an extent it couldn't have happened before or after I went to the hospital or the mental ward."

"I'll vouch for that. Go on." Jim said.

"Take a look at this." Vince said, handing Jim the package of Winston's he'd found on his nightstand.

The Continent Of St. Louis - The Search For Answers

"What about it?" Jim asked.

"Look at the tax stamp on the bottom." Vince said.

"They're from, Missouri, so what? That doesn't mean anything." Jim said.

"I agree, they could have come from anywhere, but the box would mean something to a smoker. Do you notice anything strange about the box?" Vince asked.

"It's a flip top box. Am I missing something?" Jim asked.

"Look at what it says on the top and read it." Vince said.

"It says it's a 2-Way box, open like a box or a soft pack. What's important about that?" Jim asked.

"R.J. Reynolds doesn't make boxes like that yet. I don't know when they started making them, but I got that package and a lot more, out of cigarette machine at Lambert Field in St. Louis, the day I found the penny." Vince said.

"Did you show the package to anyone else?" Donna asked.

"No, I didn't have the opportunity. I found the cigarettes, my billfold and this lighter on the nightstand, at my house, the night I escaped." Vince replied.

"Let me see them." Donna said to Jim, and Vince went on."Other than the penny and those cigarettes, it's just a memory with a story that I can't prove beyond having what I've showed you, what I've told you about your lives and, Dr. Leyland's Model, which I had no way of knowing about."

"We believe you, Vince." Jim said. "You don't need to go on."

"Yes, I do, Jim. There's more to it, than what I've explained so far. The reality of all of this is, that it did happen to me. It wasn't a dream such as you two have been experiencing lately. Although from what you've told, me it seems to verify that both of you were there with me in 2009, and probably still are."

"The one I had last night was a nightmare." Donna said.

Vince laughed and asked. "What did I do this time?"

"You didn't do anything! You weren't even in it. I was blamed for the disaster and found guilty of treason at a court martial and placed in front of a firing squad."

"That was a nightmare!" Vince exclaimed. "But it wasn't you that was guilty of treason at Area 51. It was, Lawson and Randall."

113

"Do you think we'll have more dreams?" Jim asked.

"Since both of you must still be there, I would say it would be very likely. None of it makes any sense, Jim. Believe me, when I tell you, it twists my mind just to think about it." Vince replied.

"Why do you think you came back and we didn't?" Donna asked.

"I can't think of any reason and I've wondered if the others that were there, are having dreams, like the two of you were having." Vince replied.

"Are they anyone we know?" Donna asked.

"Other than Dr. Leyland, no." Vince replied.

"Where did you say you were before you came back?" Jim asked.

"All three of us were standing in front of the destroyed Gateway Arch in St. Louis." Vince replied.

"What were we doing there?" Donna asked.

"Celebrating survival. Jim had set his camera and had just taken a victory photo of the three of us."

"Man, if you had that photo, what could anybody say, then?" Jim asked.

"That it was fake, I would imagine." Vince replied.

"What happened then?" Donna asked.

"We were looking at the photo in the LCD of Jim's camera and joking about what we would name the land mass we were on." Vince replied.

"Did we name it?" Jim asked.

"We didn't, you did." Vince said.

"Jesus Christ! I named it?" Jim asked.

"Well what I mean is, you suggested a name. Donna agreed and was asking me what I thought, when I blacked out." Vince replied.

"Don't keep me hanging! Tell me what I suggested!" Jim said impatiently.

"The Continent Of St. Louis." Vince replied.

"Jesus Christ! What kind of name is that?" Jim asked.

"A good one, considering it was all that we knew, or thought, was left of the world." Vince replied.

"It doesn't sound that good to me." Jim said with a disappointed look on his face.

"It sounded good to you at the time. You had made a photo journal of our struggle, with photos and descriptions of the people we met along the way, who had joined forces with us. That's what you said you were naming the journal." Vince replied.

"Hey, that's a good idea!" Jim said.

"What's a good idea?" Donna asked, Jim.

"A photo journal! I'm going to do the same thing now. I brought my camera, the three of us will be the first picture."

Jim set up the camera, the three posed and the flash went off. Jim retrieved the camera and showed the photo to Vince and Donna, and asked. "What do you think?"

Vince looked at the photo. They were all smiling, but he couldn't help noticing how different he looked. His confinement at Gifford had hardened his face and it showed. It looked nothing like the victory photo.

"It's good, Jim." Donna said.

"What's next?" Jim asked.

"I'd like go on with what we were discussing." Vince said.

"Where did you leave off?" Jim asked.

"The two of you were with me at the Arch, but you're also here with me now. I don't think there's a logical explanation for what happened and as far as I know, there aren't any stories like ours except in books of fiction. No one has believed my story and no one will believe yours, if you tell them." Vince said.

"I wasn't going to tell anyone about my dreams." Jim said.

"It's a good thing you neither of you told anyone, or all three of us would have been getting the third degree from Woitasczyk."

"Who did you say, Woitasczyk was?" Donna asked.

"My brilliant psychiatrist at the mental ward. He wrote an article about my presumed psychosis. He personally named my disorder Mental Post-Forming. I'm going to be in the record books as the first human diagnosed with the disorder." Vince replied.

"Post-Forming?" Jim questioned. "Isn't that a term that's used for a machine process that forms a countertop out of Formica?" Without waiting for an answer, he went on. "What did Woitasczyk do, put your head in a press and squeeze out the diagnosis, to come to that conclusion?"

They all three laughed at Jim's joke, and then Vince got serious again.

"It's good to laugh." He said. "But I wasn't laughing when I was in there. Being locked up and alone with nothing but my thoughts for 24 hours, a day almost got to me. I had some dreams that were lu-lus. I thought I was going insane and I think I came very close to going off the deep end. But after having those dreams, I started looking for a way to escape, found the way, and we're here now. The part of all of this I haven't been able to reconcile is how I'm able to be back here, when I was in 2009. You two were there with me, and that leaves me with no other conclusion than to believe that you're still there in 2009 along with Dr. Leyland, and the rest. Since I'm back here in 2005, I have no way of knowing if I'm still there in body and going along with my daily life or if I mysteriously disappeared and you're looking for me and baffled, the same as I was here, when I woke up in, El Cajon."

"Jesus!" Jim said.

"I know, Jim, but consider this. If I had not come back to this time, ending up in the mental ward for telling about my experience, this is not how your lives or mine would have played out, had I not returned. If I'm in both time frames as the two of you must be and had not returned to this time frame as I did, I suppose, I would have no knowledge of any of this except the possibility of having some odd dreams like the two of you are having, with no explanation for the cause."

The two looked at Vince, then looked at each other, then Jim spoke. "I'm getting confused." He said.

"It gets worse." Vince said, and went on. "Without any knowledge for the cause of the dreams, we might have seen a shrink, and hearing what we were dreaming about, the shrink would have prescribed some kind of behavior or sleep modification drug. In that case, the dreams might have gone away, but even if they didn't, we would be going on with our normal day-to-day lives, just as you two were, before I ended up in the mental institution."

Vince paused for a second, giving the two time to absorb what he had said, and then went on. "Get ready, here comes the kicker."

"It can't get any deeper!" Jim contended.

"Oh yes it can! If I hadn't come back with the knowledge of what I experienced in 2009, the original me that would be here now wouldn't have ended up in Gifford."

"Why not?" Jim asked with a puzzled look on his face.

"Simply because, that me wouldn't have talked about what that me didn't know, about the future. We and the world would have went forward just the same as we did the first time I was in 2005. I'd still be there at the lab with the two of you and Dr. Leyland, without so much of a hint of what lay in store, just like it was the first time for all of us."

"Aw, Damn!" Jim said. "I'm really confused with this first time me and second time me, stuff."

"You can say that again." Donna said.

"Who wouldn't be? I am too." Vince said, and went on. "This time it will be a different 2005 for me. I know the mistakes that were made the first time and with your help, we can find a way to warn the world, making sure it doesn't go down the way it did the first time."

"How are we going to do that?" Donna asked.

"Your lives aren't going to be the same this time. They've already changed. You're here with Jim talking to me today. In the other 2005, you, Jim and I would have been plugging away at our jobs, like we always had before. I wasn't put in the mental ward the first time, but the fact I was this time, has changed everything." Vince said.

"How?" Jim asked.

"None of us will live the same lives that we would have and did in my first experience in 2005, all that's changed now. The fact that you're here now and I'm speaking to you today never happened in the first 2005, but neither of you can know that for sure. As far as either of you could possibly know, beyond what I have told and showed you, you're both doing what you must be assuming you would both would have done today, but in the reality of 2009, you didn't do."

Vince could see that what he was telling Jim and Donna was unimaginable and most likely unbelievable. But he felt if he had any chance of convincing them beyond any doubt, he had to go on. "Jim, you know I've never had any mental problems."

Jim nodded his head in agreement and Vince went on. "Donna doesn't know that, and I wouldn't blame her if she thought I did. This all sounds like the ravings of a lunatic, I know, but it's not. I keep referring to the first time I was in 2005, but for you two, as far as you know, this is your first and only time in 2005. I was never put in a mental ward, my first time in 2005. I didn't know how to fly a helicopter either, but I do now. Had I not had my experience and had I not come back, you wouldn't be here today and neither would I. I'd be in 2009 at this very moment along with you two and the others and yet you'd both still be in San Diego going on with your day-to-day life, which would eventually lead to 2009. For that matter, so would I, I guess. What boggles my mind even more is that I realize the two of you are in both time frames, but I don't know if I am. If I hadn't come back to 2005 from 2009, would there still be a duplicate of me here in 2005, who would still be working there along side, Donna and you? If so, would my duplicate be there with you two and have no knowledge or premonition of what was going to happen in 2009? That's one question I can't answer."

Vince let what he had said soak in for a few seconds and then said. "Here's the most baffling part, as far as I'm concerned. I don't know if I'm still there in 2009 looking at the Arch and living at the motel with you two and here at the same, time or not."

"I don't' get it, Vince." Jim said, seconded by Donna.

"Okay, I know it's confusing, so let me put it this way. You've both seen movies, where an individual dies or is dying and then is brought back in some form or another, to view their self and given an opportunity to change their ways."

"Sure, like Scrooge in The Christmas Carol." Jim said.

"Exactly." Vince replied. "But I'm not looking down on the Vince of 2005 and seeing the mistakes he made, there is no other Vince in 2005. The mistakes that were made the first time will still be made this time and I know that, because it has already happened to all of us in 2009, catching us and the world unaware, but that's where the comparison ends."

"Why?" Jim asked.

"Of the three of us here now, I'm the only one that has really experienced the things I've told you about. You've both had dreams, but from what you've told me, the dreams aren't a true picture of what happened and is still going to happen. Since there is no other me here, yet the both of you are here with me now, both of you and I, are experiencing a completely new set of events that neither of you or I experienced in that 2005. Aside from the proof I have that I was there, I'd say I was dreaming and made it all up, like everyone thought when I was locked up. It almost drove me crazy, just thinking about. I don't know if it's a paradox, but I guess you could call it that."

The Continent Of St. Louis - The Search For Answers

"Damn! That's enough to make anyone go nuts." Jim said.

Vince smiled at Jim and said. "It does sound nuts and I've had a lot of weird thoughts, that's for sure. One that crossed my mind was, that if I had died in 2009 from the infection in my arm or in any other way, would I have died only there or in both places. Think about that!" Vince said.

"Did you come up with an answer?" Jim asked.

"There is no answer, because I didn't die." Vince replied. "All I can say for sure is, that we became different people in 2009, from the choices we made in 2005. In spite of the fact, Donna joined the Air Force, our lives were intertwined as they did then and have been now. I believe that the three of us are connected somehow, by some force we don't or can't understand. I not going to call it a miracle or providence or the work of God or the Devil. I don't believe in any of that. There is good and evil in this world, but it's human good and evil. I don't believe in spirits, ghosts or that humans have a soul. What I've experienced before and is continuing to this day, is unexplainable. Other people have reported similar experiences, and they've been ridiculed for telling about it, or as in my case, locked up. It's a terrible feeling to know that you've actually experienced something and no one believes you because it doesn't seem possible."

"What are you going to do?" Donna asked.

"I'm going to try to do what my psychiatrist at Gifford said I was imagining I was trying to do. I've got to inform people, try to change what happened the first time, and hope that it will make a difference, this time. Jim and I are going to study, Dr. Leyland's Model, and try to get the information to the right people, much sooner than the first time. I still can't believe I sat around on my duff and let it blow right past me the first time. When, Dr. Leyland retired, I was a complete failure as Director of the Seismic Center." Vince said.

"If Dr. Leyland didn't pass the information on to you, it wasn't your fault." Donna replied.

"He couldn't tell me or anyone. He was sworn to secrecy, but regardless, I should have picked up on the signs. It was all there, I blew it!" Vince said.

Do you think he will help you now?" She asked.

"I can only hope so, Donna. I don't know how he's going to react when he finds out, Jim copied his Model."

"He said he wanted your help, and was looking forward to you coming back to work. I don't think it will bother him." Jim said.

"I hope not, but we'll find out. I'm going to make a list of the other significant participants from 2009. I'm going to try and find out if they really exist, and get in touch with them if they do. We know Sullivan does, the others may also. I knew who Sullivan was, and of course I knew, Jim and Dr. Leyland, before I had the experience, but regrettably, I never knew you, Donna."

"I noticed that! What does it take for a girl to get noticed? I should have done this." She laughed, and poked Vince, in the ribs.

Vince, laughed embarrassedly, and kept on talking. "I didn't know any of the others before the disaster. If I find out they don't exist, well… I'll have to deal with that when the time comes."

"Make the list. I'll start running the names on the internet." Jim said.

"Thanks, Jim. I'll make the list tonight. You can start on it tomorrow."

"What can I do?" Donna asked.

"I'm going to rent a light plane tomorrow. If you want, you can come with me. I have a camera, you could take photographs for me, if you decide to come along." Vince said.

"Where are you going?" She asked.

"I'm going to check out Area 51. I'd like to try and get some pictures of the place." Vince replied.

"Hey!" Jim said. "I want to go too. I can take photographs for my journal. I can work on the list when we get back."

"Are you sure Area 51 exists? Donna asked. "I've heard it's nothing but a rumor. Where is Area 51?"

"It exists all right." Vince said. "It's northwest of here, I looked it up on the internet last night. There was one photo of it and a map showing the general area and other pictures of signs indicating it was Government Property."

"Will you get in trouble flying over Area 51?" Donna asked.

"I'm sure it's a no fly zone so we can't fly over it. I just want to try and get close enough to take some telephoto shots of it."

"What about me? May I go?" Jim Asked.

"We can all go." Vince replied.

"Okay, that's settled. What's it going to be, the casino or work tonight?" Jim asked.

"Why don't you and Donna go on down to the casino. I'll get the list made up for you, Jim."

"Suits me." Jim answered.

"Don't you want to come along, Vince?" Donna asked.

"No, I was there earlier today. I have one favor to ask though."

"What's that?" Donna asked.

"Do you have a secret compartment in your purse to hide the penny?"

"I could put it in my compact behind the lining." She answered.

"That will work." Vince said. "I don't want to keep it in my room, I don't like the way that security guard was watching us. If you see him snooping around, call me when you get to the casino."

AN ENEMY AT THE DOOR

THE TWO LEFT AND Vince got busy making the list on his laptop, thinking about the ones he'd like to locate. *It won't be hard to check up on people like Lemming or Clemmons and perhaps Max. But others like Ray, Dana, Bob and George are going to be hard to find.*

He knew that Dana's folks lived either in St. Louis or Highlandville, Missouri. *They won't be hard to find.* He thought. *Bob never said what his parent's names were or where he was from. Ray, George, Lawson, Randall and Sgt. Collins were all assigned to Area 51 with top-secret clearances. Jim probably won't be able to find anything on them. Other lesser figures like General Wright and Barnes will be easier. Barnes said he was from Independence, Missouri. He'll be easy to find. It really doesn't make any difference if I can find them all. Just enough to verify that some of them exist and are not some figment of my imagination, will do.*

The phone rang, he saw it was, Jim and answered.

"No sign of the Security Guard." Jim said.

"Good, maybe I'm just being jumpy." Vince replied.

"Why don't you come on down? Donna just won a thousand dollars, but I'm losing my ass. I could use some company."

"All right, Jim. I've got the list finished. I'll put it on a disc and bring it with me. See you in a few minutes."

He put the finishing touches on the list and copied it to CD. He put it in his pocket and headed for the elevators, not noticing the two surly looking figures that watched him all the way down the hall, and then board the elevator.

Vince joined them in the casino and watched as Donna lost the thousand dollars she had won. With a matter of fact air, she said. "Easy come, easy go."

"I quit!" Jim said. "I've lost all I can afford."

The three left and walked back to the lobby and took an elevator back to their floor. As they rounded the corner and started down the corridor, the two men, Vince hadn't noticed earlier, came out of his room and walked toward them in a hurry. One had Vince's laptop clutched in his hand.

"Vince!" Jim whispered. "They've been in your room."

"I see that." Vince whispered back. "Donna, slow down, get behind us."

The men came toward them both smiling and said. "Evening folks." As if, they were the room occupant.

Jim returned the greeting as Vince and he separated as if to let the two pass. As they did, Vince jumped one and Jim jumped the other, wrestling both men to the floor.

"What the hell?" One yelled, as he went down, dropping Vince's laptop and his hotel room swipe card. As the two cussed and struggled trying to escape, Vince slugged the one he was wrestling with. The man's head hit the floor and he was out for the count. Jim had the other down with his knee on his chest, telling him not to move. The man pushed Jim off, pulled a gun out of his belt and pointed at Jim. Before he could fire, Vince kicked the gun out of his hand and then kicked the offender in the side, ending the struggle.

"Damn! He meant business." Jim said, getting to his feet.

"You're damn right he did!" Vince replied, and then said to, Donna."Get the gun, and go to your room! Call security as soon as you lock your door, and hurry!"

As Donna left, Vince said. "Watch them, Jim, while I check my room."

The Continent Of St. Louis - The Search For Answers

He went in and found the room ransacked. His bags were lying open, with the contents strewn across the floor. The blankets, sheets and pillowcases were scattered everywhere, the mattress had been cut open and gutted of its stuffing. All the drawers in the chest were laying upside down with their contents spilled on the floor. The bathroom had also been ransacked.

They must have been looking for the penny! Vince thought.

His phone rang, Donna was on the line and said. "Security's on the way, Vince."

"What did you do with the gun?" He asked.

"It's in my underwear drawer. Do you want it?" She asked.

"No, it's mine. Just keep it for now and don't mention it. Those two thugs took it when they ransacked my room."

"What do you want me to do?" She asked.

"Wait there, I've got to get back out with, Jim."

He went out and joined Jim in the hallway, just as two security guards arrived. "What's going on?" The first asked.

"These men broke in my room." Vince said. "They took my laptop and ransacked my room."

"What's your name, and room number, sir?" The guard asked.

"Davis, room 904." Vince answered.

The guard called in the attempted robbery on his radio and requested police back up. A well-dressed man stepped from the elevator and came down the corridor, joining them, and was told of the situation.

"Cuff them and take them downstairs. Police are on the way." He said to the guards, then turned and asked. "Which of you is, Mr. Davis?"

"I'm, Davis." Vince replied.

"I'm the assistant manager, Mr. Davis. My name is, Royce Adams. Please accept my personal apology and that of the hotel for this inconvenience. May I ask if you've checked your room? If anything is missing, our insurance carrier will pay for anything they might have stolen or damaged."

"They messed up the room, but it looks like the only thing they took was my laptop, laying there." Vince bent down and picked it up along with the swipe card.

"Is the laptop damaged? The hotel will have it repaired or buy you a new one if it can't be repaired." Adams said.

123

"It looks like it's all right. I'll check it later. Would you mind explaining where they got this swipe card to my room?"

"That card isn't yours?" Adams asked.

"No, one of them dropped it when I slugged him." Vince reached in his pocket, and produced his swipe card. "This is mine." He said.

Adams took both swipe cards from his hand and said. "I need to try these in the door."

He tried them both, the green light came on both times.

"I'm afraid someone's made a mistake and made a duplicate, in error, Mr. Davis." Adams said.

"I don't think it was a mistake." Vince replied. "I think it was done with the

intention of breaking in my room without making any noise. The swipe cards, have no room number on them. Those two men would have had to try every door in the hotel to see what door it worked in."

"Mr. Davis, I don't know what you're saying." Adams replied.

"I'm saying one of your desk clerks made a duplicate for those thugs. They were after something else I have, but it wasn't in my room. I guess they took the laptop when they didn't find what they came after." Vince said.

"Our employees are above reproach, Mr. Davis. This has never happened in the past." Adams said.

Vince explained the situation he had encountered with the coin dealer and described the guard the coin dealer had been talking with when they left.

"The guard followed me to my room when we came up earlier. I'm sure his intentions were to find out which room I was staying in." Vince said.

"It's hard to imagine those thugs would single out your room and then only steal a laptop, Mr. Davis." Adams said.

"They weren't after the laptop. It was the rare coin I have they were after, but they didn't find it." Vince said.

"Well thank goodness for that." Adams said. "I'm going to move you to a different room, Mr. Davis. There will be no charge for your stay. The hotel will comp your room while you're here, for the inconvenience."

"I appreciate that, but my associates and I are leaving. We'll be checking out, just as soon as we can get our belongings."

The Continent Of St. Louis - The Search For Answers

"I understand and again I apologize." Adams said. "There'll be no charge to you, for any of the rooms. When you check out, have the clerk page me. I'll give you a voucher, good for any hotel you'd rather stay in, while you're in Las Vegas. The voucher will be good for the three of you for as long as you want to stay. I completely understand why you wouldn't want to stay here any longer."

"Thank you, Mr. Adams, we'll be down in a few minutes."

"Thank you, Mr. Davis. I hope this won't discourage you from staying with us in the future. I'll see you downstairs."

As Adams left, Vince said. "Okay, let's get packed."

"We just got here. I liked this place!" Jim complained.

A police officer was waiting at the desk when they arrived to check out, and said. "The Hotel has filed charges against the two men, Mr. Davis. Would you like to file a complaint also?"

"No, nothing was damaged or missing from the room. Who were those men?" Vince asked. "Do they work for the hotel?"

"No, they're just a couple of local, petty thieves. That coin you have must be pretty valuable, Mr. Davis." The officer replied.

"How did you know about that?" Vince asked.

"One of them started talking. The coin dealer hired a security guard from the hotel, who hired them. The guard let them use his passkey to get in your room. They've all been arrested and taken downtown."

"Thanks." Vince said.

"If there's nothing else, I'll be going." The officer said.

Before the officer walked away the desk clerk came up to Vince and said. "Here's your credit card printout, Mr. Davis. As you can see, I have refunded the charge for the rooms. This is your voucher, that Mr. Adams authorized and your envelope from the lock box. The hotel again would like to extend a sincere apology to you. If you should ever wish to stay here again as our guest, please reference the code number on your receipt. You will be given a room at no cost for a week and a five hundred dollar credit, good toward gambling in the casino."

"Is that transferable?" Jim asked.

"I'm afraid not, sir." The clerk replied.

"Is that the rare coin in the envelope, Mr. Davis?" The officer asked.

"Yes." Vince lied.

"Mind if I look at it? I'm a coin collector myself. I'd like to see what that coin dealer thought breaking the law was worth, to get it." The officer said.

"Not at all." Vince replied, looking at the envelope and seeing it had been opened previously. *No wonder they ransacked my room.* He thought, as he opened the envelope and handed the police officer the penny.

"What's special about this? It's a 2005. It's not worth anything." The officer said.

"Only in sentimental value." Vince replied. "It's, Miss Stevens and my lucky penny."

"Well I'll be damned! The coin dealer said you had a 2009 penny." The officer replied.

"A 2009? His eyesight must be going bad." Vince said.

"I guess so." The officer replied. "If you two are getting married, Las Vegas is the place to do it. So long."

Donna looked at Vince. "Our special penny, huh?" She asked.

"Well it was yours, and you gave it to me." He replied.

They walked out front and waited for the valet to bring Vince's car around. As the valet drove up, Vince said. "See if anyone's watching us, Donna."

She looked around as Vince tossed their bags in the trunk. "I don't see anyone." She said.

"Good. Let's go." Vince said.

"Where are we going to stay? Can we stay at that hotel that looks like a Pyramid?" Jim asked.

"No, we can't. We've attracted to much attention as it is. I'm going to get a Vegas map, locate a small airport, and get motel rooms close to it. Watch and see if anyone follows us." Vince replied.

"A motel?" Jim asked, in a disappointed tone.

Vince smiled as he drove away. Jim was sounding more like the Jim he'd known. It still wasn't like old times, but things were getting better all the time.

"Yes, a motel, Jim. We've got to lay low. I don't want to have to talk to any more policemen, if I can help it. I'm going to try to become anonymous from now on. See if anyone is following us."

Jim looked behind them and said. "There's no one on our tail."

CHAPTER TEN

DR. WOITASCZYK'S OFFICE...GIFFORD MENTAL CENTER

IT WAS FOUR P.M., Friday evening. Dr. Woitasczyk was sitting at his desk, desperately trying to come up with an answer for Vince's disappearance. The longer he thought, the more paranoid he became. *The whole damn thing is like a plot against me! Norton didn't find any way, Davis could have escaped, so someone helped him and that someone is trying to steal my glory. I know goddamned well those brainless orderlies had something to do with it, but they're too damn stupid to have done it on their own. Some other doctor's found out about Davis and his condition and is trying to take credit for my discovery. The only way it could have been done, was with Crischell and Dawdry's help. They both hate me and probably want to see me ruined. They must have helped smuggle him out during the night, and the bomb scare was probably the cover they used to get him out. There's no other explanation.*

He went over the list of doctors that knew about Vince, eliminated most of them, and came up with a thought. *I'll bet Dr. Benjamin had something to do with the escape! It would be just like some third rate, hayseed, psychiatrist from Missouri, looking to gain some glory and trying to steal mine. I'll get the bastard, if he did! I shouldn't have revealed Davis's condition on the Psychiatric blog. If Benjamin's patient doesn't show up, I'll know he* had something to do with Davis's escape, and they'll all do some time up the river, if I have anything to say about it!

He had gone over the surveillance recordings of Vince's room, those of the corridor and the nurse's station, for the night of Vince's escape. The recording of Vince's room showed what looked like a figure laying in the bed, all night. The corridor recording showed no movement other than two police officers with dogs going down the hall and coming back, and then much later, when Dawdry and Crischell had gone to wake Vince up. Woitasczyk had put the recording from the nurses' station in last, and was looking at it. He saw Dawdry going into the inner office and then saw Crischell leaning back in his chair and going to sleep. He speeded up the display, watching the complete recording, in fast forward. Crischell hadn't moved for hours until he suddenly woke up and answered the phone. He spoke for a few minutes and then tapped his baton on the inner office window and his mouthed moved as if he were talking.

Why don't they have audio on these recordings, like they do for the patient's rooms? Woitasczyk fumed as he watched Dawdry come out of the office, scratching his balls and rubbing his eyes. His hair was matted down and his whites looked filthy.

"You're both going to be fired!" Woitasczyk screamed as he watched the two converse. "What are you two dumkoph's talking about?"

He saw the two, waving their arms as if they were in an argument and wanted desperately to know what they were saying. *I'll hire a lip reading expert and then I'll get some answers!* He thought.

He watched as the two left the nurses' station and headed down the hall, toward Vince's room. Disgustedly, Woitasczyk turned off the recording and called the director of human resources, saying he was charging the two with dereliction of duty, saying he had a recording that proved the charges. He demanded that they be dismissed immediately.

"I'm sorry, Dr. Woitasczyk, but we can't dismiss them without a hearing." The director replied.

"All right! Set the hearings up for tonight and do it now!" Woitasczyk blared.

"We'll have to notify them first, and schedule the hearings, after their shift is over." The director replied.

"If we notify them and wait till they get off duty, they'll have time to talk it over and make up some damn lie. Don't tell them a damn thing! I'll be here when they come in, and I'll bring them straight to your office."

"What time do they report for duty?" The director asked.

"They're on duty from eight p.m. until eight a.m." Woitasczyk replied.

"Human Resources closes at five p.m. You'll have to hold them over, after their shift, and bring them to my office at nine a.m. tomorrow morning. Saturday is one of my days off, but I'll come in if you don't think this can wait until Monday." The director said.

"Jesus Christ!" Woitasczyk screamed. "They're off duty at eight. Why can't we hold the hearings the minute their shift is over?"

"I'd be doing you a favor to come in at all. If you want to schedule it for Monday, that's fine with me." The director replied.

"This can't wait until Monday! I'll have them there at nine sharp." Woitasczyk replied.

"You'll have to authorize overtime payment for them, until the hearings are concluded." The director said.

"Overtime! The bastard's don't deserve what they get for straight time! They were both sleeping on the job and I have surveillance tapes to prove it!" Woitasczyk snarled.

"Be sure to bring the tapes to the hearings. I have the equipment to watch them."The director said.

"You're goddamned right we'll watch them! I want their asses off the payroll the second the hearings are over!" Woitasczyk spat back.

"I'll make that decision after reviewing the tapes. If what you say is true, I have the authority to dismiss them, but only if the dereliction and violation you say they've committed, is flagrant and intentional. If otherwise, my recommendations will have to be submitted to a review board, for the final decision."

"Review board, my ass!" Woitasczyk screamed.

"Dr. Woitasczyk! You're behaving very unprofessional, and your language, I must say, is vulgar at the least. I won't allow you to attend the hearing unless you give me your assurance that you will behave in a professional manner and refrain from the use of vulgar language. Do I have that assurance?"

Goddamned, pencil pushing, bastard! Is what Woitasczyk thought, but what he said was. "Ya, you do. I apologize for my behavior. I'll conduct myself in a professional manner. You have my assurance of that."

"Thank you Dr. Woitasczyk. You do seem very upset though." The director said.

"You're damned right I'm upset! They're worthless!" Woitasczyk spat back.

"If you can furnish my office with any additional information or other recordings that also substantiates your charges, I can almost guarantee you, they will be dismissed after the hearings." The director said.

"I'll get more tapes for you and I'm bringing David Norton to the hearings. He is head of security. He'll testify that the tapes are genuine." Woitasczyk said.

"I'm familiar with Mr. Norton. His testimony will be above reproach."

"Good. I want the bastard's gone the second the hearings are over!" Woitasczyk hissed.

"What's prompted this anger and contempt you seem to hold for these two orderlies? Is there something you're not telling me?" The director asked.

"They're not worth a damn and I can't imagine how they were ever hired in the first place." Woitasczyk complained.

"I see. Then there's nothing personal or anything other than their dereliction of duty, involved in your request for their dismissal?" The director asked.

"Nothing that I'm allowed to say or reveal, at this time." Woitasczyk replied.

"Don't you think all evidence of any misdoing by the two, should be presented at their hearings?" The director asked.

"This isn't going to be a goddamned trial in a court of law! They won't be able to deny they were sleeping on the job! I'll bring additional tapes of preceding nights, I'm sure those tapes will show the exact, same behavior!" Woitasczyk snarled.

"Very well. I have my office notify the two of them and I'll see you and Mr. Norton in my office at nine in the morning."

Woitasczyk hung up and called Norton, and said. "I want all recordings of the nightshift for the complete week before Davis escaped."

"What in the hell do you need those for?" Norton asked.

Woitasczyk explained and then said. "I want you to hire a lip reading expert and have him tell me what those two idiots were saying to each other, the night Davis escaped. I know damn well those two bastard's were in on it and they were probably talking about it."

"I can't do that!" Norton said.

"Why not? You're the head of security aren't you?" Woitasczyk retorted.

"I'd have to get authorization from up top and get them to cut a check for his fee. I'm not going one-step further with this. If you want those two fired to cover your ass, all right, I'll go along with that, but that's it. The tapes will be good enough to get the job done."

"I want to know what they were saying, goddamnit!" Woitasczyk hissed.

"Ask them at the hearing, when the tapes are shown." Norton replied.

"You know goddamned well I can't do that. I don't want one word of Davis's escape brought up. Neither of us can afford that."

"Then drop the charges against them and call off the hearings." Norton replied.

"I can't do that! No one knows Davis escaped but those two assholes and us. I would look like a fool." Woitasczyk replied.

"What about the two day shift orderlies that work that wing? They know Davis escaped don't they?" Norton asked.

"No they don't. They think Davis was moved to the men's wing." Woitasczyk replied.

"Okay, I'll take care of it for you. I'll call the director of Human Recourses and tell him I've reviewed the tapes of the preceding nights and found they had been asleep only the one time. I'll smooth it over and tell him I advised you to drop the charges and cancel the hearings. I'll tell him we're going to have an informal meeting with the two and at most, they'll get a warning and a couple days off without pay and a disciplinary letter in their file."

"Okay, do it, but he'll still think I was a fool for carrying on the way I was." Woitasczyk replied.

"I'll take care of that by simply telling him what a responsible medical professional you are, and that you were incensed, thinking the welfare of the patients in your care, could have been in jeopardy." Norton said.

"Jesus Christ! You should have been a lawyer!" Woitasczyk declared.

"I've been told that before. I'll see you in your office, later tonight. Thank you, Dr. Woitasczyk." Norton replied.

Crischell and Dawdry were being questioned separately by Norton and Woitasczyk. Norton was using techniques he learned from police training, interrogation CD's he'd purchased. "Listen Dawdry! Crischell has already spilled his guts, so you better start coming clean. Otherwise you going to face the rap by yourself."

"He's a lying, son-of-a-bitch!" Dawdry replied. "I was asleep all night and I sleep every night. I have to, I have a day job. If anyone helped sneak, Davis, out of his room, it was Crischell."

The trick hadn't worked on either of them. Norton had finally taken Woitasczyk aside and said. "We're not going to get anything out of them. They must have been in on it together. That stupid Dawdry is still saying, Davis, has to be a time traveler."

Woitasczyk agreed and recommended they be given two days off without pay along with the warning and the letter in their file. Norton concurred and the two were sent home. Industrial Relations cut the penalty down to one day without pay, citing staff shortages. Their duty pay for the night of interrogation was forfeited and counted as the day off they would have to incur for the policy violation. They both reported for duty again that night.

At home that evening, Woitasczyk sat and brooded while he thought. *I'll get rid of their asses if it's the last thing I do.*

He found himself considering what Dawdry had said, regarding time travel, and caught himself. "No! It isn't possible!" He said aloud.

"What's that dear?" His wife asked looking up from her magazine.

"Nothing! Leave me alone!" He snapped.

"What's wrong dear? Is it something I could help you with?" She asked.

"Not unless you can tell me where, Davis is." He shouted back.

"Davis? Who is this person you're talking about?" She asked.

Woitasczyk realized he had made a slip. "No one dear. Forget it." He said in a sweet tone.

"Why don't I fix us some nice hot tea? Would you like that, dear?" She asked.

He sighed and agreed. She left to fix the tea and he went to his bar and poured himself a stiff drink, swallowing it in one gulp. He had several more by the time she got back and he was feeling better. He'd been thinking about Vince while she was gone. The liquor had mellowed him out and he was no longer on edge. As he sipped the spicy tea, he started thinking the situation over. *Dawdry and Blake are complete dumkoph's. Davis isn't a goddamned time traveler! The son-of-a-bitch was holding down a steady job until he went off the deep end. Davis is unlike any patient I have ever treated, but he's not a time traveler. An illusionist or magician, would be more likely, having escaped without a trace. He'll show up. He'll be proud of what he did and want to tell everyone how he outsmarted the best psychiatrist in the world. He'll show back up at his office, where in the hell else would an insane seismologist go?*

He called, Dr. Leyland again, not even thinking of how late it was. Dr. Leyland, answered and he asked if Vince, had shown up. Dr. Leyland, said he hadn't.

"Do you know if any of your staff members have seen or talked to him, Dr. Leyland?" Woitasczyk asked.

"Not that I know of. No one has mentioned it." Dr. Leyland said.

"What about, Mr. Lewis? Has he mentioned seeing or talking to, Davis?" Woitasczyk asked.

"No he hasn't." Leyland replied.

"Is, Mr. Lewis, in? May I speak with him?" Woitasczyk asked.

"I'm sorry, Dr. Woitasczyk. Mr. Lewis, is on vacation." Dr. Leyland replied.

Another goddamned dead end! Woitasczyk thought, but asked. "When will he be back?"

"In two weeks." Dr. Leyland replied.

"Goddamn! I can't wait two weeks! I need to speak with him, now! Where the hell did he go on vacation?" Woitasczyk shouted.

"What was that?" Dr. Leyland asked.

"I said, where in the hell did he go, on vacation?" Woitasczyk snarled back.

"I'm sorry, Dr. Woitasczyk. I can't help you. I'm a busy man." Dr. Leyland said.

"Busy? You don't know what busy is!" Woitasczyk spat back. "I need to know where, Davis, is!"

"If you released him, why are you calling around here looking for him in that tone of voice and using profane language?" Dr. Leyland asked.

"I want to make sure he's okay, that's all. I'm his doctor, remember?" Woitasczyk arrogantly replied.

"If he comes in, I'll call you. Otherwise, leave me alone, I'm busy." Dr. Leyland hung up.

Woitasczyk was furious again. "Lousy, seismologist, PhD's!" He shouted. "They've got their noses in books and figures all the time, that don't mean shit! I'm doing something important, and all he can think about is some damn crack in the Earth, that's not going anywhere!"

He kicked his trashcan across the floor, shouting obscenities in German. *"Hahn Saugen Arschloche!"* He shouted over and over, enraged by what he considered to be, Dr. Leyland's insolent dismissal of him.

His wife walked in the room after hearing his outburst. She saw the overturned trash can and asked. "What's wrong dear?"

"Everything's wrong!" He shouted and left the room without saying another word.

POLICE HEADQUARTERS...SAN DIEGO

CHIEF BREWER WAS STILL in his office when he should have been at home. Brewer had every detective available, looking for the suspect who had hi-jacked the Medi-vac. He had issued orders to bring every teenager with a pilot license in for questioning, but it had led nowhere. There were only four in the greater San Diego area, none of them attended the Granite Hills High School and none of them had, helicopter certification. The four had been released back to their enraged parent's custody, when none were found to resemble the individual in the surveillance photo.

Despite the fact, they had no suspects in the Medi-vac hi-jacking, Brewer was resting easier about one thing. The bomb scare item had died down, and no one was talking about it anymore. Regardless, the heat was still on Brewer from the Police Commissioner and the Mayor's Office. He needed to find the person who had hi-jacked the Medi-vac, but so far, his men had found nothing and no one had called in and identified the person from the photo that had been released.

"Get a goddamned photo expert and get the pictured cleaned up!" The Mayor had told Brewer.

Brewer needed the original video to take to a professional lab. The hospital refused to release the video and he had asked Claude Forrester, the District Attorney, to get a judge to issue a court order to get the video. The judge had denied Forrester's request, finding no fault with the hospital's decision, since they had provided photo copies of the hi-jacker.

Again, at a dead end, Brewer was going over a copy of the field officers report of the evidence found in the hi-jacked Medi-vac. He hoped he could find something the detectives had overlooked. He found what he was looking for, in the officer's comment.

San Diego, California Police Department.

Case No. 12103-05   Date. 30, August, 05

Field Officers Evidence Report

Physical evidence: None

Fingerprints: None, other than pilot, John Workman

Inventory of personal property recovered from scene:

Duffle bag: Black, Canvas
Contents: Wallet, two hundred dollars in cash, 3 credit cards - Visa, Master Card Discover. CA. driver license, pilot license, address book, cigarettes, lighter, sunglasses, cell phone, iPod, earphones, 2 – Hustler Magazines, 1 – Prescription bottle containing 25, 100 mg Viagra tablets, Portable DVD Player, 3 – Pornographic DVD's, 10 -Trojan condoms, 2 oz tube Astro-Glide lubricant. All items identified as property belonging

to Medi-vac Pilot, John Workman, 2102 Rio Drive, San Diego, California, 92139.

End of inventory: No other items found.

Officers comments: *I find it highly unusual, that no money or credit cards were removed from the wallet. In addition to that, no items of value were taken, such as the DVD player, pornographic DVD's or the bottle of Viagra I would strongly, suggest ruling out robbery as the motive for the hi-jacking of the Medi-vac. I would also suggest, the ruling out of juveniles, as suspects in the investigation. Juveniles' would have stolen the duffle bag and contents*

Investigating Officers Signature: Sgt. Arnold Rodriguez

"Goddamn!" Brewer yelled aloud. He depressed his intercom button and said to his secretary. "Get Captain Jennings on the phone for me."

"Yes, Chief."

Jennings called five minutes later and asked. "What's up, Chief?"

"Get those clowns that are working on the Medi-vac case, in my office now! And get your ass in here with them!" Brewer barked.

"You mean Harper and Edwards, sir?" Jennings asked.

"Who else would I mean? You assigned those two morons to the case, didn't you?" Brewer snarled.

"Yes, sir. They're good men." Jennings said.

"Well, get them, and get your ass in my office, now!" Brewer snapped.

Five minutes later the two detective and Jennings came in the Chief's office. They started to sit down, when Brewer roared. "Get your asses up out of those chairs! This isn't a goddamned social visit!"

Jennings didn't like the Chief's tone or the look on his face. "What's wrong?" He asked.

"You bastard's are what's wrong! What have you got on the Medi-vac case, Jennings?" Brewer asked.

"Nothing. There wasn't any evidence at the hospital and there wasn't any prints or other evidence in the Medi-vac." Jennings answered

"Nothing? Nothing, is all I hear from you and these two clowns. Did you read the evidence report, Jennings?" Brewer asked.

"Yes, sir, there wasn't any evidence connected to the hi-jacker. The chopper was clean." Jennings replied.

"What the hell do you call that?" Brewer asked pointing to the evidence report.

"You mean the pilot's duffle bag?" Jennings asked.

"What was in the duffle bag? What else do you see, Jennings?"

"His cell phone…" Jennings said as he was interrupted.

"Before that, Jennings! Open your eyes, goddamnit! What do you see before that?" Brewer barked.

"His wallet, sir?" Jennings asked hesitantly.

"Yes, his wallet, you dumb shit! What was in his wallet? Did you read that?" Brewer asked.

"Yes, sir, cash, credit cards, his lic…" Jennings was again interrupted.

"That's enough, Jennings! Every goddamned thing that belonged to the pilot was still in his wallet and the wallet was in the bag. Didn't you read the investigating officers statement?"

"Well, yes I looked it over, but I assigned the case to…"

"To these two dumb shits! Isn't that right, Jennings?" Brewer yelled, glaring at Harper and Edwards.

"Yes, sir, I did. That's their jobs." Jennings said.

"What's your job then? What else are you getting paid for besides sitting on your fat ass and taking up space in your office all day, Jennings?" Brewer asked.

"Well, I…."

"You're still a detective aren't you?" Brewer shouted.

"Yes." Jennings replied.

"Well, act the hell like one! Juveniles, didn't steal that chopper you idiots! Rodriguez said that in his report! They would have taken the money and the credit cards if they hi-jacked the Medi-vac and they damn sure wouldn't have passed up the Viagra, cell phone, the DVD player and porno movies. Have you got your heads up your asses? You've been looking for the wrong person you morons, and you call yourselves detectives! I had to do your jobs for you! All three of you are worthless, dumb shits! I ought to put all of you back out on the street and put in a voucher for your pay! It was right under your noses and you couldn't see it! Look how much time we've lost!" Brewer moaned.

"Where do we look Chief?" Jennings asked. "It's like finding a needle in a haystack. The guy is a phantom, nobody's I.D.'d him. Where do we start?"

"Did any of you read the officers report?" Brewer yelled.

"I did." Edwards said.

"What did it say?" Brewer asked.

"I don't remember." Edwards replied.

"Aw, goddamnit!" Brewer complained. "You're a bunch of morons! Rodriquez said to quit looking for a juvenile! Who would you look for next?"

"I don't know." Jennings said.

"The perp had on scrubs, right?" Brewer asked.

"Right." Jennings said.

"He wasn't hospital staff, right?" Brewer asked.

"Right." Jennings said.

"Who does that leave, Jennings?" Brewer asked.

"I don't know, Chief." Jennings replied.

"Do either of you two morons have the answer?" Brewer asked Edwards and Harper.

"No." They both replied.

"Well think about it, if any of you are capable of thinking!" Brewer spat back. "It was eleven o'clock at night. It might have been a visitor, but not likely. It damn sure wasn't a terrorist and it wasn't a kid. Who does that leave Jennings?" Brewer asked again.

"I don't know, Chief." Jennings answered.

"What a bunch of morons I have for detectives!" Brewer said shaking his head. "It had to be a disgruntled employee of the Medi-vac company or a patient! A patient is coming in dead last in my mind, they're locked up! Put two and two together you idiots."

"What are you getting at, Chief?" Jennings asked.

"Something any one of you should have seen if you were really detectives, which you aren't! A fellow worker wouldn't steal the pilot's wallet. They were probably friends. The pilot was probably in on it. What was his alibi?"

"He was supposed to be inside taking a leak or something." Jennings said.

"How convenient! He left his Medi-vac unattended and had to take a piss, then the Medi-vac gets hi-jacked while he's gone. That means his ass is covered, right?"

"Right." Jennings said.

"I didn't ask you for an answer, Jennings!" Brewer barked. "I just wanted to see if you're listening!"

"I'm listening, Chief." Jennings replied and then yelled. "Pay attention!" To Harper, who was picking his nose.

"All right, now that I have everybody's attention, this is the way it was. Workman conveniently wasn't anywhere in sight when the Medi-vac was hi-jacked. So he can't I.D. the suspect and he thinks that gives him a perfect alibi and the three of you were buying it." Brewer said.

"What were we supposed to think?" Edwards asked. "Rowland looked at the tape, he said he saw the pilot get out of the Medi-vac and he was heading toward the hospital entrance. He doesn't remember seeing anyone else in the Medi-vac."

"Have you got anything else to say, Edwards?" Brewer asked.

"Yeah, the only other person he saw was the suspect coming out of that door. They make a lot of trips to the hospital in those Medi-vac's, each day. The suspect could have been on an earlier flight and waited in the room till Workman arrived."

"I'm not buying that. You're going to have to come up with a better idea than that." Brewer said. "Am I the only one that's doing any thinking here?" He asked.

"I've got an idea how we can find out if he was on an earlier flight, Chief." Jennings said.

"This better be good." Brewer said.

"We can check the hospital's tapes." Jennings said. "If he was on an earlier flight, he would have been recorded by the surveillance camera."

"Hell no! That's out! It would be a waste of time even if the hospital would give us the tapes. Whoever helped the pilot could have been on an earlier flight, but I doubt it. They would know that they were being taped and wouldn't be that stupid, like some people I know!" He waited a second to let his last statement soak in, which didn't, and went on. "My guess is, whoever helped him, walked right in the front door in uniform and went to the service shaft and climbed to the top, and waited."

"He had on scrubs, Chief." Harper said.

"Oh, that's brilliant! He could have had some scrubs hidden under his jacket and put them on over his other clothes, after he reached the top, couldn't he?"

Harper had no reply. He knew he'd made a stupid statement. Brewer went on. "They probably had some beef with the company and they wouldn't have been stupid enough to fly there together. Unless one of you has a better idea, I think they were screwing with the Medi-vac company. Probably over some grievance or something. They're probably laughing their asses off right now while we go around looking for a teenager, we ain't ever going to find. Get your asses out there, and bring Workman in for questioning." He said to Harper and Edwards. "Jennings, you call the Medi-vac office. Find out if Workman or any other employees have a grievance against the company. While you're at it, find out who the paramedics are and send some other men out and bring them in too. One of them will talk."

"It's getting late in the day." Edwards said, looking at Harper, but talking to Brewer. "Our shift is almost over, we'll be on overtime if we stay. Could you assign the detail to the weekend detectives?"

"Hell no! You've screwed this case up so far and you're not getting a dammed dime of overtime pay! You can take compensating time off when you find and arrest the suspect."

"Damn, Chief! You know we never get to take any comp time!" Edwards complained. "I've got an AA meeting tonight, I shouldn't miss it."

"That's commendable. I'm glad you've straightened your ass out. How are your feet, Edwards?" Brewer asked in a soothing tone.

"They're fine, Chief." Edwards replied.

"That's because you've been sitting on your ass since this case broke! Now get out of here and find the suspect!" Brewer bellowed.

"Yes sir." The three said and started for the door, but not fast enough for Brewer, who yelled. "Move like you mean business! Get me a collar, or your asses are back in Blues and you'll be wearing Dr. Scholl's foot pads, pounding a beat."

"Yes, sir." Was heard in unison.

Why do I have a Police Force? Brewer wondered, after they left. *I have to do all the thinking for those worthless bastards.* He called, the Mayor, and explained what he suspected, telling him the detective unit was already looking into the lead.

"You better, damn well, be right his time!" The Mayor said, and hung up.

What a bastard! Brewer thought. *He sits up there in City Hall on his fat ass all day, throwing orders around, like he's a king!*

Brewer was in his fourth month as head of the San Diego Police Department. He had started at age 21 and had spent thirty-five years of his life working for the police department. He had started as a rookie and had moved up through the ranks, till he had been appointed Chief. He was 56 years old, and had kept himself in good shape over the years, but wasn't used to the kind of pressure the Mayor and the Commissioner were now putting on him. The media had been eating him alive as well. He knew if he could crack the case, he would be back in everyone's good graces. But so far, the prospect of solving the case, didn't look good.

CHAPTER ELEVEN

EL CAJON, CALIFORNIA...THE DAY BEFORE

BOB AND MARGARET EPPERSON pulled into El Cajon on Friday. They had checked into the Motel 6, off Interstate 8 at Magnolia for the night. Margaret had calmed down remarkably after taking her medication and asking the clerk if there had been any murders reported in El Cajon for the past two or three days. She relaxed and her mood changed after hearing there had been none reported. Bob saw the change and welcomed it.

Saturday morning Margaret got up bright and cheery. They drove to Vince's house and pulled up in front. Bob had no difficulty figuring out where the neighbor lived. He saw the mailbox with the Chargers helmet on it and went to the neighbor's house, introduced himself, told him the details of the arrangement they had and showed him, Vince's note.

"How is he?" Williams asked.

"What do you mean? Who are you talking about?" Bob asked.

"I'm talking about Davis. I didn't know he had gotten out of the hospital. He fell and hit his head and was in a coma. I didn't know he had been released." Williams said.

"He looked fine to me. He said he'd been transferred to the Midwest for a while. He didn't say what he did." Bob said.

The Continent Of St. Louis - The Search For Answers

"He's a seismologist. He works at the Seismic Center at UCSD." Williams replied.

"Oh, I'm the new Principal at Granite Hills High School. That's my wife Margaret in the truck. I'm not wishing Mr. Davis any bad luck, but I hope he stays a while. His place looks great, it's close to the school, and it's perfect."

"Granite Hills, huh? Did you hear the latest news?" Williams asked.

"About the helicopter that was landed on the football field?" Bob asked.

"Yes, but did you hear the latest?" Williams asked.

"I guess not. What's happened?" Bob asked.

"The police have brought the pilot in for questioning. He's the one that reported the Medi-vac hi-jacking. Looks like it wasn't a school kid after all." Williams said.

"I didn't think it was a school prank. Mr. Davis didn't either." Bob said.

"You know, the photo they released of the hi-jacker looked a lot like Vince, but I knew he couldn't fly a helicopter." Williams said.

"Vince?" Bob queried.

"Vince Davis, the owner of that house." Williams said.

"Oh, that's right, his name was Vince." Bob said.

"He's the assistant director at UCSD. He has a PhD. in Geology." Williams bragged, as if it added to his prominence.

"Well, he seemed very nice." Bob replied. "I thought he was some kind of professional by his manner." Bob looked at his wife in the truck and thought about her paranoid behavior the day before. *Wait till I tell her this.* He thought. *That should settle the crazy bitch down!*

"He's a great guy, I'm glad he's better." Williams said.

"He's supposed to call in a few days and let us know the arrangements." Bob said.

Williams shook Bob's hand and said. "I'm glad to meet you, Bob. Be sure and tell Vince I said hi, when you talk to him."

"I'll be sure to do that. Are you married?" Bob asked.

"Sure." Williams replied. "The old lady's inside on the crapper taking a dump. When she's through, she'll want to meet your old lady. What did you say her name is?"

J. L. Reynolds

"Margaret." Bob replied, not particularly caring for Williams' reference to his wife or for his revealing reference to his own wife's whereabouts.

"Oh yeah, that's right. My old lady's name is Cindy, Bob. When she gets through taking her dump, I'll tell her you're moving in." He closed the door and went back in his house. Bob could hear him calling out to his wife.

"Hey Cindy! We've got some new neighbors you need to meet. I told them you were taking a dump and would meet them later!"

Bob could hear the woman screaming obscenities but couldn't make out the rest of what she said. He motioned for his wife. She got out of the truck and followed him in the house. It was stuffy and a little dusty, but Bob knew it would a good home for them, and thought. *I need to make an appointment for her with Dr. Woitasczyk as soon as we settle in. Her paranoid behavior is becoming more pronounced and more frequent.*

As they toured the house, he said. "Mr. Davis has a PhD. in Geology, dear. He was the Assistant Director in Seismology at UCSD."

"That must be why he has all these pictures of rock formations on the wall. I like the house, I'm sorry for my behavior." She said.

"I like the house too, it will be perfect." Bob replied.

They unloaded their truck into the garage and left to return the rental truck and car dolly. They passed Dr. Woitasczyk as they reached the corner. He pulled up in front of Vince's house and rang the doorbell. When no one answered, he started pounding on the door and calling out. "Dr. Davis, are you in there?"

Larry Williams heard him yelling, came outside and said. "Davis doesn't live there anymore, mister. Some other people bought the house from him. They live there now."

"Have you seen, Davis?" Woitasczyk asked.

"No. The guy that's moving in, said Vince was headed for the Midwest." Larry replied.

"If you see him, tell him to call, Dr. Woitasczyk." Woitasczyk said handing Larry his card.

"Who? The guy that's moving in?" Larry asked.

"No, not the guy that's moving in! It's Davis I want to speak to." Woitasczyk said.

"Why didn't you say so?" Larry asked.

"I thought I did. It was you that misunderstood!" Woitasczyk shot back.

"Hey! Don't get all high and mighty with me, kraut lips!" Larry snarled, spitting beer-laden saliva on Woitasczyk.

"If you see Davis, give him my card." Woitasczyk said, as he wiped the saliva off his face and headed for his car.

"I'm not going to see him! I told you, he doesn't live there anymore!" Larry yelled to Woitasczyk.

Woitasczyk got in his car, turned around, and drove off thinking. *Goddamned drunken peasants! All they do is drink beer and breed more peasants!"*

Larry had started drinking early. His attitude and breath were proof. He looked at Woitasczyk's card and wondered. *Dr. Whatashit? What kind of name is that? I wonder what that stupid bastard wanted with Vince.* He popped the top on a backup beer he'd brought with him, turned it up and chugged it down. He went back in the house wondering what he was doing before he answered the door. He saw his Chargers helmet sitting on the coffee table and it all came back to him. The Chargers were playing the Raiders the next day. He had to get his paraphernalia ready for the game. He threw Woitasczyk's card in the trash, put his Lightning Bolt Helmet on and looked at himself in the mirror and yelled. "Go Bolts."

"Starting already?" His wife asked as she walked in the room.

"We got new neighbors." He slurred.

"I heard your filthy mouth!" She fumed back.

"What?" He said, oblivious to her statement.

"Do you have to tell the whole world, when I'm going to the bathroom?" She demanded.

"Oh, that! Well you were taking a dump weren't you?" Before she could answer, he said. "I know you were! I could smell it clear outside! Bob probably smelled it too!" He laughed, while holding his nose and fanning the air with the hand that was holding his beer.

"You're despicable!" She said in disgust. "I don't know why I married you!"

"I do!" He said, cupping his crotch in his hand, then drawing it up and down.

"Stop it right now! Do you hear me?" She gasped.

"I hear you, but I don't believe you!" He said with a leer on his face as he unzipped his fly, and asked. "You want some of this, don't you?"

"Absolutely not! Don't you dare get that filthy thing out in my living room!" She exclaimed.

Larry laughed, and said. "Take it easy! I'm only kidding! I've got to get ready for the game."

"I wasn't!" She replied, and asked. "What's their name?"

Larry looked down at his crotch, and said. "Long Larum and the Twins! You know that!" He guffawed, amused at himself.

"Would you mind getting your brains out of your crotch for just one second, and tell me what their names are?" She snapped back.

"Who are you talking about?" He asked as he zipped his fly back up.

"The new neighbors, you idiot!" His wife said.

"Uh….Shit! I don't know, I've forgotten." Larry slurred.

"You're drunk! That's what you are!" She screamed.

"Don't take that tone with me! I've only had a few beers, so far!" He retorted.

"A few too many, I'd say!" She countered.

"Wait a minute! I've got it, his name is Bob. See, I'm not drunk!" Larry slurred, with a smile.

"Bob what?" His wife asked.

"Stop grilling me!" Larry ordered. "Give me a minute, I'll remember."

"You're drunk, and the only thing you think about, or ever remember is, whether you're out of beer or not!" She snapped back.

"Oh shit! I'm glad you reminded me, I'm almost out! I've got to go pick up a case for tomorrow." He slurred.

"Not today, you're not! You're too drunk to drive, and I'm not going to go get it for you!" She said defiantly.

"Please." He pleaded.

"Not after telling the new neighbors I was taking a dump! I can't believe you told him that, when you can't even remember his name!" She hissed.

"Wait! He's the new principal at Granite Hills High School. I remember that much. So there!" He slurred.

The Continent Of St. Louis - The Search For Answers

"Where's, Vince? Why are they moving in his house? I thought he was in the hospital. Did he die?"She asked.

"Hell no! He was transferred to the Midwest." Larry slurred.

"Midwest? They don't have any earthquakes there, do they?" She asked.

"Maybe he's going to start some!" He laughed raucously, and finished another beer.

"You better slow down, you'll be passed out by six and you'll have a hangover tomorrow." His wife said, and then asked. "Who was it you were just talking too outside?"

"There was a guy named Whatashit looking for Vince." He slurred.

"Who?" She asked.

"Some guy named Dr. Whatashit or something like that. Hell! I don't know, I'm drunk! I had his card here somewhere." He said patting his pockets.

"That can't be his name! Nobody would have shit as part of their name. Slow down on that beer, you're more than drunk and get that stupid helmet off!" She said, as she reached for it.

"Go Bolts! We're going to kick some Raider asses tomorrow!" He yelled, as he avoided her and ran around the dining room table.

Men! She thought. *Do they ever grow up? He'll be drunk, sitting on the couch tomorrow and screaming his head off, with that stupid helmet on.* Knowing what the next day would bring, and not looking forward to it, she went to the kitchen to bake some cookies for her new neighbors.

POLICE HEADQUARTERS...SAN DIEGO

Edwards and Harper had Workman in an interrogation room, they were giving him the third degree.

"Who was he, Workman? You might as well tell us now. We're not leaving here till you tell us!" Edwards barked.

"I told you, I went to take a piss and someone took the Medi-vac." Workman retorted.

"Who was he, Workman? You know damn well he was there waiting for you in that room, when you landed! You thought you were being real smooth, going inside to take a piss. You probably thought you'd have a perfect alibi. You knew that would be on tape and throw the suspicion off of you!" Edwards snarled.

"I didn't even know they had cameras on the roof!" Workman shot back.

"Don't hand us that line of shit! We're not stupid like you! You made your big mistake when he didn't take your bag when you landed. If it were someone else who stole the Medi-vac, they would have taken all your shit! No thief would leave your wallet behind with two hundred dollars and your credit cards in it. We know it was one of your fellow workers and we know he climbed the shaft and put on scrubs before he took the Medi-vac, which was conveniently left unattended by you!"

"That's a goddamned lie! You're making all this shit up because you can't find out who did it!" Workman protested.

Edwards went on as if hadn't heard anything, Workman said except, the word lie. "You're the one that's lying, Workman! What have you two got against the company. You better start talking! We're going to find out who was in on it with you. We've got your paramedic buddies down the hall. One of them is talking already. You better be telling the same story!" Edwards lied.

"I don't know what you're talking about, you assholes! I don't have any complaint against the company!" Workman yelled.

"Keep your voice down, you prick!" Edwards said as Harper went on went on with the questioning.

"Then why didn't whoever hi-jacked the Medi-vac, take your wallet and other shit? You know damn well you screwed up! You should have told him to take the duffle bag. That would have covered your ass. What kind of brilliant ass answer, do you have for that, dumb shit?"

"Don't forget the Viagra and the porno movies." Edwards chimed in. "They were hot!"

"I don't know, goddamnit! Leave me alone! I want a lawyer!" Workman screamed.

"You aren't under arrest yet and you can't call a lawyer! But, if you don't start telling us something, you're going to be. You'll be in the tank without your Viagra, you limp-dicked bastard! Now start talking." Edwards demanded.

Harper motioned for Edwards to step outside. "What?" He asked Harper.

"We ain't got shit on him and he's asking for a lawyer. We've either got to let him go or arrest him. If we don't he's going turn this around on us."

"He's about ready to break, I know it. Give me ten more minutes with him. The bastard's already sweating his ass off, he'll crack." Edwards said.

"You better call the Chief first. I'm telling you, if we mess this up, it's our asses, and you know it. Do you want to be back in Blues pounding the pavement?"

"Hell, no! But, we don't have anything to charge him on. If he gets a lawyer, he's going to dummy up and he ain't going to tell us shit." Edwards said.

"He hasn't told us shit anyway." Harper replied. "We need to start playing the good cop, bad cop, routine on him. Let him cool off. Let's go see if they're getting anything out of the paramedics."

Harper stuck his head in the door and said. "We'll be back in a minute, buddy. I won't let Edwards screw you over, he's a prick. I'll take care of you."

Workman sat back in his chair and thought. *The stupid assholes are going to play the good cop, bad cop, routine on me!*

Harper and Edwards went down the hall and talked to the detectives who were interrogating the paramedics. "What have you gotten from them, Bennett?" Edwards asked.

"Not much." Bennett answered.

Warner, Bennett's partner spoke up. "Listen you guys, what one of the paramedics said, made sense."

"What did he say?" Edwards asked.

"The Medi-vac company only has two Medi-vac's. They were both in service when the one was hi-jacked off the roof. They only have four pilots, also." He said.

"So, what does that prove?" Edwards asked.

"Workman was on overtime. He normally flies the day shift. The other Medi-vac had just sat down at the base when Workman called the office and reported the hi-jacking. That eliminates that pilot as an accomplice. Workman was covering for the other night shift pilot. He broke his leg, so he couldn't have hi-jacked the Medi-vac."

"What about the other day shift pilot? He could have been in on it." Edwards said.

"He was waiting at the base for Workman to return. He'd gone home and gotten some rest and was going to take over from Workman. The pilots can only be on duty twelve hours in a twenty-four period. He's eliminated too." Warner said.

"Shit! Are you sure he's right?" Edwards asked.

"I called the Medi-vac office, he's telling the truth. Workman didn't have any grudge or grievance against the company either." Warner replied.

"We better call the Chief." Edwards said.

"The Chief's going to be pissed." Harper replied.

"He's already pissed." Edwards replied. "If the paramedic's right, it will blow the Chief's theory and he ain't going to like that."

"Maybe he won't, but maybe he'll quit calling us idiots." Harper said.

"Who could it have been, that came out of the door? If it wasn't one of Workman's buddies, we're at a dead end again." Edwards said.

"We don't know that for sure. Workman could have gotten someone else to do the hi-jacking. We need a copy of the tape. Rowland probably missed something when he looked at it." Harper said.

"Call him." Edwards replied.

Harper left and came back ten minutes later. "He doesn't remember exactly. He didn't have them run the tape back and look for someone else. He doesn't remember seeing anyone else inside of, or coming out of the chopper. When he saw the guy come out the door, he assumed that he'd been hiding inside of the building. He's not sure though. He only looked at that part of the tape once. He remembered seeing the pilot get out and shut the patient door, but he can't say for sure if someone else came out of the chopper or not. He said when the pilot walked away, the camera swung right over to the door when the guy came walking out."

"How could he have run to the door from the Medi-vac without the camera seeing his movement?" Warner asked. "The camera caught the hi-jacker the moment he opened that door and came walking out. Do you really believe he could have gotten out of the chopper and went in the door without the camera seeing him?" Warner asked.

"Hey, don't look at me!" Harper said. "This is your story."

"Think about it." Warner said. "Why would he have run to the door in the first place? All he had to do was start the engine and take off, if he was inside the Medi-vac. I don't believe the paramedics are lying. What would they have to gain? I don't think Workman's lying either. He thought he was going to fly back to base and go home, that's why he left the duffle bag in the chopper. The hi-jacker either overlooked the duffle bag in his hurry, or didn't want to get any of his prints on it."

"Jesus! Have we overlooked the obvious?" Edwards asked

"What do you mean, Edwards? What's so obvious to you that we haven't figured out? Tell me you dumb shit!" Harper said.

"The perp had to be a patient!" Edwards exclaimed.

"The hospital hasn't reported any patients missing." Harper replied.

"I'll bet the hospital is covering it up. We're getting somewhere now! The Chief said a patient was coming in dead last on his list of suspects. If it was a patient that hi-jacked the Medi-vac, the Chief is going to have to eat some crow. I'm calling the Chief and rub it in." Edwards said.

"Hey, screw you, Edwards! I'm calling the Chief! I want to be the one that rubs the shit in his face, for a change. I owe him!" Harper exclaimed.

"Okay, go ahead and call him! I'd just as soon keep my name out of this, in case he turns it around on you." Edwards said.

"He won't be able to turn this one around on me. Let the paramedics go." Harper said to Warner and Bennett.

"I'm not doing it, unless the Chief says to." Bennett answered.

"What choice is the Chief going to have?" Harper asked. "The D.A. won't take the case now. There isn't any evidence the paramedics were involved. Turn them loose, Bennett."

"Not without talking to the D. A. or the Chief." Bennett said.

"Okay." Harper said. "I'll go call the Chief."

"Are you going to let Workman go?" Edwards asked, as they walked down the hall."

"Do I look stupid to you?" Harper asked.

"Now that you mention it, I...."

"Shut up! Hell no, I'm not letting Workman go!" Harper barked.

"You told, Bennett and Warner, to let the paramedics go." Edwards replied.

"They're not doing it are they? Go watch Workman, I'm calling the Chief."

CHAPTER TWELVE

INTO HIDING

VINCE BOUGHT A MAP and located the North Las Vegas Air Terminal on Tonopah, Highway. They drove by the airport and found a motel a half mile to the north. Vince had Jim register and get rooms for the night. Jim had seen no suspicious cars following them and Vince was satisfied that no one was interested in them anymore, but wasn't going to leave a paper trail with his name on it, any longer.

Jim went to work on the list of names, while Donna helped Vince with Dr. Leyland's Model. Neither having been in on the project with Dr. Leyland, didn't help. The two of them worked until midnight before they were able to get the Model running. Vince went over the details, explaining and showing each to Donna, as each event the Model predicted escalated, and put additional pressure on the weakening faults. It showed the eventuality of the disaster, which in Vince's mind, had already happened.

"It's all here." Vince said. "The North American Plate will be forced under the Pacific Plate and in turn, will cause tremendous pressure and energy to be transferred to the New Madrid fault. It's hard to believe that Caltech will reject his findings now."

"What if they don't reject the findings this time? What if they accept his findings?" Donna asked.

"You know, I never thought of that. You could be right. This is really the first time around for Dr. Leyland's Model as far as Sandra Beatty's concerned. Maybe there's some way we can help him when he contacts Caltech and goes to show them this information. With your and Jim's help we may be able to convince Sandra that Dr. Leyland is correct. What do we have to lose?" He asked.

"Nothing. Who's Sandra Beatty?" Donna asked.

"Sandra Beatty is the overall Director of Seismology for the entire West Coast. She was, Dr. Leyland's assistant, before she was promoted to Directors position at Caltech. I took her place when she left." Vince said.

"A woman? That seems odd to me." Donna said.

"Maybe so, but she was, Dr. Leyland's assistant, before I came on board. He didn't care for her and was glad when she left." Vince said.

"I didn't know her. I guess she was gone by the time I started working in the office. You were, Dr. Leyland's assistant, when I started working there." Donna replied.

"I've never met Sandra, either. Dr. Leyland was offered the job before she got it. He would have been in charge of the entire West Coast instead of Sandra, if he had taken the job. It's a very important job, but Dr. Leyland, turned it down. I don't know if he recommended, Sandra, or not, but it's ironic because she ended up being his boss, and must have been involved in rejecting his theory in 2005."

"This is 2005, Vince." Donna said. "She hasn't rejected it yet."

"I mean in my first 2005. I know it's confusing, but it's all here in my head. I know I don't make sense sometimes."

"If she rejected Dr. Leyland's theory and prediction, why did the government believe him?" Donna asked.

"I don't have the complete answer to that, but I know now that he couldn't have had the details before, that he has now. I don't really know who made the decision not to implement, Dr. Leyland's theory and suggestions. There may have been others involved. Sandra, must have had to answer to someone, but I don't know who it was."

"Don't you mean, who it is?" Donna asked.

"Here I go again slipping back to the other time frame. Yes, you're right, I mean, is. It's difficult for me to think in and keep two different time frames separated."

"Go on with what you were saying." Donna said.

"I found out that, Clemmons, wanted the whole thing kept a secret. He somehow influenced Lemming and the project got set up, in total secrecy, at Area 51. Even Congress wasn't aware of what was going on. Dr. Leyland told me that Lemming didn't want the economy of the United States jeopardized, until he was sure it was going to happen. But he never told me who it was that rejected his theory, but it had to be someone at Caltech."

"Do you think it was Lemming that stopped her from going forward with, Dr. Leyland's theory?" Donna asked.

"It couldn't have been Lemming. He's the Governor of the State of Washington right now. He won't be elected President, until 2008." Vince replied.

"Then you don't think Sandra Beatty rejected Dr. Leyland's theory, on her own?" Donna asked."

"No, not on her own. Someone else had to be involved. It doesn't seem likely she would have had the authority to make a decision of that significance on her own. She may have Federal people in Washington she has to report to. That might be the reason the government took over the project when Lemming got elected. But I don't know for sure."

"Do you think it might have been Bush, who stopped her?" Donna asked.

"If I had to guess, I'd say yes. He had a lot on his mind and I don't think it would have been a popular decision for him. He was already spending billions of dollars of taxpayer's money on the Iraq war. I don't believe he wanted to rock the boat, and ask Congress for more money to fund the project. My best guess is that it was, Bush, who sidetracked the project."

"Did you mean to say, that's what he's doing now?" Donna asked.

"Yeah, crap! I keep thinking it's already happened." Vince replied.

"How do you hope to get around that? If he was the one that forced her to reject, Dr. Leyland's findings, he'll do it again, won't he?" Donna asked.

Vince started to answer her, but she interrupted him.

"Damn! Listen to me!" She said. "You've got me thinking like you and asking questions like all of this has already happened. I'm not sure of anything anymore."

"You can be sure of this, Donna. Dr. Leyland is going to have some help this time, if he will allow us. That's the difference I'm counting on, between then and now."

Donna, stood there with her thoughts muddled from what they had discussed. Jim, knocked on the door breaking her thoughts.

"I've found most of the people you're looking for, Vince." He said.

"Good, that's a relief. It's good to know and prove, I wasn't making those people up. I have one other to add to the list." Vince said.

"Who?" Jim asked.

"Sandra Beatty." Vince replied.

"She's at Caltech, you know that." Jim said.

"I want her home address and phone number. I need to talk to her outside of her office." Vince said.

"Okay." Jim said. "That won't be any problem. I've got one other thing for you to look at."

"What is it, Jim?" Vince asked.

"Since I got the list finished I've been checking the internet on Area 51. They have some good photos of the place. You might not have to rent a plane after all. I've got the page open on my laptop in my room."

They went to his room and the three started looking at the photos and map references.

"See these satellite pictures?" Jim asked. "They were allowed to be revealed to satisfy Russian demands to see the facility, as part of the Nuclear Accord Agreement signed by Russia and the United States. Area 51 is listed as a Military site for Nuclear testing but, there are a lot of innuendos on other pages regarding the facility and it's rumored that it's used as a secret base for the testing of new Military Aircraft."

"Area 51, is used for secret testing, Jim. Gen. Johnson told me that. That's why they chose Area 51 for the Forecast Project. The whole thing was kept a top secret." Vince said.

Jim and Donna looked at each other, then Donna said. "The first time, Jim."

"Oh yeah. Damn! This is confusing."

"Not just for you and Donna, Jim. It's confusing for me also." Vince said.

They went back to looking at the photos of Area 51. "This picture's better." Jim said. "It's a color photo."

The Continent Of St. Louis - The Search For Answers

"That's the place we were, Jim. See the buildings and runways and that short mountain range. Everything's just like I told you. There aren't any tall buildings except the tower. The rest is underground."

"Do you still want to go and try to look the place over?" Jim asked.

"No, I'd have to use my license to rent a plane. I'm not leaving any more paper trails. I'm going to sell my car to a used car dealer tomorrow. I want you to rent a car at the airport in the morning and follow me to the dealer, then we're going to L.A."

"L.A.! What for?" Jim asked.

"I want to talk to Sandra Beatty. She's your number one priority. Find her for me, Jim.

POLICE HEADQUARTERS...SAN DIEGO

CHIEF BREWER WAS GRILLING David Norton in one interrogation room, while Harper and Edwards had the night shift security clerk, in another.

"You better start talking, Norton. You better tell me who's missing from the patient list?" Brewer said.

"I can't tell you anything, they'll fire my ass." Norton replied.

"Who are they?" Brewer asked.

"Talk to Hospital Administration! They're the ones who approved not releasing the patient's name. I can't tell you who it is or I'll be fired." Norton replied.

"If you don't tell me his name, you'll be charged with withholding evidence and you'll spend some time in jail. Which would you prefer?" Brewer asked.

"All right! His name is Davis." Norton said.

"What's his first name?" Brewer barked.

"Vince Davis is his name. He escaped from the mental ward."

"The mental ward! Are you kidding me, Norton? Davis is a mental patient and you let him escape and you didn't report it?"

"I was instructed not to reveal the information." Norton lied.

"Oh, that's just great! You won't be working at the hospital anymore and neither will the stupid bastard's that okayed it. What's their names?"

"Before I go any further, I want to cut a deal." Norton said.

"There's not going to be any deals, Norton. You can tell me who authorized withholding the information or I'm going to have you booked right now. Make up your mind."

"You got to do something for me, otherwise I'm not saying another damn word." Norton said.

"All right. I'll speak to the D.A. on your behalf, if you tell me right now." Brewer said.

"I want that it writing." Norton said.

"Take him away and book him!" Brewer barked to an officer who was in the room with him.

"No! Wait!" Norton cried out. "I'll tell you!"

"Make it fast, or the cuffs are going on!" Brewer threatened.

"It was, Dr. Woitasczyk. He was evaluating, Davis. He authorized not reporting it. Administration countersigned the authorization." Norton said and sighed.

"Are you saying you didn't have any hand in any of this? Don't lie to me!" Brewer said.

"No! Hell no! I don't have that kind of authority. I told Woitasczyk not to do it, but he went over my head. I was ordered not to say a word." Norton said, trying to diminish his part in the cover-up.

"Who countersigned the order?" Brewer asked.

"I don't know which official countersigned the authorization. I was told to keep it quiet, so I did." Norton lied again. "I don't make policy. My job is to see that it's enforced."

"What was Davis being treated for? Is he a criminal? You better tell me, Norton!" Brewer said.

"Dr. Woitasczyk said he was delusional. It had something to do with his job. Woitasczyk said he isn't violent or criminally insane." Norton said.

"So, you let this whole thing go on knowing Davis had escaped and stole the Medi-vac. Why in the hell's name would you do that? We were making fools out of ourselves chasing a prankster and you knew all along it was, Davis." Brewer said.

"Now wait a minute, Chief! If you're saying Davis stole the Medi-vac, this is the first I've heard of that! I didn't know Davis had anything to do with stealing the Medi-vac. I never found out how he managed to escape." Norton said.

"You're lying to me! Don't hand me that line of shit!" Brewer barked.

"Honest to God, Chief! I swear I didn't know Davis hi-jacked the Medi-vac. No one ever thought it was Davis who stole the Medi-vac. That thought never crossed our minds. It never occurred to anyone that the two were related. I swear to, God."

"Oh, really! Do you expect me to believe that shit? What did Davis do for a living? Was he a pilot?" Brewer asked.

"I don't know! Woitasczyk said he worked for UCSD in the Seismology Lab. That was why he was in the mental ward." Norton said.

"What else did he tell you about Davis?" Brewer asked.

"Woitasczyk said his condition was job related. Davis was having some kind of delusion that an earthquake was going to completely destroy the Earth and wanted to warn everybody. His co-workers' thought he was crazy, that's how he got confined to the mental ward." Norton said.

"Jesus Christ, Norton! I don't believe this! Someone's going to jail for this! I'll guarantee you that!" Brewer bellowed.

"I'm cooperating, goddamnit! I'm not taking the fall!" Norton exclaimed.

"Let me paint you a picture, Norton! The city has an escaped mental patient roaming the countryside, doing who in the hell knows what, and you were in the know from the gitgo! Tell me, how do you figure you're going to squirm your way out of that?" Brewer asked.

"You said you would put in a good word for me with the D.A. if I cooperated, and I'm cooperating. You're not going to piss backwards on me, are you?" Norton pleaded.

"I'll piss anyway I want to, Norton! You bastard's were letting us stumble around in the dark and I'll bet none of you bastard's thought we would figure it out! Well guess what, asshole! We figured it out! You're not going to skate on this one unless you can tell me where Davis is." Brewer said.

"I don't have any idea where he is and I've already told you I don't know how he escaped." Norton replied.

"Don't hand me that line of shit, Norton! You have security cameras everywhere. Someone saw him or helped him and I'm betting I'll find out who it was when we get our hands on your tapes!" Brewer yelled

"There was a lot of shit going on when he escaped. We had a riot in the mental ward and you had those dogs and the bomb squad going all over the place, I was busy taking care of that shit!" Norton spat back.

"A riot? Is that when Davis escaped?" Brewer asked.

"No it happened before he escaped." Norton replied.

"I didn't hear anything about a riot! Did you cover that up also?" Brewer asked.

"Woitasczyk didn't want any of it getting out! He knew it would ruin his reputation." Norton retorted.

"Does Woitasczyk run the goddamned hospital? Is he your boss?" Brewer asked.

"No, he's the head of the Psychiatric Department." Norton replied.

"He's not your boss, but you kept it quiet just because he told you too? Is that what you're saying?" Brewer asked.

"Yes, that's right. Look, I don't make decisions. I'm just the head of security and things were getting out of hand with the riot and the bomb scare. Administration was all over my ass and there were reporters all over the place, questioning me, as if I knew who called the bomb scare in....Wait a minute! Do you think Davis called the bomb scare in to cover his escape?" Norton asked.

"I'm asking the questions here, Norton! You better listen to me, and you better listen to me good! I want all the tapes and I want Davis's records. You got that straight?" Brewer asked.

"I can't get either for you, Chief. My office no longer has the tapes and Woitasczyk would have to okay giving you the records. I can't do that."

"Okay, you wait right here. I'll be right back." Brewer said and left.

Norton sat squirming in his chair as Brewer left. *Goddamn!* He thought. *I need to piss!*

Brewer went into the interrogation room where Harper and Edwards were interrogating the security clerk. "What have you got?" He asked.

"He said he looked at the complete tape after Rowland left. He didn't see anyone get out of the Medi-vac except the pilot and the paramedics. He doesn't know anything else." Edwards said.

"That's what I thought. Good job boys, let him go." Brewer said.

The clerk let out his breath and looked at the three of them with disdain.

"Thanks, son, we won't need you anymore." Edwards said. "Just sign the report and you can go home."

The clerk signed his name and left muttering. "Assholes." Under his breath as he walked out.

"Did you say something, son?" Brewer asked.

The clerk didn't answer and kept on walking.

"Sounded like he called us assholes, Chief." Harper said, looking at Edwards in a questioning way.

"I didn't hear him. What's next, Chief?" Edwards asked.

"Arrest, Norton. Charge him with withholding evidence and book him. I know who we're looking for now." Brewer said.

"Who?" Harper asked.

"A mental patient that escaped. His name is Davis. He has to be the one that stole the Medi-vac. Norton said Davis's doctor covered up the escape. Hospital administration is involved in it also. That's why they wouldn't release the tape."

"No shit? Why would the hospital get involved in the cover-up?" Edwards asked.

"I don't know, but you're going to find out. After you lock Norton up, go to the hospital and get Davis's records from a Dr. Woitasczyk. Norton said he's the psychiatrist who was treating Davis. Norton also said Woitasczyk is the one who authorized the cover-up of Davis's escape. Pump Woitasczyk's ass for the name of person in hospital administration who countersigned the authorization, before you arrest him." Brewer said.

"What if he won't talk, Chief?" Edwards asked.

"Then arrest him for withholding information, vital to this investigation. While you're there see if you can get that tape and I want Davis's records even if Woitasczyk won't release them. Understand?" Brewer asked.

"Yeah, we understand, but how do you spell Woitasczyk?" Edwards asked.

"Hell, I don't know! Jesus Christ! This is the second time I've done your job for you morons. Do I have to do everything for you?" Brewer asked.

"Hey, I was the one that told you I thought it was a patient." Harper said.

"You're right, Harper. That's what you get paid for, remember?" Brewer spat back.

"I'm not getting paid shit! We're on overtime and all I'll see of it is a voucher for comp time that I'll never get to take." Harper complained.

"Do you want to go back to patrol?" Brewer asked.

"No." Harper replied.

"Then get over to the hospital, find Woitasczyk and get me the information." Brewer yelled.

"We've got to get a warrant for Woitasczyk's arrest, Chief. How are we going to do that if we can't spell his name?" Edwards asked.

"Call the hospital or look it up in the phone book!" Brewer hissed. "It's not my job to teach you retards how to spell. Ask that dick-wad, Captain of yours, how you spell Woitasczyk's name. Goddamn! You're both morons, and if that kid said asshole's, he probably pegged both of you right."

"Chief, you can't use that kind of language anymore." Harper complained. "We have rights."

"Okay, I'll sugar coat it for you. After you mentally challenged, rectum appearing, so called detectives arrest Woitasczyk, book him on the same charge as Norton and lock him up. Is that better?" Brewer asked.

"Forget it, Harper." Edwards said. "What else, Chief?"

"When you find out who the administrative official was that countersigned the cover-up, arrest the bastard and book whoever it is on the same charge." Brewer said.

"By the time we get a warrant, we'll be off duty, Chief." Harper said.

"You're not off duty today, until you've gotten everything I've asked you to get done, and your report is laying on my desk." Brewer retorted.

"Jesus Christ, Chief! We've been on duty twelve hours today and we haven't had a day off in two weeks." Harper complained.

"Tough shit! You both bid on your detective jobs, nobody twisted your arms! I want your asses in here bright and early in the morning and neither of you are going home tonight until all the paperwork is finished and the case is ready for the D.A."

"I guess that will be more comp time!" Edwards said sarcastically.

"It damn sure is! Now get out of here and get over to the hospital. You don't need a warrant for Woitasczyk or anyone else. We have probable cause from Norton's admissions. Now, you morons get your asses moving, and tell Rowland, I want to see him."

"Calling us names and working us for comp time isn't right, Chief." Harper complained.

"Then I'll tell you what is right!" Brewer bellowed. "The Mayor isn't authorizing any overtime pay. You both know damn well that your boss, Captain Jennings, can't figure a damn thing out! Jennings, is the Mayor's goddamned brother-in-law. Have him ask the Mayor to sign your vouchers for overtime. Now get the hell out of here and book Norton!"

"Jesus Christ, Harper! Are you trying to get us put back in Blues?" Edwards asked as they walked down the hall.

"No, but we don't have to take the Chief's shit." Harper said.

"Maybe not, but he is the Chief and he's under a lot of pressure." Edwards replied.

"I don't care if he is the Chief! We have rights!" Harper said.

"Then file a grievance." Edwards said.

"Oh sure! Like taking a legitimate complaint to Bob Haynes, will do any good! All, Haynes does is kiss ass and do whatever he's told. He's never filed a grievance, he's afraid he'd have to go back to work if he did! He's nothing but a chickenshit!" Harper replied.

"That's because all he gets is half-ass complaints from crybabies like you, every time they get their feelings hurt!" Edwards said.

"Don't call me a crybaby, Edwards!" Harper shot back. "You know damn well all Haynes does is sit in the committee office all day. He's just feathering his own nest, trying to get a district representative appointment! I'm not taking his or your shit!"

"It's not shit! You get your feelings hurt if a mouse farts under your desk." Edwards said.

"Why in the hell do we pay union dues? The union isn't worth a damn!" Harper replied.

"Have you ever gone to a union meeting?" Edwards asked.

"Hell yes! And every time I went and wanted to say something about Haynes, they said I was out of order! Screw Haynes and the union!" Harper replied.

"You can do something about it, if you want to." Edwards said. "The Steward election is coming up, why don't you run against Haynes? If you win, you can sit on your ass all day in the committee room, like he does." Edwards said.

"Oh sure! Like I'd win! You know damn well nobody would vote for me." Harper replied.

Edwards could see the union conversation was going nowhere. He couldn't resist sticking a few more barbs in Harper and said. "That kid called you an asshole, Harper! I heard him. He was looking right at you when he said it." Edwards knew he was going to get Harper going.

"He called all of us assholes, the Chief included!" Harper shot back.

"No, he said, Harper is an asshole!" Edwards said. "I heard him and so did the Chief. We didn't want you to get your feelings hurt again, so we dropped the subject. Come on we've got to arrest Norton."

"Arrest him yourself, you miserable bastard! I don't have to take any shit off of you or the Chief! Screw the union and Bob Haynes, I'm going to Internal Affairs!" Harper whined.

"I guess I'll be getting me a new partner, when you do. You know, when you're back in Blues and pounding the pavement. It's been nice knowing you, Harper." Edwards said.

"Screw you, Edwards!" Harper replied, as they went in the interrogation room and told Norton he was under arrest.

Norton began crying as they put the cuffs on him and peed his pants as they led him down the hall to the booking desk. The thought of being locked up with deviants sent a signal to his bowels and he involuntarily shit his pants while he was standing at the booking desk.

"What have we here?" Sgt. Reese, the booking sergeant asked.

"Lock the bastard in the tank, Carl." Harper said.

It was then that the foul odor from Norton's trousers reached their nostrils.

"The lousy bastard's shit his pants and pissed all over himself!" Edwards complained, as he stood back holding his nose.

"He won't be a welcome addition to the tank and I'm not hosing his ass down!" Reese commented, and then said. "Jesus Christ! What did you eat, goddamnit?" The foul smell from Norton's trousers had reached Reese's nostrils also.

"I think he ate some Crow, Carl! Looks like it didn't agree with him!" Harper joked, and they all started laughing.

Now that Harper had a scapegoat to laugh at, he forgot about the insults the Chief and Edwards had levied at him and said. "I'd wipe my ass good if I were you Norton. You need to get the old brown eye cleaned up good, for the jailhouse bitches."

The three officers laughed till their sides hurt. Norton, completely mortified, could think of nothing better to say other than. "You're nothing but animals, all of you! You disgust me! I've never seen such unprofessional behavior."

"You'll think animals, when one the tank queens gets hung up in your ass!" Harper shot back. "They'll have to hose you down with cold water, till his dog knot goes down." They all started laughing again.

Brewer walked up and asked. "What's going on? I told you to lock him up!" Brewer smelled the odor and asked. "What the hell happened?"

"Norton shit himself, Chief!" Harper said, and started laughing again, joined by the other two.

"I'll be dammed! I can smell it now. Get him out of here, and get him cleaned up, Reese." Brewer said, laughing along with the others.

"I can't clean him up! I don't have any help!" Reese complained, as he led Norton away.

"I'm charging all of you with inhuman treatment and police brutality! I want a lawyer! I'm suing all of your asses! Do you hear me, Chief?" Norton screamed as he was led away.

"I hear you!" Brewer yelled back and then said. "Get that piss mopped up and then go get Rowland for me boys."

"I'm not a janitor!" Harper shot back.

"You will be if you don't get your ass moving! Clean up the piss and then go and get Rowland for me, before you put the collar on Woitasczyk. I'll be in my office." Brewer said.

As Brewer walked away, Edwards said. "I'll take care of the piss. Go find Rowland so we can get out of here."

Rowland came in Brewer's office and sat down. Brewer explained what they had learned and brought him up to date and then said. "I want you to go over to the UCSD campus and get me a copy of Davis's photo I.D. Get his address and talk to his boss. Find out who his friends are, and then get back to me. I'm going to ask the D.A. to get a warrant for his arrest. I'm putting out an all points on him, when you get me his photo."

"I'll get right on it, Chief." Rowland replied.

"We're going to come out of this in spite of everything." Brewer said. "I'll get public relations to schedule a press conference with the media for later. I want to furnish all of them with Davis's photo. It won't take long to run him down when his picture is in the papers and on the news, get going."

LAS VEGAS

JIM HAD RENTED A car and followed Vince to a car dealer, where Vince sold his car. With the cash in hand, he and Jim went back to the Motel, where Vince got on line and checked his bank account. He knew sooner or later, the hospital would have to report him missing. The police might even learn it was he, who hi-jacked the Medi-vac. He logged onto his account, transferring most of his savings and checking account funds to Donna's account, leaving a small balance in each to debit his utilities until he made the final arrangement with Bob and Margret Epperson. He now had plenty of cash, but was going to check back in a week's time and see if UCSD was still paying him. They packed their bags, checked out of the motel, got on Interstate 15 and headed for L.A., with Jim behind the wheel. Vince was no longer going to drive, he couldn't risk having his identity checked.

CHAPTER THIRTEEN

CHIEF BREWER'S ANNOUNCEMENT

SERGEANT ROWLAND RETURNED TO Chief Brewer's office with Vince's I.D. photo and his address. Brewer had the photo scanned for insertion into a wanted bulletin he was going to release to the media, as he had promised. He was looking at the bulletin with Vince's photo and description on it, as he stood behind the podium ready for his press conference. With an assured look on his face, he began.

"We now know the identity of the man that hi-jacked the Medi-vac. The man we're looking for is, Dr. Vince Davis. Davis escaped from his room at the Gifford Mental Health Center on August 30th. We have compared his photo to that of the man who hi-jacked the Medi-vac and it's now clear that Davis was that man. A warrant has been issued for his arrest, but at this time, we have no leads as to his whereabouts. I'm asking for the help of all media sources in the publication of his photograph and description." Brewer said, and was about to go on when, as usual, Jean Simmons interrupted him.

"How did Davis escape from his cell, and why wasn't it reported?" She yelled.

"Gifford is not a prison, Miss Simmons, it's a hospital." Brewer replied and then said. "Other than the fact he hi-jacked the Medi-vac, there are no other details available at this time." Brewer replied and asked. "May I go on?"

Burned again, Jean said nothing and Brewer continued. "We have also learned, that at least three high ranking staff members employed by the hospital where Davis was confined, have been involved in an intentional cover-up of Davis's escape."

A clamor ran through the media and Jean Simmons was back at it.

"Can you identify the individuals, Chief?" She asked.

"I was getting to that when you interrupted me, again." Brewer scolded her and then went on. "David Norton, who is the head of security at the hospital, has already been arrested and is in custody. Mr. Norton is cooperating in the investigation at this time."

"What part did Norton play in the cover-up?" Jean yelled.

"Please, Miss Simmons, Let me finish." Brewer said and went on. "The investigation into the cover-up of Davis's escape is still ongoing and my office anticipates additional arrests of other staff members who were involved in the cover-up with David Norton. I would like to commend the detectives and other officers who have spent long and tireless hours, putting the pieces of this puzzle together, that eventually lead to the arrest of David Norton. It would be premature at this time to say that the case is completely solved. However, as the investigation into this case continues in the upcoming days, the names of the other suspects involved will be released, as they are taken into custody. Captain Jennings, who I respect highly and is standing beside me, was in charge of the investigation."

Brewer turned and acknowledged Jennings presence and then went on. "Captain Jennings has assured me that every lead his office has received was investigated thoroughly. Those leads, as well as excellent detective work from Captain Jennings office, led to discovery and arrest of David Norton. Captain Jennings has also assured me, that all of those responsible for the cover-up, have been identified and will soon be in custody. He asked me to thank all of you for your help and the tips his office received."

Jennings was floored when Brewer mentioned his name, and thought. *What the hell is he talking about? I didn't get any tips!*

As those thought ran through Jennings mind, Brewer was thinking. *That will get the Mayor off of my ass, for sure!*

Reporters started firing questions at Brewer. He held up his hand for silence, and went on. "I'm not saying this investigation is complete. There may be other individuals involved, and we're looking into that aspect now. I can't reveal the names of those who are not in custody at this time, but all will face charges, when they're arrested."

Jean Simmons, shouted another question at Brewer. "What is, Davis's mental condition?"

"I don't have the exact details on Dr. Davis's mental condition, at this time. However, I want everyone to understand that this is still an ongoing police matter. I am asking anyone who sees Dr. Davis, to take extreme caution. Call 911 if you see, Dr. Davis. Do not make any attempt to apprehend, Dr. Davis on your own."

Brewer held up Vince's photo and said. "If you have seen this man, or if you have any information as to his whereabouts, call the Police Tips line."

"Is he dangerous?" Simmons shouted.

"Any fugitive can be dangerous, Miss Simmons." Brewer replied.

Flashbulbs were flashing and cameras were rolling as Brewer went on. "Although, Dr. Davis has no prior criminal record or arrests, I want to remind you that, Dr. Davis, did in fact, hi-jack the Medi-vac. He then used it for unlawful flight to avoid prosecution and both are felonies. I urge everyone again to leave this matter to police. Do not try to apprehend Dr. Davis. Call the Tips line."

"Did Davis call in the bomb scare to cover his escape?" Jean Simmons shouted.

"That has been suggested and we're looking into that, Miss Simmons." Brewer replied. "We've checked telephone records and have found the call was made from inside the hospital. It could have been Davis, or one of the staff members. We won't have that answer until we have all of them in custody. I want to remind you though, that it might not have been any of them. It may have just been coincidental. It could have been an angry patient, or an employee. At this time, we don't have any suspect in that regard. We're focusing all our efforts on the capture of, Davis."

Question after question was hurled at Brewer. He took his time and answered each in turn. He smiled as the cameras flashed. It was a great photo opportunity for him. The exposure was establishing his authority and was putting to rest the criticism his office had endured. He felt confident in his manner as each reporter got their question answered and left to file their story. At the end of the interview, he again thanked and praised Captain Jennings, Sgt. Rowland and the detectives for doing such a fine job. The bomb scare issue was now on the back burner. Simmons, unknowingly, had assisted him in putting it to rest. She would never find out that the call had been placed after the Medi-vac was hi-jacked. No one would. The heat was finally off him.

The Mayor and Police Commissioner were on hand. Both got up and praised Brewer and his subordinates for their excellent work. They all left the podium as the media clapped and cheered. Chief Brewer and the Police Department had come out smelling like a Rose. He was going to take a week off. He needed the time to relax and play a little golf.

GIFFORD MENTAL CENTER...SAN DIEGO

HARPER AND EDWARDS HAD waited three hours in Dr. Woitasczyk's office for him to return. Woitasczyk had not watched the press conference and didn't know Norton had been arrested.

"What do you men want? Who let you in my office?" Woitasczyk asked, not liking the appearance of the two shabbily dressed, scruffy looking men waiting in his office.

The two identified themselves, and Harper began explaining. "We know, Vince Davis escaped, Dr. Woitasczyk, and we know you covered it up. You're in some deep shit, so you better cooperate."

Woitasczyk was caught off guard and became defensive. "Look here! Do you know who you're talking to? I am the head of the psychiatry department. Who do you think you are barging in here with your threats? I don't have to tolerate this. I'm calling security!"

"Don't waste your time, Dr. Woitasczyk. Norton's already in jail. He spilled his guts. He told us you covered up, Davis's escape." Edwards said.

"Norton's a lying son-of-a-bitch! He's the one that covered it up!" Woitasczyk spat back.

"We're not here to argue." Harper said. "We have a warrant for your arrest. Make it easy on yourself, Woitasczyk."

"What am I being charged with?" He asked.

"Withholding evidence." Harper said.

"What evidence?" Woitasczyk asked.

"Don't play dumb, Woitasczyk." Edwards said. "You knew, Davis escaped and you ordered the cover-up. Now come along peacefully."

"Don't forget, Davis's records." Harper said to Edwards.

"Chief Brewer wants, Davis's medical records, Woitasczyk. Get them for us." Edwards said.

"I can't release Davis's records without a court order." Woitasczyk said truthfully.

"Okay, we'll get a court order, you're under arrest." Edwards said.

"I'm not responsible for any of this!" Woitasczyk said. "It was all Norton's idea."

"Tell it to the judge." Harper said. "You can also tell him why you didn't notify the police when, Davis escaped. You should have."

"It was Norton's idea to cover it up, not mine!" Woitasczyk retorted.

"You signed the authorization for him, didn't you?" Edwards asked.

"Ya, but it was not my idea! Norton forced me to sign it!" Woitasczyk replied.

"Don't hand me that line of shit!" Edwards said. "Norton couldn't have forced you to sign it! He didn't put a gun at your head did he?"

"No, but…" Woitasczyk started to answer and was interrupted by Edwards, who said. "No is right! It was your idea and you know it! Davis was your patient, not Norton's, so quit lying!"

"Yeah, and give us Davis's records. It will go easier on you if you do." Harper lied.

"I already told you, I can't." Woitasczyk replied.

"Get the cuffs on him, Harper. You're under arrest, Dr. Woitasczyk. You'll have to come with us." Edwards said and began reading him his rights.

Woitasczyk became enraged when Harper took him by the arms and attempted to put the cuffs on him. He began to struggle, swinging wildly, hitting, Harper in the mouth. They forcibly restrained him, took him down to the floor and put the cuffs on him. Woitasczyk continued to struggle as he cursed the two detectives, in English and German. They got him under control and brought him to his feet.

"I'll get you bastard's for this!" He screamed, as they dragged him out the door.

"Your ass is in deep shit now, Woitasczyk!" Harper said, as he wiped blood from his mouth. "We're going to add resisting arrest and assaulting a police officer to your charges."

Dawdry and Crischell had just come on duty. They saw Harper and Edwards, dragging Woitasczyk down the hall, cussing and crying out his innocence. The two stood back and stared at the three as they passed.

"Get to work you dumkoph's!" Woitasczyk screamed as he passed.

"Screw you, Woitasczyk!" Crischell yelled. "It doesn't look like you'll be giving any orders around here anymore!"

He was carrying a special edition of the Tribune with Vince's picture centered under the headline that stated. 'Hospital Involved. Arrests Of Staff Members To Be Made Soon.' He held it up and pointed at the headlines for Woitasczyk to see as he was being dragged by, and said.

"Read this, you asshole! Let's see how you like it when they lock your ass up! I hope they put your ass in with a bunch of crazy bastard so you'll feel at home!" He turned to Dawdry and said. "He must be one of them. Look at this."

Escaped Mental Patient Now Sought By Police…Hospital Employees Involved In Escape. Staff Members Will Face Charges. Arrests Of Staff Members To Be Made Soon.

Dr. Vince Davis, Deranged And Desperate Mental Patient, Now Charged With Hi-Jacking Of The Medi-vac. A Warrant Has Been Issued For His Arrest. High Ranking Staff Members Of Hospital To Be Charged With Withholding Of Evidence In The Case. Police Advise Caution. Call 555-TIPS

Dawdry read the headline and said. "If he isn't one of them, you'll be in deeper shit than you've ever been in before, for what you said to him. He'll hang your ass out to dry!"

"I'm not a damned bit worried. Woitasczyk must be one of the staff members they're arresting, why would they be dragging his ass down the hall otherwise?"

"Maybe so, but he's pissed. If he gets out, he'll have your ass!" Dawdry replied.

"Screw him! I'm not afraid of him! Look at this picture, they've identified Davis as the hi-jacker." Crischell said.

"That picture must be old, Crischell. He didn't look like that when he was in here, he looked older. But that's Davis coming out of that door heading for the chopper. I can see that now." Dawdry said.

"I thought you said he was a time traveler." Crischell chided Dawdry. "What have you got to say now, Mr. Science Fiction?"

"Stick it, Crischell! You didn't recognize him either. If you're so smart, how did he get on the roof?" Dawdry asked.

"It sounds like the hospital was in on it. Why would they arrest Woitasczyk otherwise?" Crischell asked.

"You're right. Woitasczyk must have come in and got him while we were asleep." Dawdry said.

"Oh, so now you don't think, Davis was a time traveler!" Crischell said.

"Blake thought he was." Dawdry said.

"Screw, Blake! He's and idiot and so are you!" Crischell replied

"I'm tired of you and Woitasczyk calling me an idiot! You didn't know how Davis escaped. Woitasczyk must have done it, so lay off my ass!" Dawdry snapped.

"If Woitasczyk did it, he was pretty slick. It wasn't on the corridor tape." Crischell replied.

"They could have altered that tape." Dawdry said. "I've seen it done in movies. It says here, high-ranking staff members will be charged in the case. Someone else was involved. Probably, Norton. I'll bet he altered the tape."

"Who cares? Personally, I never liked Woitasczyk. He's always been a prick. Things will be quieter around here without him." Crischell replied.

The two went to the nurses' station and reported for duty.

J. L. Reynolds

WORKMAN'S HOUSE

JOHN WORKMAN HAD READ the headlines also. His boss had given him a letter of reprimand and two weeks off without pay, and he was still stinging from the third degree he'd been confronted with, in the interrogation room. He turned on his TV and caught the coverage of the unfolding, live story.

"We've just been informed that, Dr. Gunderich Woitasczyk is the second person from the hospital, to be arrested, in the continuing investigation into the hi-jacking of the Medi-vac." Jean Simmons said.

A clip of Woitasczyk was shown. He was in handcuffs, being led into Police Headquarters, and Jean went on. "One other suspect, David Norton, who is head of security for the hospital, has already been arrested and is now in custody. Police as yet, have not named a third hospital staff member they are seeking in relationship to the case. We have learned that there may be more arrests forthcoming as the investigation develops. Hospital spokesperson, Dr. Jesse Ferguson, has not commented in regard to the hospital's alleged involvement in the escape. His office has indicated, that at this time, an internal investigation is in place and he will issue a statement when the investigation is concluded. His office did say however, that the hospital will cooperate fully with the police investigation."

A photo of the hospital was shown on screen, and Jean went on.

"In other news relating to this case, Captain Jennings, who is charge of the investigation into the hi-jacking, has said that all previous suspects in the case have now been released, and are no longer considered suspects in the hi-jacking of the Medi-vac."

The studio showed a clip of Workman as he left police headquarters after being interrogated. His face showed anger as he shouted derogatory, four letter words at the cameraman, which had been bleeped out.

"That was John Workman, the Medi-vac pilot who was brought in for questioning and initially thought to have played a key part in the hi-jacking." Jean said and went on. "As you can see, he wasn't happy as he left police headquarters. However, he was later cleared of all charges, which led to his arrest."

"I wasn't arrested, you worthless bitch!" Workman screamed at the TV.

Jean wasn't through and went on. "As a result of his arrest, it is our understanding, that Mr. Workman was disciplined and suspended from his employment with Air Flight Rescue, who operates the Medi-vac service under license to San Diego County. We have not been able to contact Mr. Workman for his comment at this time. Stay tuned for further developments in this case, as they occur. This is Jean Simmons, reporting live from San Diego, Police Headquarters."

"Goddamn you!" Workman screamed at Jean, as the studio returned to local programming. He was livid as he turned off the TV and threw the remote on the floor, shouting. "Goddamnit! If it's not bad enough to have my name plastered all over the front page and TV yesterday, now that bitch has to show my picture and tell everyone I was arrested and got suspended."

Just then, his phone rang. He picked it up and answered. It was his boss.

"John, I'm glad I caught you." His boss said.

Workman was still mad and almost hung up. His boss sensed his anger by the sound of his voice when he had answered, and said. "Don't hang up, I've got something important to tell you."

"What do you want?" Workman asked.

"Hey, man, I want to say I'm sorry and I want to apologize! We heard the news and we've taken you off suspension, you've been reinstated. I've authorized a week off with pay for you, but if you want to come on in to work, you'll get the extra weeks pay, in addition to your regular pay, plus overtime for the week. We're shorthanded here. You know you're our best pilot. What do you say?"

Workman's anger subsided quickly as he heard the news. Relieved, he said. "Thanks, boss. I've got to go down to Police Headquarters first, and try to get my duffle bag. They're holding it as evidence."

"I've already called the, Chief." His boss replied. "He's sending it out to your house with a patrolman."

"Who is this, Davis anyway?" Workman asked. "How did he know how to fly the Medi-vac? They say he's a mental patient. Is he insane or something?"

"He was a mental patient all right, but the Chief, doesn't know how he did it. He doesn't have a helicopter certification. Just a multi engine fixed wing aircraft license." His boss said.

"Jesus! That's scary." Workman said. "He could have crashed and killed a lot of people."

"That's the really odd thing." His boss said. "He knew what he was doing. The Medi-vac doesn't have a scratch on it. He made a perfect landing, but we still have to have it re-certified for service."

The doorbell rang. "I've got to go, someone's at the door. It must be the cop with my duffle bag. I'll be in as soon as he leaves. Thanks, again."

He opened his door expecting to see a patrolman with his duffle bag. Instead, it was a camera crew and Jean Simmons from KQTV.

"Mr. Workman? I'm Jean Simmons with KQTV. We'd like to interview you and get your comments regarding the Medi-vac hi-jacking, now that you've been cleared and released. We're live right now do you have any comments?"

"Get that mic out of my face, you bitch!" Workman roared. "All you do is invade people's private lives and feed off people's misery to get a goddamned story! Get the hell off my porch, and get off my goddamned property!"

"Cut the feed." Jean said disregarding Workman's order to get off his property. "Mr. Workman, won't you reconsider? There are a lot of people that would like to hear your side of the story."

The cameraman turned his camera back on as Jean put the mic in Workman's face.

"My side of the story is, screw you!" Workman retorted. He shoved the mic out of his face and in so doing, shoved Jean into the cameraman, who fell over backwards, dropping the camera and cussing. As the cameraman was getting up, the patrolman Brewer had sent over, came running up.

"What the hell's going on here?" He asked.

"I asked them to leave and they didn't. She pushed her mic in my face and I pushed it away, she fell into the cameraman and he fell down." Workman said in his own defense.

"Are you, John Workman?" The patrolman asked.

"Yes, I am."

"Is what he said true?" The patrolman asked Jean.

"Not exactly." She replied. "He was angry when he did it. It was more like assault."

The Continent Of St. Louis - The Search For Answers

"Ask her to play back the video, it's all on tape." Workman said.

"What about it?" The patrolman asked Jean. "Do you have it on tape?"

"Yes, but it's copyrighted video. It belongs to KQTV. I can't play it back without the station's authorization." Jean replied.

"Do you want them to leave, Mr. Workman?" The patrolman asked.

"Your damned right I do! I've already told them to get off my property."

The patrolman turned to Jean, and said. "You're going to have to leave, Ma'am. You're on private property, he's within his rights."

She turned to the cameraman and said. "let's go." As the two walked away, Jean turned and said. "You haven't heard the last of this, Workman!"

"Ma'am if you don't get off this man's property right now, I'm going to have to arrest you." The patrolman said.

"I have rights too." She snapped back at the officer. "The public has the right to know. I'll get the story whether he wants me to or not!"

The policeman started walking her way. "You've got one minute to leave, starting now!" He said looking at his watch.

Jean turned without saying another word and got in the van.

The patrolman watched as the van drove away and turned the corner. He hadn't seen Jean flipping him off.

"What in the hell's wrong with you?" Her cameraman asked. "You're going to get us arrested."

"Shut up and drive!" She snarled.

The policeman went back to the patrol car and returned with Workman's duffle bag. "Here's your duffle bag, Mr. Workman and here's a letter from the Chief, with his apology, as well as those of the Mayor and Police Commissioner."

"Thanks. I hope I don't have to see or talk to another cop in my life." Workman said.

"I understand. Thank you for your cooperation in the investigation." The patrolman said as he left.

Cooperation my ass! Workman thought. *The lousy bastard's were ready to use a rubber hose on me and beat a confession out of me!*

He shut the door and opened his duffle bag. He pulled out his wallet and counted his money, fully expecting to find some of it missing, but it was all there. He checked the contents of the bag, everything was there except his porno DVD's. He opened his bottle of Viagra and found half of it was missing. "Goddamn those detectives!" He muttered

POLICE HEADQUARTERS...SAN DIEGO

HARPER HAD BOOKED WOITASCZYK and he'd been taken to a cell. The judge had ordered him and Norton held without bond, until their arraignment. Claude Forrester, the District Attorney, was in Chief Brewer's office and they were going over the case. The Commissioner had not given Brewer the week off, he had asked for.

"Anything on, Davis yet?" Forrester asked.

"No. I sent a patrolman out to his house and no one was home. A neighbor said he doesn't live there anymore. Someone named Epperson lives there now. I've been going over Davis's medical records. He was living there when he was first taken to the Hospital. I also pulled up a report of a 911 call the morning he was taken to the hospital. The Sheriff's Department found him unconscious in the bathroom. That's why he ended up in the hospital." Brewer replied.

"What happened to him?" Forrester asked

"The report said it was an accident." Brewer replied.

"How did he end up at Gifford?" Forrester asked

"Rowland asked his boss that question." Brewer replied. "He hit his head when he fell in his bathroom. He was in a coma and didn't wake up for a week. His boss said he went off the deep end after that. How could someone have moved into his house with him at Gifford in the psychiatric ward?"

"I don't know, Chief. Maybe they're relatives and came to town to look after him." Forrester said.

"The only relatives he has are his parents who live in, Missouri. I checked." Brewer said.

"None of this makes any sense. I've looked at his records too. He never did anything against the law until he stole the Medi-vac. There's not a spot on his record, not even a traffic ticket. The thing that has me puzzled most, is how he was able to fly the Medi-vac after he stole it. He's never been certified in a helicopter, yet he took off from Gifford and set it down at Granite Hills, without putting a scratch on it." Forrester said.

"Davis has a pilot license." Brewer said.

"I realize that, but not for flying helicopters and there's more to this than meets the eye. Someone had to be in on the escape, he couldn't have done it on his own. I don't know who helped him or why they thought, using the Medi-vac was a good idea. They could have walked him right out the front door with scrubs on." Forrester said.

"You're right. Davis got to the roof without being seen. Obviously, Woitasczyk and Norton helped him get out of his room. He couldn't have escaped otherwise." Brewer replied.

"Have you checked to see if Woitasczyk or Norton has a helicopter license?" Forrester asked.

"Neither of them do." Brewer replied.

"Have you checked the tapes for accomplices?" Forrester asked.

"I sent them to the lab. They checked them and didn't come up with any evidence, but I sent the tapes to your office anyway." Brewer replied.

"Why was Davis committed to Gifford in the first place?" Forrester asked.

"His records say he was in there because he insisted the world was coming to an end." Brewer replied. "He said he was in the year 2009, when the whole thing went down. He insists he was somehow returned to 2005, and wants to warn everyone, before it's too late. How does someone with no record of that kind of behavior and no previous arrests, go off the deep end like that?"

"I don't know. I'm not a shrink." Forrester replied.

"Here's the kicker." Brewer said. "Woitasczyk's records of his examinations of Davis, say that Davis insisted he had a Lincoln Penny that he had found in the future and it was dated 2009. He said it would prove what he was saying."

"I know that, but they never found it, did they?" Forrester asked.

"No they didn't." Brewer replied. "They sent a team from the hospital to his house to look for it. Davis said it had to be in the bathroom on the floor. It was never found in the bathroom or anywhere else in the house. All they found were some CD's in jewel cases."

"What was on them?" Forrester asked.

"Some files they couldn't open. The hospital records show they forwarded them to Woitasczyk, at his request." Brewer replied.

"What did Woitasczyk want them for?" Forrester asked.

"I don't know. Maybe, Davis told him what the passwords were." Brewer replied.

"Was there any reference or notes pertaining to the discs in Woitasczyk's office?" Forrester asked.

"His office was tossed. They didn't find anything but patient records, Psychiatric books, the C.D.'s and a receipt for an article he sent to the International Psychiatric Journal." Brewer replied.

"Call the Journal and get a me copy of the article." The D. A. said and then asked. "Where are the discs?"

"I have the discs in my office with the other evidence. Do you want me to send Rowland down to Woitasczyk's cell and see if he knows what was on the discs?" Brewer asked.

"Don't waste the time." Forrester replied. "It wouldn't make any difference what was on them anyway. Davis, must be nuts, they wouldn't have put him Gifford otherwise."

"You're probably right." Brewer said. "I read all of Woitasczyk's written evaluation reports. I also listened to the tapes he made when he was evaluating, Davis. Davis sounded crazy most of the time, but at other times, he sounded normal. You should listen to the tapes. It's a hell of a story. It would make a damn good disaster movie and it's got my curiosity stirred up. I'm going to send the discs to crypto and see if they can crack them."

"You don't believe the shit, Davis, is putting out, do you?" Forrester asked.

"No, I don't. His story is unbelievable." Brewer replied.

"I don't either. Woitasczyk said Davis is insane and I believe him. A sane man would never make the claims he has, but there's one thing I don't get. How did he fly the Medi-vac, if he wasn't a chopper pilot?" Forrester asked.

"Listen to Woitasczyk's tapes." Brewer replied. "Davis said he was flying Blackhawk's in 2009. He said an Air Force Captain showed him how. He even has a name for the Captain."

"No shit! A Blackhawk is a military chopper, isn't it?" Forrester asked.

The Continent Of St. Louis - The Search For Answers

"Yes it is, and I'm not shitting you!" Brewer replied.

"Did you check with military authorities and ask if this Captain exists?" Forrester asked.

"Not yet. I didn't think it was important." Brewer replied.

"Was, Davis, ever in the military?" Forrester asked.

"No, he wasn't." Brewer replied.

"Then how in the hell did he learn to fly a chopper? You know what he's saying is bullshit, and I'm not buying it." Forrester said.

"If you think that's bullshit, listen to this! Davis said he was taken to Area 51 when the disaster hit, San Diego." Brewer said and laughed.

"Aw damn! He is nuts!" Forrester exclaimed.

"Nuts or not, if we had known it was him that stole the Medi-vac and landed at the high school, then we would have known he was trying to get to his house. I'll give odds that he went there before he left, for wherever he is now." Brewer said.

"And the neighbors haven't seen him?" Forrester asked.

"No, I sent a patrolman out to question his neighbors." Brewer replied. "The neighbor lady just south of Davis's house, told the patrolman that Bob and Margaret Epperson are living in the house, and they would know how to contact Davis."

"Did the officer talk to the Epperson's?" Forrester asked.

"They weren't home when he was there." Brewer said.

"Did the neighbor lady say where Epperson worked?" Forrester asked.

"No she didn't." Brewer replied. "After the patrolman had talked to the rest of the neighbors, he went back to the neighbor lady to ask her if she knew where Epperson worked. Her husband answered the door, and said his wife wasn't home. He was drunk and he was wearing a Chargers helmet. He offered the patrolman a beer and invited him in to watch the game. The patrolman tried to question him, but he was too drunk to remember anything."

"Have you ran a phone check on the Epperson's?" Forrester asked.

"I checked with all the cell companies and Pac Bell. None of them could find a phone listing for a Bob, Robert or Margaret Epperson in the San Diego area, so I ran both their names through the computer. We don't have anything on them and there aren't many Epperson's in our database." Brewer replied.

"What about the utility companies?" Forrester asked.

"They're all still in Davis's name." Brewer replied.

"Did Davis have a phone in his name?" Forrester asked.

"Yeah, we've called the number several times and no one answers." Brewer replied.

"What about a cell phone?" Forrester asked.

"I tried it. It's turned off, wherever it is." Brewer replied.

"Do you think the neighbor got their names wrong? You said he was drunk." Forrester said.

"No, his wife was there the first time. She was the one that gave their names." Brewer replied.

"This doesn't add up! Davis escapes and the next thing you know, some different people are living in his house and we can't find a thing on those people. Something's screwy here." Forrester said.

"I've been thinking the same thing." Brewer replied. "But I haven't been able to come up with any ideas. Can you think of any?" He asked.

"No…Wait a minute! What if Davis has disguised himself, got a woman to go along with the masquerade, and is calling himself, Epperson?" Forrester asked.

"Jeez! Why didn't I think of that! You could be right! I better get someone back out there!" Brewer exclaimed.

"You'll need a search warrant." Forrester replied. "I'll get the judge to give us one. If no one's home, break the door down, and go on in."

"You think I should send the SWAT team?" Brewer asked.

"It wouldn't hurt." Forrester replied.

"Okay, get the warrant and I'll call the SWAT team." Brewer said. A half hour later, he was going over the details with the team leader.

"Remember, he's not reported to be dangerous. Don't go in there with your guns blazing. This office has had enough bad publicity already. Give him a chance to surrender, if he's there." Brewer ordered.

"Right, Chief."

Forrester returned with the warrant and handed it to the team leader.

"Okay, get out there, and see if you can find him." Brewer said. "Remember, no Rambo shit, and I mean it."

Forrester sat down and asked. "What have you heard from Ferguson?

"Ferguson? Who's that?" Brewer asked.

"The hospital spokesman." Forrester said. "Did he tell you who the third person is?"

"Oh yeah, he said it was a secretary in the Public Relations Office. Her boss was gone and she rubber stamped his name and filed it." Brewer replied.

"Then that means Woitasczyk and Norton are the only ones in on the escape and cover-up?" Forrester said.

"Looks like it." Brewer replied.

"I better get back to my office and get the case prepared against them. I'll have my experts go over the tapes from the roof, the one from the mental ward corridors and Davis's room. If Norton edited the tapes to remove any evidence of him and Woitasczyk getting Davis out of there, the time sequence will be altered and my boys will find it. Norton was the one who was withholding the tapes, they were locked in his desk. I think he was the primary player in all of this." Forrester said.

"Even if it was Norton's idea, he couldn't have gotten away with it on his own. I think Woitasczyk is the key player." Brewer said.

"Why do you think that?" Forrester asked.

"He had more to lose, but in any case, he'll be doing some time on the assault charges." Brewer said.

"I'm arraigning the two of them Wednesday. If the tapes were edited, Norton will probably try to cop a plea. They both have Lawyers now." Forrester said.

"I still can't figure out why they would help Davis escape." Brewer replied. "What did they have to gain? Davis clearly sounded like he belonged there, with his doomsday shit. What would be the advantage of helping him get out of there?"

"I've thought that angle over." Forrester replied. "The only conclusion I've been able to come to is maybe they did find the penny. Maybe Woitasczyk has some plan to cash in on the publicity when Davis escaped and couldn't be found and then they would miraculously come up with the penny proving he wasn't nuts. Think of the money they could make. Books, Movies, speaking engagements. Hell they'd be Millionaires."

"Then you think they're hiding, Davis somewhere." Brewer said.

"Maybe and maybe not." Forrester replied. "If we find Davis hiding in his house, then I'd say they didn't have anything to do with his escape.

If they were in on it, why would they hide him in his own house. That would be a little too obvious, and I don't think they would be that dumb. I don't really believe he's hiding there, but we have to check it out, and if he is, it would leave us with no other conclusion, than he actually escaped on his own, and the penny story is bullshit."

"There was no way out of the room. The windows were barred and the door was locked. He couldn't have escaped on his own? Woitasczyk and Norton helped him, I'm sure of it." Brewer said.

"What about the other staff members who work in the wing where Davis was confined?" Have you questioned them?" Forrester asked.

"Those bastard's should have been locked up there with him." Brewer replied. "One of the night shift orderlies looks just like a Neanderthal. It wasn't them who helped, Davis, the bastard's were asleep on the job when Davis escaped. I'm going to send my own team over there and check out the room after I call Ferguson and get the plans for the building."

"Let me know what the SWAT team comes up with." Forrester said and left.

CHAPTER FOURTEEN

ON THE ROAD

JIM WAS BEHIND THE wheel, they were on Interstate 15, heading for Los Angeles. Before reaching the Cajon Pass, they stopped in Victorville to get something to eat. On the way into the restaurant, Vince bought a newspaper, and saw the headlines.

"Wait a minute, I can't go in there!" He said as he looked at his face staring back at him.

"What's wrong?" Donna asked.

"They've figured it out. Look!" Vince said.

She and Jim looked at the headlines. Vince's face and the photo of him running for the Medi-vac, were front-page news.

"We'll have to eat later." Vince said. "We've got to get a room in the motel and hole up till it gets dark. It won't be safe for me to be seen in the daytime anymore."

Jim and Vince got back in the car as Donna went inside and checked in, under her name. In their room, Vince sat on the bed looking at his I.D. image staring back at him in full color on the front page and decided he had to change his appearance. "I've got to find some way to change my appearance. Anyone would know who I am if they see this photo."

Donna suggested lightening his hair. She and Jim went shopping for hair coloring and sunglasses.

He sat and read the whole story while they were gone. The part about Woitasczyk and Norton being arrested for concealing his escape amused him. He had never heard of Norton, but read that he was the Head of Security for the hospital and wondered how he had become involved with Woitasczyk. He now realized why it had taken so long for him to become headline news, but had no idea why Woitasczyk and Norton, had kept his escape a secret. It bothered him that the headline said he was deranged and desperate. He had no idea why they would have labeled him in that regard. As he put the paper down, he wondered if the Epperson's or Dr. Leyland, had read the news. Contacting either of them was out of the question now. His house was not a concern, but he wondered what Dr. Leyland might be thinking of him. He wanted to call his parents and tell them he was all right, but knew the police would be checking with them sooner or later. The story now made it far more difficult to accomplish anything, he needed to do. Anyone who read the story would think he was, indeed insane, as well as deranged and desperate.

Donna and Jim returned with the items, as well as some pizza and drinks. Vince flipped on the TV and selected CNN Headline News. The second story they reported was his. He was now on nationwide news, hiding was going to be very difficult.

They ate the pizza and decided to go no further until it was well after dark. Donna lightened Vince's dark hair to sandy blonde, he put on the sunglasses and tried out his new look in the mirror. He held the color photo of him next to his face. When he grew a beard and mustache, he felt that no one, would recognize him. *Not even my own mother could pick me out of a line-up.* He thought as he looked at himself in the mirror.

EPPERSON RESIDENCE...EL CAJON

The SWAT team arrived in front of Vince's house, then dispersed around the perimeter and covered all exits. When all were in place, the team leader approached the front door and rang the doorbell and yelled. "Police Department, open up! We have a search warrant!"

Getting no response, he pounded on the door and called out again. "Police Department, I have a search warrant, open up!"

Again, he got no response and by that, time neighbors had started coming out of their houses. Two officers still on post beside their vehicles got on bullhorns and yelled. "Get back inside your homes! This is a police matter! Get back inside your homes!"

"Screw you! I'm not going anywhere!" Larry Williams yelled.

The officer started toward, Williams, when his radio came alive.

"This is Team Leader. We're going inside in one minute. Hold your positions!"

"Roger that, Team Leader!" He replied, then said to Williams. "I'll deal with your smart ass, when this is over!"

Williams cussed the officer, gave him the finger and went back into his house.

"What's going on?" His wife asked.

"I don't know. There's a bunch of SWAT assholes in front of Vince's house."

She pulled the blinds up and watched the SWAT Team leader pounding on the front door.

"Okay, bust it down." He said to the officer holding the battering ram.

One swing of the ram knocked the door open. The three officers, with guns ready, moved slowly through the door and checked inside. There was no one in the living room and they saw no movement. The team leader called out again.

"Police Department! I have a search warrant! If there's anyone in this house, show yourself, and come out with your hands up!"

Again, there was no answer. The team leader motioned to the two support officers to fan out and make a sweep of the bedrooms, while he checked the kitchen. Seconds later, he got a call.

"Team leader, this is Niner-Two. I have a body in the back bedroom."

"Hold your position Niner-Two." The team leader replied. "What have you got, Niner-Three?"

"Clear." Niner-Three replied.

"Rear positions! Come in through the garage and back door. We're clear inside." The team leader said over his radio.

"Roger that, Team Leader."

A few seconds passed, then the Team Leader received a call. "Team leader, this is Niner-Five. I have a woman's body hanging in the garage. Niner-Four is with me."

"Hold your position. I'm coming to you." The Team Leader replied.

The Team leader checked the body in the bedroom, then went to the garage and called dispatch.

"This is, SWAT, Niner-One. Patch me through to the Chief."

Brewer's phone rang and he answered.

"Niner-One reporting, Chief. We have two bodies here. Male victim, in bedroom, has been stabbed repeatedly. Female victim is hanging from the rafters in the garage."

"Is the male victim, Davis?" Brewer asked.

"Negative, sir. Male victim's I.D., says he's Robert Epperson. Female victim has been I.D.'d, as Margaret Epperson. Looks like murder suicide."

"Any signs of Davis?" Brewer asked.

"Negative, sir!"

"Secure the place and put up perimeter tape. I'm sending a control squad and the lab boys out. Hold your position until they get there." Brewer said.

"Roger that, Niner-One out."

A crowd had gathered in the street despite the officer's warning and watched as the SWAT team encompassed the property with yellow warning tape. Before the police back-up squad arrived, Jean Simmons, from KQTV was on the scene, with her cameraman. The SWAT leader wouldn't give her any details, so she started interviewing neighbors, trying to learn who lived at the house. Vince's next-door neighbor and his wife, were the first she interviewed. "Do you know who lives in the house?" She asked.

"I think he said his name was, Epperson. He and his wife just moved in, we live next door, my name is Larry Williams." Larry said, making sure he was on camera.

"Bob and Margaret Epperson is their names." Larry's wife said. "I made them some cookies and took them over when they moved in. I'm Larry's wife, Cindy." She said smiling for the camera.

More police cars began to arrive as Jean talked to the couple. Jean saw, Lt. Traxler step from the lead car, thanked the couple, and rushed to find out the details from the Lieutenant.

"What's going on, Lt. Traxler?" She asked thrusting the mic in his face.

"Give us a minute here, Jean." He replied.

"Can't you tell me what's happened here?" Jean asked, getting anxious as other camera crews began arriving.

"Apparently there has been a murder and suicide in the house. That's all I have for now, excuse me, Jean." Traxler said.

"Is it the Epperson's?" She shouted behind him.

He turned and said. "Jean, I'll let you know when I have the details!"

"Go live." She said wanting to be the first to report the story. The cameraman indicated they were transmitting the signal.

"This is Jean Simmons, live in El Cajon. I'm on the scene of an apparent murder-suicide." The cameraman zoomed in on Vince's house. "I don't have all the details yet." She continued. "But I have just spoken with Lt. Traxler, who's going inside the residence now. He's confirmed there has been a murder-suicide inside."

The cameraman cut to the interview she had just had with Larry and Cindy Williams, then the brief interview with Traxler and then went back live. She called the neighbors back and began a live interview with them.

"This is Larry and Cindy Williams. They live in the house just south of where the victims were found." Talking to Cindy, she said. "I believe you said the couple who live in the house are Bob and Margaret Epperson?"

"Yes, that's right." Cindy said straightening her hair.

"Do you know anything about the couple?" Jean asked.

"They just moved here from the Midwest. Bob was the new Principal of Granite Hills High School. I took them some cookies when they moved in, too welcome them to our neighborhood." Cindy said again.

"Did they seem unusual in any way? Did you hear any arguments between the couple?" Jean asked.

"Why, no! They just moved in. We really don't know anything other than what I told you." Cindy replied.

"And you, sir?" Jean asked Larry.

"It was like she said, they just moved in. I talked to Bob when they first got here. He had a note from Vince, explaining they were moving in."

"Vince? Who would Vince be, Mr. Williams?" Jean asked.

"Vince Davis. The one the police are looking for. He used to live here." Larry said.

"This was Vince Davis's house? The Vince Davis who escaped from the Mental Hospital? Is that what you said?" Jean asked, with an astonished look on her face.

"Yeah, Bob had a note from Vince that explained everything." Larry said.

"You're sure it's the same Vince Davis the police are looking for?" Jean asked Larry.

"Yes, he was Assistant Director of the Seismology lab at UCSD."

"Thank you both, excuse me." Jean said when she saw Lt. Traxler coming back out of the house.

"Lt. Traxler! Do you have any comment?" She shouted as she rushed to talk to him.

Traxler saw an opportunity to get his name and face on the news. He had more seniority in the detective unit that any other officer, but had been passed over for promotion to Captain, when Jennings had gotten the undeserved promotion ahead of him. He was still burning from that injustice, having felt that everyone had known that he was next up and assumed he would get the promotion, but Jennings had gotten it instead. Although Jennings was now holding down the Captain's desk, Traxler had been the acting Captain until the appointment had been made and still felt it was he that was making the day-to-day decisions, which Jennings was implementing. He smiled as he thought of the golden opportunity that lay before him and motioned for Jean to come over.

"Okay Jean, here's the deal. It looks like the wife stabbed her husband to death in the back bedroom, then took her own life, by hanging herself in the garage." He saw the cameraman recording his comments, smiled and went on. "I can't give any more details, or release their names until family members are notified."

"This is Lt. Traxler of the San Diego Police Department I'm speaking with." Jean said. "Lieutenant can you confirm the house was previously occupied by Vince Davis, the escaped mental patient, police are looking for?" Jean asked.

"I have no comment on that." Traxler replied, having been caught off guard.

The Continent Of St. Louis - The Search For Answers

"The neighbors said the couple who lived in the house are Bob and Margaret Epperson. I've already reported that live. Is that correct, Lt. Traxler?" Jean asked.

"Traxler immediately became defensive and lost control of his temper. "Goddamnit, Jean!" He said angrily. "Don't you have any decency? The family members need to be notified before we can release the victim's names. You shouldn't have done that! That's all I have to say for now!" Traxler turned and started to leave muttering about Jean's behavior under his breath.

"Wait a minute, Lieutenant! Is this part of the Medi-vac hi-jacking case?" Jean asked.

Traxler turned around and said. "You know I can't comment on that."

Jean went on as if Traxler hadn't said a word.

"The neighbor next door said Mr. Epperson, was the Principal at Granite Hills. Can you confirm that?" Jean asked.

"Absolutely not!" Traxler snarled back, with an ever-increasing look of contempt on his face.

Jean turned and faced the camera and continued on. "As you all know by now, Vince Davis was the man who hi-jacked the Medi-vac and landed it at the Granite Hills Football Field. I'm talking with Lt. Traxler of the San Diego, Police Department, in an effort to confirm or deny the statement made by neighbors regarding the house once belonging to the same Vince Davis that police are now seeking. This house is now being investigated as murder-suicide scene. Can you confirm the neighbors claim?" Jean asked Traxler.

"You know better than to ask questions like that!" Traxler spat back.

Unabashed, Jean went on. "Do you know if the victims inside were involved in the hi-jacking?" Jean asked, knowing she was fishing for information and also knowing Traxler was getting mad, but she didn't care, she had a scoop and she was running with it.

Traxler saw the interview was going sour and knew he had to stop her comments. He was now sorry he had agreed to talk to her.

"That's it Jean. The interview is over!" Traxler barked.

"I'm not finished yet!" She snapped back.

"Yes you are!" Traxler retorted.

Jean motioned for the cameraman to zoom in on her face, and said. "Lt. Traxler, for some reason, is being un-cooperative. We already know the identity of the victims, but Lt. Traxler has refused to confirm the identities."

Traxler interrupted her and said. "Hold it right there, Jean! I'm warning you! If you don't quit putting your hearsay, allegations out over the air, I'm going to place you under arrest."

"On what charges?" She demanded.

"For interfering with a police investigation." Traxler retaliated.

"You can't do that! The public has the right to know!" Jean argued.

"I agree, the public does have the right to know. But you, as a reporter, don't have the right to make allegations and assumptions, based solely on conjecture, on your part. I think that's called gossip and something more in line with stories in the, Tattler!" He chided her, but thought. *Maybe that will shut the bitch up!*

Jean became enraged and lost control as her temper flared. She turned, facing the camera, and said. "Apparently the Police Department made a bad choice in sending, Lt. Traxler to investigate this murder-suicide scene. Perhaps his behavior is an indication of the reason he wasn't promoted to Captain!"

"Shut up, Jean!" Her cameraman said, as Jean went on.

"I have already discovered that Vince Davis once lived here. I have confirmed that with his neighbors. What I haven't learned yet, is whether the Epperson's helped Davis in his escape and he then murdered them."

"I warned you!" Traxler barked. "Arrest the mouthy bitch, Unroe!"

The cameraman kept rolling as Sgt. Unroe stepped forward, and said to Jean. "Come with me. You're under arrest."

Jean started fighting and hit Sgt. Unroe with her mic, making a loud thud, heard and seen by the TV viewers at home.

KQTV NEWS ROOM

"JESUS CHRIST! CUT THE feed! Get her off the air, goddamnit!" The studio director yelled to the feed technician as Traxler was seen taking Jean down to the ground, and cuffing her.

The Continent Of St. Louis - The Search For Answers

"I told you to shut up, you bitch!" Traxler hissed in Jean's ear, which was also heard by the TV viewers, just as the live feed was cut.

"Did you see that? She's screwed up good and got herself in some deep shit this time!" The studio director said.

"She usually turns it around and squirms out of it." The technician replied.

"If she gets any help on this one, it won't come from me! I think she's slit her own throat this time." The director said.

"Maybe, maybe not." The technician said. "She's in solid with management. Her numbers are always up."

"I don't think that's going to help this time, she slugged that cop with her mic." The director said as they both watched the cameraman's feed that was still coming in, but no longer live. As the camera rolled, they watched Traxler wrestle Jean up, and half drag her to a police cruiser.

"She isn't going to get away with claiming police brutality on this one! She threw the first punch!" The director exclaimed.

"What about the cameraman?" Sgt. Unroe asked from behind the scene, as they watched.

"Impound his camera and call a tow truck for the van!" Traxler yelled back as he shoved Jean's head down and pushed her in the cruiser, which was also caught on tape just before the camera was shut off and impounded.

"She's screwed now! The director said. "Get someone down to Police Headquarters and find out what lot they're towing the van to."

"What about her cameraman? Do you want me to send another unit by to pick him up?" The technician asked.

"Hell no! I don't want Traxler seeing another KQTV van out there! Call the cameraman and tell him to find a ride!" The director ordered.

"I don't have his cell number." The technician replied.

"Then he can walk or take a cab." The director said.

"He'll put in a voucher for the cab ride." The technician replied.

"Then call upstairs! Tell them to dock his pay for the rest of the day and tell them not to pay any vouchers, if he turns any in!" The director shouted.

"He's going to bitch about it. What excuse can I give payroll for docking him?" The technician asked.

"You've got it all recorded, don't you?" The director asked.

193

"Yeah, sure." The technician replied.

"Then let him bitch! Tell payroll, he didn't try hard enough to stop her. We've got it on tape!" The director said and left the room.

VINCE'S HOUSE

"HOW AM I GETTING back to the station?" The cameraman asked Sgt. Unroe, who was now holding his camera.

"I guess you better find a ride." Unroe replied.

The cameraman walked over to a second crew, from a rival station that had also caught the entire scene on tape and asked. "Can you give me a ride?"

"You'll have to wait till we wrap this up." The reporter replied.

"No problem, I'm getting paid." He said with a smile.

"Jean got her tits all the way in the wringer, this time." The reporter said.

"She deserved it. I told her to shut up, but she didn't. I hope they lock her up and throw away the key." The cameraman replied as he thought about the easy money he was going to get for the rest of the day.

"Where did she come up with all that shit, she was putting out?" The reporter asked.

"She talked to that guy and his wife before you got here." The cameraman said, pointing to Larry and Cindy Williams and then asked. "Do you mind if I kick back in your van, till it's time to leave?"

"Sure, help yourself. Thanks for the tip." She said to Jean's cameraman and then said. "Come on." To her cameraman as she headed toward Larry and Cindy Williams.

"Don't ask, Traxler anything!" Jean's cameraman called out to them, as they walked away.

Traxler and Unroe were talking, as they watched Jean being driven away in the cruiser. "You're going to catch some shit for that, Traxler!" Unroe said.

"I don't give a shit! Screw her!" Traxler retorted. "She came within an inch of being arrested over at Workman's house today. She's a major pain in the ass, Unroe. All reporters are! They don't give a damn who gets hurt, as long as they get the story first. Take charge out here. Don't give out anymore information until I get all the details, and tell the rest of those vultures, the same thing's going to happen to them if they don't stay back."

"All right, but I still think you're crapping in your own nest!" Unroe replied.

Traxler walked to Vince's house mumbling under his breath, regretting having let his ego and desire to be in the limelight, get the better of him. *What a bitch!* He thought, as he saw the cruiser turn the corner and head downtown.

Detectives arrived and started questioning the neighbors. None had any information other than Larry and Cindy. Reporters' interest in the story ebbed, as Ambulances arrived to take the bodies to the morgue. Later in the day, the detectives and lab technicians left with the evidence gathered.

Except for one of Jean's high heels that had come off and now lay in the grass where Traxler had taken her down, the yellow warning tape surrounding Vince's house, was the only sign that police had been there.

POLICE HEADQUARTERS...SAN DIEGO

JENNINGS HAD HARPER AND Edwards with him and they were going over the evidence with Chief Brewer, in his office.

"Here's the note Davis wrote to the neighbor and here's the Epperson woman's suicide note, Chief." Jennings said.

Brewer read the two notes and shook his head and said. "Davis didn't have anything to do with the deaths of the two. The woman's handwriting is altogether different, so here's what we've got. Davis met those people sometime after he escaped. They must have told him they were going to El Cajon and he made a deal to sell his house to them. They were coming from the Midwest, so Davis must have headed east when he left town and they must have been somewhere on Interstate 8 when they met."

"How do you know that, Chief?" Edwards asked.

"I don't know that for sure, goddamnit, but we can guess that much! Jesus Christ, Edwards! Do I have to explain everything to you personally?"

"No, I just wondered what made you think he went east on the 8."

"Which way would you go if you were trying to get out of California?" Before Edwards could answer, Brewer said. "You damn sure wouldn't try to cross the border, would you?"

"No, I wouldn't, but it would be closer."

"Goddamnit, Edwards! I know damn well he wouldn't go to Mexico! He's not that stupid. He's from Missouri, I'll bet he's on his way there, now." Brewer replied.

"How are we going to find out?" Edwards asked.

"Run his credit cards and check with his parents. They live outside of St. Louis. While you're at it, run the Epperson's cards, see where they stayed along Interstate 8. There has to be a connection between them and Davis. He had to have made a deal with them somewhere along the 8." Brewer said.

"Why would they have made a deal with Davis, Chief? The woman's note said she mistook her husband for Davis in the dark and killed him by accident." Jennings said.

"They already had the note from Davis, they showed to his neighbor when they got there. That means they must have met before the news got out that Davis was an escaped mental patient." Brewer said. "You saw how the media exaggerated his condition."

"Speaking of the media what are you going to do with, Simmons?" Jennings asked.

"The TV station's been all over my ass about that, but she's staying in jail! The commissioner told Forrester to charge her with interfering with a police investigation. Forrester's going to ask the judge not to let her post out and she's not going to get out on a Habeas Corpus either. The commissioner wants to make an example of her and send a message to the rest of those blood-sucking reporters. We've got her tapes and there's enough evidence on them to hang her ass out to dry. Traxler told her he couldn't reveal the couples names, then she found out who they were and put their names out live and then tried to tie them in with Davis's escape. She's going to do some time for that little escapade." Brewer replied.

"She's the hottest reporter in town, Chief. Do you think the public is going to go along with this?" Jennings asked.

"I don't give a damn what the public says!" Brewer retorted. "Simmons is a nosey, bitch and Traxler did the right thing. She had to be ordered off Workman's property by a patrolman earlier in the day. I'm tired of her and the rest of them using the, horseshit excuse, that the public has the right to know. We're in the middle of an investigation where two people ended up dead and all she could do is make up suppositions and allegations. Screw her, maybe some of the other hot shot reporters will think twice before they start barging in to get the story first."

"Chief, I think we should put a caller I.D. trace on Davis's phone and loop it back to the station. Sooner or later he's going to call and we can get the number he's calling from." Edwards said.

"Good idea, Edwards." Brewer replied. "Get on it and get the Epperson's and Davis's credit cards checked out. Let's find out where they met Davis. They must have stayed at the same motel or gassed up at the same station. I'm going to have Forrester put a freeze on Davis's credit cards along with the funds in his bank account. He'll start feeling the pinch before long."

INTERSTATE 15…VICTORVILLE, CALIFORNIA

VINCE WAS NERVOUS WHEN they left the motel. Darkness had set in and Jim was back behind the wheel as they got back on Interstate 15. As they descended down the Cajon Pass, Vince thought about the San Andreas Fault, which ran along the edge of the mountain range they were leaving. It had completely ruptured and disappeared along with the rest of Southern California during the massive earthquakes and landslides that caused the mighty Tsunami's that destroyed the world. He felt the car picking up speed as they descended lower.

"Keep it under the speed limit, Jim." Vince said as big rigs sped past them on the downgrade.

At the speed they were traveling, they would be in Los Angeles in a couple hours. When they got there, he had to find a way to talk to Sandra Beatty in private. He didn't know the exact date that Dr. Leyland had presented his findings and recommendations to Caltech, but he knew it would be soon. He needed to talk to, Sandra, and show her the Model before Dr. Leyland did. He hoped he could convince her that Dr. Leyland wasn't going off the deep end, like she and everyone had thought, in his first 2005.

Maybe if I had been more involved and understood what he had discovered and had gone with him, perhaps they wouldn't have turned him down. He thought and then remembered Dr. Leyland had told him Sandra Beatty was a status seeking individual, and realized he might not be any better persuading, Sandra Beatty this time than, Dr. Leyland had been the first time. Even with better facts and proof, he knew it wasn't going to be easy. As it was, he had already been locked up for telling his story and he'd be locked up again if they caught him. Sandra Beatty and everyone else, now knew he was escaped mental patient. His job wasn't going to be easy, perhaps impossible, and he knew that.

The miles slipped away as the thoughts rolled over in his mind. They were nearing Interstate 10, for the last leg to L.A.

"How about a restroom break?" Donna asked.

Jim pulled off at the next exit and gassed up the car while Donna went inside. She returned with an San Diego, Union Tribune and handed it to Vince.

"Look at this." She said. His picture was still on the front page, but there were bold, new headlines under it, that read.

Midwestern Couple Found Dead In Davis Home

Robert Epperson and wife Margaret were found dead in the home of Vince Davis, mental patient, escapee. Davis is still at large as police seek clues to his disappearance and whereabouts. KQTV Reporter, Jean Simmons, of San Diego was arrested today at the Davis home and initially charged with interfering with a police investigation. San Diego County District Attorney, Claude Forrester, later filed resisting arrest, as well as felony assault charges against Ms. Simmons for striking an officer of the law with her microphone, while in performance of his duty. She was also cited for criminally releasing the deceased couple's names and other damaging allegations in a live broadcast made, from the Davis home. No further information is available regarding what, if any part, Davis might have played in the deaths of the couple. San Diego Police Chief, Wayne Brewer, has not released any information, other than the couple's names. KQTV officials, could not be reached for comment.

The article went on, but Vince quit reading and laid the paper down.

"Did you know them, Vince?" Donna asked

"Not really, I met them in Yuma. They were on their way to El Cajon. They were going to see if they liked my house and possibly buy it."

"What will you do now?" Donna asked.

"There's not much I can do. The police, will impound the house as a crime scene. I can't go back there anyway." He replied.

"Do you think, Sandra will want to talk to you now?" Donna asked.

"Not likely and it's probably best not to risk it. I think the best course now is to talk to Dr. Leyland, and see when he's going to present his Model to her. We can figure out what to do then, and go from there."

"I can call Dr. Leyland, Vince." Jim said.

"Okay, let's find a place to hole up close to Caltech. We better use pay phones from now on." Vince said.

The three got back on Interstate 10 and continued on their trip to L.A. Donna looked at Vince from the back seat, and thought. *What have I gotten myself into? The Air Force is sounding better all the time.*

CHAPTER FIFTEEN

POLICE HEADQUARTERS...EARLIER IN THE DAY

HARPER AND EDWARDS WERE in Chief Brewer's office going over the case and looking through the evidence that had been collected. Brewer was going to have to make a statement regarding the Epperson's soon.

"Here's the Epperson's credit card records." Harper said.

Brewer compared Epperson's records to Vince's credit card records, and said. "Here's the link. They both stayed at the same motel in Yuma and they both checked out the day after Davis escaped. That has to be how the Epperson's met him and ended up at his house."

"You don't think he knew them before that day, Chief?" Edwards asked.

"It's not likely, Edwards." Brewer replied.

"Are you forgetting what, Jean Simmons said?" Jennings asked. "Epperson was the new Principal for Granite Hills. Davis landed the Medi-vac there!"

"I haven't forgot a damn thing, Jennings! She's in jail for making that statement!" Brewer retorted. "I imagine everyone in the city believes that, but the dates don't coincide. Davis and the Epperson's were in Yuma the morning after Davis escaped. They couldn't have picked him up at the football field. Didn't you hear me tell you that, just now?"

"Yeah, I heard you." Jennings replied, and then said. "But they could have met him there and then drove to Davis's house, where he killed them. He could have forced the woman to write the suicide note."

"Jesus, Jennings! How in the hell did you get to be Captain? Davis stayed in Needles the next night and in Las Vegas at the Grand after that. How in the hell would he have had time to drive back to El Cajon with the Epperson's, kill them and then drive to Needles and check in early in the day? He was in his own car the whole time. Goddamn! I don't believe this." Brewer said leaning his head on his hands.

"I ran his car tag, Chief. He sold his car in Las Vegas to a used car dealer for cash, the day after he checked out of the MGM Grand, and that's not all. The car dealer found a trash bag in the trunk of Davis's car when they were detailing it. The scrubs and tennis shoes Davis was wearing when he hi-jacked the Medi-vac, were in the trash bag. I told him to turn the bag over to the Vegas Police." Edwards said.

"What for? We know it was Davis who hi-jacked the Medi-vac." Brewer said.

"I know, but I thought the D.A. might want them for evidence for Davis's trial when we catch him." Edwards replied

"There isn't going to be a trial when we catch him. He'll go right back into Gifford. We can't prosecute an insane person for any crimes they commit, it would be a waste of time and money. Any lawyer could pin it on his mental condition. Forrester's not stupid enough to put him on trial." Brewer said.

"All right, maybe this doesn't mean anything either." Edwards said.

"If you've got something to say, say it, Edwards!" Brewer barked.

"Two men broke into Davis's room at the Grand while he was there and tried to steal a penny he had showed to a rare coin dealer. He captured the two and held them till the police arrived and then he checked out."

"A penny! What kind of penny?" Brewer asked.

"That's the odd part, Chief." Edwards said. "The desk clerk at the Grand said it was a 2005 penny. The Vegas Police arrested the coin dealer and one of the Security Guards at the Grand. Seems like the coin dealer had hired the two thieves to break into Davis's room and the Security Guard had let them use his pass key to do it."

"Jesus! All of that for a 2005 penny?" Brewer asked.

"I got a copy of the police report, Chief." Edwards said. "The coin dealer swears the penny, Davis, had was a 2009. He said it was a Mint error and he wanted it bad. He offered Davis big bucks for it and when Davis wouldn't sell it, he hired the thieves and the security guard to steal it."

"A 2009? Are you sure?" Brewer asked.

"Yeah, Chief. That's what the coin dealer said, but it wasn't. The penny was a 2005." Edwards said.

"How do you know?" Brewer asked.

"Davis showed it to the arresting officer. It was a 2005." Edwards replied.

"Let's back up here for a minute." Brewer said. "Davis swore he had a 2009 penny that proved what he was saying about the future. He said he had it when he tripped and hit his head in his bathroom."

"Hold on, Chief!" Jennings said. "The lab guys didn't find a penny or anything else on the floor of the bathroom, when Davis's house was searched."

"I know that, goddamnit! Shut up for a minute and listen!" Brewer barked.

"Sorry, Chief. Go on." Jennings said.

"Woitasczyk got Davis's permission and sent a crew out to his house to search for the penny. They never found the penny either. Woitasczyk, asshole that he is, wanted to give Davis every chance to prove to himself that he was imagining the stuff about the future. All they found in Davis's bathroom was some computer discs. When they didn't find the penny, Davis got worse. It's in Davis's records, I read it. Now, some coin dealer says he's seen it, tries to steal it and ends up in jail. I don't think the coin dealer would have went to all that trouble, unless it was a 2009. Did Davis file the complaint?" Brewer asked.

"No. The Grand did." Edwards said. "The thieves trashed Davis's room. It was one of them that fingered the coin dealer and the guard."

"Get over to Vegas." Brewer said. "Talk to that coin dealer, I want to find out what else he knows."

"I already know he isn't talking, Chief." Edwards said. "The local cops thinks he's nuts. They don't believe he saw a 2009 penny."

"Think about it, Edwards." Brewer said. "Woitasczyk said Davis was crazy and now the Vegas Police think the coin dealer is crazy. Why would the coin dealer say he saw a 2009 penny if it was a 2005? He wouldn't goddamnit, and he wouldn't have hired someone to steal it unless he had. Get your asses moving and get me some information!"

"Can we get a voucher for plane fare and a hotel room?" Harper asked.

"This ain't no vacation, Harper!" Brewer yelled. "You and Edwards can take your department car!"

"It will take five or six hours to get there in a car! Maybe more if traffic is tied up!" Edwards protested.

"I don't care how long it takes, and I don't want to get any feedback saying you two were shooting craps or doing any kind of gambling. Are we clear?" Brewer barked.

"I hate driving the 15, Chief." Harper said.

"Everyone does! That's tough shit, Harper! Get going and call me as soon as you talk to the coin dealer." Brewer ordered.

"Oh, by the way, Chief." Harper said. "The local cop said Davis is traveling with a good looking blonde and a younger guy. He thinks Davis and the blonde were getting married."

"Well, check the county courthouse, find out if they got a license." Brewer barked.

"I already have, they didn't." Harper replied.

"Try to find out who the two other people are. See if the Grand has any security tapes with them on it." Brewer suggested.

"I already have, Chief." Harper said. "They're over-nighting you a copy of the lobby recording, when Davis checked out." Harper said.

"Well what are you two standing there for? Get going!" Brewer yelled.

As the two walked out of Brewer's office, and went down the hall, Harper was feeling slightly abused again. Chief Brewer's harsh tones had struck home. "Goddamn!" Harper complained. "The least he could do was say, good job, or something. I'm tired of him eating our asses out all the time!"

"He's in a tight spot, Harper. This is his first big case and it just keeps getting deeper. He's just passing his ass eating's on down to us. But the Chief's right about one thing."

"What thing?" Harper asked.

"Jennings is a stupid bastard!" Edwards replied. "How in the hell did he get to be Captain?"

"You better not let him hear you saying that, or you'll be back in Blues. Jennings is the Mayor's brother in law. If the Chief screws this one up, Jennings will probably be the next Chief. You're driving, I hate the 15 traffic."

"It's your turn!" Edwards shot back.

"Okay, fine! I'm driving on the shoulder if I have to, and I'm running the red light and siren all the way to Vegas."

As the two Detectives headed north, they passed the Interstate 10 exit with their siren screaming and red light flashing in the darkness. Jim instinctively pulled his foot off the accelerator and looked at the speedometer as the police car passed them at high speed going in the opposite direction, then relaxed when he remembered he was in cruise control.

"Where do you think they're going?" Jim asked Vince.

"Probably a wreck. Pick it up a little, everyone's speeding. We don't want to stick out like a sore thumb." Vince said.

As the two detective sped on weaving in and out of traffic, Edwards had finally had enough. He had been holding his hands over his ears for the last hour and a half. "

"Goddamnit! Turn off that siren. I'm going deaf!" He screamed to Harper.

"You want to drive, Edwards?" Harper asked.

"Hell yes! You're damned right I do! Pull over you crazy bastard!" Edwards yelled.

"Okay, I need to piss anyway." Harper replied.

LAS VEGAS

THE TWO DETECTIVES ARRIVED in Vegas three hours later and went straight to Vegas Police Headquarters. They were sent on to the County Jail where the coin dealer was being held for arraignment. The jailer looked at his watch, noting the late hour, he said. "He might have posted bond, I'll check for you."

The Continent Of St. Louis - The Search For Answers

"Give me his home address and phone number, in case he has." Harper said.

After looking through the released files and not finding the coin dealers name, he said. "I won't have to, he's still being held. I'll have him brought up."

A deputy brought the coin dealer to an interrogation room and the two began questioning him about the attempted theft, and the penny.

"I'm not crazy! The penny was a 2009, goddamnit!" The dealer exclaimed.

"What kind of penny was it? Harper asked.

"What?" The dealer asked.

"What kind of penny was it that you looked at?" Harper asked again.

"The only kind there is in the United States, you moron! Jesus Christ, do you know what time it is? I had finally gone to sleep and you two morons show up asking stupid questions! Screw both of you! I want to go back to my cell!" The dealer spat back.

Harper was ready to backhand the coin dealer when Edwards grabbed his arm, and said. "He's right, Harper."

"The hell he is! I'm not a moron and that bastard's not calling me one!" Harper snapped back.

"I don't mean that, goddamnit! I was talking about the penny. Lincoln Pennies are the only ones they make in the United States." Edwards said.

Harper shook Edwards arm away and said. "Well how in the hell was I supposed to know that, Edwards?"

The coin dealer rolled his eyes and started to speak, but Harper cut him off and said. "Don't get smart with me anymore, you asshole! I'm just doing my job! Now, for the record, what kind of penny was it?"

"It was a goddamned, 2009, Lincoln Penny. It was a Mint error. The Goddamned thing is worth a fortune." The dealer said.

"Why did the arresting officer and the hotel clerk say it was a 2005?" Harper asked

"Hell, I don't know, maybe he…wait a minute! What was the guy's name?" The dealer asked.

"The arresting officer?" Harper asked.

"No! The guy with the penny. What's his name?" The dealer asked.

"Do you mean, Davis?" Harper answered.

"Yeah, Davis, that was his name. He must have switched it. Is he a magician? They have magicians in Vegas all the time." The dealer said.

"Some people think he is, but no, he isn't." Edwards said.

"I'm telling you the penny he showed me was 2009. He switched them somehow." The dealer said.

"Was it worth breaking into his room and trying to steal it?" Harper asked.

"Hell yes! I'm not denying that. It's worth a fortune! It's worth more than any coin I've ever had my hands on, and the bastard wouldn't sell it." The dealer complained.

"If it was a Mint error, how do you know there aren't others?" Edwards asked.

"If there were others, it would be all over the internet. I checked." The dealer replied.

"Did anyone else see it besides you?" Edwards asked.

"The blonde and the guy that was with him did." The dealer replied.

"Anybody else?" Harper asked.

"How the hell would I know where he'd been or who he showed it to?" The dealer blurted out. "He might have shown it to someone else besides me. Why is that so important? Why hasn't my Lawyer shown up?"

"Our Chief wants to know all he can about the penny." Harper said. "Davis claimed he had it before he was placed in a mental institution, but no one has reported seeing it except you."

"Well isn't that the shits!" The dealer exclaimed. "Some crazy guy comes in my store with a 2009 penny, an ex-mental patient at that, and I end up in jail…Hey, wait a minute!"

"He's not an ex-mental patient, he escaped, and we're looking for him." Edwards said.

"I don't care about that!" The dealer exclaimed. "What I mean is, when he showed me the penny in my shop, I got a picture of it."

"How did you get a picture of it?" Edwards asked.

"I have a camera over the counter in the ceiling that photographs the coin and one behind the counter that photographs the person who has brought it in. I do it for insurance reasons in case someone says I switched their coin or in case it's stolen. I'd like to cooperate with the police if I can, but you're going to have to cut me a deal."

"Have you told anyone else about this? Do the local police know you have the cameras?" Edwards asked.

"No, you two are the only ones that have mentioned the penny other than the smart ass local cops. They said I must be losing my eyesight. They kept showing me 2005 pennies and asking me if they looked like a 2009. The bastard's have been laughing their asses off at me." The dealer said.

"Are you willing to cooperate with our investigation?" Edwards asked.

"I told you I would. I'll do anything to help me beat this rap." The dealer replied.

"I think you're going to have to face the charges. When are you going to be arraigned? Harper asked.

"In the morning."

"If you help us, we'll be at your arraignment. We'll talk to the judge for you and tell him you're helping us. Maybe he'll let you off with a misdemeanor if you've never been in trouble before. Have you?" Harper asked.

"No, hell no! I don't know what got into me." The dealer said with a sheepish look on his face. "I saw that penny and had to have it. That lousy security guard said he could get it for me for a price. I didn't know he was going to hire those thugs and break into the room. He said Davis put the penny in a lock box and he could get it for me."

"Will you give us your permission to have the smart cards removed from your cameras and have a technician make copies of the photos?" Harper asked.

"Yes, if it will help get me out of this mess."

"I'm not promising you anything." Harper said. "But, if you give us your permission in writing, to have them removed, we'll be there in the morning with you when you go before the judge."

With permission given in writing, the two detectives accompanied by a police technician, entered the coin store and removed the smart cards and returned to Police Headquarters and uploaded the photos.

"That's him, that's Davis." Harper said to the technician.

"Then this is the coin that corresponds to Davis." The technician said.

"Can you enlarge it?" Harper asked.

"Sure." The technician said blowing the image up on the computer screen.

"Jesus Christ! Look at that, It's a 2009! Can you make me some color prints of that?" Harper asked.

"No problem." The technician said.

"Print me some of his face and some of that blonde beside him." Harper said.

"Can you fax copies to our Chief?" Edwards asked.

"Sure what's the number?"

POLICE HEADQUARTERS...SAN DIEGO

CHIEF BREWER STOOD OVER his fax machine as the photos were being received. He picked up the photo of the penny, and said. "Jesus Christ! The penny is real!" He got on the phone and called the Commissioner, the D.A. and the Mayor and faxed copies to each. An hour later, all three were in Chief Brewer's office.

"Do you know what time it is? I was just getting ready to knock some off when you called, this better be good!" The Mayor said to Brewer.

"No shit?" Forrester said, thinking about the Mayor's less than desirable looking wife.

"Get on with it, Chief!" The Mayor barked. He knew Forrester was messing with him.

"Did you look at the faxes I sent you?" Brewer asked.

"Yes, goddamnit! Get on with it!" The Mayor barked.

"Then you all realize the penny is real?" Brewer asked.

"Yes, so what?" The Mayor asked.

"He was telling the truth about the penny, maybe he didn't belong in Gifford after all." Brewer said.

"Okay, so he wasn't lying about the penny or making it up. He's still guilty of stealing that Medi-vac, and those people ended up dead in his house. He may have had something to do with that." The Mayor said.

"I've ruled out any involvement on Davis's part in the Epperson case." Brewer said.

"He's made a fool out of the Police Force and the City of San Diego, hasn't he?" The Mayor asked.

"Yes, he did, but from the evidence we have now, it doesn't look like he belonged in that mental hospital." Brewer said.

"Why? Because you have a photo of a penny, dated 2009? It could be fake for Christ's sake! I've read his record, he sounds mental to me. When did you become a psychiatrist?" The Mayor barked back.

Brewer could see he was getting in over his head and didn't answer the Mayor. Instead, he said. "Harper and Edwards will be back tomorrow. They taped their conversation with the coin dealer in the County Jail. He said the penny isn't a fake. He was willing to pay thousands to get it."

"Why is he in jail?" The Mayor asked.

"He hired some thugs to steal the penny." Brewer answered.

"Well I'll be go to hell! Do you expect me to believe some thieving ass coin dealer who got caught? Is that it? He'd say anything to try and save his ass! You know that!" The Mayor shot back.

"I don't think he's lying." Brewer said.

"I'd lie like hell wouldn't have it, if I was in jail! You know goddamned well everyone in jail says they're innocent." The Mayor barked.

"I know they all lie, but I don't think the coin dealer's lying." Brewer replied.

"Was he given a polygraph?" The Mayor asked.

"No, he wasn't given a polygraph and he wasn't actually the one that hired the thugs. Vegas Police have the MGM Grand Security Guard in custody, that set the break-in up. The coin dealer had no idea the security guard was going to hire the thugs to do the job. The security guard said he would get the coin for him. He didn't say how he was going to get it." Brewer said.

"So that makes the coin dealer a saint! Is that what you're telling me?" The Mayor asked.

"No, he's just as guilty as the rest of them, your Honor. I'd just like for the three of you to listen to the tape, and then make up your minds." Brewer said.

"What have we got to lose, your Honor?" The Commissioner asked.

The Mayor thought about the relaxing evening he'd missed out on, looked at his watch, and knew he wasn't going to get another offer when he got home. He sighed and said. "Nothing I guess. What about Davis? Where is he?" He asked.

"We don't know, your Honor. He's disappeared." Brewer replied.

"Disappeared! How can he disappear with his face all over the goddamn television and in the papers?" The Mayor yelled.

"Nobody said he's dumb, your Honor. He managed to pick a lock in an access panel in his shower ceiling and find his way to the roof of the hospital and fly a helicopter, he had no training or certification to fly and land it without putting a scratch on it." Brewer said.

"All right! He's a goddamned genius, so what? He's still an escaped mental patient, and a Felon. If he's not crazy, then he belongs in jail! Find him, and I mean soon! The goddamned media's all over my ass as it is!" The Mayor barked, and then thought for a second and went on. "I want you to release that Simmons bitch and drop the charges, and I mean now!" He ordered.

"Why? Forrester asked.

"To get the media off my ass, that's why!" The Mayor replied.

"She'll sue the Police Department and the City of San Diego, if we drop the charges." Forrester said.

"No she won't." The Mayor replied. "I've already taken care of that. The station manager said he will reprimand her if we drop the charges and release her. She can't sue anybody if the company she works for, agrees she was wrong in what she did. She can't claim police brutality, can she?" The Mayor asked.

"No." Brewer replied. "She hit the officer that was arresting her with her microphone. Traxler ordered her arrest and the officer was doing what he was told to do."

"All right, let her go." The Mayor said.

"Yes, your Honor." Brewer said.

"What about the Medi-vac pilot, those lame ass detectives of yours, brow beat down in interrogation? Has he given any indication he's going to sue? Did they use a rubber hose on him?" The Mayor asked.

"We don't use rubber hoses anymore, your Honor. But I'm sure Traxler would have liked to have used one on Simmons. She's a mouthy bitch!" Brewer said.

"What about the pilot? Is he going to sue?" The Mayor asked.

"Workman won't sue either." Forrester said. "I got his company to give him a week off with pay and re-instate him, when I dropped the charges against him."

"You better tell Harper and Edwards to lay off that brow beating routine they put Workman through, Chief. We may not be so lucky next time." The Commissioner said.

"Norton's lawyer said he's going to sue the city." Forrester said.

"What for?" The Mayor asked.

"He shit and pissed his pants when Harper and Edwards arrested him. They had him put in the tank without letting him clean himself up." Forrester said.

"Typical!" The Mayor bellowed. "That's some more great police work from those two! You better straighten their asses out, Chief!"

"Norton's lawyer said you were in on it, Chief." Forrester said.

"I wasn't in on it! Norton was already at the booking desk when I arrived and he'd already shit his pants and pissed all over the floor. I ordered Harper and Edwards to go and arrest Woitasczyk. The jailor is the one who didn't get him cleaned up!" Brewer replied.

"Norton's lawyer said you were laughing at Norton." The D. A. said.

"Hell yes I was! I admit it. It was pretty damn funny seeing Norton standing there with his britches full of shit, and a puddle of piss on the floor. Hell yes I laughed, you would too." Brewer chuckled.

The Mayor started laughing. "No shit?" He said. "I probably would have laughed too, but that's off the record! You're going to have to do something with Edwards and Harper, Chief. They're getting out of hand."

"I'll tell them, and their boss also. Jennings is just as big a screw-up as they are." Brewer said.

"Watch it, Chief!" The Mayor said. "I know Jennings is a loser, but don't go too far out on a limb with him! He's my brother-in-law and I don't want him to go crying to my wife, and have her crawling up my ass! Let me know the second you find Davis and have him under arrest. I want to go on Television as soon as he's in custody and let the public know they're safe."

"Davis isn't dangerous, your Honor" Brewer said.

"Tell that to Bob Epperson, Chief!" The Mayor spat back. "Just being in contact with Davis, got the man killed."

"Davis didn't have anything to do with it." Brewer said.

"She murdered her husband because she thought he was Davis, didn't she?" The Mayor asked.

"Yes, your Honor, she did." Brewer replied.

"That's because she was afraid of Davis. The whole damn city is afraid of him!" The Mayor yelled. "Now find him! If he resists arrest, shoot him! Put out that order right now!"

"Yes, your Honor." Brewer said.

"What about, Woitasczyk and Norton?" Forrester asked.

"They lied to cover up Davis's escape didn't they?" The Mayor asked.

"Well, Norton didn't after the police brought him in." Forrester said. "He said he was under orders from Woitasczyk to keep it from the public."

"Okay, let him go, but before you do, cut a deal with his lawyer. Tell him the charges will be dropped against him if he signs an agreement he won't sue the city. Tell him you're going to throw the book at him otherwise." The Mayor turned to Brewer and asked. "He really shit his pants, huh?"

"Yeah. He was crying too." Brewer replied, and they both started laughing again.

"I don't want to spoil your fun and games." Forrester said as the two laughed. "But, what about Woitasczyk?"

The Mayor stopped laughing, and said. "He's responsible for this whole mess! He knew Davis had escaped and he alone, made the decision, not to notify authorities. He resisted arrest and assaulted the officers. That alone will be enough to put him behind bars for a while. The rest will keep him there longer, and he deserves it."

"Yes, that's true, your Honor." Forrester said. "But, he's tops in his field. He's a well-respected psychiatrist. He's known worldwide."

The Mayor wasn't deterred and said. "Throw the book at the bastard! I want an example made of someone in this case and he's going to be that example! The last thing we need in this city is a medical professional that's has sworn to be responsible, a psychiatrist for Christ's sake, letting a crazy mental patient escape and covering it up. The only plea you'll accept from Woitasczyk is an agreement to give up his license to practice in the State of California and he has to agree to leave the state. If he doesn't, then put him on trial. The board will take his license away anyway, when he's convicted. He will be convicted won't he?" The Mayor asked.

"Yes, your Honor." Forrester replied. "His signature is only one on the document authorizing Davis's escape to be kept secret from the public, and authorities."

"Then forget making any deal with him. Hang the bastard!" The Mayor told Forrester.

"Mayor, I'd like to ask you to re-consider your shoot to kill order on Davis." Brewer said.

"What in hell for?" The Mayor barked.

"If he's crazy, he can't be held responsible for what he's done. Forrester will tell you we can't put him on trial for any of it anyway. He'll just have to go back to Gifford when we catch him." Brewer said.

"I distinctly remember you saying you don't think he belonged in Gifford." The Mayor said.

"You're right, I did say that and I still don't think he belongs there." Brewer replied.

"If he's not crazy, then he's a criminal and most likely a dangerous one. As far as I'm concerned, Davis is public enemy number one! The order stands! Are we clear?" The Mayor barked.

"Yes, your Honor." Brewer replied.

The next morning, Chief Brewer was in his office. He was holding the photos of the penny and the other of Vince with the blonde. He buzzed his Secretary and said. "Get Rowland in here." The elated feeling, he had experienced after looking at the photo of the penny the day before, was gone. He felt fairly certain, that there was something more to Vince's story than just the penny. He didn't feel good at all about the Mayor's order to shoot Vince if he resisted arrest, and wondered. *What if what Davis is saying about the disaster is true? No matter how he came up with the information, we'd be killing the only hope of being prepared for what lies ahead, if it is true.*

There was a knock at his door and Rowland came in. "You want to see me, Chief?" He asked.

"Yes, and this is important. The Mayor has given orders to shoot and kill Davis if he resists arrest. We can't let that happen. We've got to find Davis before he runs into some trigger-happy rookie. Find this girl, and we find Davis." He handed Rowland the photo of Donna standing beside Vince at the coin shop.

"Who is she, Chief?" Rowland asked.

"I don't know, but she's traveling with him. They were last seen in Vegas, that's where the photo was taken."

"When was the photo taken?" Rowland asked.

"A couple days ago. Look at this." Brewer showed Rowland the photo of the penny and explained the story about the coin dealer in Vegas, and went on. "The coin dealer claims it's a Mint error, but I don't think so. If it was, there would have been a lot more of them stamped out. I checked it on the internet and there's nothing regarding a Mint error, so I checked with the mint. There was no such error made. They told me it would have been impossible to get a six upside down when it was engraved into the die. The penny is real, Rowland."

"If it is, then Davis isn't crazy." Rowland said.

"Exactly! I told the Mayor that, but I think he's so tired of this whole mess he would prefer for Davis to be shot. I want you to make sure that doesn't happen. We need to hear what he has to say about the future. Nobody could make a penny like that except the, U.S. Mint, and they say they didn't make it. I don't know for sure, if I believe everything, Davis said in Woitasczyk's reports, but we can't let him get killed. We have to hear what he has to say, Rowland."

"How can I make sure some hot shot doesn't pull the trigger, Chief?"

"Our best hope of getting in contact with Davis, is through his boss, Dr. Leyland. If Davis is so sure of what he's saying is going to happen, then he's going to have to talk to someone that would understand what he's talking about. Leyland, will be our best bet. Take the photo of the penny and the one of him and the blonde with you. See if, Leyland, knows who she is and tell him what the Mayor has said about shooting, Davis. I know he won't want to see Davis killed and we need, Dr. Leyland's help, in setting up a private meeting with Davis. Word of this, can't get out of this office, or we'll both be in deep shit. You're on your own on this one, Rowland. Are you up to it? Can I count on you?" Brewer asked.

"I owe you one on that bomb scare mess-up. You can count on me." Rowland replied.

"I thought you said it was, Corporal Burton's fault. I ate his ass out royally." Brewer said.

"I should have known better, I didn't have to let him call it in. But the goddamned President's got us all scared shitless of terrorists. I wasn't thinking clearly I guess." Rowland said.

"All's well that ends well. It didn't hurt, Burton, to get his ass ate out. We all have at one time or another. Mine is raw right now from all of the ass eating's the Mayor's given me. It doesn't get a chance to heal up before he chews on it again. Go see Dr. Leyland, and find out what he knows about the blonde."

CHAPTER SIXTEEN

CLARK COUNTY COURTHOUSE...LAS VEGAS

EDWARDS AND HARPER SHOWED up at the coin dealers arraignment and explained to the judge that he was helping them with their investigation and that he had been taken advantage of by the security guard in his eagerness to acquire the penny, which they showed him the photo of.

"I don't blame him for wanting the penny." The judge said. "But I can't let him off without paying some sort of penalty. If he'll plead guilty to a reduced charge of being in the company of convicted felons, which is a misdemeanor, I'll let him off for time served and a five hundred dollar fine."

The coin dealer's attorney, who was present, agreed to the plea. The coin dealer plead guilty, and was released into the custody of his attorney. Edwards and Harper walked with them on the way to the clerk's office to pay his fine. They thanked and shook hands with him on the courthouse steps, and then headed for their patrol car with the tape recording of their conversation safely tucked away. As they were leaving the parking lot, Harper said. "The Chief won't know it if we shoot some Craps or something. We've done a good job up here and we deserve a little R and R, while we're here"

"Listen, Dick Wad! I don't make enough to lose it here on the Crap tables. I'm putting in for Per Diem when we get back and get what I've spent here and a little more to boot." Edwards replied.

"You're a pain in the ass, Edwards!" Harper complained. "We get this golden opportunity and all you want to do is leave. We're stopping at the state line if I have anything to say about it."

"You don't and we're not stopping!" Edwards said as he pulled on to Interstate 15 for the drive back. He wasn't going to allow Harper to drive. His ears were still ringing from the trip to Vegas.

UCSD SEISMOLOGY CENTER...SAN DIEGO

ROWLAND SAT IN DR. Leyland's office, ready to begin his questioning. He had showed Dr. Leyland the two photos and asked if could record the conversation they were having. Dr. Leyland, shook his head yes, and said. "The poor boy. How could anyone have believed his story. It still isn't believable, but how could anyone explain that penny any other way?"

"Do you know the girl?" Rowland asked.

"Yes. She's, Miss Stevens. She works in our lab offices. The other man is, Jim Lewis, he works here also."

"Did she work for, Davis?" Rowland asked.

"No, she doesn't work here in the lab. Her job is to make sure all of our equipment is kept up to date with all refinements, as they come along. I don't think she knew Vince at all. But the night I called Vince, the night he fell, he asked me about her."

"What did he want to know?" Rowland asked.

"That was really odd, Sergeant. He asked me if a, Donna Stevens, worked in our offices. He called her by her first, name as if he knew her. Later, when I talked to him, after he had recovered and came out of the coma, he told me that he, Miss Stevens and Jim Lewis, the other man in the photo, had all been in 2009 working together, at Area 51, trying to escape the advance of a world ending catastrophe."

"You weren't included?" Rowland asked.

"He said I had been, but that I had been drugged and kidnapped by the time he got to Area 51. He said a plot had been put in place to make it appear I had died in a fire. How could I believe that? How could anyone? He said government officials were behind the plot."

"Government officials?" Rowland questioned.

"Yes, he said it was the Vice President of the United States. I don't recall who he said it was, but it wasn't, Cheney." Dr. Leyland said.

"And this all happens in 2009?" Rowland asked.

"Yes, he said it all began on August 18th, 2009 and was over by the twenty-second of September." Dr. Leyland said.

Rowland, did some quick math and said. "That means the whole thing would have happened in thirty-five days. How could that be possible?" He asked unbelievably.

"It doesn't seem possible that the Earth could be completely destroyed in that short of time span. That part was just as unbelievable to me, as me being involved and being at Area 51. I've studied the Earth's faults for many years and I don't want to say what he told me is impossible, but it doesn't seem probable. Every Tectonic Plate that dissects the Earth would have had to have been involved for that to happen. But even then, it would have to be triggered simultaneously, by some other underground, cataclysmic event, to have occurred in such catastrophic proportions, as he said it did. He could tell I didn't believe him, when he told me of the disaster, I could see it in his eyes. I suppose I was his last hope, but I couldn't encourage or endorse what he was saying."

"It does seem impossible." Rowland said.

"Quite so, Sgt. Rowland. But, as I was leaving, he told me one last thing that did make sense."

"What was that?" Rowland asked.

"To watch what was going on in Mexico, closely. I did take that seriously. I have been watching what's going on in Mexico, far more closely than any of us would have been, normally. You're aware that we had some cluster quake activity around the Salton Sea, in August."

"No, I didn't hear about that." Rowland said.

"Most people didn't and those that did, didn't pay any attention to it, but that's why I had called Vince, that night. I wanted him to come in and help me work on a Model I was preparing. At the time, his answer was preposterous." Leyland said.

"What did he tell you?" Rowland asked.

"That he and others already knew about the activity in the Salton Sea area, which I thought impossible, and of course, didn't believe. I was the one that called 911 and sent the Sheriff's Deputies to check on him. They found him unconscious and he was taken to the hospital. I wasn't able to speak with him until a week later, and that's when he told me the disaster he was referring to, would start in the Salton Sea area in 2009. He said it would be triggered by previous seismic activity in Mexico that we had overlooked. At the time, I thought he had been working too hard, but after thinking over what he had said, I looked into the Mexico angle and I saw what he was referring to. I've been watching it since then and have a new Model prepared. "

"I don't know what a Model is. Would you mind explaining that to me?" Rowland asked.

"Well, an easy explanation would be, that we input all the data we have acquired over several months, in this case it was a year. The computer then correlates all the data and events through a special program and displays the results on the screen in a graphic mode. A sort of prediction can be accessed from the results of past events. If escalation is seen, then a picture of future activity can be predicated within the Model by what's come before, and what's currently seen."

"I'm afraid I still don't understand Doctor. I'm not into computers." Rowland said.

"Here, I'll show you." Dr. Leyland said. He slid his computer around on his desk and showed Rowland the screen. Rowland looked and still couldn't see what it represented. "I don't understand." He said.

"What you see is a Model I have completed and I'm in the final stages of preparing it to present to my colleagues at Caltech. I must say, what Vince told me threw a new light on the whole project. I believe we are in the first stages of what looks like an accelerated movement of the plates. I'm planning a trip to Los Angeles to show my results to my colleagues as soon as I complete the final touches. I've already printed out a specification spread sheet for them to read and compare to the Model."

"Plates? I don't understand, Doctor." Rowland said.

"What I'm saying is, Vince's story has some merit. In fact, I've come to realize it has significant merit. I know what he said was so unimaginable at the time that none of us could comprehend what he was saying. Therefore, everyone thought he had suffered brain trauma from his fall, and it was affecting his thinking."

"So, you're saying you believe Davis now, and this Model proves it?" Rowland asked.

"Not exactly, and not to the degree he said happened in 2009. But none the less it is beginning to appear that we may be moving in that direction." Leyland replied.

"The Chief would like to setup a meeting with you and Davis. If Davis calls you, will you assure him that Chief Brewer will listen to him and he won't be locked up?" Rowland asked.

"Yes, I will, Sergeant. Dr. Woitasczyk is looking for him also, he asked me to call him if I talked to Vince. Should I notify him also?" Dr. Leyland asked.

"Dr. Woitasczyk is in jail. He won't be calling you anymore." Rowland said.

"In jail? What did he do?" Leyland asked.

"He authorized covering up Davis's escape, and fought with the officers when they came to arrest him." Rowland replied.

"Why did he do that? He told me Vince was on a provisional release." Leyland said.

"He lied to you about Davis. We don't know why he did it, but he did and he's in jail." Rowland replied.

"I didn't care for him very much anyway. He was arrogant." Dr. Leyland said.

"Chief Brewer, doesn't want anyone besides the three of us to know, if Davis, contacts you. We have to be very careful and keep this under wraps. Davis is in grave danger. The Mayor has given orders to shoot him if he resists arrest. If he calls, tell him he needs to come in from hiding. We'll arrange a safe place for him where we can all talk this out, and the sooner, the better."

"I understand, Sergeant. If I hear from him, I'll let you know. I thought it was odd that, Jim and Miss Stevens, took a vacation at the same time. I can see now they're with, Vince."

"Jim? Who's he?" Rowland asked.

"The man in the photo with, Vince and Miss Stevens." Dr. Leyland replied.

The Continent Of St. Louis - The Search For Answers

"Oh yeah, that's right. Can you get me addresses and phone numbers for, Miss Stevens and Mr. Lewis." Rowland asked.

"Mr. Lewis, moved very recently, I may not have his address, but I can get, Miss Stevens, address and phone number for you."

"How do you think they made contact with, Davis? No one's seen him until he showed up in Vegas, at the Grand." Rowland said.

"I have no idea. As far as I know, Vince never called this office."

"It appears they are accompanying him voluntarily. I wish I knew how they got in touch with each other." Rowland said.

"I would guess it was done by email." Dr. Leyland replied.

"Do you have, Davis's, email address?" Rowland asked.

"No, I don't. I don't use email." Dr. Leyland replied.

Rowland knew it was no use asking him if he had, Miss Stevens or Lewis's, email addresses and went on. "Is there anything else you would like to add?"

"Only that, Vince and Jim, were more than co-workers, they're best friends."

"Thank you, Dr. Leyland. We can count on you then?" Rowland asked.

"Yes you can, Sergeant." Leyland replied.

"Here's my card and Chief Brewer's card." Rowland said. "Call us, if you hear from Davis, but don't leave any messages. If we're not in, keep calling till you get one of us. The Chief and I are the only two that can assure Davis's safety."

POLICE HEADQUARTERS...CHIEF BREWER'S OFFICE

EDWARDS AND HARPER ARRIVED back at headquarters and played the tape for Chief Brewer. After listening to the tape, he didn't eat their asses out like the Mayor had told him to do, instead, he complimented them on their work and told them to take a couple days off. For once, they had done a good job and had helped more than they knew, but he wasn't going to go overboard in his praise. He knew they were both smart asses, who acted very juvenile at times. He did chuckle under his breath when he thought of Norton standing there with his pants full of shit. He composed himself and listened to the tape again and looked at the photos on his desk and wondered to himself. *Where are you Davis?* He had a feeling Vince would be coming back to San Diego. He had no ties anywhere else except in St. Louis, but his parents hadn't heard from him. He thought it was unlikely, Vince would return to Missouri, but he had alerted the authorities and they were watching his parent's farm.

CHIEF BREWER'S OFFICE...LATER THAT DAY

Monitoring Vince's home phone had proved useless. There had been no calls to the Epperson's from Vince, and no new leads through his credit cards. He had not made any attempt to use the now frozen cards since he had left the Grand and had not tried to make any withdrawals from the minimal balance in his checking account. Chief Brewer was not worried that police from other cities might shoot Vince if they caught him. He was concerned that Vince would be shot if he returned to San Diego and was cornered and tried to run. Brewer had no choice but to issue the Mayor's order to shoot and kill, and had reluctantly done so. All San Diego Police Officers, now had Vince's photo, and were on the lookout for him. Brewer was at a dead end until Vince called, or he was shot or captured.

Rowland returned from UCSD with the personal information on Donna and Jim. Using their Social Security numbers, he checked their credit card activity and received credit reports on both. He entered Brewer's office with the information he had received, and laid it out on the Chief's desk.

"Lewis and Miss Stevens both bought one way airline tickets to Vegas. Lewis rented motel rooms near the Las Vegas Air Terminal and got a rental a car at the terminal the next day." Rowland said.

"The day, Davis sold his car?" Brewer asked.

"Yes, they're together all right." Rowland said. "Miss Stevens rented a motel suite in Victorville the next day. They stayed a few hours then checked out later the same night."

"Anything else?" Brewer asked.

"No, they must be paying cash, now." Rowland said.

"Did you check with the motel? Did they leave anything behind?" Brewer asked.

"It was too late." Rowland replied. "The rooms were cleaned and re-rented the next night."

"Okay, they were on Interstate 15 and had been going west." Brewer said. "They could have been headed for L.A. or San Diego. Check with the rental car company. Get the tag number and model of the car. See if Lewis is going to return it to Vegas or some other city."

"I've already done that, Chief. It's a 2005 Buick. It's brand new, it has a temporary tag in the window and it's a one way rental to L.A."

"L.A.! Has he turned it in yet?" Brewer asked.

"No, they're going to call when he does." Rowland replied.

"You better keep calling them. If we're not here when the call comes in anyone could take it." Brewer said.

"It won't make any difference if they do, Chief. I told Avis to ask for you or me, and call our cell phones, if we're not in. No one will connect Lewis to Davis anyway. No one knows yet."

"I know you're right, but I don't want to mess this up. We have to find him, and soon. I'm going home and rest for a few hours. Call me if you hear anything, and keep calling Avis." Brewer said.

LOS ANGELES

JIM, CHECKED INTO A seedy motel that required no identification. Donna, waited at the motel while, Vince and Jim, went looking for transportation. Vince, was certain they would tie Jim and Donna to him, if they started checking and was in a hurry to get rid of the rental car. They stopped at a used car lot, where Vince, bought a used car, for cash. He knew it would take several weeks for the DMV to get it recorded and onto their database. They then went back to the motel and spent the night. Jim, returned the rental car the next day and took a cab back to a strip mall, where, Vince and Donna met him and the three drove to another similar motel and checked in. Vince was taking no chances, since he had learned the San Diego Police had a standing order to shoot, if he resisted arrest. He planned to move from one seedy motel to another, on a daily basis, until he could make contact with, Dr. Leyland. He had sent Jim to the motel pay phone in an attempt to contact Dr. Leyland, and ask if arrangements could be made to meet with him in Los Angeles, before he presented his Model and analysis to, Sandra Beatty.

Donna was becoming progressively more nervous as time went by. The stories in the newspapers and on TV were disturbing. The fact that Vince was now a hunted man, with the possibility of gunfire being involved if he were caught, only heightened her worries. She, expressed her concerns and her doubt that she would be of any value or use in contacting, Sandra Beatty. She, had never met the woman and knew nothing about her and saw little reason to remain and decided it would be better for her to return to San Diego. Vince had reluctantly agreed to take her the airport, the next morning. Donna felt better, but at the same time felt like a deserter. She didn't understand her feelings and doubts about her decision to leave and now it haunted her mind. *Why am I so attracted to him.* She wondered. *I don't even know him other than for the last few days, but I can't deny the attraction I have for him. Is it from the dreams or just being this close to him?*

Vince, saw the look of concern that now clouded, Donna's face. He didn't want her to go, but knew he didn't have the right to ask her to stay. *She, has no way of knowing about the relationship we had in 2009.* He thought and realized it was dangerous for her and Jim to remain with him. *When Jim returns, I'm going to tell him to leave with Donna, tomorrow.*

Jim burst into the room catching Vince and Donna by surprise, catapulting them out of their thoughts and back to reality.

"Come on, Vince!" He said. "Dr. Leyland's on the phone. He wants to talk to you!"

"Me? What about?" Vince asked.

"It's a long story, Vince. Let him tell you."

Vince, went to the pay phone, picked the receiver and started talking to, Dr. Leyland.

"What's this all about?" Donna asked Jim.

"Dr. Leyland and the San Diego Police Chief believe, Vince." Jim said. "They want him to come back to San Diego. They have a safe place for him to stay until they can get other people to understand."

"How did that happen?" Donna asked suspiciously.

"The police showed Dr. Leyland a photo of the penny." Jim said.

"How did they get a photo of the penny? It's still in my purse." She replied.

"From the coin dealers shop. When Vince showed it to the coin dealer, a camera in his shop photographed it. The police have the photo. We can go back to San Diego!" Jim said excitedly.

"How do you know it's not a trap?" Donna asked, and was instantly back to her old self. The thought of Vince walking into a trap and being captured or shot re-instilled her resolve.

"Dr. Leyland wouldn't be in on something like that. He said he's been doing what Vince told him to do when, Vince was still in the hospital. He said Vince was right. The faults are becoming more unstable in Mexico. It's all in his new Model." Jim said.

"He can see the disaster coming?" Donna asked not quite believing what Jim was saying.

"He said he can see what might be the beginning of what Vince said happened. He's told the police that he believes what Vince is saying."

Donna was not convinced. It all seemed too easy. She, could understand how Dr. Leyland might believe Vince, but not the police. They had a shoot to kill order in place. *This sounds like a trap to me.* She thought and said. "I don't know, Jim. I don't think it will be safe to just take Dr. Leyland's word on it. The police may be using him."

"I never thought of that. Let's see what Vince has to say." Jim said.

Vince had concluded his talk with Dr. Leyland. He came back to the room and said. "Come on, we're getting out of here now!"

"What's wrong?" Donna asked. "Did Dr. Leyland say something wrong?"

"No, he said he wants me to come to San Diego and meet with him and the Chief of police. He said a sergeant came to see him and said the police department would provide me with a safe-house until they can straighten all of this out." Vince replied.

"Why do we have to leave then?" Jim asked.

"I'm not going to be lulled into a feeling of safety, Jim. We were on that phone long enough for the police to trace the call. Dr. Leyland seemed sincere, but the police might be using him to flush me out. They could have his phone tapped."

"My exact thought." Donna said. "I just told Jim that. I'm not flying back to San Diego tomorrow. I'm staying with you, Vince. Forgive me for doubting you."

"No, this works out better, Donna. I want you to take that flight in the morning." Vince said.

"Are you mad at me for how I behaved?" Donna asked.

"No, that's not it. I'm not mad at you at all. I want you to go and meet Dr. Leyland at the airport tomorrow. He's supposed to be alone. He said he's not going to tell the police I'm in town until he has me in his own, safe place."

"Don't you trust Dr. Leyland?" Donna asked.

"I trust him, but I don't trust the police. If they did tap his phone, I'm sure it would have been done without his knowledge. They could be using him thinking he would be the first person I would call."

"I never thought of that." Donna said.

"How did you get so savvy, Vince?" Jim asked.

"From a lot of bad experiences in 2009. I don't trust any type of government officials, the police included. Pack your bags, and let's get out of here." Vince replied.

"What do you want me to do tomorrow?" Donna asked.

"I told Dr. Leyland I was catching a flight to San Diego from Ontario in the morning, but you're going to be on that flight, not me. I'll tell you the rest on the way." Vince replied.

CHAPTER SEVENTEEN

POLICE DEPARTMENT...SAN DIEGO...MINUTES LATER

"WE GOT HIM!" A police officer exclaimed.

"Where is he?" Lt. Traxler asked.

"He was on a pay phone at a motel in South L.A." The officer replied.

"Get the L.A. Police over there. Tell them to shoot the bastard if he tries to get away. Fax them a copy of that order right now!" Traxler barked.

"Shouldn't we get the Chief in on this?" The officer asked.

"Screw the Chief!" Traxler retorted. "He pissed me off when he let Simmons go."

"He had to! The Mayor told him to do it!" The officer replied.

"Screw the Mayor too! Brewer shouldn't even be Chief!" Traxler snapped. "He never thought of tapping Leyland's phone, I did. When we get Davis, dead or alive, without the Chief's help, it won't be the Chief the Mayor will be patting on the back, it will be me. Call L.A. and do it now! Get the L.A. Sheriff's department in on it too."

"Yes, Sir." The officer replied.

Traxler left the office thinking. *There may be a promotion in this for me. Screw Brewer! Who knows, the Mayor might fire the bastard and make me Chief.*

LOS ANGELES...TEN MINUTES LATER

VINCE TOLD DONNA HIS plan, as they drove east on Interstate 10. "I'm dropping you off at a hotel close to the Ontario Airport. You can take the shuttle bus in the morning to catch your flight. Jim and I are driving to San Diego tonight. I'll be at Lindbergh Field in the morning when your flight arrives. If it's a trap, I'll be ready for it."

"Is Jim going in with you?" Donna asked.

"No, I can't risk it. If they have a photo of the penny then they have a photo of us in the coin shop or in the Grand. They could spot Jim, so I'm going to have him wait in the car. but who's going to recognize me in a crowd like that?" Vince asked. He now had a three-day growth of whiskers on his face.

Donna admitted even she wouldn't know him if they met and didn't know he had lightened his hair. He now looked more like a beach bum dressed the way he was. She approved of his plan, and for some unknown reason felt compelled to kiss him goodbye as she wished him good luck, then got out of the car, and carried her bag into the hotel.

THE SEEDY MOTEL...SOUTH LOS ANGELES

THE LOS ANGELES POLICE Department SWAT Team along with the Sheriff's Department arrived at the motel and set up a perimeter. The Sergeant in charge, went in the office and showed the clerk, Vince, Jim and Donna's photos. The clerk denied seeing any of them.

"One of them made a call from that pay phone outside, not a half hour ago." The Sergeant said.

"I told you, I haven't seen them." The clerk replied.

"Look, I'm not going to mess with you any longer! If you saw any of them, you better say so. Harboring a fugitive is a pretty serious rap!" The sergeant said.

"Okay, goddamnit! He made the phone call." The clerk said pointing to Jim.

"Is he staying at the motel?"

"Yeah, so is the blonde. But I haven't seen the other guy."

"What's their room numbers?"

"The blonde's in 108. The guy that made the call is in 110."

"What about him?" The Sergeant asked pointing to Vince.

"He wasn't with them." The clerk replied.

"Take a closer look!" The Sergeant demanded.

"I haven't seen him for Christ's sake! I told you that! You cops are all the same. Everyone's a goddamned criminal to the police department! You come in here throwing your weight around like I'm guilty of something. If he was here I would have told you, goddamnit!"

"It was just the two of them then?" The Sergeant asked. "No one else was with them? Don't lie to me you asshole!"

"There was another guy with them. He's in 112, but he isn't the guy in the photo."

"What did he look like?" The Sergeant asked.

"I can't remember. He didn't come in the office."

The Sergeant started to leave, then stopped, turned around and said. "You better not be screwing with me! I'm going to have a man watch you, if you pick up that phone, your ass is in jail."

"Wait!" The clerk pleaded. "Don't break down the doors! I'll get you the keys to the rooms."

"Screw the keys, asshole! We don't need them!" The Sergeant snarled, then went outside and ordered his men to break down the doors of the three rooms. They rushed into the rooms, guns ready, and found the rooms empty. He assembled his men back outside and ordered them to fan out and check any restaurants or other public places nearby. The Sergeant went back into the motel office, and asked to see their registration forms.

"We don't keep records, Sergeant." The clerk said. "If you've got the money, then you've got the room. Besides they all get to looking the same after a while. Who cares who they are, it's the money I look at."

"I've got to check all the rooms then." The Sergeant said. "I better not find any Hookers with Johns in their rooms. You'll all go to jail if I do!"

"Wait a minute Sergeant!" The clerk blurted out. "Who's going to pay for the doors you busted down? You aren't going to bust anymore down are you?"

"Tell me which ones have your regular Hookers in them and I'll just check the other rooms." The Sergeant replied.

"Damn, Sergeant! They all have Hookers in them. They rent a room for the night and do all the business they can. They're regulars. Don't bust down anymore doors, please." The clerk pleaded.

The Sergeant hesitated, and then said. "Okay, I'll give you a break if you tell me what kind of car the three were driving!"

"Hell I don't know! It was an old Junker." The clerk replied.

"You better pay more attention to who you rent rooms to in the future! This guy's an escaped lunatic with a shoot to kill order on him, and he was with the other two." The Sergeant said, showing the clerk Vince's picture again.

"I told you he wasn't with them." The clerk replied.

"Okay, I'm cutting you some slack this time. If you see any of them, call this number." The Sergeant said and handed the clerk his card. He went outside and yelled. "Pack it up, we missed them. I've got to call in and tell them they got away."

POLICE HEADQUARTERS...SAN DIEGO

LT. TRAXLER WAS NOT pleased when he learned Vince had eluded the L.A. Police. He was dressing down the officer, who had set up the raid. "If you hadn't been arguing with me about telling the Chief and called sooner, they would have gotten there and caught, Davis!"

"It isn't my fault! You shouldn't be doing this without telling the Chief." The officer said.

"Do you like your job, you pencil pushing, desk jockey? Traxler hissed.

"Yes, sir, I do." He replied.

"Well, you better stop arguing with me and do what I tell you or I'll have your ass out on the street, walking a beat! Do you get my meaning?" Traxler threatened

"Yes, I do, Lieutenant."

"All right, then. I'll get them at the airport in the morning. I don't want any of this to get out. I want to make the collar personally in the morning. Do you understand?"

"Yes, sir, I won't say a word without your approval." He replied.

"Good, make sure you don't!" Traxler said as he left, mumbling to himself, and thinking. *What a stupid bastard he is! I could have had Davis's* carcass on a morgue slab, if he had called when I told him to. I've got to do everything my goddamned self, if I want to get it done right. As he walked, the last thought left his mind and he smiled as another took its place. *I can't wait to see the look the Chief's going to have on his face tomorrow, when I get Davis single handedly. I'm going to be waiting beside the jet-way exit when Davis walks past. If he tries anything, I'll put a bullet in the side of his head.*

He studied the photo of Vince that was taken in the coin store. "You won't get away this time." He said aloud.

He left the station for home. He needed to get some sleep, although he didn't imagine he'd get much, with the biggest opportunity of his life, knocking on his door.

RETURNING TO SAN DIEGO

VINCE AND JIM CONTINUED on their way to San Diego on Interstate 15. The freeway was packed with cars, and all were exceeding the speed limit by at least fifteen miles an hour. They fell in with the traffic, two hours later they were passing by Miramar Air Base and exited south on 163.

"Take Interstate 8, to the 5, Jim. I want to avoid the downtown area. We can find a cheap motel on Morena, Boulevard."

Jim checked into a double, they ordered pizza and crashed for the night.

Vince got up at seven. He had tossed and turned all night, as dream after crazy dream, had woke him. He woke Jim up and sent him out to get breakfast. He went through the yellow pages and found a beach shop located just down the road. After eating, he sent Jim to the shop to purchase some beach attire, including a visor with open top, wanting his newly colored hair to show.

After donning his new attire, he looked at himself in the mirror and passed his own inspection. They left for the airport at ten. Donna's flight was scheduled to land at eleven thirty. Vince wanted plenty of spare time to check the terminal, before Donna arrived. If the police were setting up a trap, he'd be there to watch them.

There was no sign of the police as they blended in with the regular morning traffic arriving at the airport. They pulled into the airport parking lot across from the terminal and parked.

"I'll call you if things go wrong." Vince said. "Otherwise, leave the parking lot at eleven thirty five, and circle around the terminal exit until you see Donna and Dr. Leyland coming out. If you see them, you'll know everything is okay and you can go back to the motel and wait for my call."

LINDBERGH FIELD

VINCE WALKED INTO THE terminal knowing it would be impossible for him to get to the jet-way, without a boarding pass and I.D. He waited in a concession stand just ahead of the screening area, where anyone going in or deplaning, would have to pass. At eleven-twenty, he saw Dr. Leyland pass by, heading for the screening area. He was alone and Vince watched him as he showed his I.D. The agent waved him through and he continued up the stairs toward the gates. Vince was feeling better, but wondered how Dr. Leyland had gotten through security without a boarding pass. Dr. Leyland hadn't looked nervous, or showed any signs of anxiety, as he walked by and went through security. He nervously looked around for any signs of police activity and was caught off guard when his cell phone rang. Everyone was pulling their phones out, he put his to his ear and answered. It was Jim, who said.

"Dr. Leyland walked past me a few minutes ago, he was alone and went into the terminal. I don't think he saw me, did you see him come in?"

"Yes, I saw him. Did you see what kind of car he got out of?" Vince asked.

"No, he must have parked at the back of the lot." Jim replied.

"He just passed me and went through security. He's on his way to the gates. I'll call you back." Vince said.

The time was passing slowly. Vince was getting edgy from waiting and was rolling all kinds of scenarios around in his mind and looked at his watch. *It doesn't look like a trap.* He thought, wondering if he should wait or try to get through security as Dr. Leyland had, and try to get to the passenger concourse. He decided against trying to, and walked across

The Continent Of St. Louis - The Search For Answers

the hall to the men's restroom. As he entered the door, he bumped into a man who was hurriedly leaving. The man cursed as his paperwork fell to the floor.

"Get out of my way you goddamned bum!" The angry man shouted and bent down to retrieve the dropped items. Vince's jaw dropped open when he saw the man pick up a photo of him from the floor along with the other paperwork. The man was mumbling obscenities as he pulled his suit jacket open, put the paperwork in the inside pocket, pulled out his Police Badge and said. "Find someplace else to piss mister! The airport's closed! Get your stinking ass out of here!"

Without a word, Vince turned and started to walk back across the hall to the concession stand. He was met by a stream of patrons who were hurriedly leaving and heading for the terminal exit.

"What's going on?" He asked one of the patrons.

"I heard there's a bomb on a plane that's landing. I'm getting out of here!"

Damn! Vince thought. *I better get out of here too.*

A concession stand attendant was rolling down the gate as the last patron left. Vince looked back at the policeman who had told him to leave. He was now talking to two other men in suits. They looked his way and he felt his heart begin pounding in his ears. He nervously looked around and found he was standing there alone.

"Hey you!" The policeman yelled. "I told you to get your ass out of here! Now get going!"

Vince turned and headed for the exit, catching up with the crowd of others, going in the same direction. He pulled his cell phone out to call Jim. It rang in his shaking hand, catching him off guard.

The last thing I need is attention! He thought, as he quickened his pace. He saw Jim's number in the view screen and answered. "Yeah, Jim."

"Something's going on out here, Vince! There's four police cars parked in front of the terminal. Four cops in suits got out of each car and went into the terminal. Did you see them?" Jim asked.

"I bumped into one of them going in the restroom. I wouldn't have known he was a policemen otherwise. He had my picture and he's talking to two other cops right now. It's a trap, Jim and Dr. Leyland's in on it!"

"How do you know? I don't think he would knowingly, be doing something like that. It's not like him at all." Jim replied.

"You may be right, but I don't think so." Vince said.

"Why? Did he do something that made you suspicious?" Jim asked.

"When I saw him go by a few minutes ago, he breezed right through the screening area. They just waved him on through without any kind of metal tests or anything. I'm getting out of here. The place must be crawling with plain clothes cops."

"Be careful." Jim said. "The cops are watching all the entrances. It's eleven thirty, Donna's plane should be on the ground, I'm going to start circling in five minutes, I'll call you back."

As he walked, Vince noticed that there were no more passengers coming into the terminal.

They think I'm on the plane! He thought. *But Jim could be right. Dr. Leyland could be setting me up, without knowing he is. The police could have tapped his phone, but that would take a court order. It's not likely they could have gotten one, since Dr. Leyland's not suspected of anything. Maybe he thinks he's doing the right thing helping them catch me. With all the media, hype that's going on, he might have thought I'd be safer in the hands of the police. But then again, he may think I'm crazy. He may have been handing me a line of shit saying he believed me. Either way I've got to get out of here. I can't let them catch me.*

He now felt coming to the terminal had been a bad idea. He didn't like the way things were stacking up and he knew there was no way he could continue playing the waiting game. *Things are getting to dangerous.* He thought, as he merged into a line of disgruntled passengers coming from the passenger concourse. His phone rang again and he answered. "Yeah, Jim."

"Where are you?"

"I'm coming out." Vince replied.

"Stay put!" Jim said. "They've got the terminal approach closed off, I can't get back around. There's cop cars and camera crews from the TV stations everywhere."

"I can't stay in here, Jim. They're making everyone leave." Vince said, as he continued walking toward the exit. He looked ahead and saw a policeman outside the door with a picture in his hand, scanning the passengers as they exited.

The Continent Of St. Louis - The Search For Answers

"It's now, or never, Jim. I don't have any choice." He said and kept talking on his phone as he went out the door, passing the policeman, who didn't give him a second glance.

"Where are you, Jim?" Vince asked.

"On, Harbor Drive. I couldn't get back around to the parking lot."

"Go on back to the motel, I'll get a taxi. I'll see you there in a little while."

"What do you think went wrong?" Jim asked.

"I don't know. I'm going to hang around outside and try to find out. Donna should be off the plane by now. I'll call you later."

He walked to the center lane island and got in line for a taxi. He kept the phone up to his ear and kept talking as if someone was still listening. His turn came for a taxi and he motioned the party behind him to take the taxi and crossed to the parking lot side of the street, climbing the stairs to the upper deck and went out on the overhead walkway. He could see the traffic jam of police cars and television studio vans on the approach ramp. Traffic was backed up on Harbor Drive for as far as he could see. The entrance to the airport was sealed off as the last passenger left.

I walked right past them and they didn't even look twice at me. He thought and relaxed, as he looked down on the exit and waited.

INSIDE THE TERMINAL

GETTING CONTROL OF THE airport had been easy for Traxler. All he had to do was show his credentials and say the police department had gotten a tip saying a terrorist was on board Donna's flight and he had been sent as commander of the police task force of SWAT members. He then told them to hold Donna's flight at the gate until he was in position at the jet-way. Without hesitation, airport authorities cooperated fully, giving him complete control and followed his orders to close down the terminal.

Traxler then went to the gate, where his men waited, with a handcuffed, and protesting Dr. Leyland in custody. As the last waiting passenger was escorted out of the gate by airport authorities, Traxler said. "Get him out of sight. Take him back up the corridor and wait for me."

Traxler radioed airport officials, telling them he was in position and gave the go-ahead to begin unloading Donna's flight. He waited, gun in hand, with his back against the wall, on the side of the jet-way exit. As passengers from Donna's flight started filing out of the jet-way door, they barely noticed Traxler as he stood waiting. Donna didn't see Traxler, but sensed something was wrong the second she walked through the jet-way door and walked into the waiting area. It was empty except for the line of passengers that had got off the plane ahead of her, who were being quietly ushered out by airport security. She looked ahead and saw Dr. Leyland surrounded by police and noticed he was handcuffed. She moved over, walking on the outside of a cluster of passengers, passing Dr. Leyland without him seeing her, and kept walking without looking back. She went down the stairs, passed by the empty screening area and continued walking, till she reached the street outside. Vince saw her come out the door and immediately dialed her cell phone number. She answered and asked. "Where are you?"

"I'm on the upper level walkway outside of the parking garage. Get in line for a taxi, I'll come down and meet you."

Traxler became anxious as he scanned the faces of the last few male passengers as the exited the jet-way and hadn't seen Vince. As the line slowly trickled down and then came to a stop, he became alarmed. *Where are you, you son-of-a-bitch!* He wondered as he peered around the corner and looked down the jet-way ramp, which was now empty.

He had been so certain Vince would be on the flight, he hadn't asked the airline for an outbound passenger list, He was now regretting that decision, wondering what had went wrong, but he hadn't given up. He decided to board the plane and make sure Vince wasn't hiding somewhere inside. He cautiously went down the ramp holding his gun at his side, and entered the plane. He showed his badge and Vince's photo to the flight attendants, asking if they had seen him. None of them recognized the face in the photo. He then ordered the flight crew off the plane and called for backup, on his radio. Two officers arrived and he sent them to check the lavatories.

"Clear." Both men said, finding the lavatories empty.

"Goddamnit!" Traxler bellowed, as he stormed back up the jet-way ramp, and went directly to the officers who were holding Dr. Leyland. "Where is the son-of-a-bitch, Leyland?" Traxler barked.

"Who?" Dr. Leyland asked.

"Don't give me that line of shit! You know who I mean!" Traxler snapped.

"What's this all about?" Dr. Leyland asked. "Am I under arrest?"

"Where's Davis? You know goddamned well you were here to meet him!" Traxler hissed.

"You must be mistaken officer. I wasn't here to meet…"

"Shut your lying mouth, you bastard!" Traxler yelled cutting him off. "You know goddamned well you talked to Davis on the phone last night."

"Wasn't he on the plane, Lieutenant?" One of the policemen asked.

"Hell, no!" Traxler bellowed. "They've made a fool out of me. Take him downtown. He'll start talking before I'm through with him!"

TAXI WAITING AREA…OUTSIDE THE TERMINAL

VINCE AND DONNA HAD just gotten in their cab and watched as Dr. Leyland was led out of the terminal, in handcuffs, and placed in a police car. The police car sped past them as they exited the airport onto Harbor, Drive.

"That was close." Vince whispered to Donna.

"I just about died when I saw Dr. Leyland being held by the police. They had him in handcuffs, but he didn't see me go past him. Do you think he was in on it?" She asked.

"I don't think so, he was arguing with them when they put him in the police car. Did you call him and tell him what flight you were on?"

"Yes, I called him. I said I was a reservations clerk and told him that you would be arriving on the eleven-thirty flight."

"His phone was tapped. That's why they weren't looking for you, they thought I was alone. Good going, Donna."

AIRPORT ENTRANCE…HARBOR DRIVE.

KQTV WAS AMONG THE throng of TV crews that had assembled at the airport entrance, hoping to cover an unconfirmed report of a terrorist on board an incoming flight. No one knew where the rumor had started, but it had leaked out and spread through the news media community, like a wildfire. Police had stopped the clamoring, news crews as they arrived, denying them access to the passenger drop off or pickup area. Every station had gone live, as the rumor spread. The alleged seriousness of the threat was escalating by the minute, as the irresponsible reporters, fed fuel to the already out of control situation. TV stations were soon airing live comments from professional terrorist experts, who were giving their profound opinions and criticizing the police authorities for not warning citizens, before storming and closing the airport.

CHIEF BREWER'S OFFICE

SAN DIEGO'S FBI AGENT in charge, called Chief Brewer, asking why the FBI hadn't been informed and asked to assist in the capture of the terrorist. Brewer was dumbfounded and didn't know what to say, as he was redressed for handling the situation, without Federal support. "I don't know what you're talking about." He said.

"What in the hell's the matter with you? It's on all the TV stations! Turn your goddamned TV on! CNN has gone nationwide with the story! I'm getting calls from my boss in Washington and he wants some answers! You get me the answers, and you better damn well make it fast!" The agent barked.

"I'll get back to you." Brewer said, and hung up. His intercom buzzed and his secretary said. "The Mayor's on line two and he's pissed!"

"Tell him I'm not in." Brewer said.

"I can't! I've already told him you were on the phone. He's been waiting for you to hang up."

"Aw shit!" Brewer depressed line one and said. "Yes, your Honor. What can I do for you?"

"What the hell's going on at the airport, Brewer?"

"I don't know, your Honor." Brewer answered.

"You don't know!" What the hell do you mean, you don't know?" The Mayor screamed.

"The FBI just called me! I don't know what's going on down there." Brewer replied.

"Oh, the FBI's handling it then. Who have you got down there?" The Mayor asked.

"No one that I know of." Brewer replied.

"What do you mean, you don't know who's down there? I can see our squad cars and policemen on the goddamned TV screen, right now! How can they be there and you don't know a damned thing about it?" The Mayor yelled in his ear.

"I have no idea, your Honor." Brewer replied.

"No idea? The goddamned TV reporter said there's a terrorist on board an incoming flight. How in the hell can the TV stations know about it and you don't?" The Mayor yelled louder

"I don't know. I didn't send the squad cars to the airport, your Honor. No call has come through my office regarding a terrorist situation." Brewer replied.

"Then what the hell are San Diego Policemen doing there, if you don't know about it?" The Mayor screamed.

"I don't know, your Honor. I'll find out and get back to you." Brewer said.

"Get me some answers, and be damned quick about it! Do you understand, me?" The Mayor hissed in his ear.

"Yes, your Honor." Brewer said and hung up. He buzzed his secretary and said. "Get all the department heads in my office, right now!"

"Yes, sir. What's going on at the airport?" She asked.

"Just get them." Brewer said.

"Yes, sir."

AIRPORT ENTRANCE...HARBOR DRIVE

THE CONFUSION WORSENED AT the airport, as policemen waited for orders regarding the situation. Jean Simmons was interviewing Sergeant Jack Unroe, who was in charge of blocking the entrance.

"What's the situation, Sergeant?" She asked.

"I have no comment." Unroe replied.

"We've heard reports, that it's a hostage situation. Can you confirm that?" She asked.

"No, I cannot." Unroe replied.

"Who's in charge here?" Jean asked.

"Lt. Traxler. Please step back, you'll be informed as soon as the situation is under control." Unroe said, and then answered a call on his radio. Traxler was on the other end. "We're clear, let them through, Jack." Traxler said.

"That Simmons bitch is all over my ass again, looking for answers! Did you get, Davis?" Unroe asked.

"I've got a suspect in custody. Don't tell her a damn thing other than that, Jack! Let the traffic through! I'm leaving!" Traxler replied.

"Okay, let them through." Unroe said, motioning to the other policemen.

"Can you tell me now, Sergeant Unroe?" Jean asked. "Was that Traxler you talked to?"

"Yes, it was. Lt. Traxler said the terminal is clear. The suspect is in custody and is being taken to headquarters." Unroe replied.

"Who is the suspect, Sergeant? Is it a male or female? What are they being charged with?" Jean asked knowing she wouldn't get anything from Traxler.

"I have no further comment." Unroe said, and walked away.

"Wrap it up and step on it!" Jean barked to her cameraman.

"Why? We just got here!" The cameraman protested.

"Shut up and do what you're told! We're going downtown to headquarters. I want to beat the other crews there." Jean snarled.

CHAPTER EIGHTEEN

POLICE HEADQUARTERS...SAN DIEGO

THE PHONES AT POLICE Headquarters became jammed as the calls flooded in. The lobby was overflowing with reporters trying to get the story. Lt. Traxler had to fight his way through traffic with his red light and siren blaring, to gain access to the lower garage entry. The street in front of Police Headquarters became gridlocked as police officers attempted, without success to keep traffic moving. Traxler knew he was going to have to do some tall talking to explain away the mess he was in. He shoved Dr. Leyland through the doors, into the station and was met by Sgt. Rowland as he came in the door.

"The Chief wants you in his office right now, Traxler!" Rowland said.

"I've got to question this suspect." Traxler argued.

"I'll take custody of, Dr. Leyland." Rowland said. "The Chief's pissed and he wants you in his office now!"

Damn! Traxler thought, and said. "Tell the Chief you haven't seen me yet. I need a few minutes alone with Leyland and I'll be able to clear this whole mess up."

"It's too late for that, and I'm not covering for your ass!" Rowland replied.

"Look, Rowland! I don't want to pull rank on you, but I will if you force me to. Leyland is working with Davis and I can prove it. All I need is a few minutes with him and he'll spill his guts."

"Do you want to go on your own, or do you want me to arrest you?" Rowland asked. "The Chief said to get you to his office one way or the other. It's your choice."

"Listen to me! Davis is back in town and Leyland knows where he is. All I need is five minutes with Leyland and the Chief will be thanking me. The Chief doesn't know I'm here yet, so just give me five minutes, what do you say?" Traxler asked.

"The hell with you, is what I say! You're not getting me mixed up in this. The Chief is already pissed at me." Rowland said.

"I'll get you for this, Rowland! You'll be back out on the beat when I'm through with you and I'll be wiping my ass with your Sergeant's stripes." Traxler threatened.

"You're not giving me any choice, Traxler. Place Lt. Traxler under arrest." Rowland said to the officer with him.

"All right, goddamnit! I'm going!" Traxler retorted. "But you haven't heard the last from me, Rowland. I'll tend to your ass later."

"Go with him." Rowland said to the officer. "Don't let him out of your sight."

When Traxler and the officer got on the elevator, Rowland removed Dr. Leyland's handcuffs and said. "I apologize for Traxler's behavior. Come with me, Dr. Leyland."

Traxler walked into Chief Brewer's office, where the ranking members of the Police Department had gathered.

"Sit down, Traxler." Brewer said.

"I can explain everything, Chief." Traxler said as he sat down.

"Everything, Traxler?" Brewer fired back. "Like the calls from FBI Headquarters and Homeland Security? The President wants to know what the hell's going on in San Diego, Traxler! The Mayor's on my ass, and all of our telephone lines are jammed. I'd like to hear you explain all of that."

"Davis was supposed to be on the plane, Chief." Traxler said.

"Well, was he?" Brewer asked.

The Continent Of St. Louis - The Search For Answers

"No, but I arrested his boss at the airport. He was there waiting to meet Davis." Traxler said.

"If, Davis wasn't on the plane, why would his boss be there to meet him? That doesn't make any sense, Traxler." Brewer replied.

"They're in cahoots, Chief! Davis's boss is helping him and I know it." Traxler said and went on. "They must have cooked up this whole thing to divert attention so Davis could slip into town unnoticed. Davis must have taken a different flight."

"Do you think you're the Lone Ranger?" Brewer asked.

"No, I don't! But let me explain!" Traxler whined.

"You're damn right you're not!" Brewer barked back. "But you went out and stirred up all this shit, closed down the airport and started a nationwide terrorist scare, all on your own, like some damned TV cop, playing a hero!"

"It's not like that, Chief! I saw the chance to get Davis and acted on it, that's all." Traxler replied.

"You're suspended! Give me your badge and gun!" Brewer barked.

"Chief, wait! Let me explain! I've got Davis's boss downstairs. He was going help Davis and hide him." Traxler begged.

"Are referring to Dr. Leyland?" Brewer asked.

"Yes, he's, Davis's boss! I collared him at the airport." Traxler replied with an assured look on his face.

"I know he's Davis's boss! What made you think he was supposed to be meeting Davis at the airport and how do you know he was going to hide him?" Brewer fired back.

"I did what you should have done, Chief! I had Leyland's phone tapped!" Traxler spat back.

"On whose orders? It damn sure wasn't mine!" Brewer barked.

"Wait a minute, Chief! Give me a chance to explain!" Traxler said and went on. "Leyland got a call last night from airline reservations. They said Davis would be on the flight. You weren't here and Jennings authorized the tap." Traxler replied.

"Did Jennings get a court order?" Brewer asked.

"I didn't need one, I had probable cause. I tapped the calls to and from Leyland and he talked to Davis and agreed to meet him. That's all the evidence I needed!" Traxler replied defiantly.

"I suppose you set up that fiasco in L.A. last night, too." Brewer snarled.

"Davis was staying at the motel, Chief! He called Leyland from the pay phone outside the motel office." Traxler fired back.

"Oh, is that right?" Brewer retorted.

"I'm telling you the truth, Chief! Davis was there!" Traxler insisted.

"L.A. faxed us a bill for three replacement doors for the motel. Are you going to pay for them?" Brewer asked.

"No, Chief! We don't have to pay for the doors, Davis was there!" Traxler replied.

"Then, how come the motel manager couldn't identify, Davis?" Brewer asked.

"I don't know, he was probably lying! Davis was there and I know it!" Traxler insisted.

"That won't float, Traxler! Without a witness to identify Davis being there, you didn't have a damn thing! You didn't get a warrant to tap Leyland's phone and I know you didn't ask L.A. to get a warrant to search the motel. We're liable for the doors they broke down at the motel." Brewer said.

"I didn't need warrants! I had probable cause!" Traxler retorted.

"Probable cause my ass! You're going to face charges at a review hearing, Traxler! No one is going to take the fall for this, except you. You exceeded your authority by miles and got the Federal Government down on the San Diego Police Department and the Mayor." Brewer said.

"What about, Leyland? He's in on it! He talked to Davis and didn't report it! I didn't do anything wrong!" Traxler whined.

"Dr. Leyland's cooperating with the department, Traxler! We've already made a deal with him. What you've done is screw everything up! I'd be talking to Davis right now if it weren't for you and your stupidity. Give me your gun and badge, you're suspended without pay!" Brewer barked.

Traxler jumped up out of his chair and pulled his gun and pointed it at Brewer, and yelled. "This is bullshit, Chief! I was doing my job like you should have been doing yours! I would have captured Davis if he'd been on that plane. I'd be a hero now instead of being in here getting my ass ate out! Stand back, I'm leaving, and don't any of you try to stop me or I'll shoot your asses! I mean it, goddamnit! My career's over, I've got nothing to lose!"

Brewer moved back as Traxler's shaking hand attempted to pull the receiver back to cock his automatic, and accidentally hit the release button, causing the clip to fall out. Traxler looked on in disbelief as the clip fell, while everyone standing before him, stood paralyzed. A split second, later, the clip hit the floor and Brewer knocked the gun out of Traxler's hand, took him down to the floor, held him there and yelled. "Help me cuff the bastard!"

The other officers recovered their composure and assisted Brewer in cuffing and pulling Traxler up to his feet.

"Lock his ass up! Charge him with assault, with intent to kill." Brewer ordered. He pulled Traxler's badge and I.D. from his jacket pocket, and then said. "Get down to Traxler's office and find out who else besides Jennings was in on the wire tapping, then find Rowland and tell him to bring Dr. Leyland to my office."

As they led Traxler out of the office, he turned and said. "Screw you, Chief! You're nothing but a pussy for letting that bitch Simmons out of jail. She was down at the airport this morning sticking her nose in Police business again. If I had caught Davis, I'd be sitting in your chair, you'd be looking for a job and she'd be asking you why you got fired, you bastard!"

"Get him out of here." Brewer said, thinking to himself. *That's the best collar I've ever made. Damn, I need to piss!*

He went to the restroom, looked at himself in the mirror, straightened his uniform and said. "Not bad for an old man. Not bad at all."

He went back to his office, buzzed his secretary and said. "Get Forrester on the phone for me, I've got to over the charges against Traxler, with him."

"Are you all right, Chief?" His secretary asked.

"Never better!" Brewer replied, still thinking about his collar of, Traxler.

MORENA BOULEVARD MOTEL

VINCE AND DONNA ARRIVED at the motel and Vince gave the driver a sizable tip as the stepped out. The driver had seen Vince and

Donna, hug and eagerly kiss, in his mirror on the way to the motel and had assumed the two were heading to the motel for some sex. He winked at Vince and said. "Thanks for the tip, dude. I'd like to trade places with you." He was eyeing Donna at the time.

"Trading places with me might not be as good as you think." Vince answered and smiled.

"I'd take the chance." He replied. "The worst I've ever had was fabulous!"

They both laughed and the cab driver left.

"You both thought you were pretty amusing, didn't you?" Donna asked. She put her arm around him and said. "You don't need to answer that, big boy! I know men never grow up, when it comes to conquering a woman."

"We were just joking." Vince said defensively.

"He wasn't." She said "He thought I was a hooker! I wonder what he would say, if he knew the truth."

Jim was glued to the TV as they came in the room, and said. "Jesus! It's been all over the TV. The airport was shut down because they thought a terrorist was on Donna's plane."

"They led Dr. Leyland away in handcuffs." Vince said. "It wasn't a terrorist, it was me they were after. The police must have tapped Dr. Leyland's phone. They wouldn't have been there otherwise."

"He was in handcuffs?" Jim questioned. "Do you think that was that for your benefit, in case you saw them? Do you think he was in on it and they didn't want to give him away so they could use him again?"

"It wasn't an act, Jim." Donna said. "They had him cuffed when I walked off the plane. Dr. Leyland didn't see me, but I saw him."

"Hell, it's been on CNN! They've talked to terrorist experts and everything. They sure jump to conclusions." Jim said.

They kept watching the TV, discussing what they would do next, now that Dr. Leyland wouldn't be safe to contact.

"I can go in to the office in the morning and talk to him." Donna said. "Apparently they're not looking for me."

"That's probably the best idea, but we better move again. I don't want anyone who has seen any of us to be able to say we're staying at this motel."

"How about my place?" Donna asked. "We can stay there. We can go after it's dark. I have a garage you can put your car in."

"Can you drop me off at my place on the way?" Jim asked.

Vince didn't like the idea of breaking up the trio, he was uncertain what their next move would be and asked. "Do you think that's a good idea, Jim? We haven't figured out our next move yet."

"I wanted to work on your list tonight, Vince. I'd rather use my desktop for that. Besides, I can go back in to work tomorrow with Donna. I can talk to Dr. Leyland too."

Vince agreed. He couldn't come up with a better plan. With the decision made, they ordered Chinese delivered and sat back and watched the news. Jean Simmons came on live, in front of Police Headquarters.

"I have breaking news regarding the closing of the airport. I've learned that it was nothing more than a false rumor of a terrorist on board flight 287 that arrived at eleven thirty today."

"Damn! She didn't stay in jail long." Jim said, as Jean continued.

"It now appears that a renegade, San Diego Policeman, now identified as Lt. Ronald Traxler was responsible for the whole thing. Apparently, he thought Dr. Vince Davis, the escaped mental patient and fugitive, was on the flight. Lt. Traxler closed down the airport, and was planning to capture Dr. Davis, single handedly. With security being tightened more each day at airports and the seemingly, ever escalating fear being spread by our Federal Government in regard to terrorist attacks, Lt. Traxler was able to convince airport authorities to close the airport, while he waited by the jet-way for Dr. Davis, to exit the plane. We now know that Dr. Davis was not on the plane, nor had he purchased a ticket in Ontario where the flight originated. We have secured surveillance tape from the airport showing the event unfolding."

Just before the taped rolled a heckler in the crowd yelled. "Isn't Traxler the one that arrested your ass, Jean?"

The screen now displayed the airport security tape that showed Traxler standing beside the jet-way, gun in hand, as the passengers exited.

"That's a pretty good picture of you, Donna." Jim said pointing at the screen. The station went back live to Jean after showing some of the passengers leaving the plane.

"As you have just seen." Jean went on. "Vince Davis was not on board the plane and as yet, we have not learned why police thought he was. Chief Brewer has promised to hold a press conference on the Police Station steps, where he is expected to make a statement regarding the situation. I'll be here and I'll be back live when he does so. This is Jean Simmons reporting live." She smiled as she waited for the studio to take over, giving the heckler another opportunity to again, ridicule her.

"Hey Jean!" He yelled. "Did you get a jailhouse bitch when you were in locked in the slammer?"

"Who was that bastard?" She shouted at her cameraman, as the crowd broke into laughter and hooted additional catcalls, that were heard by the TV audience, along with the sullied comment, she had made.

"Shut up, Jean!" Her cameraman said, as the station went back to the studio anchors, who apologized for Jean's poor choice of words and then continued talking about the incident, showing tapes of Lt. Traxler at Vince's house when he had talked to Jean, but hadn't arrested her yet.

"The police officer you're now watching, is Lt. Ronald Traxler." The anchor said. "As you'll recall, he was the officer involved in the wrongful arrest of our roaming correspondent, Jean Simmons, who at this time is waiting for San Diego Police Chief, Wayne Brewer's statement, which we will air live, in its entirety."

The station displayed a photo of Brewer on the screen momentarily and then went back to the anchor as a Breaking News sign started flashing at the bottom of the screen.

"This is just in!" The anchor said, reading from a paper she held in her hand. "Our news director has just learned from informed sources, that Lt. Traxler has been placed under arrest and is being held in the city jail, awaiting arraignment on, as yet, unknown charges. The Police Department has not released any information, at this time, regarding what Lt. Traxler was charged with, or what the circumstances were that resulted in his arrest. KQTV will break that news as soon as more details are provided. We do know however, that Lt. Traxler has had an authority problem recently and in the past, as we all know." The camera shifted to a second anchor who continued.

"In other news, police are still seeking the mental patient who escaped from the mental facilities at Gifford and hi-jacked the Medi-vac."

A photo of Vince popped up in a window to the side of the anchor on the screen as the anchor said. "The man you see on your screen, is Dr. Vince Davis, the subject of an intense police search. As yet, he has not been captured, or seen. Local police have received no tips from the public, regarding his whereabouts and are still asking the public for assistance in his capture. Call the Police Tips Line number you now see on your screen if you have any information regarding, Dr. Davis's, whereabouts. KQTV has been asked to remind you, that the warrant for Dr. Davis capture has been modified and now includes the use of lethal force, should it become necessary. Police have also asked that we remind you again, not try to apprehend Dr. Davis on your own. He is described as being delusional, desperate and could possibly be armed and dangerous. In an update, informed sources close to the Police Department say Dr. Davis was last seen in Las Vegas, and was known to be traveling toward Los Angeles on the 15, in the company of two other persons, as yet unnamed."

The camera went back to the first anchor who continued.

"In related news, we have learned that a police raid was made at the Siesta Grande Motel in south Los Angeles, last night. The Los Angeles Police Department and the Los Angeles County Sheriff's Department, working in cooperation, made the raid. Although neither department would make any comment on the raid, our sister station, KQLA, interviewed the motel manager who verified the raid did take place and said the police were looking for Dr. Davis. The manager confirmed that police officers who arrived at the scene, used force, to break into three rooms at the motel, even though he had offered them the keys to the rooms. No one, however, was found in the three rooms and no arrest were made. We haven't learned yet if the raid was made in response to a tip from the public, or from police intelligence. The motel manager, who prefers to remain anonymous, said the police made the illegal raid without a warrant. He also said that he was threatened with arrest if he didn't cooperate. The angry manager, told reporters, the motel owner was planning to sue the City Of Los Angeles, if restitution for the damaged doors wasn't made."

A video rolled on the screen, showing the seedy motel, and then zooming in on the rooms with the broken doors. Two Hookers standing in the camera's view, made provocative movements with their bodies, displaying their wares and blowing kisses at the cameraman.

"Who authorized rolling that goddamned clip?" The studio manager yelled in the technician's ears as the station went back to the studio anchor.

"We're going back live to Jean Simmons, who is waiting at the police headquarters for San Diego Police Chief, Wayne Brewer's comment on the terrorist situation at Lindbergh Field. Are you there, Jean?"

"Thank you Pamela." Jean said and went on. "I am standing in front of San Diego Police Headquarters, where the Mayor, District Attorney, Police Commissioner and Police Chief, Wayne Brewer have assembled. Chief Brewer is about to speak."

Chief Brewer started off by introducing the F.B.I Agent in charge, for San Diego. He then introduced a Sub Director of Homeland Security who had flown in specifically for the news conference. He then turned the podium over to the Sub Director.

For what seemed like hours, the Sub Director rambled on about how the Federal Government was doing everything within its power to make the airports safe. He assured the TV audience as well as those attending the press conference, that the San Diego Airport was safe. He said there were no terrorist involved, placing the blame for the scare and resulting melee, directly on the shoulders of a rouge police officer, he referred to as, Baxter.

He then turned the mic over to the F.B.I. agent in charge, who now was lauding Chief Brewer for his single-handed work in restraining Baxter, and placing him in custody.

He gave up the mic to Brewer, who corrected the mispronunciation of Traxler's name and then went through the complete story of the events, also laying all the blame on Traxler and confirming him to be a known rogue, and at times, hot-head.

"Lt. Traxler has never been a team player and has shown signs of stress lately." Brewer said. "Of course, the department has been aware of the situation and we were watching Lt. Traxler closely, but we had no idea that he was that close to the edge. You may recall, that just recently, Lt. Traxler inappropriately arrested Jean Simmons of KQTV." He pointed to Jean and the cameras swung her way, as he went on. "Lt. Traxler's performance, and lack of professionalism in that situation, has been under review by internal affairs. At this time, I would personally like to extend my apology and that of the Police Department and the City of San Diego to Ms. Simmons for the misunderstanding in that matter."

As the assembled group clapped and cheered, Jean smiled for the camera and mouthed an unheard thank you to Chief Brewer, but thought. *I'll get even with you, you bastard!*

"I'd like to say a few words." The Mayor whispered to Brewer, who ignored him and went on. "Although we don't know the exact whereabouts of Dr. Davis, my office is working closely and covertly, with associates of Dr. Davis, to try and reach a peaceful resolution in the on-going case."

"What exactly do you mean?" Jean Simmons yelled, as the Mayor and others gathered were wondering, at the same time.

"Certain evidence has come to light that may possibly vindicate, Dr. Davis." Brewer replied.

"What evidence is that?" Jean asked.

"At this time, I'm only at liberty to say that, Dr. Davis, may have been held an unreasonably length of time, against his will, at Gifford." Brewer replied.

"He was crazy, wasn't he?" Jean yelled.

"Dr. Davis was never diagnosed as being insane, Ms. Simmons." Brewer replied.

"Why was he in Gifford, then?" Jean yelled.

"As part of this investigation, Dr. Davis's medical records were turned over to the Police Department for evaluation. In going over those records, our psychiatric department found that Dr. Davis had been committed to Gifford against his will. He had fallen accidentally in his own home, striking his head in the fall, and suffered a severe concussion. When he regained consciousness some days later, he was delusional and made some unfounded claims about a disaster that he insisted was going to take place sometime in the future. For his own good, he was committed involuntarily to Gifford, for evaluation only. His records indicated he improved remarkably in a very short time but he was not released. Instead, he was kept isolated from the other patients and was not allowed visitors. It appears that a staff member at Gifford, might have been using Dr. Davis as a guinea pig, and the subject of a Psychiatric Journal article, he was writing." Brewer said.

Sensing a juicy, character smearing story, Jean interrupted Chief Brewer, and asked. "Can you name this person, Chief?"

"I can only say that the person is now in police custody." Brewer replied.

A throng of questions erupted from the media. "Which one is it, Chief? Is it Woitasczyk?" Jean yelled over the throng. "It has to be, he's a psychiatrist!"

"I'm sorry, I have no further comments in that regard." Brewer replied knowing he had set the stage for sympathy toward Vince. The thought of Dr. Frankenstein crossed his mind. He couldn't help smiling and said. "I'm not saying we have a Dr. Frankenstein in our midst. What I am saying is Dr. Davis may not have received the best treatment while he was confined at Gifford." He hoped the media and the public would pick up on his suggestive comments.

"Is Dr. Woitasczyk a mad scientist?" Jean yelled.

Bingo! Brewer thought, and said. "I have no further comments on that subject, Jean."

He went on and announced that the order to shoot Vince was rescinded. He looked directly into the camera and said. "Dr. Davis, if you're watching, call San Diego Police Headquarters, and make arrangements to give yourself up. No harm will come to you and you will be placed under police protection for your own safety."

The media went wild and Jean screamed the loudest. "Is this an offer from the Mayor's office, Chief? Are the charges against Dr. Davis going to be dropped?"

"I'm sure, the Mayor's Office and the District Attorney's Office, will cooperate in any way." Brewer said. "I am going to ask the District Attorney to drop the charges against Dr. Davis in regard to the hijacking of the Medi-vac. Other than that, Dr. Davis has done nothing to violate the laws of the City of San Diego or the State of California. He is not a criminal, but rather I think, a victim of circumstances and misunderstanding. Thank you."

He then turned the mic over to the Mayor who praised Chief Brewer for the great job he did in handling Traxler, and said he would cooperate in any way that would help the city heal and help it get back on an even keel. The District Attorney had no comments and the group left the podium.

"Well you heard it!" Jean Simmons said. "The police and the city have taken a one eighty on Dr. Vince Davis. I for one would like to meet this man." She signed off and the station returned to the local anchors who continued to hash over the story.

"Hell of a speech, Chief." The Mayor said as they walked back inside. "But you should have consulted with me, before you put me in a position I can't back out of." He complained.

"That goes twice for me, Chief." Forrester said. "I can't just drop the charges. The Medi-vac company lawyers will have something to say about that."

"Do it." The Mayor said. "We can't piss backwards on this. You're up for re-election aren't you?" The Mayor asked.

"Yes, but goddamnit, Mayor! He stole the Medi-vac. That's a felony!" Forrester countered.

"Don't give your opponent anything to throw back in your face, Claude." The Mayor said to Forrester. "Show them you're a team player."

The Mayor turned to Chief Brewer and asked. "Team player, do you like the sound of that, Chief?"

"Yes, I do, your Honor." Brewer replied.

"Good! You keep me in the loop from now on! Are we clear?" The Mayor asked and went on without an answer from Brewer. "You did a good job out there today, Chief. The media ate it up and I'm sure it went out nationwide. It doesn't hurt to let other cities know we're doing our job here in San Diego and that we have a heart."

"Thanks." Brewer said.

"Now, what's this new evidence you were talking about?" The Mayor asked.

"I'll give you a written report tomorrow, sir. Right now, I need to get some sleep. I haven't slept good in days." Brewer said.

"Your Honor, Chief." The Mayor said.

"What?" Brewer asked.

"You called me sir a second ago. I like, your Honor better." The Mayor replied.

"Yes, your Honor." Brewer said.

The three laughed and parted company.

Brewer looked at his clock after they had left. It was nearing quitting time, and he was thinking of the conversation between he and Dr.

Leyland. earlier in the day. He had asked Dr. Leyland for a further explanation and Dr. Leyland had laid it all out to him in terms that anyone could have understood.

"I compared the difference between what I had previously calculated, and thought correct, and then compared those results with the Model I made using Vince's recommendations. The results convinced me that Vince wasn't making the story up." Dr. Leyland had told Brewer, and had went on saying. "Vince's story of the rapidly escalating events that brought the world to its knees and the near extinction of mankind, is entirely possible. There would be few survivors left, the world over."

"How could it happen that fast?" Brewer had asked.

"The timeframe in which Vince said it happened, while incredible, would still be possible if all of the Earth's faults began moving at one time, triggered by a cataclysmic, underground event, in the molten core. At this time, science doesn't have a way of knowing what's occurring in the depths of the Earth. We unfortunately learn of these events, only after events such as Vince says will happen, actually occurs."

Dr. Leyland's explanation had hit Brewer hard. He didn't doubt any of it anymore, although he knew he might be alone, in that belief. He knew others would not believe it and understood why they wouldn't, but it explained how Vince could fly the helicopter. Brewer had first heard that fact on Woitasczyk's tapes, and had not believed it. Woitasczyk had considered the claim to be a concoction, of Vince's disturbed mind, and had blown it all off as well, but it was true.

Brewer sat in his office after listening to the recording he had made of the conversation between he and Dr. Leyland. He looked at the at the photo of the penny, and thought. *How things can change.* With that thought, he had come to a completely new reality. *We move and we live, or we stay here and die. I'm going to retire! We need to get the hell out of here!*

He put the photo of the penny in his pocket, planning to show his wife the photo and have her listen to the recording, when he got home. Afterward, he was going to tell her he was retiring, suggest they sell their house, and move slightly west of St. Louis, which wouldn't be easy for his wife, she was a native Californian. Nevertheless, he would have to convince his wife to go along with him. His intercom buzzed breaking his thoughts. "What is it?" Brewer asked.

"Crypto just called. They've cracked the passwords on the discs." His secretary said.

"Did they say what's on them?" Brewer asked.

"Classified government information." She replied. "Captain Glazier wants to know what you want him to do with the discs."

"Call him back and tell him I'll be down to pick them up. Tell him I want the passwords too." Brewer replied.

"He said they should be turned over to the Fed's." She replied.

"Tell him I'll take care of that and I'll be there in five minutes." Brewer said, hanging up the phone, and thought. *Jesus Christ! Classified government shit!*

He got up to leave and remembered the report on the new evidence he had promised the Mayor. *If I tell him, he'll think I'm crazy. Screw him! He won't remember anyway.*

He picked the discs up from a reluctant, Glazier, went to his car and headed for home.

CHAPTER NINETEEN

MORENA BOULEVARD MOTEL...SAN DIEGO

VINCE HAD HEARD CHIEF Brewer's message, and his appeal to him. All three had sat watching and had listened without saying a word. Vince turned the TV off when it went back to the studio.

"What do you think, Vince?" Jim asked. "Do you believe him?"

"He sounded sincere." Donna said.

"It all sounds too easy." Vince replied. "One minute I'm a hunted fugitive and the next, everything's forgiven. I can't think of any reason for them to change their mind."

"They didn't mention Dr. Leyland, Vince." Donna said. "They took him to the police station. Maybe he's the reason for the change."

"Could be. If he's at the lab when you go in tomorrow, we'll find out." Vince answered. "Let's pack up and get out of this motel. It'll be dark in an hour."

The three finalized their plans for the following day as they drove to Jim's apartment to drop him off. Donna was going to cut her vacation short, go back to work to check on things, try to get Dr. Leyland alone and get his story. Jim was going to work further on the list of individuals, Vince had given him, before going back to work.

Although, Vince felt better after hearing the Chief's speech, he still felt uneasy and let Donna do the driving on the way to her house. She moved her car out of the garage and parked Vince's car inside. Vince had an odd feeling and thought as they went inside. *This is all new. This is not the life any of us would be leading if I hadn't woke back in this time frame.*

Donna saw the look on his face and asked. "What's wrong? Don't you feel comfortable here?"

"It's not that." He replied. "I just had an odd thought."

"What was it?" She asked.

"None of us would be doing what we're doing now if I hadn't woke up from the dream or experience or whatever you want to call it." He replied.

"Well we're here now, and I don't mind at all." She said.

"I know, it's not that I don't want to be here, I do. It's just the questions that I can't answer." He said.

"Like what?" She asked.

"The whole thing is bothering me. If I hadn't accepted the position with Dr. Leyland, I might still be in Missouri teaching or something, and I wouldn't have ever known anything about any of this." He said.

"You wouldn't have been happy doing that, would you?" She asked.

"Teaching? No, probably not." He replied. "But why did this happen to me?"

"What did your psychiatrist say? Did he have an explanation?" She asked.

"He said it was Mental Post-Forming." Vince said with a frown on his face.

"You said that before. What exactly is Mental Post-Forming?" She asked.

"A pile of shit, Dr. Woitasczyk came up with! He said it was an elevated case of turning ones daily life and job into something grandiose, then placing one's self in it as a hero or world saver. I can't remember if that what he said exactly, but it was something like that." Vince said.

"I don't know anything about Psychology. Do many people have the problem?" She asked.

"He said I was the first case ever diagnosed, but he told me a woman from the Midwest was making similar claims about a disaster and was being referred to him for treatment. I guess that stupid article he wrote on his great discovery was published." He replied.

"Is he the doctor, Chief Brewer, was talking about. The one that was arrested for helping you escape?" She asked.

"Yes, Woitasczyk's his name, but he didn't help me escape. He just covered it up." He replied.

"Why would he have done that?" She asked.

"I haven't figured that out yet." He replied.

"Do you think he might have believed you?" She asked.

"Oh, I doubt that. He had a reputation to uphold. Believing my story might have gotten him in the mental ward too." He replied.

They both laughed. Talking to Donna about his concerns had lightened him up. He hadn't shown the attraction or feelings he had for her until they kissed in the taxi earlier in the day and he hadn't explained the relationship they had in 2009. The timing hadn't been right and she hadn't experienced what he had. The closeness of her, and being alone together had brought it all back.

"Donna, I need to explain something else to you." He said.

"What is it?" She asked.

"Even though we both worked for UCSD, I had never met you. I don't think I even noticed you."

"Like I said, Vince! What's a girl have to do to get noticed." She said and laughed.

Vince smiled and he went on. "We went through some trying times together in 2009. We became close, very close, we were in love. We shared a room together and we were going to get married. I still love you, Donna. That hasn't changed."

Donna let out her breath in a loud whoosh, and said. "Damn Vince! I admit in my dreams we made love and I embarrassedly told Jim that, but you're right. I really don't know you either and I can't explain my dreams, it was weird. Even though we worked at the same place, I really just met you in person a few days ago. I admit, I was interested in you, but you never noticed me, not once, that's reality for me. I was in your office just before you went in the hospital and you didn't even look up from your laptop."

"I can't explain that any better than I can explain the rest." He replied.

"Didn't you find me attractive? Was I the only one you could find attractive in 2009?" She asked in an affronted voice.

"What about the kiss at the airport and in the cab?" Vince asked in a hurt voice.

"That was an act." She replied.

"An act? It didn't seem like an act to me!" He said.

She laughed, and then said. "I think we're having our first lovers' quarrel, Vince. Come here, of course I love you! Men are so silly. You should have seen the hurt look on your face."

Vince took her in his arms and kissed her. For the first time since waking up in August, he felt like he was where he belonged.

"I've only have one bed and one shower. We can both fit in them." She said.

Vince had an alarming thought as they walked to the bedroom, with their arms around each other. *If this is a dream, I hope I don't wake up till it's over. The hell with 2009!*

UCSD SEISMOLOGY CENTER...SAN DIEGO

DONNA WAS WALKING UP the sidewalk to the lab, when she saw a uniformed policeman come out of the entrance. She became suspicious, turned and walked back to her car She watched as the policeman got in a plain, undercover police car and drove out of the parking lot. She immediately called Vince's cell phone number and he answered.

"Vince, there was a policeman who came out of the lab entrance when I was walking up the sidewalk. I don't think he saw me and I haven't gone in yet."

"A policeman was here too. He rang the doorbell right after you left. I didn't answer the door. He was a Sergeant in an undercover car."

"So was the one here." She said.

"What did he look like?" Vince asked.

Donna described the policeman she had seen, and Vince said. "He's the same one, Donna. How did he get there before you?"

"I stopped off at the market on the way here. He could have gotten here before me if he left there and came straight here." She said.

"Right after the policeman left, Chief Brewer left a message on your phone. He wants to talk to you about me. They've tied you to me, Donna." Vince said

"What should I do?" She asked.

"I'll call, Jim and see if they've tied him in as well. I'll call you right back."

Anxious moments passed while she waited and kept watching for the policeman. Her phone rang and she answered. "Yes, Vince."

"Jim said no one's been at his place or called. He was coming over with the information I asked him to get." He said.

"Do you think that's a good idea?" She asked.

"No, I told him not to go out. He's sending me an email with the information. Why don't you call, Dr. Leyland from your car, and see what he has to say." Vince said.

"Okay, I'll call you back." Dr. Leyland answered his phone and Donna identified herself.

"Hello, Miss Stevens. Are you back in town?" He asked.

"No. I'm still in Vegas." She lied. "I was just checking to see if you were having any problems with the new software."

"I'm glad you called. Everything is running smoothly here, but there was a Police Sergeant named Rowland, who came by looking for you. He wants to see if you can help the police get Vince to come out of hiding."

"Why was he looking for me? What makes the police think I know where Vince is?" She asked.

"They know you were with Vince in Las Vegas. They showed me a photo of both of you at the Grand. They're sure you know where Vince is." Dr. Leyland said.

"Are they going to arrest him?" Donna asked.

"No. They want to place him in protective custody. Do you know where he is?" Dr. Leyland asked.

"No." She lied again.

"Did you see the media broadcast from Police Headquarters yesterday?" Dr. Leyland asked.

"No, I didn't. What was it about?" Donna lied and asked.

"Chief Brewer is dropping the charges against, Vince. If you know, where he is, you better tell him to give himself up. He won't be totally safe until all the police agencies they sent the APB's to, take him off their watch lists. The sergeant said, Vince won't come off the list as fast as he was put on, so it will remain dangerous for him out there." Dr. Leyland said.

"You mean someone might still shoot him?" Donna asked.

"I'm afraid so. May I have Sgt. Rowland call you?" Dr. Leyland asked.

"Why don't I call him. Do you have his number?" Donna wrote the number down, thanked Dr. Leyland, and was about to hang up.

"Wait, Miss Stevens." Dr. Leyland said. "If you see Vince, tell him I really need him here to help me before I go to Los Angeles to present my Model. I also want him to go with me if he will. He would be better than me, explaining how and when the results I have now, will escalate. He's a better seismologist than I am and he's nothing short of brilliant. I want him to take over the project and I'll go with him and introduce him to Sandra Beatty. I can't do this without him."

"I'll tell him what you said." Donna replied.

"Tell him this also. Chief Brewer is going assign Sgt. Rowland to Vince as his personal bodyguard. He will take us to Los Angeles when we're ready. They have a safe house ready that Vince can stay in and they'll change his identity if he wants them to. He'll be driven anywhere he needs to go and always under police protection. Please talk to him, tell him it's safe. He knows I wouldn't lie about a thing like this." Dr. Leyland said.

"Vince doesn't know who he can trust. Especially the police." Donna said.

"Maybe this will help him decide. Tell him his bank accounts and credit cards are no longer frozen. The police are no longer trying to track him through his accounts. They want him to trust them and come in on his own. They want his help as much as I do. If what he says comes true in 2009, the police want as much advance knowledge as possible to make preparations." Dr. Leyland said.

"I'll tell him when I talk to him, but I can't promise you when that will be." Donna lied, thinking Dr. Leyland's phone might still be tapped.

"One last thing, Miss Stevens. Tell Vince I saw you get off the plane at the airport yesterday. I didn't tell the police and they still don't know you were on the flight. I had no idea Lt. Traxler had tapped my phone illegally. He was looking for Vince, not you. Please call the Sergeant and he'll explain everything, as I have."

"Thank you, Doctor, I will." She hung up and called Vince. She explained what Dr. Leyland had said, including seeing her get off the plane, and not telling the police.

"I'm sure you can trust him, Vince. You know him, he would never ask for someone's help, but he said he needs your help. He said he can't do it without you."

"He said that?" Vince asked.

"Yes, and he also said you're brilliant. He said you're the best seismologist there is, even better than himself. He said he would never have thought of checking into what you told him." She said.

"What?" Vince asked. "I can't believe he would say that."

"Don't start getting a big head now." Donna said and laughed. "You're the best and you know it."

"I never thought I was, but it's unusual for him to say something like that and I'm flattered."

"He needs your help and I believe him." She said.

"I think you're right, Donna. He was asking for my help the night he called, before I fell and hit my head."

"Another thing, Vince. He said you're bank accounts are no longer frozen and you're still on the payroll. I think you should go back to work and earn your pay."

"This all sounds good, Donna. In fact, it sounds almost too good to be true, so I'm not letting down my guard yet. I'll be at the Seven-Eleven down the street from your place, I want you to meet me there. I'll call the police and tell them to pick me up at the AM/PM down the street from Seven-Eleven. We can watch them from a safe distance and see if their telling the truth. I'll call, Jim and tell him what you told me, and where we'll be."

"Okay, I'll see you there, be careful!" Donna said an hung up.

SEVEN/ELEVEN...CLAREMONT MESA BOULEVARD

Donna saw Vince standing outside the Seven-Eleven when she drove up. Vince got in, and said. "Jim will be here in a few minutes. I've already called the policeman, he should be showing up before long."

As they waited, Jim drove up, got in the car with them, and asked. "Have you seen him yet?"

"A policeman just pulled into the AM/PM, in an undercover car, it must be him." Vince replied.

"It's him." Donna said as she watched the policeman get out of his car and look around.

"He's the same one that came to your house." Vince said.

"Who is he?" Jim asked.

"Sergeant Rowland." Donna answered.

They sat and watched, looking for other patrol cars trying to spring a trap. As the minutes rolled by, Sergeant Rowland looked at his watch and then looked around. Seeing no one, he got back in his car and started buckling his seat belt.

"Pull up alongside him, before he leaves, Donna." Vince said.

Sergeant Rowland had just started moving as they pulled up beside his car. Vince called to him and asked. "Are you Sergeant Rowland?"

"Yes, who are you?" He asked.

"Vince Davis."

"Davis?" Rowland questioned. He held up Vince's picture and looked at the man sitting in the next car, with his blonde hair sticking out of his visor and a week's growth of whiskers on his face, and asked. "Is this a joke?"

"No, Sergeant, it's not a joke. I'm, Davis. If you want to talk to me, you're going to have to go with us. Get in our car, we're going for a ride."

Sergeant Rowland saw Donna behind the wheel. "Miss Stevens?" He asked.

"Yes, Sergeant, get in." She said.

Vince got out and said "Get up front with Donna, Jim."

Jim moved to the front seat as Vince and Sgt. Rowland got in the back.

"Where are we going?" Donna asked.

"Balboa park. Keep your eyes open in case someone is following us." Vince replied.

"No one will be following us, Dr. Davis." Rowland said.

"I want to make sure." Vince replied. "Call me, Vince, Sergeant."

"Okay, Vince. I'm David." He stuck out his hand, shook with Vince, and went on. "I'm not worried anymore, thinking someone would recognize you. Hell, you could walk right past the police station, and they'd think you were just another beach bum."

263

Jim kept looking behind them, and down each side street, they passed. They saw one patrol car going in the opposite direction. The officer didn't even look at them. Ten minutes later, they arrived in Balboa Park and all four got out. It was a balmy day with a breeze coming in from the ocean.

"Here's the deal." Rowland said. "Chief Brewer wants you to go back to work at the lab. We know you can't go back to your house, not yet anyway. The department has safe houses for trial witnesses. You can stay in one until the crime scene department releases your house."

"You mean I could come and go as I please." Vince asked.

"Not at first. Chief Brewer wants me to stay with you a few days. At least until we're sure no police agencies are looking for you, anymore." Rowland replied.

"He can stay with me." Donna said. "You didn't recognize him, neither will anyone else."

"You're probably right about that." Rowland replied. "Okay take me back to my car. I'll radio the Chief and see if he'll go along with that. He has no idea that you've changed your appearance."

"I've got a better idea." Vince said. "We'll take you back to your car and follow you to the station and see if the Chief or anyone else recognizes me."

"That's a good idea, Davis. He wants to talk to you anyway." Rowland said.

POLICE HEADQUARTERS...SAN DIEGO

THE GROUP WALKED INTO Police Headquarters with Rowland in the lead. Rowland cleared the three with security and they continued on to Chief Brewer's office. Donna and Jim waited in the outer office, as Rowland took Vince in to see Brewer.

"What are you doing here?" Brewer asked Rowland. "I thought you were going to meet with Davis. Who is this guy?"

"Chief, I'd like you to meet, Dr. Vince Davis." Rowland said.

"Davis? Are you kidding? That isn't Davis." Brewer replied. "Someone's pulling your leg Rowland."

Brewer held up Vince's photo. "That's Davis!" He said pointing to the photo. "What are you trying to pull, mister?" He asked Vince.

"It's him, Chief." Rowland said. "His friends are outside. I just came from the meeting with him. I told him you had a safe house for him, but he wants to stay at Miss Steven's house."

Brewer looked closer at Vince, and said. "He doesn't look like Davis to me. Are you sure Rowland? He looks like a beach bum to me."

"I know, Chief." Rowland said. "That's the beauty of it. No one will recognize him. He showed me his California driver's license, his pilot's license and ATM card. It's him, Chief. There isn't any doubt."

"Are you sure, Rowland?" Brewer asked, still in doubt.

"I'm positive, Chief. He's told me things that only Davis could know."

"Like what?" Brewer asked.

"He knows Dr. Leyland's working on a Model and needs his help."

"Anything else?" Brewer asked.

"He's got the penny." Rowland said.

"No shit!" Brewer said, getting out of his chair. "Let me see it."

Vince laid the plastic bag on Brewer's desk. Brewer picked it up and examined the coin through the clear plastic, and said. "Goddamn! It is you! Well I'll be go to hell! You could walk through a police line and not be stopped."

"I have." Vince said.

"When? Where?" Brewer asked.

"At the airport, yesterday." Vince replied.

"The hell you say! Were you on the plane?" Brewer asked.

Vince explained the whole story to Brewer, including his whereabouts since his escape, and the events leading up to the present.

"I'm impressed, Davis." Brewer said. "You must have had some anxious moments along the way."

"I'm not fully relaxed yet." Vince said and asked. "Can I go now?"

"Well, yes, you're not going to held against your will, but I want to make sure you're safe. Are you sure about staying with your lady friend?" Brewer asked.

"There's no place I'd rather be." Vince replied.

"Okay, that's settled. What about the penny? Do you want me to lock it up?" Brewer asked.

J. L. Reynolds

"Not for now, I'm going to need it." Vince said and explained about the rest of the people he needed to contact who had played major roles in the events of 2009.

"I can help you with some of them, Dr. Davis." Brewer said.

"He'd rather you'd call him, Vince, Chief." Rowland said.

"Okay, Vince it is. I can probably find the ones in the military for you. I can get Washington in on this."

"I may need your help in the end, Chief. But I still want to go this alone for a while. The less we involve Federal people the better off I'll be." Vince said.

"Okay, but if you need any assistance, just call me." Brewer handed Vince his office card, the plastic bag with the penny, and said. "Rowland, get Davis's things we took in the search of his home."

"I'm on it, Chief." Rowland said.

"When you get some time I'd like to hear your complete story in person, Vince. I'd like for you to have dinner with my wife and I, at our house. I want her to hear it from you first hand." Brewer said.

"Anytime, Chief." Vince replied. "It'll be good to tell the story without being locked up in a mental ward."

"Thanks, Vince." Brewer said and shook his hand. "I'll call you at the lab with the arrangements."

"What are you going to do with Woitasczyk?" Vince asked.

"The shrink? He's only facing assault charges since we found out he didn't help you escape. But he's lost his license and position with the hospital for not reporting it." Brewer said.

"Can I convince you to drop the charges against him." Vince asked.

"Why? He resisted arrest and fought with the officers." Brewer said.

"Did he hurt them?" Vince asked.

"Him? No way! Do you feel sorry for him?" Brewer asked.

"I look at it this way." Vince replied. "He, of course didn't believe me, no one did. He came up with a new theory regarding what he thought my psychosis was. He wrote an article describing my condition, and the procedure he was taking to treat me. The article is coming out in a Psychiatric Journal soon, if not already. I'd like to talk to him and see what he has to say now."

"One of his associates told me about that article. I called the journal, they're not printing it. Are you sure you want to talk to him?" Brewer asked.

"I guess you could say it's ironic, but yes, I do. He said I had some kind of Mental Post-Forming, which I don't have. I escaped on my own and he's lost his license and position for covering it up, as well as being arrested for doing it. I'm not crazy and I've proved that, but I'd really like to talk to him, if only to see what his position is now, regarding his diagnosis of me and I'd prefer it not to be in jail." Vince said.

"The Mayor wants his ass hung out to dry, but I'll talk to the D.A. for you. That's all I can promise you now." Brewer replied.

"That's good enough." Vince said.

They shook hands again and walked out to the outer office and Vince introduced Chief Brewer to, Jim and Donna. Rowland was waiting with them and handed Vince the evidence bag with his things in it and they left.

"We would have never found him." Rowland said as the elevator door closed.

"No, we wouldn't have. Good job, David." Brewer replied and suddenly remembered the discs he'd forgotten at home, in his rush to get back to the station.

"Goddamnit! Go after them!" Brewer blurted out to Rowland.

Rowland jumped like he was shot, when Brewer suddenly barked out his order. He was holding his chest, and wheezing. "Jesus Christ! You scared the shit out of me! You damn near gave me a heart attack! What the hell's wrong?" He asked.

"I forgot to tell, Davis something." Brewer said, and started laughing when he saw the distress in Rowland's eyes.

"That isn't funny, Chief!" Rowland complained.

"Go after them." Brewer said.

"Shit! I'll have a heart attack if I do! My heart's beating a mile a minute. Can't you just call him when he gets home? Miss Stevens' number is on your desk with his file." Rowland said.

"You're a good man, Rowland." Brewer said as he shook his hand and started sniffing the air.

Rowland looked at him and asked. "What the hell are you sniffing for?"

"I just wanted to see if you had shit your pants like Norton did!" Brewer replied and started laughing again.

"Harper and Edwards are assholes, Chief, but they're right!" Rowland blurted out.

"What do mean?" Brewer asked.

"You can be a prick sometimes!" Rowland replied, and started to leave.

"Hey wait a minute! They said that, did they? They said I was a prick?" Brewer asked.

Rowland was about to answer when the Chief's secretary stuck her head out the door and said. "Chief, your wife called and said to get your ass home!"

"Bye, Chief!" Rowland said. "The master calls."

"Hey wait a minute, I'm not through with you, Rowland!" Brewer said.

"She said now, Chief!" His secretary yelled.

"Aw shit! Get out of here, Rowland!" Brewer said, and went back in his office, got Donna's phone number and headed home.

CHAPTER TWENTY

RETURN TO THE UCSD SIESMOLOGY CENTER

VINCE FELT ODD WALKING back into the lab. Donna and Jim had cut their vacations short and the three had walked in the office together.

Dr. Leyland had a hard time adjusting to Vince's new look and attire, but soon forgot it, as he and Vince got down to business. Vince made a graph and time line of the future events as they had unfolded. He knew similar things must have happened around the globe, but he had never known that for sure. He knew what started it all, and that fact was what mattered most. The graph was a 35-day chronicle that escalated rapidly from August, 18th, 2009, or day one.

"That's really bizarre." Dr. Leyland said. "That's exactly four years to the hour from the Salton Sea activity last month."

"To the minute." Vince corrected him.

The two incorporated Vince's graph into Dr. Leyland's Model and were going over the changes it presented.

"Do you think it will take four years to become unstable this time?" Dr. Leyland asked.

It was an odd question coming from his mentor and the genius of his field. Vince felt somewhat strange, considering the fact that Dr. Leyland was his boss and was now asking for his subordinates' conclusions. The question asked for a hypothetical answer. Vince thought for minute then answered.

"Nothing has been the same for me this time, Doctor. Nor has it for you or the others. Everyone I've come in contact with is leading a different life than they did the first time in 2005. I've met people this time, I would have never met, and things have happened to those people this time, that didn't the first time." He thought of the Epperson's and then finished his answer. "I suppose things could escalate sooner, but I doubt it. We should have four years to prepare this time."

"For me there wasn't a first time, Vince." Dr. Leyland said. "This is the only time that I know of. The only thing that is clear to me is I wouldn't have done some of things that I have. I've changed my direction after talking to you, and reached some conclusions I wouldn't have, if it had not been for you. The things you have pointed out makes perfect sense now. I wouldn't have even thought of them without your suggestions. I'd like to turn the whole project over to you. I'm not getting any younger and I need some rest. The last few days have been very exhausting for me. Will you take over the project and present it to Sandra Beatty?"

"Not without you. I'll go with you, but you're still in charge. It didn't go down that way the first time and I wasn't even involved then. You did it on your own." Vince replied.

"I know you've told me that and knowing that, only confirms what I feared could happen. I don't think I could subject myself to the ridicule and disbelief you said happened to me in your first experience. Knowing ahead of time makes it that much harder for me to go through with it." Dr. Leyland said.

"That's just it, Doctor." Vince said. "Nothing has gone the same way as the first time. This may not either."

"But we don't know for sure, do we?" Dr. Leyland asked.

"No, sir, we don't."

"I'd still like for you to take over the project, but not entirely for the reason I said. For some time now, I've been tinkering around with some ideas for new equipment, just as you said I did, and they are satellite based, also just as you said they were. I drew the schematic up a while back and I just received an order of ten motherboards for the receiving units, as well two boards for the satellite transmitter. That's another reason why I couldn't deny what you were saying. No one knew that

I have a Doctorate in Electrical Engineering, but you knew I did, you also knew I developed the new equipment, and no one knows I'm doing that either. This is all mind-boggling and that's why I'd like you to be in charge. I hadn't thought of it before, but now I'm thinking of retiring from Seismology and spend all my time on the new equipment. You said yourself that you took over after I retired."

"I know I did, but I didn't see it coming." Vince replied. "No one did, except you, and I didn't know that either."

"If you hadn't explained what you know to me, I still would have made that mistake. You're on top of this, not me, won't you please reconsider?" Dr. Leyland asked.

"Not at this juncture." Vince replied. "We have to let this all play out as if I didn't know, even though I do. You didn't retire the first time until your theory and predictions were rejected. You have to wait it out and you'll have to present your findings to Sandra Beatty, but I'll go with you. All three of us will."

"Do you mean that?" Dr. Leyland asked.

"Yes, we'll all go with you." Vince said. "What do you say? Deal or no deal?"

"It's a deal." Dr. Leyland said.

"How long will it take you to get your equipment up and running?" Vince asked.

"It won't be soon. I have the motherboards, but I'm still waiting on the new cases to house them. The manufacturer said it will be another ninety days."

"Okay, I'll make another deal with you. We'll work on the Model and paperwork until you get the equipment ready."

They shook hands and Dr. Leyland excused himself, to take a nap in his office.

DONNA'S HOUSE

"I'M WORRIED." VINCE SAID to Donna and Jim, later that evening.

"About what?" Donna asked.

"Dr. Leyland." Vince replied. "He looks older and more feeble than he did the first time."

"The first time?" Jim queried.

"You know what I mean." Vince said. "The first time I was in 2005, he seemed younger and more enthused. This time he seems like he's ready to give up and he didn't look at all well today. He looked more like when you found him at Scott Air Force Base, Jim."

Jim had heard the story more than once, but every time Vince said something about him personally being in 2009, it didn't compute. It was still unimaginable for him to think that way. It was all right for him to think Vince, had been there, he had a penny to prove it. His involvement to his knowledge had only been a few odd dreams and for the most part, he had forgotten them.

"Jim, are you listening?" Vince asked.

"Yeah, what? Oh, the first time, yeah, okay." He said.

"Do you think Dr. Leyland needs to see a physician, Vince?" Donna asked.

"I doubt that would help. Taking some time off would probably be better. We have to make sure he doesn't get depressed and give up on his work. He played a big a role in what happened in 2009. Without him, the new equipment will never come to be and we need it much sooner than it was put on line, the first time. We need it to show the world that neither he, nor we, are crackpots."

"Why don't you put off showing Sandra what you've come up with?" Donna asked. "Why don't you let Dr. Leyland work on his equipment and get the transmitter and receiver completed? You said we don't have to worry about the big one until 2009. I think you should present the new equipment to Caltech first. Maybe they could get the government to get behind production and get a satellite up before we tell the world anything about the disaster. We would have better proof if the equipment works as good as you said it did. We have a lot of time to get ready, Vince. Why not wait?"

"You're right. I'm rushing things." Vince replied. "I already know Dr. Leyland's theory will be rejected and what the results will be in 2009 using the equipment we have now. If we wait until we can provide a clearer picture like Dr. Leyland's new equipment will furnish, I don't see how they could reject his theory then."

"It's your theory now, Vince." Donna said. "You're the boss, you heard what Dr. Leyland said and I don't think he's up to it, do you?"

"He didn't look like it today." Jim said before Vince could answer. "He was ready to quit. Without his equipment we may as well throw in our cards."

"Don't go off the deep end, Jim." Vince replied. "That all depends on how much time it will take Dr. Leyland to complete his equipment."

"How much time do we have?" Jim asked.

"All we need." Vince replied. "Our best bet will be to wait and help Dr. Leyland in any way we can. If we can convince Sandra and Caltech with the new equipment, it won't end up in the hands of Lemming and Clemmons to bungle. We have to hope the present administration will do a better job."

"That's not going to be easy." Jim said. "You know who we have running this country."

"I know, Jim. The damn war in Iraq is all they're concerned with. But all of that will become secondary, once we can prove what's going to happen."

"How can you be sure Sandra and Caltech will go along with any of this?" Jim asked.

"I'm not sure of anything, Jim. We'll just have to do our best to get the equipment ready and hope it will convince them. All Dr. Leyland had was a Model and a theory the first time. If the equipment works as good as it did in 2009, we shouldn't have any problem convincing them."

"I hope you're right, but if they're not convinced, what do you plan on doing?"

"We'll cross that bridge when we come to it, Jim. The United States isn't the only country that would be interested in Dr. Leyland's equipment. No matter what though, I still have to try and contact, Max. He may hold the key to the White House."

"Max, who is he?" Jim asked.

"General Maxwell Morgan." Vince replied. "He was Chief of Staff in 2009 and he was the General who was in charge of the meeting at Area 51 when we went there."

Jim was caught off guard again. Vince's references to 2009 always came out of the blue. "Oh, that's right." Jim said. "His name is on your list."

Donna spoke up and said. "If Sandra Beatty endorses Dr. Leyland's theory when we go to Caltech, you're going to change history. Do you realize that, Vince?"

"History from my viewpoint only." Vince replied. "So far nothing's happened like it did the first time. Maybe the big one won't either and I'd like to hope and think it won't. Sometimes I think it was all a dream, but I've got the penny and this scar to make me think otherwise."

"Where do we start?" Donna Asked.

"When Dr. Leyland is ready, I want you to encourage him to go on with his work on his new equipment and offer to help him with the software for his new equipment. We don't have the capability or means to fabricate new housings for his new design, and we don't have the time to wait for a manufacturing company to produce them, so we're going to have to try to use the units we have on hand. We'll have to try to jury rig them to work with the new design."

"I can help with that end of it." Jim said. "Basically what you're talking about is configuring the new design to work in the old housings. I've been spending my spare time learning computer design. I've got all the electronic testing equipment at home. I'm sure I can do it."

"I'll get you an older unit that's in for upgrades, Jim." Donna said.

"Sandra would be familiar with the older units." Vince said. "What if she doesn't believe we've come up with something new, and won't go along with testing it even if it is a new prototype?"

"We've got to make sure she does." Donna replied. "We're only going to get one shot at doing this right, so we're going to have to make sure we get it right the first time."

"Okay, I agree." Vince said. "We have to take it slow and try to avoid or correct any problems along the way. We'll go at this right and take the time to make sure everything works before we go see Sandra."

"It would still be better if what we showed Sandra didn't look like something that was jury rigged, Vince." Jim said.

"I know, but we can't wait to get the new cases Dr. Leyland is having manufactured, just so we can take a new, shiny looking, case with us. We'll have to depend on Dr. Leyland's clout and hope he still swings enough weight to get us in the door." Vince replied.

"Do you mind if I surf the internet and see if there's any generic cases out there for sale?" Jim asked.

"That's a good idea, Jim. If you find one that will work, Dr. Leyland can order it, if not, we'll use what we have on hand." Vince replied.

"Dr. Leyland said he has more than one motherboard, Vince. If Jim finds a generic case, okay, but I think, we should get started converting an old one. That way if we run into any configuration problems, we'll know what Jim should look for." Donna said.

"Okay, we all know what we have to do. Let's get busy and get it done." Vince said.

Donna and Jim left to get the old unit. Vince called, Chief Brewer and told him of their plans and asked for his help with his list of names.

"I'll get on the names for you as soon as I get the list." Brewer replied.

"Thanks, Chief. I've got to go, we're going to start working on the new equipment today." Vince said.

"Wait! There's something else I need to tell you. I have the discs that were found in your bathroom." Brewer said.

"Where did you get them? Who had them?" Vince asked.

"Woitasczyk had the discs in your files and they became police property during the investigation." Brewer said.

Vince was stunned, but at the same time offended, and said. "Woitasczyk never told me he had them! Man that pisses me off!"

"Cool down, Vince." Brewer said. "My guess is that he never told you because they didn't find the penny and were never able to open the discs."

"I'm okay, Chief." Vince replied. "I guess it doesn't make much difference now, I'm out and Woitasczyk's career is ruined."

"I've got some more news for you." Brewer said. "My crypto man recovered the passwords and opened the discs."

"What did he find on them?" Vince asked.

"He said the files contained classified Federal information. Two of them were property of a Vice President, named John Clemmons and the other belonged to a Secret Service Agent named, David Lindsey." Brewer said.

"I knew that. They were taken off their bodies at Lambert Field. Clemmons and Lindsey were working hand in hand to take control of the government, like I told you." Vince said.

"The head of the crypto department wanted me to turn the discs over to Feds." Brewer replied.

"Did you?" Vince asked.

"No, I took them home with me last night. I thought you might want to see them. They're at my house." Brewer replied.

"You're right, I do want to see them." Vince said.

"I knew you would, but my crypto man said viewing the files was a Federal Offense. Do you still want them?" Brewer asked.

"Yes, there's nothing on them that anybody would understand or want, except me." Vince replied.

"You already know what happened. What do you expect to learn from the discs." Brewer asked.

"How those bastard's were able to manipulate the system and get Dr. Leyland turned down. I want to know who the people were that did it and how they did it, so I can avoid the pitfalls that happened last time." Vince replied.

"I understand, but this shit is way over my head! You're talking about discs that were created in 2009 as if they're history. I felt strange holding the discs knowing they were from the future." Brewer said.

"I know, Jim and Donna feel the same way when I talk about things they were involved in, in 2009." Vince replied.

"I've got to ask you a question." Brewer said.

"Shoot." Vince replied. "I'll do my best to answer it."

"What happened to me in 2009?" Brewer asked.

"I don't know for certain, but you must have gotten killed along with everyone else in the San Diego area." Vince replied.

"Damn! That's what I thought. I'm putting in my retirement papers and moving to St. Louis." Brewer said.

"You've got time, but it's a good idea. I can tell you the best place to relocate. My folks live there and they survived the first quakes." Vince replied.

"What do you mean? You said they were still alive when you came back to 2005." Brewer said.

"They were and probably still are. We'll have to get into that later. Do you mind if we got back to the discs?" Vince asked.

"Sure, go ahead." Brewer said.

The Continent Of St. Louis - The Search For Answers

"Do you know if the crypto boys read any of the files?" Vince asked.

"Captain Glazier didn't say. He was anxious to get rid of them, since they were classified, Federal property." Brewer replied.

"I would have opened them and I'll bet they did also." Vince said.

"Captain Glazier is in charge of Cryptology. He's a good man, I think he would have told me if he had opened the files." Brewer replied.

"Would he have been the one that recovered the passwords?" Vince asked.

"I doubt it. He has a full staff that do the day to day work." Brewer replied.

"Find out who actually did the work. If word of the discs gets out, the Feds are going to be all over this like stink on shit. I, for one, don't need the Feds breathing down my neck, you don't either." Vince said.

"I'll take care of it on my end." Brewer said, and then asked. "What do you want me to do with the discs? Do you want me to bring them back to the office?"

"Did you get the passwords?" Vince asked.

"Yes, I have them with the discs." Brewer replied.

"Do me a big favor, then." Vince said.

"What is it you need?" Brewer asked.

"Can you copy the discs at home?" Vince asked.

"No way, I'm not into computers." Brewer replied.

"Can you have it done at Police Headquarters without arousing suspicion?" Vince asked.

"No, I'd have to ask the crypto boys to do that and the discs are marked as evidence and they're Federal property. The crypto boys would draw the line if I asked them to do that. I don't even think they'd make a printout of the files either, since they're classified." Brewer replied.

"Then the only other choice would be to mail the discs to Jim Lewis's apartment. He can make copies and then I can give the originals back to you." Vince said.

"Why would I need the originals?" Brewer asked.

"To cover yourself, in case the Feds come looking." Vince replied.

"You don't trust anybody, do you, Vince?" Brewer asked.

"If you could read the files on the discs, you'd see why." Vince replied.

"I'd rather not. "Brewer replied. "Give me Mr. Lewis's address and I'll call my wife and have her take them to the post office and mail them."

"Have her send them in the overnight mail and tell her to get rid of the receipt." Vince said.

"Why would she need to get rid of the receipt?" Brewer asked.

"In case the Feds come looking sooner than we think." Vince replied.

"Goddamn! Do you suspect one of the boys in crypto has already called the Feds?" Brewer asked.

"I'll bet on it." Vince replied.

"Okay, you may be right. I'm going home right now and I'll get the discs and take them to Mr. Lewis myself." Brewer said.

"How long will it take you?" Vince asked.

"A couple hours. I've got some paperwork to go over." Brewer replied.

"I've got a bad feeling about this, Chief. Can you leave now?" Vince asked.

"Yeah, I guess I can." Brewer replied.

"Okay, get out of there now and don't tell anyone where you're going. I'm sending Jim home, as soon as I hang up." Vince said.

Brewer locked his desk and buzzed his secretary and said. "I'll be gone for a couple hours. If anyone calls, tell them I'll call them back."

"I've had someone on hold, while you were on the phone. Do you want to take the call?" She asked.

Brewer thought about what Vince had said and knew if he answered the call he might get tied up. "Who is it?" He asked.

"I don't know. They didn't say." She replied.

"It wasn't the Mayor's office or the D.A.?" He asked.

"They wouldn't wait on hold. They would call back." She replied.

He was doubly suspicious now, and said. "Keep them on hold for five minutes and then drop the connection. If they call back, tell them I'm not available and take a message."

"What's going on, Chief?" She asked.

"Nothing you need to know about, right now. I'll tell you when I get back." He headed for the rear entrance to his office, opened the door slightly, peered out in both directions and found the hallway empty. He took the back stairs down to the parking lot, got in his car and left.

Thirty minutes later, two deputies from the U.S. Marshall's Office entered Brewer's office, showed their credentials, and asked to speak with Chief Brewer.

"He stepped out a while ago." His secretary replied. "I'm sure he'll be back soon. Please have a seat."

The two sat down and waited. A half hour later one stood up and asked. "Where did he go?"

"I'm not sure. He didn't say, but he did say he was returning. Why don't you sit back down? I'm sure he'll be back soon." She said and smiled.

"Is he in the building somewhere?" He asked.

"I'm not sure, but he didn't say he was leaving the building." She replied.

"Can you page him?" He asked.

"No. We don't have an internal paging system." She lied.

"What are the speakers on the wall for then?" He asked.

"Muzak. Do you want to listen to some music?" She asked.

"No." He replied.

"Would you mind closing the door for me? It's drafty in here." She said.

"Not at all." He replied and went to close the door. While his back was turned and the other mans attention was drawn away, she turned the switch for the speaker off, hoping the Federal Agents wouldn't hear any pages from down the hall, once the door was closed.

The time dragged for the two agents as they waited. They had both looked through all the magazines and one said to the other. "What do you want to do?"

"We have to wait. We don't have any other choice." The other replied.

"I'd better call in." The first man said and pulled out his cell and hit send.

"This is Stewart." He said and then said. "No, not yet. And then said. "I don't know." He listened for a few seconds and then said. "Okay." and shut his phone.

"What did he say?" The other asked.

"He said to wait." He sat down and picked up a magazine he'd already looked through and started looking through it again.

Chief Brewer walked in the back door of his office and saw the light blinking on his telephone. He picked up the receiver and his secretary said. "There are two Deputies from the U.S. Marshall's Office, waiting to see you, Chief. I told them you'd be back soon."

"Jesus Christ! How long have they been here?" He asked and then said. "Never mind! I'm going out the back way and circle around and come in the front door. I think I know what they're after. Tell them it will be a few minutes."

"Yes, sir." She hung up the phone and said. "Chief Brewer will be here in a few minutes. I've told him you're here."

"Thank you." One politely replied.

Brewer went out the back door of his office, stopped at the restroom, took a leak and washed his hands. *Let the bastard's wait!* He thought as he dried his hands.

He left and walked down the back corridor, came around the front to his door, walked in and said. "I'm Chief Brewer. What may I do for you, gentlemen?"

"We need to speak to you in private in your office." One said and flashed his badge and I.D.

"I think that can be arranged." Brewer replied and then said "I'd like a closer look at your credentials, if you don't mind."

The man pulled his credentials back out and handed it to Brewer, who looked at the other man, and said. "And yours?"

The other took his credentials out and handed them to Brewer.

"Deputies Stewart and Landreth are with the U.S. Marshall's office." He said to his secretary and winked. She wrote their names down on a pad while Brewer had their attention. He handed them back their credentials, and said. "Come on in boys." The three walked in his office and Brewer said. "Have a seat."

"We've been sitting for two goddamned hours waiting for you!" Stewart complained.

"Where's the discs?" Landreth demanded.

"What discs?" Brewer asked with a puzzled look on his face.

"The one's Captain Glazier gave you." Landreth retorted.

"Oh, you had me going there for a minute. They're locked in my desk with some other evidence I was going over." Brewer replied.

"Give them to us!" Landreth demanded "They have classified information on them. They're Federal property and we're taking custody of them."

"Not without a receipt for chain of custody." Brewer replied. "They're evidence in an ongoing case."

"Get the goddamned custody papers and we'll sign for them!" Stewart barked.

Brewer called his secretary and told her to prepare the chain of custody papers for the discs and thought. *Jesus! I didn't get back a minute to soon. Vince was right! I've got to call him.*

"Did you open the discs?" Stewart asked.

"Do you see a computer in here?" Brewer asked.

"Don't get smart with me, Brewer! Did you open them or not?" Stewart demanded.

"Hell no I didn't! I don't know a damned thing about computers." He replied, and then said. "That's why we have people that do. Did you ask Captain Glazier if any of his boys did?"

"It was one of his boys that called us and said you had them." Stewart replied.

"Which one called you? Did he say whether he looked at files?" Brewer asked.

"Both questions are really none of your business, Chief?" Landreth snapped back.

"I'll make it my business if he opened classified government files! Did he?" Brewer barked.

"Don't get your dander up, Chief! It was Earl Lucas. He said he didn't open the files." Landreth said.

"I'll have his ass on the carpet anyway!" Brewer bellowed.

"What for?" Stewart asked.

"For not following the chain of command! I'm the Chief here, goddamnit! I make the decisions around here! It was my job to call you, not his!" Brewer yelled putting on his best face of anger.

"Jesus Christ, Chief! Calm down! No laws have been broken here. He did the right thing!" Landreth said.

"Right thing, my ass! Brewer snarled. "He went over his commander's head and blew right past my office, when he called the Feds! His ass is mine!"

The Chief's secretary, who had been listening to the conversation on the intercom, walked in with the papers, and said. "I have the custody transfer papers. Are you having a problem with these men, Chief?"

"No, they're just doing their job and I'm going to do mine." Brewer replied and went on." Get Glazier up here to witness the transfer of custody of these discs. They're Federal property with classified information on them and one of his men broke the password and looked at the discs. Tell Glazier to bring Lucas with him."

"Yes, sir." She replied.

"Jesus Christ, Brewer! You don't have to go to all that trouble." Landreth said.

"You run your office and I'll run mine!" Brewer spat back. "Take a seat! The discs are yours, when I do my job and say they are!"

Chief Brewer called Vince, after the Federal Marshall's left, and filled him in on what had happened. "The crypto technician said he didn't open the files on the discs, so he won't be able to provide them with any information."

"That's good news." Vince said.

"Well this is better." Brewer said. "The Feds aren't going to find any classified information on them either. Jim copied them and then erased everything beyond the classified warning and replaced the information in each file with porno photos and video's he downloaded off the internet. They'll shit when they open those files." He laughed and Vince joined him and then he went on.

"I hate those smart ass Feds! The bastard's are always throwing their weight around and trying to intimidate people. It didn't work on me, I showed them who was running this office. They left like whipped pups and thanked me as they left." Brewer said, and started laughing again.

"Thanks, Chief. I know what I asked you to do would have been wrong in most cases, but this was information from the future and my name is in the files. If they had found my name and told Lindsey or Clemmons, I would have been arrested and taken to wherever they take people who said they've been probed by an alien, or whatever. You know what I mean." Vince said.

"I do know what you mean." Brewer replied. "We've had a few of those pass through here over the years, but you don't have to worry. I removed the case number from the jewel cases of the discs. If they come back asking questions, no one will be able to tell them what case they were related to. Fortunately no one but me and Forrester knew where they came from and he wasn't interested in them since all of the charges have been dropped."

"I wasn't talking about reference to my name in regard to the case number, Chief. My name is in the files on the disc." Vince said.

"Oh, I see what you mean." Brewer replied.

"I'll bring the list of names by tomorrow. Thanks again, Chief." Vince said and hung up.

Brewer was puzzled. *How the hell does he know his name is in the files, on the disc.* He wondered and then thought. *Maybe Jim told him.*

CHAPTER TWENTY-ONE

UCSD SIESMOLOGY CENTER...SAN DIEGO

The next morning, Jim told Donna about the CD's he now had, and how he gotten them. "Do you know what this means?" He asked.

"More proof of what Vince already knows?" She asked.

"More than that." He replied. "Vince is going to go through the files and find out who was involved in rejecting Dr. Leyland's theory."

"Who did the CD's belong to?" She asked.

"Clemmons and Lindsey." Jim replied.

"Who?" Donna asked and then said. "Oh, I remember! Vince said Clemmons was responsible for the cover-up. Who is, Lindsey?"

"A Secret Service Agent that worked for Lemming. He was the team leader at the White House and responsible for Lemming's safety." Jim replied.

They heard Dr. Leyland's office door open, he came out and headed their way. They both noticed Dr. Leyland looked better, as he walked toward them.

"Good morning. What are we working on today?" He asked.

Jim explained his idea of converting one of the old housings for use with his new designs. "If your new design will fit in the old equipment, it will save us lot of time and speed up the whole process of getting a working model to Sandra Beatty."

"With a small amount of re-configuring, an old case should work, Jim." Dr. Leyland replied.

"I thought it might." Jim said. "I couldn't find a new case we could use, so I got a case from the stores department. I'm ready to start working on it."

"The case is the least of my worries, Jim. It suddenly dawned on me that Vince might be a detriment to the project, when we go to see Sandra Beatty." Dr. Leyland said.

"Why?" Jim asked.

"If she's heard of Vince escaping from Gifford and being hunted by the police, she won't be receptive to any of this." He replied.

"Aren't there others besides her that would be required to be in on the meeting?" Donna asked.

"If someone other than I had discovered what's going on, I'm sure there would be others involved. Anyone but me would get her full attention, but we're talking about Sandra Beatty and her dislike for me." He replied.

"Have you talked to Vince about your concern?" Donna asked.

"Not yet. I was planning on talking to him the first thing this morning. Where is he?" Dr. Leyland asked.

"He went to see, Chief Brewer." Donna replied.

"I'll have to talk to him about it as soon as he returns and that's another worry." Dr. Leyland said.

"What do you mean?" Donna asked.

"I don't know how to tell Vince that he shouldn't be with us when we go to see Sandra." Dr. Leyland said.

"It won't bother him. He wanted you to stay in charge of the project." Jim said.

"Yes, I know. But I just the same as twisted his arm into going, now I'm going to have to tell him he shouldn't." Dr. Leyland said.

"Maybe Sandra doesn't know about Vince." Donna said.

"You don't know Sandra like I do." Dr. Leyland replied. "She is well aware of the fact that Vince is my assistant, no one including her, could have missed the news coverage of his escape and the police hunt for him. Sandra wouldn't even agree to a meeting, if she knew Vince was going to be there."

"Is she really that pig headed?" Donna asked.

"Yes, every bit so and I don't know how to explain to Vince, that his presence or even his name being associated with the project, could cause its failure. I'm afraid he'll end up back in Gifford if I tell him that no one, outside of this room, believes him." Dr. Leyland said.

"Chief Brewer believes him." Donna said.

"That's all well and good." Dr. Leyland replied. "But I think we'll be better off if he doesn't go to the meeting with Sandra. I also feel it's best to keep his name out of the whole thing as far as the L.A. offices are concerned."

"Do you have second thoughts about what Vince has told you?" Donna asked.

"Not at all." Dr. Leyland replied. "What he's told me has proven out so far, but for me it's still a theory, and one I can't prove beyond what the Model will predict. I can't use Vince's experience as a basis for proof and I don't have any hope that Sandra will believe Vince was in 2009 and has returned to warn the world."

"What are you going to tell Vince?" Donna asked.

"I'm going to tell him that I think it best that he remain in San Diego when we go to see Sandra. Tell me the truth, do you think that will upset him?"

"It shouldn't, but I can't say for sure." Donna replied. "He said he didn't want to take the project over, maybe he realizes he could jeopardize things if he was involved."

"I'll talk to him when he gets back." Dr. Leyland replied. "I hope you're right."

"Wait a minute." Jim said. "There's something you don't know, Dr. Leyland."

"What's that?" Dr. Leyland asked.

"I made some copies of the CD's they found in Vince's bathroom. The files on them will prove everything that Vince has said is true!" Jim said.

"How on Earth could information on CD's prove what he said is true?" Dr. Leyland asked.

"Vince brought them back with him from 2009."

POLICE DEPARTMENT...SAN DIEGO

VINCE ENTERED CHIEF BREWER'S office and thanked him again for the CD's.

"Have you looked at them yet?" Brewer asked.

"Not yet. Jim still has them at his apartment." Vince replied.

"Oh, I thought you had." Brewer said, still wondering how Vince knew his name was on the discs.

"Jim's bringing them in to work. I'll take a look at them later." Vince replied.

"Jim's a whiz on a computer. He had them copied and put the phony information on the originals in less than an hour." Brewer said.

"I know he's good. He's going to set up a new device for monitoring seismic activity that Dr. Leyland designed." Vince replied.

"As fast as he was, I was cutting it close and I barely got my ass back here on time. Those Feds were waiting in the outer office when I got back. All's well that ends well." He said and laughed.

Vince handed him the list with Max, Ray, George, Dana and Bob's names on it and said. "These are the people I want to find first." He also had Lemming, Clemmons, Lawson and Randall's names on it as secondary figures to run down.

"Lemming is the Governor of Washington." Brewer said. "I've never heard of any of the others."

"Except for Gray and Segar they're all military. Gray may be in the military also. He and Segar were the Secret Service Agents that were assigned to me in 2009." Vince said, and filled Chief Brewer in on some of the details of the part he and the others had played in the disaster. He noted which of the persons he was seeking were allies and those that were enemies.

"I imagine most of the information on Clemmons and Lindsey's discs will pertain to the cover-up. I don't expect to find much real information about the disaster. Clemmons didn't believe Dr. Leyland's predictions, although he was planning to use the disaster to take over power, if Dr. Leyland's predictions came true, even to the slightest degree."

"If all the Feds are like those two that were in my office yesterday, I can see why you don't like or trust authority figures." Brewer said.

"The higher up the ladder they are, the more corrupt they are." Vince replied and went on. "For the time being, I just want to try to contact my allies. I want to see if any of them have had any dreams, like Donna and Jim have."

"The big shots won't be easy. I'll do my best, but I might have to get the FBI involved to get clearance for the military information."

"Get what you can without involving any Federal help, for now." Vince said. "Morgan is the one I'd like you to concentrate on first."

"All right, I'll let you know as soon as I have something. Maybe I'll have some news for you when you come to my house for dinner." Brewer said.

"Chief, I can't come to your house for dinner." Vince said. "I'm sorry and I apologize. I have too much to do and not enough time to do it in. We have to get that new piece of equipment up and running before we can go to L.A. and try to convince them at Caltech."

"That's all right, I understand." Brewer replied. "My wife has already agreed to move to Missouri when I retire."

"When do you plan on retiring?" Vince asked.

"Not until you have everything my office can provide." He replied "I haven't mentioned retiring to anyone but, Rowland. I've been trying to convince him to retire and move there also."

"I'll give you a list of things you'll need to have when you get there and the safest place to locate." Vince said. "If I can't accomplish anything with Caltech or the government, my intentions are to go there also. My parents own a farm west of St. Louis. That's where I intend to be in 2009, if none of this works out. Get a temporary place when you move, and make sure you give me your address as soon as you relocate."

"Thanks, Vince." Brewer replied. "I sort of feel like a rat deserting a ship, but if what you say comes true, what could I do? What use would I be here?"

"You could do absolutely nothing unless the government believes me. Even then, there won't be enough land left to support the masses that would try and reach the St. Louis area. There's no way of stopping what's going to happen and even if the government believes me, the only thing they could do is warn the world." Vince replied.

Brewer was astonished. What Dr. Leyland had told him seemed more technical. What Vince was telling him sounded hopeless and surreal. "What hope does the world have?" He asked.

"More lives will be saved, that's all, but to what end? There wouldn't be enough resources left to support the ones that survive. I really have no idea what was left of the world, but I know what was left was mostly under water. I've got mixed feelings about all of this. Sometimes I feel like I should forget about all of this and just cut and run, but I can't and I know it. The downside of all of this is, if Sandra believes us in the slightest and they build the equipment, they'll come to realize how serious it will be. When they do, they'll have to warn other countries and I know another type of disaster will develop, before the final one."

"What do you mean? What other type of disaster will occur?" Brewer asked.

"When they warn everyone, the result will be anarchy and chaos." Vince replied. "There aren't enough people in uniform, military and civilian combined, to stop an uprising, if one starts, so don't let leaving concern you. If you stayed you wouldn't be able to do anything about it, anymore than anyone else could."

"Thanks, Vince." Brewer said shaking hands. "That makes me feel better about leaving, but damn, you don't paint a very pretty picture."

"It wasn't a pretty picture and it isn't going to be, believe me." Vince replied as he headed for the door.

"Hold on, Vince. Forrester has dropped the charges against Woitasczyk. He might get his license back now. Here's his address and phone number if you want to contact him."

Vince somehow knew the charges against Woitasczyk has been dropped, but he didn't know why. He remembered thinking that and perhaps mentioning it sometime, but he couldn't recall when. *Probably in my dreams!* He thought. He looked at the address, Chief Brewer had given him. *La Jolla! Where else would a cocky bastard like him live? I wonder what his autocratic neighbors think of him now.*

He slipped the card in his pocket and said. "Thanks, Chief. I'll call him later."

Vince was thinking about Woitasczyk as he drove back to the lab. He remembered all of the things Woitasczyk had said regarding his diagnosis. *All of it was wrong, but nevertheless, as wrong as he was, he must have believed his was right.*

Vince could see and hear him, spitting out his orders to the orderlies, in his guttural accent, with contempt written into every word. *My name is Dr. Vatasheck, not Dr. Whatasheck, und you vill do it my vay! Do you understand, dumkoph? My vay! Shiest! Vill you eber gidt dit hrright?*

Vince laughed out loud, thinking of Hitler, pounding on his podium and bellowing out his orders of world domination and hate. Hitler had almost brought the world to its knees, with his paranoid master plan, that had included the annihilation of the Jews and the return of the Aryan race. Hitler demanded full cooperation and obedience from all that surrounded him, or they were not true Germans and were delt with accordingly. Hitler had doctors that played with the human mind, using drugs and deprivation in experiments to find the causes of human difference. The doctors had camps where they bred the fairest skinned and bluest eyed young women to men with the same features in an effort to bring back the Aryan race. Millions were tortured and slaughtered on Hitler's orders. Intellectuals were looked down on and books were burned, as hate and contempt was spread to the masses, that were required to his attend his Nazi rallies. Citizens were ordered to tell on each other and report any activity not benefiting the Fuehrer and his ideals. Woitasczyk reminded Vince of Hitler. He didn't know Woitasczyk's age, but he was almost certain, Woitasczyk had been in Hitler's Jugend, the name applied to Hitler's Youth Corp. If not, then his attitude and behavior, must had been ingrained into him by parents, who must have been loyal to Hitler. *Where did Woitasczyk's, Germanic, know it all, upbringing and attitude, get him?* Vince wondered and answered his own thought. *He wound up in jail, lost his license and will probably never practice medicine again.*

Vince thought about the woman who was coming from the Midwest to seek treatment from Woitasczyk. *She doesn't know how lucky she is! Woitasczyk will never be able to see her or miss-diagnose her problems now. All the patients at Gifford will benefit from him being gone.*

Woitasczyk had told him that the woman was suffering with a similar delusional, disaster related problem. *Woitasczyk now has his own disaster to deal with, but it's not delusional.* He laughed out loud again when that thought crossed his mind.

The Continent Of St. Louis - The Search For Answers

He saw a police cruiser pass and momentarily, felt panicked. The cruiser went by, without the officer ever looking at him. *Will I ever get over the feeling of being a hunted man?* He wondered.

He stopped at a convenience store and bought a newspaper. Woitasczyk's story had slipped to the second page and his story was gone entirely. He ordered a cup of coffee and pack of Winston's. The clerk handed him a soft pack of Winston's, he looked at them thinking of the ones he'd gotten from the cigarette machine at Lambert Field, and thought. *They're going to stop making soft packs.*

He got back in his car, lit a cigarette and sipped his coffee, thinking. *My troubles with Woitasczyk are over. I'm not going to talk to him, what good would it do? I don't need to gain a feeling of vindication or reprisal by seeing him. He's already given me that by covering up my escape and being locked up for it.*

He threw the newspaper, and the card with Woitasczyk's address and phone number, in the trash as he left the convenience store parking lot. *Good riddance.* He thought as he pulled out onto the street and continued heading for the lab. A van pulled up beside him at a stop light and the driver looked at him and said. "Hey, that's him, that's Davis!"

Vince felt the hair raise on his neck. The man looked exactly like Clemmons. He was pointing at him, and yelling at his passenger. "That's Davis! I'm telling you it's Davis!"

The light turned green and Vince floor-boarded his car. He jumped forward as his tires squealed, peeling rubber, leaving the van behind. His heart was pounding in his chest as the Van caught up with him.

"Hey, Davis!" The driver yelled. "I've got Jean Simmons in the van! How about an interview?"

Vince looked at him again. The man didn't look anything like Clemmons and he saw the KQTV logo on the side of the van.

"I don't know what you're talking about!" Vince yelled back as he speeded, up leaving them behind.

"That was him, Jean. I swear to God." Her cameraman said.

"He didn't look anything like Davis!" She replied.

"It's his eyes. I'd know them anywhere. You'd better follow him." The cameraman said.

"Bullshit! I've got better things to do." She replied and turned at the next corner.

"Didn't you see the way he looked at me? He looked like he'd seen ghost! I swear it was him. Get his license number." The cameraman insisted.

"I don't want his license number! If I listened to you, I would have been interviewing that guy, you said was Elvis." Jean said.

"It was Elvis!" The cameraman replied.

"Then why didn't anybody else say they saw him?" Jean asked.

"That's the way Elvis is! He shows himself to someone and then he's gone." The cameraman retorted.

"You're the one that's gone! Turn right at the next corner. I've got a feeling a big story's going to break today." Jean said

Vince saw the van turn and breathed a sigh of relief, but the image of Clemmons staring at him was still in his mind. *Now it's happening in the daytime.* He thought.

He pulled into the parking lot of the lab and went inside. He walked up to Jim and said. "Give me the discs, I want to take a look at them in my office."

CHAPTER TWENTY-TWO

DR. WOITASCZYK'S HOUSE...LA JOLLA, CALIFORNIA

WOITASCZYK'S LAWYER HAD CALLED and informed him that the charges against him had been dropped. He was surprised and relieved, as one would be, facing jail time. His moment of elation had subsided, when he learned the charges had been dropped at Vince's request. His attorney had also told him he was working on getting his license re-instated, and was sure it would just be a matter of days before it happened. Despite the fact everything seemed to be going his way, he was still angry after speaking with his attorney, and thought. *Davis made a fool of me. I'll still be a laughing stock, even if I get my license back.*

The thought of his colleagues and the hospital staff laughing behind his back, set him off further. *I'll get Davis for this! I'm not through with that bastard yet!*

"Who was it that called?" His wife asked breaking his thoughts.

"My Lawyer. The D.A. has dropped the charges against me." He said.

"Why, that's wonderful, dear. You don't look happy, why?" She asked.

"That goddamned, Davis got them to drop the charges. That's why!" He snapped.

"Wasn't he the mental patient you were treating, that escaped?" His wife asked.

"Ya, goddamnit!" Woitasczyk snarled.

"He was an escapee and a criminal. How could he have done that?" His wife asked.

"I don't know and I don't give a shit!" Woitasczyk spat back.

"Calm down dear. Don't get your blood pressure up." His wife said.

"Fuck my blood pressure! The bastard made a fool of me and I know goddamned well that every psychiatrist on the West Coast is laughing their asses off at me." Woitasczyk complained.

"Is, Davis in custody." His wife asked.

"Hell no!" Woitasczyk shouted. "My Lawyer said they were handling him with kid gloves. They dropped all the charges against him too. He's a goddamned escaped mental patient and a felon, but he can do no wrong! I ended up in jail, because of the bastard escaping, and lost my license! I'm going to get even with him, goddamnit!"

"You won't do any such thing, Gunder! Now you listen to me! You're getting yourself all worked up and it's not good for you. I know what's happened to you is embarrassing, but you were just trying to do as you thought best. Since they dropped the charges against you, they must know you didn't do anything wrong."

"I don't give a shit what they think!" Woitasczyk snapped.

"Will you get your license back, dear?" His wife asked.

"My lawyer is working on it, but I don't give a shit if they do give it back!" Woitasczyk shot back.

"You're an important man, dear. I know they will re-instate your license. When they do, you can go back to the hospital and continue your practice. Then we can get back to a normal life." His wife said.

"I'll never go back to that goddamned place!" Woitasczyk yelled. "I'll be the laughing stock of the hospital! Everyone there would ridicule me, goddamnit! The orderlies already have!"

"Calm down, dear. Everything will be all right. Would you like a nice cup of coffee?" She asked, trying to get him off the subject.

"Hell no, I don't want any goddamned cup of coffee!" He screamed. "My article on Davis came out in the Psychiatric Journal while I was in jail. By now, I must be considered the biggest quack in Psychiatric Medicine. No one's going to refer any patients to me now! Why would they? All the doctors will think I'm as crazy as the goddamned patients, I've been treating. Davis has ruined my life, and I'm going to make him pay for that, goddamnit!"

"Why, I thought the Chief of Police said they weren't going to print the article." His wife said.

"They did it anyway! They did it to make a fool out of me! They're nothing but a bunch of jealous sons-of-bitches. The asshole that's in charge of the articles they print is an old enemy of mine. He was always reminding me of where I came from and that Germany lost the war. He called me a Nazi once, and he compared me to Mengele! I should have killed the lousy bastard for that! He's ruined me for good now! My life is over, goddamnit!" Woitasczyk wailed.

Woitasczyk was going off the deep end. His wife had never seen him behave as he was. She was beginning to worry that he would have a stroke or heart attack. He was shaking all over and his face had turn bright red.

"Gunder! Get a hold of yourself!" She insisted. "You'll be in the hospital or dead if you don't calm down. You better take a couple Xanax and lay down."

"Fuck you and fuck your advice! I don't need any Xanax or anything else! I've got some things I need to take care of, so quit trying to sooth me and get the hell out of my way!" Woitasczyk screamed.

"What do you mean? What are you planning to do?" She asked.

"I know what I'm going to do and you better stay out of my way!" He screamed as he walked into their bedroom and pulled his .44 magnum out of the nightstand drawer and started loading it.

"What are you doing, dear?" His wife asked as she followed him in the bedroom and saw the gun. "You aren't thinking of killing yourself are you? Please don't do that." She pleaded.

"Hell no! Just leave me alone, you bitch! I'm not going to kill myself!" He spat back. "Now, get the hell out of here!"

"Why do you need the gun? Could you at least tell me that?" She asked.

"I am going to clean the goddamned thing, all right? Now leave me alone, goddamnit!" He screamed.

"You shouldn't clean a gun when it's loaded, dear. You could shoot yourself, accidentally." She said.

"Will you leave me the hell alone? I know what I'm doing!" He screamed.

"All right, I'll leave. You aren't thinking of doing something rash are you? Please, Gunder. Tell me you aren't." His wife pleaded.

"Rash!" Woitasczyk bellowed. "I'll tell you what's rash! I have practiced medicine in California for twenty-five goddamned years and I reached the top of my field. Everyone except that quack at the Psychiatric Journal admitted I was the best. He knew it too, but he's just a lazy, jealous bastard or he wouldn't have given up his practice to sit on the board of that worthless rag!"

"Stop it, dear! Just listen to yourself! This isn't you and you know it!" His wife said.

"How would you know?" He hissed. "You don't even know me and you know it! All you ever married me for was my money and position!"

"You know that's not true, Gunder! I love you dear and I don't want to see you do something you'll regret. Give me the gun, please."

"Go to hell! I am not giving you the gun! Get back in the kitchen and mind your own damned business!" Woitasczyk barked.

"Please listen to me, Gunder! You're not yourself!" She pleaded.

"This is me all right! I'm Gunderich, really fucked, Woitasczyk, MD, PhD!" He screamed.

"Gunder! Stop it and I mean now! I don't know why you thought you needed a gun anyway. Now look at what's happening to you. Please give me the gun before something bad happens! She pleaded.

"Something bad!" Woitasczyk screamed. "I'll tell you what's bad, goddamnit! Everything was fine and then along comes that son-of-a-bitch, Davis! The bastard was crazy, and he's still crazy! Do you hear me?"

"I hear you, but why are you using that word, dear?" She asked.

"What word?" He screamed.

"Crazy! You never wanted your patients referred to as crazy. You said so yourself. I heard you." She said, trying to get his mind off whatever had stirred him up.

"The bastard is crazy! He said the world is coming to an end and it is for him! I can goddamned well, guarantee you that! Do you hear me?" He roared.

"Yes, Dear, I hear you, so does everyone in the neighborhood! Please calm down!" His wife said.

"I don't give a shit who hears me! I am calm and I know what I'm doing, so shut up!" He barked.

"I can't take any more of this, Gunder! Please stop!" She begged.

"You can't take it? That's a laugh! Try walking in my shoes!" He screamed. "I'm disgraced and Davis is being treated like he's something special. I won't be able to show my face or tell anyone who the hell I am, for the rest of my goddamned life! I don't give a shit if I get my license back, It won't do me any damned good now!"

"Gunder! You're shouting! The neighbors will hear!" His wife said.

"Fuck the neighbors!" He roared as he slid the patio door open, stuck his head outside, and screamed. "Fuck all of you La Jolla, motherfucking, snobs!" He ranted on, working himself into a frenzy, and continued screaming, louder. "Gunderich Woitasczyk says, all of you are a bunch of no good, cocksucking, motherfuckers!"

"Gunder! Close that door!" His wife demanded. "Get back in here this minute! You're embarrassing me! The neighbors will think you're drunk or you went crazy."

He slid the door shut and turned to his wife and asked. "Crazy? Are you calling me crazy?"

"No dear, but what you're saying and doing sounds crazy. Please give me the gun, dear." She said again.

"Get out of my way, bitch!" He said as he pushed past her and headed for the garage.

"Where are you going, Gunder?" She asked. "Please come back. Whatever you're thinking of doing, please don't do it. Please stop and think about it before you do anything rash. Please stop and think of me at least. What will the neighbors think? What will I tell them? Please don't do something you'll regret!" She pleaded again.

He stopped and turned around facing her. His face was masked in a rage.

"Please, Gunder." She pleaded and started crying. "Please don't do what you're thinking of doing, whatever it is. You need help, dear. Please, let me call a doctor, let me call someone that can help you."

He raised the .44 magnum and without a word, shot her once in the forehead. She was dead before she hit the floor. Woitasczyk turned and went to the garage and backed his car out of the driveway.

Neighbors who had heard the screaming and gunshot were already standing outside their homes. As a crowd began to gather, the Mayor, who was attending a social function two houses down, went out with his host and joined the others standing along the curb, and asked. "Was that a gunshot, I heard?"

"It sounded like a gunshot to me, your Honor." One in the group replied.

"Has anyone called the police?" The Mayor asked.

"I'll do it." His host said and pulled his cell phone out.

Woitasczyk recognized the Mayor as he approached the group and pulled to a stop in front of them. "Your, Honor?" Woitasczyk asked as he rolled down his window.

"Yes, what's happened? What's the trouble?" The Mayor asked.

"You're a big part of the trouble, you asshole!" Woitasczyk said vengefully. He raised his gun and shot the Mayor in the forehead, and then sped off down the street. *I'll get them all!* He thought to himself as he picked up speed. *I'll get that bastard, Davis, next! Then I'll get the Police Chief and that pompas ass, D.A.! They're all going to pay for this, including the asshole that revoked my license! They're as good as dead, right now!*

The Mayor's host, who had been standing beside the Mayor when Woitasczyk gunned him down, had fallen down, dropping his cell phone, when Woitasczyk had fired his .44 Magnum. His ears were ringing so loudly, he couldn't hear the crowd screaming in horror, as they watched blood spurt from the Mayor's forehead, and run down his face. The deafened man looked sideways in horror and saw the Mayor's lifeless eyes staring directly at him, as if to blame him, for the bullet that had ended his life. Panic shot through the Mayor's host as he jumped to his feet and ran his hands over his head and body, feeling for blood and screaming. "Jesus Christ! Have I been shot? Tell me, goddamnit! Have I been shot?"

"Hell no, you're not shot! Call 911, you stupid asshole!" A man yelled to him, who was leaning over the Mayor and checking his pulse.

The Mayor's host couldn't hear the man, but he saw him pointing at his cell phone and got the message. His hands were shaking so badly it took three attempts to finally get through. His ears were ringing so loudly, he could barely hear the operator answer the call. He handed the phone to the man that was leaning over the Mayor's body.

"He's dead, the Mayor's dead!" The man yelled to the 911 operator. "Some crazy bastard just shot the Mayor, and drove off!"

The operator got the details, saying police and an ambulance were already on the way. By then a large crowd had gathered around the Mayor's body.

"Who is he?" Another neighbor asked.

"What did you say? I can't hear you!" The Mayor's host replied, now feeling foolish, for his panicked outburst.

"Who the hell is he?" The man yelled.

"That's the Mayor, you idiot! The Mayor's host retorted. "Don't you ever watch the goddamned news?"

Before the man could answer, a cruiser turned the corner with siren blaring, and came to a screeching halt in the middle of the street in front of the crowd of people. The policeman stepped from the cruiser and drew his gun.

"Get back!" He ordered and then asked. "Who made the call?"

"He did!" A neighbor said, pointing to Mayor's host.

"All right! Everybody get back! Give me some room!" The officer yelled as he leaned down and checked the Mayor's pulse.

"He's dead!" The Mayor's host said.

"I can see that! What happened? Who shot the Mayor?" The officer asked.

"What?" I can't hear you!" The man replied.

"What happened?" The officer yelled.

"I was standing right beside the Mayor when that asshole drove up, and murdered him in cold blood!" He yelled back.

"All right! Everyone else step back, right now!" The officer shouted and then asked. "Who did it?"

The crowd was slowly backing up when one of them yelled. "He's coming back!"

A car resembling Woitasczyk's car turned the corner and was slowly driving down the street.

"Get down, everybody!" The officer yelled, and keyed his lapel radio. "This is Sgt. Unroe! The Mayor is dead and I need some back-up, right now, goddamnit! The perp's on his way back down the street!"

He pointed his gun at the approaching car and thought. *Shit! My vest is in the goddamned trunk!*

The car slowed down and came to a stop as Unroe ran to his cruiser and popped the trunk. He grabbed his vest and a riot gun, then turned back facing the car. He fired a shot in the air and then pointed the riot gun directly at the driver's side of the vehicle.

"Hold it right there!" Unroe yelled. "Get out of the car with your hands on your head!"

The car door opened slowly and a man stepped out of the car with his hands in the air.

"Turn around and put your hands on the roof of your vehicle!" Unroe yelled.

The man complied, but asked. "What the hell's going on? I haven't done anything!"

Unroe approached him cautiously, and said. "Spread your legs!"

As the man complied, Unroe walked up to the man and pulled one of his arms down and snapped his cuffs around one wrist, then the other, pushing him down on the car's hood and started patting him down. By then three more cruisers were arriving to back Unroe up.

"Where's the gun you, asshole?" Unroe demanded.

"I don't know what you're talking about." The man replied shakily. "I don't own a gun." A puddle of urine started forming at the man's feet.

"Tell it to the judge, you bastard! You're under arrest, you're going to jail!" Unroe barked as he led the man to his cruiser.

"That's not him! Look out his car is rolling!" The deafened neighbor yelled as Unroe reached his cruiser and locked the suspect in the back seat.

The suspect's car started picking up speed, as it rolled down the hill, slamming into the front of Unroe's cruiser. Unroe jumped back, as the car struck his cruiser, and yelled at the suspect. "You didn't put your car in park, you stupid bastard!"

The suspect inside had been pitched forward on impact, causing him strike his head on the mesh security divider. A large knot was forming on his forehead as he moaned in pain.

"Goddamnit!" Unroe mumbled as he looked at the damage the suspect's car had caused to his cruiser. "What did you say?" Unroe yelled at the deafened man.

"I said his car was rolling!" He yelled back.

"I can see that, goddamnit! What did you say before that?" Unroe yelled.

"I said you've got the wrong man! That's not the man who shot the Mayor!" He yelled back.

"What do mean, it's not him?" Unroe yelled.

"It wasn't him. You've got the wrong man!" He yelled back.

"Aw shit! Watch him." Unroe said to an officer who had come to assist him, and then yelled. "Are you sure?" As he was walked up to the deafened man.

"Yes, I'm sure! I was standing right beside the Mayor when he was shot! I can't hear a goddamned thing now!" He complained.

"Which one of the neighbors said he was the shooter?" Unroe asked, under his breath, while pointing to the group.

"What? The defended man asked.

"Forget it!" Unroe said, and then yelled to the officer that was watching the suspect. "Take the cuffs off that guy and let him go."

"Are you sure, Jack?" The officer yelled back.

"Yes, I'm sure! Let him go!" Unroe yelled back.

The officer unlocked the cruiser, got the man out, unlocked his handcuffs and said. "You're free to go."

"Thank you officer." The man said politely, as he straightened his jacket, and pulled his wet trousers away from his leg. He pulled a small notebook and pen from inside his jacket pocket and then handed the officer his business card.

"What's this for?" The officer asked.

"I'll need all of your names and badge numbers." He said as the officer looked at his card. "I'll also need you to fill out an accident report in regard to the damage my vehicle has sustained."

"Hey, that's not our fault! You didn't put your car in park!" The officer retorted.

"How could I have? I was dragged from my car with a shotgun pointed at my face and arrested, and I wasn't read my rights. Therefore it was an illegal arrest."

"You weren't arrested." The officer retorted.

"What would you call it then? I had a riot gun fired over my head and then pointed at me. I was told I was under arrest, I was handled roughly, causing me to urinate in my trousers, handcuffed and then thrown headfirst into the back seat of a cruiser. Look at the knot on my head!" Before the officer could answer the man started up again. "I'll tell you what it is! It's false arrest, police negligence and police brutality! I'm suing the city and the police department."

"You were I.D.'d as the shooter. Unroe had probable cause, but you weren't arrested, you were just detained so he ask some questions and find out what happened. I'd suggest you get out of here, while you still can." The officer replied.

"I'm not going anywhere until I have the information I need." The man said. "I want your names and badge numbers and I want the accident report before I leave."

"Oh, shit! All right!" The officer said. He walked up to Unroe and showed him the man's business card, and said. "Listen Jack, he's Alex Lazlo, that ambulance chasing lawyer, and he's got us by the balls. He said he's going to sue the police department and the city. He said you fired the riot gun at him. Did you?"

"Hell no! I shot it in the air to get his attention." Unroe protested.

"What the hell did you do that for, Jack?" The officer asked.

"One of those rubber-necking assholes, said he was the shooter." Unroe said.

"Which one?" The officer asked.

"Hell, I don't know." Unroe replied and then yelled. "Which one of you said that man was the shooter?"

The crowd started mumbling and looking at each other, but no one admitted saying the man was the shooter.

"You're ass will be in a sling if you don't come up with a good reason for cuffing him, Jack!" The other officer said. "He said you didn't read him his rights, either."

"I didn't read him his rights, because I didn't arrest the bastard! I was detaining him till I could see what happened." Unroe lied.

"He said you arrested him. You should have waited for back-up, Jack." The other officer said.

"Back-up, my ass!" Unroe retorted. "The Mayor is laying there in a pool of blood and one of the witnesses said he was the shooter! I wasn't waiting for back-up. That was a good enough reason for me! Put him back in the cuffs and arrest him."

"You're not going to let him go?" The other officer asked

"Not now! Screw him!" Unroe said. "Cuff him and don't let him talk to any of these people. Take the bastard downtown and book him. I'll have his car impounded. Everyone knows that Lazlo's an ambulance chaser with a police scanner in his car."

"On what charges?" The other officer asked.

"Interfering in a police investigation." Unroe replied.

"That isn't going to hold up! He'll have your ass on a platter." The other officer said.

"He drove through that yellow police tape and crashed into a police car right in the middle of a crime scene." Unroe said.

"What yellow tape?" The other officer asked.

"The tape I'm going to put up when you get his ass out of here. Hurry up and get out of here before the news media shows up." Unroe said.

The officer returned to Lazlo and told him he was arresting him for interfering in a crime scene. He cuffed the protesting Lazlo again, read him rights, put him in his cruiser, and headed for downtown. After he left, two officers began taping off the area, making sure the tape was torn and broken where Lazlo's car had crashed into the cruiser.

"Have the lab boys take a few pictures of the broken tape and his car for the D.A. when they get here." Unroe told one of the other officers, and then told the another. "Question the neighbors and see what they know."

The officer started questioning the neighbors, and learned it was Dr. Gunderich Woitasczyk who had gunned the Mayor down.

"He lives right there." The deafened host said, pointing to Woitasczyk's house, while he patted his ears.

"What are you patting your ears for?" The officer asked.

"What?" The man asked drawing closer to the officer.

"Why are you patting your ears." The officer asked in a louder voice.

"I think I'm deaf." He replied. "I was standing right beside the Mayor when Woitasczyk shot him."

"What else can you tell me about Woitasczyk?" The officer shouted.

"He's a crazy bastard! I can tell you that!" The host replied.

"If it was him that shot the Mayor, that's apparent. Are you sure it was Woitasczyk that shot the Mayor?" The officer shouted.

"Hell yes I'm sure! I watched the crazy bastard roll down his window. The next thing I knew he had a gun in his hand and shot the Mayor!" He yelled back.

"Okay, what happened before the mayor was shot?" The officer shouted.

"I was hosting a small get together in honor of the Mayor, when we heard a lot of screaming and cussing coming from Woitasczyk's house and then a gunshot. That kind of shit never happens in this neighborhood, so everyone came outside to see what was going on. We were just standing here beside the street when Woitasczyk drove up and shot the Mayor. Hell, I thought I'd been shot too!"

"Did the Mayor say anything to anger, Woitasczyk?" The officer yelled.

"Woitasczyk said something to the Mayor, but I don't know what he said. The Mayor had just told me to call 911 to report the disturbance and gunshot. I was dialing when Woitasczyk drove up, rolled down his window, and shot the Mayor. Jesus Christ! I don't believe it! I think I have permanent damage to my ears, I can't hear a thing."

"Okay, thanks. You better see a doctor about your ears. That's all for now." The officer gave his notes to Unroe who had been advised to take command of the crime scene. Unroe called dispatch and identified Woitasczyk as the suspected shooter.

An officer who had been sent to check Woitasczyk's house returned and said. "There's another body inside the house, Sarge. It must be Woitasczyk's wife. He shot her in the forehead too."

Unroe requested crime scene investigators, after advising dispatch of the second, and as yet, unidentified body, that had been found in Woitasczyk's residence. He then began questioning neighbors, asking what they knew or had heard. One related hearing Woitasczyk yelling at the top of his lungs, identifying himself and telling all of the, La Jolla motherfuckers, to get fucked, before he had heard the first gunshot. Other neighbors had nothing additional to add.

As Unroe called dispatch and related the information regarding Woitasczyk's behavior, Jean Simmons arrived in her KQTV van. She immediately went live and started questioning Unroe, who was less than happy to see her.

"Can you tell me what's happened here, Sergeant?"

"The Mayor was murdered, while he was standing there beside the street." Unroe replied, pointing to the Mayor's dead body, that had now been covered.

"Do you know who the murderer is?" Jean asked.

"That's all I have to say for now." Unroe replied.

As Unroe finished talking to Jean, detectives and crime scene crewmembers arrived to take over the Woitasczyk's residence. Jean watched as they pulled into the driveway of the house and entered. She knew something else was going on and intended to find out what it was, and yelled. "Wait Sergeant! Why are the other officers going in that house?"

Unroe turned around and said. "There's been another murder inside the house. That's all I'm telling you for now. You and your crew are going to have to get back and stay behind the crime scene tape."

As Unroe walked away, Jean signaled the cameraman to go in close on her face and continued live. "Although I don't agree, the Sergeant has asked my crew and I, to stand back while the investigation goes on. I'll be back live with more breaking news, momentarily. I'm Jean Simmons reporting live from the grizzly scene of the Mayor's murder, here in La Jolla, and you heard it first on KQTV."

Unroe saw that Jean was still on camera and speaking into her mic. *That bitch never does what she's told to do!* He thought and yelled to her. "I'm not going to warn you again, Jean! If you don't move back, you'll be arrested!"

Jean signaled the cameraman to cut the feed and said. "Wait a minute, Sergeant! I'm a reporter and I have rights! You can't talk to me like that and you can't arrest me for doing my job! Do you know who I am?" She yelled back.

"I know exactly who and what you are and you're wrong about your rights, Jean!" Unroe replied as he walked up and pulled out his cuffs.

"Get it on camera!" Jean yelled to cameraman.

"Are you going to hit me in the head with your mic like you did at Davis's house when I was arresting your ass? I'm sure you remember that little fiasco you got into for running your mouth?" Unroe said.

Jean hadn't recognized Unroe. She was affronted by his words, but wasn't giving up. "You had it coming! I was wrongfully arrested! You and Traxler had no right to do that and they dropped the charges! If you arrest me again, I'll sue the city and the police department. " She retorted.

"Your bluff isn't working, Jean. Just keep running your mouth like you did at Davis's house, and I'll see that you spend some more time in jail! Now get back! I'm not going to tell you again!" Unroe threatened, and walked away.

Screw him! I'm glad I hit the bastard with my mic! Jean thought, as she moved back a few feet, called the studio and gave the cameraman the go-ahead.

"This is Jean Simmons. I'm reporting live again from the tragic scene of the brutal murder of the Mayor of San Diego, which took place here in this affluent neighborhood in La Jolla, just minutes ago. We haven't learned why the Mayor was here in this neighborhood, but apparently he was standing beside the road just a few feet from here when a crazed gunman drove up and shot him down, in cold blood."

The cameraman zoomed in on the blanket-covered body lying in the grass a few yards away, and then went back to Jean who continued speaking.

"As yet, we don't know who shot the Mayor or why the Mayor was murdered. All we know for sure at this time, is that the Mayor was gunned down for no apparent reason, as he stood beside the street in this affluent, usually quiet, neighborhood in La Jolla. The so far, unidentified body, of a second victim has been found in a house, just up the street. We don't know at this time if there was any connection between the two deaths. Detectives and crime scene investigation crews have arrived and they are inside the house now."

She looked over the cameraman's shoulder and saw Unroe looking her way and said. "I've been threatened with arrest by Sergeant Unroe, of the San Diego Police Department, for trying to do my job. I'm going to have to pack up our equipment and move back. I'll be back live with more information as it's released by the police."

Jean stalled for time hoping she'd find out who the murder victim in the house was. "Don't get in any hurry to pack up." She told the cameraman. A few minutes later, Unroe yelled at her again.. "Get your ass out of there, Simmons!"

She waved at Unroe and yelled back. "We're going as soon as we've got our equipment packed."

Unroe became angered by her insolence and disregard for his orders. He started walking her way, intending to arrest her, and was stopped by another Sergeant, who said. "Hold on Jack! The Chief's watching her broadcast in his office. He told me to tell you not to screw with her anymore."

"For Christ's sake! Is he out of his mind? The bitch will mess everything up again, with her innuendos and allegations. Tell the Chief you couldn't find me, I'm arresting her ass!" Unroe replied.

"I've told you what he said, Jack. Go ahead and be a screw up like Traxler, for all I care. You'll lose those stripes if you do." He said.

Unroe was up for promotion. He wanted Traxler's job and the Lieutenants pay grade that went with it. He knew he wouldn't get it, if he stirred up some more shit for the Chief, and said. "Screw her! She isn't worth it. She'll mess up again somewhere down the line, and I'll get her when the Chief's not watching."

Jean and her cameraman saw Unroe turn and walk away with the other officer, just as the ambulance arrived.

"Should I keep taping?" The cameraman asked.

"Hell yes! Somebody has shut Unroe's ass down. Get a close-up of that house's mailbox. What the number?" She asked.

"Fourteen-thirty." He replied.

"Let get some background information. Maybe someone can tell me who lives there." She said and started questioning the neighbors. She was told that someone was shouting obscenities from up the street and thought it had come from the house police were inside of. Another neighbor said he thought the first shot had came from the same house, before the Mayor was murdered. Neither person could give her the names of the couple that lived in the house.

"Did you get that?" She asked the cameraman, who said that he had.

More police cars from the Sheriff's Department arrived, followed by another ambulance. Paramedics checked the Mayor's vital signs. Finding no signs of life, the Mayor was put in a body bag, lifted onto a gurney and placed in an ambulance, for the trip to the Morgue.

Jean was getting anxious as the minutes slipped away. She knew she was sitting on a hot story and wanted to scoop the other stations. She flipped her cell phone open, called the research department of KQTV and said. " This is Jean Simmons. Let me speak to Russell Vetterling."

"This is Russell, what do you need, Jean?" He asked.

"I'm in La Jolla at the Mayor's murder scene. There's been another murder inside a house two doors up. The number on the house is fourteen-thirty, La Jolla Rancho Drive. Find out who owns the house and call me back."

Jean had the cameraman keep taping the residence as crime scene technicians were dispensing yellow warning tape, sealing the area off. Her phone rang, it was an answer she didn't expect to get.

"The house is owned by Dr. Gunderich Woitasczyk, and his wife. He's the shrink who was involved in Davis's escape at Gifford. Forrester just dropped the charges against him this morning." Russell said.

"Goddamn!" Jean whispered. "It must have been Woitasczyk that shot the Mayor!"

"Has someone identified Woitasczyk as the shooter?" Russell asked.

"No, but I'll bet my last dollar, that he did it." Jean replied.

"Don't put that out over the air until it's been confirmed!" Russell said.

"Why not?" Jean asked.

"You'll get me tangled up in the mess if you do. As far as I'm concerned, I didn't tell you anything! Don't put it out! I mean it, goddamnit!" He snarled.

"Shit! We're sitting on the hottest story to hit San Diego in decades." She said, looking around and seeing other news vans unloading their equipment. "The other stations are here! I'm going live with this!" Jean said.

"You're not going to say Woitasczyk shot the Mayor, are you?" He asked.

"It had to be him! Neighbors heard a man screaming obscenities at the neighborhood and then they heard a shot come from his house!" She replied.

"Did they say it was Woitasczyk?" He asked.

"They weren't sure." She replied.

"When did that happen?" He asked.

"Just before the Mayor was murdered." She replied.

"That doesn't mean Woitasczyk did it!"He snapped back.

"Woitasczyk's garage door is open and the car's gone. It had to be him that shot the Mayor. I've got to go. I'm going live with this!" She said.

"I'm telling you to wait until you get a confirmation from the police, before saying anything! Do you hear me, Jean?" He yelled.

Jean heard what he saying, couldn't believe it, and said. "What was that? I didn't hear you! You're breaking up! Are you there?" She yelled.

"Yes, I'm here, goddamnit! Listen to me, Jean! Don't say anything about Woitasczyk, until you have verification from the police! You know goddamned well they told you to get an okay from your boss, before putting out any information at crime scenes." He yelled.

Jean wasn't going to be put off by Russell. She sensed a scoop in the making and said."I've lost him. I'm not getting a signal. Get us back live." She said to her cameraman.

The cameraman heard the last part of the conversation that was yelled at Jean before she closed her cell phone. "You're not going to report the house belonging to Woitasczyk are you?" He asked.

"You're goddamned right I am! Get us back live!" She ordered.

"Russell said not to do it! I heard him." The cameraman replied.

"Screw Russell! That's Woitasczyk's house. I'm going for it." She said.

"I thought he was in jail." The cameraman said.

"He was out on bail. It had to be him that murdered the Mayor. I'm going to break this story first. Get me back live and do it now!" She hissed.

"Are you sure, Jean? Don't you remember what happened last time?" The cameraman asked.

"Yes, I'm sure! Traxler's locked up and Unroe's off my ass. Besides, Unroe didn't tell me not to put out any information." She said.

"Unroe doesn't know you've identified Woitasczyk's house, Jean. He probably doesn't even know who lives there yet. You better not do it." The cameraman said.

"You don't get anywhere holding back when you get a story as hot as this." Jean said. "Get the studio and get us back live, right now!"

"Your boss told you not to report anything before it was confirmed by the police. Russell just told you the same thing. You'll get fired!" Her cameraman warned her.

"The hell I will! When I break this story, they'll be kissing my ass at the studio. Get me back live now, or I'll get your ass fired!" She threatened.

"If you mess this one up, it'll be your ass that gets fired, not mine!" He replied.

"Do it, goddamnit!" She hissed.

"Remember, it's your funeral." He replied.

She was again in front of the camera and they went live. "We have now learned from neighbors that the house where the second victim of this terrible shooting spree was found, is owned by, Dr. Gunderich Woitasczyk." She waited while the cameraman zoomed in on Woitasczyk's house and then continued. "You'll recall, Dr. Woitasczyk, was recently arrested for withholding evidence, resisting arrest and charged with assault against a police officer, in connection with the Vince Davis escape. The victim inside the house has not yet been identified, but neighbors suspect it might be Dr. Woitasczyk's wife. Neighbors here at the scene, reported hearing a loud male voice, identifying itself as Gunderich Woitasczyk, yelling threats and obscenities from the house before hearing the first gunshot that is thought to have come from the inside the house. It's not clear at this time what the motive might have been, if indeed, it is Dr. Woitasczyk that fired the shots killing the unidentified victim and the Mayor."

Jean was feeling her oats, having scooped the other media present at the scene and went on. "I have just learned today, that all charges against Dr. Woitasczyk were dropped in an unprecedented move by District Attorney, Claude Forrester. If, indeed Dr. Woitasczyk is the killer it would make one wonder why he would have done such a heinous thing, having been cleared of all the charges pending against him. We'll be back live as soon as the case becomes more clear and the unidentified victims name is released by police. This has been a very unusual day here in La Jolla. Reporting live with breaking news, this is Jean Simmons and you heard it first, here on KQTV."

"Goddamnit, Jean!" Her cameraman protested as they went off the air. "The neighbors didn't tell you it was Woitasczyk that was yelling and they didn't know who lived in the house, but you made it sound like they did. You don't know who it is that's dead in there. What if it's not Woitasczyk who did it or his wife that's dead inside the house?"

"I'll make a bet on this one and we got it out first. If I'm wrong, I can correct what I said and lay it off on the neighbors jumping to conclusions. But if I'm right, I scooped the whole city on this one. Let's get out of here. Woitasczyk's going to show up someplace else and I know it. I want to be close when he pulls his gun out again."

The cameraman started walking back toward the van and then turned to her and said. "Go to hell, Jean! I'm not going along with anymore of your bullshit. I heard them tell you not to reveal Woitasczyk's name."

"I don't give a damn what you thought you heard! I didn't hear a thing and I know I'm right on this one. Get in the goddamned van and drive." She ordered.

"My pay was docked the last time you pulled this bullshit." He replied.

"Well isn't that too bad! Listen to the baby cry!" She said. "That's why you're not a reporter. You haven't got any balls and you worry about things too much!"

CHAPTER TWENTY-THREE

POLICE HEADQUARTERS...SAN DIEGO

THE CITY REELED, WHEN Jean Simmons broke the news of the Mayor's murder. Chief Brewer had been watching Jean, as she reported live on the story, and revealed Woitasczyk's name.

"How does that bitch get there first, and where in the hell did she get Woitasczyk's name as the killer? We don't know for sure if it was him." Brewer said to his secretary, who was watching the broadcast with him.

"I don't know, Chief." She answered. "You should have let, Sergeant Unroe, arrest her."

"That would have started another stink. The bitch is too cunning to mess with and I've got other fish to fry. If Woitasczyk killed his wife and the Mayor, we've got to find him. Call down and have then put out an APB on Woitasczyk. Find out what make and model his car is, get the license number before you do."

"Okay. But as far as I'm concerned, you shouldn't have let that Simmons bitch out of jail. She was right where she belonged." His secretary said.

Brewer rolled his eyes and said. "Thank you for your input, Ms. Billings. Let me know when you've got what I've asked you to do, done."

"Don't forget, I covered your ass with those Fed's. You haven't told me what that was all about." She replied.

"I'll tell you when I retire." Brewer replied.

"And when might that be?" She asked.

"Sooner than you think. Now get going. I want to find Woitasczyk."

"Yes, sir!"

INTERSTATE 5…NORTH OF SAN DIEGO

DR. WOITASCZYK WAS SPEEDING south on Interstate 5, heading straight for the hospital. He was going to settle the score with Norton first, and then find Davis. He had four bullets left in his gun, enough to settle the score with all of them, including the Chief and the D.A. He felt empowered as he rubbed his hand over the cold blue steel of the barrel and cylinder of his gun.

Dirty Harry couldn't have done a better job with his .44 Magnum! He thought looking down at the gun beside him. He had bought it recently for home protection, against his wife's wishes. *I'm glad I killed her!* He thought. *The status-seeking bitch deserved it. I should have never married her anyway.* The more he thought about her, the angrier he became. *The insolent bitch called me crazy and wanted me to calm down so she could get me some help! The only help I'm going to need is a little luck in killing those other bastard's! I'll get that quack at the Psychiatric Journal, when I'm finished with the others!* His patted his box of shells that were laying on the seat beside his gun, and smiled.

As he sped toward the hospital, he saw an ambulance and police cars, streaking toward him, in the opposite lanes. Their lights were blinking and their sirens were blaring, as they blazed past him, heading north. Woitasczyk smiled as they went by, thinking. *They're probably on their way to pickup his majesty, the Mayor. He doesn't need an ambulance, what he needs is a hearse!*

He laughed as he thought of the Mayor, standing beside the curb, with the rest of the neighborhood gawkers. *The stupid bastard found out what was going on, when I splattered his brains all over the sidewalk!*

He looked in his mirror for any sign of police in pursuit, and thought. *I can't let the bastard's catch me. I've got to finish this job.*

He pushed the accelerator to the floorboard and watched the speedometer, in his Mercedes, pass the hundred mile an hour mark. He was weaving in and out of traffic, with no concern for the safety other drivers on the freeway.

Suddenly a car ahead, changed lanes in front of him, he slammed on the brakes, but it was too late. He hit the car in front of him, sending his car catapulting into the air and twisting, as it flipped over and came crashing down on the convertible top, killing him instantly. He had not fastened his seat belt when he had left on his deadly errand, not that it mattered now, he would have been killed either way. As his car skidded, top down, showering sparks, it was struck from behind and crushed by a semi, hauling fuel. The gas tank of his car exploded, engulfing his car, and the tanker, in an inferno of flames. Traffic piled up, on both sides of the freeway as one chain reaction accident after the other occurred, leaving Interstate 5, hopelessly snarled. Unknowingly, Woitasczyk had caused the worst traffic accident in the history of San Diego, and with it, his shooting spree had come to an end.

THE CHIEF CALLS VINCE

CHIEF BREWER CALLED VINCE at the lab and told him what had happened to Woitasczyk. "You won't be talking to him now, and it's probably a good thing you didn't. The crime scene boys found a list of names at his house. We think it was a hit list. It looks like he intended to kill you, me, the D.A. and Norton. The Mayor and his wife's names weren't on the list, but he shot her first and the Mayor next. The Mayor was in the wrong place, that's for sure."

"Damn! And he said I was crazy!" Vince replied.

"Somehow that Simmons bitch, found out about his list." Brewer said. "She's already trying to get an interview with me and Forrester. She's asked for your new address. I didn't give it out, but she'll put two and two together. She'll be looking for you at the lab before you know it. Don't tell her anything, Vince. We can't have your story spread all over the airways."

"Don't worry, I won't. Thanks, Chief." He didn't tell the Chief about seeing Jean Simmons in her van earlier in day, and thinking her driver was Clemmons. He'd been thinking of Woitasczyk before he had seen

Jean's van, and had thrown the card with Woitasczyk's name and address on it, in the trash. The Mayor's murder and Woitasczyk's death was another bizarre turn of events, that had happened since he had escaped, and Jean Simmons had covered all of them. He had no idea why he thought her driver was Clemmons. He knew Clemmons was somewhere in D.C., but he sure as hell wouldn't be driving a KQTV van, and asking for an interview. He also knew that he had killed Clemmons at Lambert Field in 2009. *I'm seeing things! What's next?* He wondered.

He began to feel like he was a plague or grim reaper that had come to San Diego, with a vengeance, so that Jean Simmons would have one bizarre story after another, connected to him, which she could report on. He thought of the individuals, who were now dead that he had came in contact with since he had come back. The whole thing was unimaginable to him. *The Epperson's are dead and now the Mayor. Woitasczyk killed his wife and now he's dead. I've had contact with all of them, in one way or another, except Woitasczyk's wife. This new version of 2005 isn't panning out the way it did before. I didn't know any of them the first time. But even for those I did know, things are going different. Donna and Jim have lead different lives this time. I didn't even know Donna the first time and I'm not doing what I did the first time. None of this makes any sense. Maybe Woitasczyk was right. Maybe I am going off the deep end.*

He sat and continued to ponder what he should do next. He didn't want to cause more harm or ill effects on anyone else's life. He was sure he was doing more harm than good. It showed on his face as Donna walked up.

"What's bothering you, Vince?" She asked.

He laid out the whole story. She knew the Mayor had been killed, but hadn't known it was Woitasczyk who had done it.

"I just don't know, Donna." He said. "Am I doing more harm than good? Look at Dr. Leyland. He looks worse than he did after he recovered in 2009."

Donna had no way of knowing what Dr. Leyland looked like in 2009, but she let Vince continue talking, without interrupting.

"If something happens to him, we can't go on. Without his new equipment, credentials and reputation, we might as well piss in the wind." He said.

"Boy, are you down." She said.

"With good reason." He replied. "I don't like the way things are stacking up. I've changed everybody's life around me. What's next?"

"I like the way my life's changed." Donna said and smiled. "Why don't we just take the rest of the day off and do some sightseeing. I'd like to go down to the beach or something. Maybe ride the roller coaster at Mission Beach. What do you say?"

He agreed and they left, after telling Jim, they'd see him in the morning.

MISSION BEACH

THE BEACH WAS PACKED, it was a beautiful day with children playing in the surf and sand. Screams of delight sounded as the roller coaster topped the summit and plummeted down, taking the riders breath away. It was all just like he had dreamed it was, when he was riding back to Camp Davis in the Blackhawk, from Lambert field. He remembered being jolted awake after seeing the surgeons' masked face looking down and reassuring him, everything was going to be okay. That part of the dream had not been welcome. That dream had began from fond memories of his first life in 2005, and then had been intertwined with things he was experiencing in 2009. His mind wasn't on the beach or roller coaster. He was trying to sort out why the things that were happening to him now, were happening and trying to figure out what the things he was dreaming about could possible mean. Neither had any real life connection to the other, especially the dreams. *Dreams are usually about real things that have happened in your life or imaginary things from your life that have never happened to you at all. Now I'm dreaming about things from the future that never happened, with people that were never associated with the events in the future, but somehow, they've been connected to what's going to happen in the future.*

He had been dreaming almost every night about what had happened in 2009. He hadn't told Donna, he didn't want to worry her. The events in those dreams weren't playing out as they actually had in 2009. In his new dreams, he was losing ground at every turn and was continually struggling to overcome new challenges that faced him, in events that had never occurred in 2009. He usually woke up when someone from the camp was killed and each night had been a continuing chapter from the night before. It was like the serial movies that were made in the 1940's, but the hero in the serials, always escaped and was back the next week fighting, till he ultimately won out in the end, but he wasn't winning in his dreams. Lately, in his new dreams, some of the individuals around him were different people. People that had never been at Camp Davis, but regardless, they were people he had known at some time in his life in 2005 or 2009. His dreams were now mixing those people in with the camp members at Camp Davis. Larry Williams and his wife and the Epperson's were among those people and they were dying along side of the familiar faces. There was nothing he could do to prevent it and to make matters worse, Woitasczyk had replaced Dr. Lucas as the camp doctor and had eagerly fallen in league with Randall, as Camp Davis took on the look of a Nazi concentration camp.

He had that dream, two nights before and thought it had been the worst. Jim had been killed in that dream, as Randall's column had reached their camp, and had taken it over. He knew he had killed Randall, but there he was, in his dreams, fulfilling his mission. He had pondered and dismissed the absurdity of Randall, still being alive, but that didn't help matters. Woitasczyk being the camp doctor and turning it into a concentration camp, to carry out his deadly experiments as Josef Mengele had, was even more absurd. When he woke up, he had felt as though he was losing his mind.

He had struggled through the following day, telling no one and not wanting to fall asleep that night, but he did and he dreamed again. That dream, his most recent, had been last night and had been the worst of all. Randall had captured him and Donna, and was planning to execute both of them. They were both bound and tied to posts, driven in the ground at the camp, and were facing a firing squad of Randall's men. Lawson, Clemmons and Woitasczyk, looked on approvingly, as Randall was barking out the commands. In defeat, he and Donna had looked helplessly at each other, as he told her he loved her and was sorry. Then the count came. Ready, aim, fire! As the rifles fired, he had woke up frantically and jumped out of bed, with the sound of the gunshots, ringing in his ears, yelling. "Jesus Christ! This has got to stop!"

He had wakened Donna, and had told her it was another bad dream and had considered he might actually go crazy, if the dreams didn't stop. He had sat down on the edge of the bed and began rubbing his head, trying uselessly, to erase the memory of the dreams. He had wanted to discuss the dreams with Woitasczyk or some other psychiatrist. He knew Woitasczyk would have been the best choice, since he had heard the whole story time and again. He now realized it wasn't vindication he was seeking from Woitasczyk, it was help with his problems. That wasn't going to happen now, Woitasczyk was dead. He knew he needed to talk to someone about the dreams, and he knew he needed to talk to someone soon.

The screams from roller coaster broke through his thoughts, as Donna said. "Something's bothering you again, Vince. What is it?"

He came out of his thoughts, realizing Donna was looking at him with a concerned look on her face.

"Nothing really, I was just thinking." He replied.

"What were you thinking about?" She asked.

"The bad dreams, I've had." He replied.

"They're just dreams, Vince! Everyone has bad dreams, some time or another." Donna said.

"Not like mine. Let's get out of here and go home. We can pick up some hamburgers on the way. I need to talk to you, in private."

POLICE DEPARTMENT…SAN DIEGO

CHIEF BREWER WAS GIVING the media, the interview they were clamoring for. He officially released the names of the victims, as he stood in front of Police Headquarters, where the flags hung at half-staff. He had first thanked all of the press and media members for being there, and then released the findings.

"The official findings of the coroner's office, is a double homicide in the deaths of the Mayor and Mrs. Gunderich Woitasczyk. Those murders were committed by, Dr. Gunderich Woitasczyk. The coroner has also found that the death of Dr. Gunderich Woitasczyk while driving south on the 5, was accidental and the result of a collision he was involved in while driving at a high rate of speed after leaving the scene of the two murders he committed. A charred .44 Magnum handgun was recovered in the wreckage of Dr. Woitasczyk's automobile. Forensics has determined it was the gun used to commit the murders of the Mayor and Dr. Woitasczyk's wife."

Jean Simmons was in the forefront of the media members and posed her first question before Brewer could go on.

"Chief! Do you think if you hadn't released Dr. Woitasczyk, none of this would have happened?"

How does that bitch always get the first, pointed question in? Brewer thought, but said."Dr. Woitasczyk was released on bond, Miss Simmons. He was not released on his own recognizance. His regrettable actions reflect no misconduct on the part of the police department. The court set the bond and Dr. Woitasczyk posted the bond, as any citizens, has the right to do. Next question." He said.

Jean wasn't through, and said."Wait a minute, Chief! I wasn't finished."

Goddamnit! Brewer thought, but said. "Continue, Miss Simmons."

"I've learned the District Attorney had dropped all the charges against Dr. Woitasczyk. Is that correct?"

"That's correct, Miss Simmons."

"Had Dr. Woitasczyk been informed of the charges being dropped, before he went on his rampage?" Jean asked.

"The District Attorney would have that answer, Miss Simmons, not I." Brewer replied.

"Do you think that letting Dr. Woitasczyk out on bond, was a responsible or wise decision, in view of what's happened?" Jean asked.

"Hindsight is much better than foresight, Miss Simmons. We don't have crystal balls we can look into. No one could have known or suspected, Dr. Woitasczyk would have committed the crimes he did. He was a well respected psychiatrist." Brewer replied.

"It was you that suggested the charges against him be dropped, if I recall correctly." Jean said.

"That is correct." Brewer said, becoming aggravated by Jean's, innuendos. "I did suggest the charges be dropped against Dr. Woitasczyk. I based my suggestions on his professional standing in the community, having found he had lead an exemplary life, here in San Diego. While what's happened today is reprehensible and very regrettable, the Police Department Psychiatrist has examined all the facts and feels that, Dr. Woitasczyk, would have still committed the heinous crimes he did today, even if the charges against him, were still standing. As I said, the Police Department and the District Attorney's Office do not have crystal balls we can look into, Miss Simmons. No one can predict future events or human behavior. It's long been known by all law enforcement agencies and prosecuting attorney's offices, that the criminal mind can't be predicted, nor can acts of violence that are spontaneously triggered by some contributing circumstance. Dr. Woitasczyk was not a criminal and had no background of violence. The man standing there next to you, could commit a crime tomorrow, you wouldn't know that today, but you would be reporting on it tomorrow. The fact the charges were dropped against Dr. Woitasczyk, bore no relationship or had any bearing, on the fact that he committed the crimes. Think about it, Miss Simmons. Why would Dr. Woitasczyk kill the Mayor? They didn't know each other and in fact, had never met, therefore Dr. Woitasczyk's actions didn't appear to be premeditated. The Mayor went on record just as I did recommending the charges against Dr. Woitasczyk be dropped. For whatever reason, and perhaps we'll never know, Dr. Woitasczyk was somehow ignited into his acts of violence. Perhaps he and his wife weren't getting along. They may have had a quarrel that ended up in her death. We don't know, and I don't presume we ever will."

"Are you saying you don't have any idea or know of any reason why he would have committed the murders?" Jean interrupted.

"If you'll give me the opportunity, I'll finish what I was saying, Miss Simmons."

Jean was rebuffed and she didn't like it. *Bastard!* She thought, as he went on.

"Miss Simmons, I believe it was you that first reported on a loud disturbance that seemed to be taking place in the Woitasczyk residence, before he murdered his wife. Is that correct?"

"Yes, I did. His neighbors told me they had heard the disturbance, before they heard the gunshot."

"Well it would seem to me that those facts would answer your question. As you reported, a quarrel was heard and then a gunshot. Apparently the Woitasczyk's were having a domestic dispute, before he killed his wife, but there was no physical evidence found in the house that would indicate a sign of a struggle. The house was pristine and nothing was found that supported an argument or violent behavior other than, Mrs. Woitasczyk's body. Dr. Woitasczyk's following action of murdering the Mayor, appears to simply be, that the Mayor was in the wrong place and was a victim of random violence. If he had not been there, it might have been one of the neighbors. No more questions."

Brewer started to leave the podium, when Jean Simmons shouted. "Chief! Didn't Woitasczyk have a hit list in his house with your name on it as well as, Vince Davis's, The D.A.'s and Dr. Carson."

I wondered when she was going to get around to that. Brewer thought. He stepped back to the microphone and said. "I think you have misunderstood the purpose of that list, Miss Simmons. You're right, there was a list, but it wasn't a hit list."

"Perhaps you'd like to explain what that list was for, Chief." Jean said with a smug look on her face.

"I'll be glad to, Miss Simmons. The hit list, as you refer to it, was nothing other than a list of names, Dr. Woitasczyk was going to write letters of thanks to, for the fair treatment, he received, while in custody. One to myself and the department. One to the District Attorney, for dropping the charges against him, and one to Dr. Carson for restoring his license to practice. Dr. Woitasczyk's Attorney had called Dr. Woitasczyk this morning, prior to the his incomprehensible acts, and had informed him his license would be restored, since the charges had been dropped."

Jean interrupted the Chief before he could go on. "Hold on, Chief! Informed sources told me that you would say that, and also said you were covering up the truth!"

"Once again you've interrupted me before I was finished, Miss Simmons. With your permission, may I go on?" Brewer asked.

"Well yes, certainly, I thought you were finished." Jean replied.

"Thank you, Miss Simmons! What I was going to say before you interrupted me was, Dr. Woitasczyk had called his attorney back after he had been told the charges were dropped. He read the names off that list to his attorney and asked him to draft and send those letters. I'm afraid you were off base on that one, Miss Simmons. The Mayor's name wasn't on the list, nor was Dr. Woitasczyk's wife's name, yet they're both dead. The murders were a random act of violence and nothing more, yet, you choose to question the truth and float un-substantiated allegations as if it were the truth. While I don't object to a reporter doing their job and I wholeheartedly support the First Amendment, what you're doing is reporting those allegations as if they were true, in hopes of putting public figures in an embarrassing situation. Damaging news, filled with unsubstantiated allegations, seems to be your forte of late. I believe you were arrested for that recently, were you not?" Brewer asked, staring right at her.

Jean was furious. Chief Brewer had struck a nerve, but she hadn't given up, despite the fact, that the Chief had just publicly embarrassed her, and replied in rebuttal. "Yes I was, and wrongfully so! The charges against me were dropped. Lt. Traxler's in jail now, not me! What about Davis? He was on the list, but you didn't mention him."

"Let me get this straight, Miss Simmons." Brewer said. "You're saying it's okay for the D.A. to drop the charges against you, because you thought it was wrong in your case, but not in the case of Dr. Woitasczyk. Is that what you're saying?" Brewer asked.

"The public has the right to know, Chief. What about, Davis?" Jean asked, avoiding the Chief's question.

"Dr. Woitasczyk's lawyer was instructed to draft a letter to him also." Brewer replied. "Dr. Woitasczyk wanted to apologize to Dr. Davis for misdiagnosing his condition."

"And what is Dr. Davis's condition, Chief?" Jean asked.

"I'm not qualified to answer that. I'm not a doctor." Brewer replied.

"Doesn't the Police Department consider Davis a soothsayer or some kind of psychic?" Jean asked.

"No, Miss Simmons, that's not true. Dr. Davis is a seismologist. It's his job to study the Earth's faults and try to determine where the next earthquake might occur. He's not a psychic or soothsayer as you referred to him. His job is to try and anticipate when and where the next earthquake could happen." Brewer replied.

"Hasn't he predicted a massive earthquake for some time in the future? One that will destroy the Earth?" Jean asked.

"Yes he did." Brewer replied. "But those statements were made after he had suffered a concussion, in a fall. At first, he did say that, but he was delirious and not himself, when he made those statements. That's why he was placed in Dr. Woitasczyk's care. That's all. No further questions." Brewer said and started walking away.

"Wait Chief! Why did he escape?" Jean yelled after him. "Why didn't Dr. Woitasczyk release him, if he was cured?"

Brewer stopped and turned around. He had an angry look on his face. He returned to the mic and said. "Miss Simmons, if you were on top of things, you would realize that medical records are confidential. A patient of any medical professional has a right to keep their medical history between their doctor and themselves. You or no one has a right to that information, and I'm sure, Dr. Davis wouldn't approve of you trying to dig into his personal life. What is your job and responsibilities, Miss Simmons? Is it to report facts or is your job to dig up all the dirt you can and muddy up the facts? It was my understanding that a reporter's job was to report genuine facts, in an ethical way, but from your past exploits, I would think you don't appear to have any ethics. It also appears to me, that you enjoy and gain some sort of devious satisfaction, from hurting people. You're free today to do your job, because I intervened, when Sergeant Unroe was going to arrest you at the at the crime scene in Dr. Woitasczyk's neighborhood. The next time you interfere in a police investigation, you won't be so lucky. Do I make myself clear?"

"Yes." Was all Jean could say, but she was thinking other things. *I'll get you for that, you lousy, bastard!*

"Is there anything else you would like to ask, Miss Simmons?" Brewer asked.

"No!" Jean replied in an angry tone.

"Then this news conference is over." Brewer said and left the podium.

The other reporters were no longer interested in the murders. They were all busy finishing their notes and making final comments into their recorders for the latest story that had been dropped in their laps. Jean Simmons was going to be on television, but she wouldn't be reporting. She was going to the subject of all the stories on the other radio and television stations.

While the reporters ran for their vehicles, Chief Brewer leaned over and whispered to Forrester. "She's was trying to screw things up again. I've got to find out who she's been getting her information from at headquarters. When I find out who it is, I'll zip her lip, and whoever's been leaking the information, will be gone."

"I think you zipped her lip, Chief." Forrester said. "You ripped her a new asshole out there and I think you pretty much discredited her. I don't think anyone is going to pay much attention to her allegations anymore. Hey, I'm thinking of running for Mayor, will you back me?" Forrester asked.

"Jesus Christ, Claude! Let them get the Mayor buried first!" Brewer replied, but thought. *What an asshole!*

KQTV VAN

"I'M GETTING THAT BASTARD!" Jean said to her cameraman as they packed their equipment. "He hasn't heard the last of me yet. Get Davis's work and home address for me."

"His home address? It's a crime scene, remember?" He replied.

"I mean where he's living now, you stupid, idiot! Do I have to spell everything out for you?" Jean asked sarcastically.

"Hey, go to hell, Jean!" He said.

"I'll see you there!" She sneered.

Her cameraman was fed up with her insults, and said. "The Chief buggered you up pretty good. I'll bet all of the other stations are going live, with the ass reaming, he gave you."

The thought hadn't crossed Jean's mind. She flipped on the radio and listened to a competitors broadcast.

"That right folks! You heard me right! San Diego Police Chief, Wayne Brewer, just finished his dressing down of and warning to Jean Simmons of KQTV. Jean had been asking absurd and irresponsible questions, at the Chief's news conference, and as always, Jean wasn't willing to let a sleeping dog lie. She got paid back for her disrespectful behavior, by Chief Brewer, who warned her she would be arrested again and returned to jail, if she continued to interfere in police matters. You will recall she was just recently released from jail, after having interfered in police matters at another location in the city. Today she refused to follow orders from Police Sergeant Jack Unroe, who was in charge at the scene of the Mayor's murder. It was only because Chief Brewer intervened, that she was not arrested today. Chief Brewer gave Jean her final warning at the news conference today. Jean, if you're out there and you're listening, you've been a naughty girl."

Jean was enraged as her cameraman laughed.

"I told you!" He said and continued laughing.

"Stop laughing, goddamnit! It isn't funny!" She yelled.

"What's the matter, Jean? Don't you like getting the shitty end of the stick?" The cameraman asked and went on laughing.

"I'm not taking any more of your shit, you asshole! Drop me off at the corner!" She shouted.

He pulled up at the corner and let her out and said. "Get yourself another cameraman! I'm too embarrassed to work with you any longer!"

"You bet I will, and you'll be looking for a job when I do!" She yelled, slammed the door and gave him the finger, as he drove away laughing.

CHAPTER TWENTY-FOUR

CITY JAIL...SAN DIEGO POLICE DEPARTMENT

Traxler sat in his cell awaiting arraignment. He could hear, but not see the TV, Reese was watching. He had heard Jean Simmons as she interviewed the Chief outside the Police Department. Having heard Simmons remark about him being in jail and her being free stung him deeply, as the thought of revenge went though his mind. *I'll get that worthless bitch, if it's the last thing I do!*

His angered welled up dramatically, and he started pacing his cell trying to think of a way to escape. *I've got to get out of here! I've got to get even with them!*

His focus was now on escaping and killing Simmons, then the Chief and anyone else that got in his way.

There might be a way to get out of here, if I play it right." He thought.

CHIEF BREWER'S OFFICE

The Chief's secretary buzzed Chief Brewer, and said. "Rowland's on the phone. He said it's urgent."

"Shit! What now?" Brewer asked.

"I don't know. He didn't say."

Brewer picked up his phone and asked. "What is it Rowland?"

"Traxler's had a seizure of some kind. He was foaming at the mouth and having convulsions. They've taken him to the Hospital."

"Jesus Christ! How bad is he?" Brewer asked.

"I don't know! He was still having seizures when they loaded him in the ambulance. Reese said he was unconscious, but he was still breathing." Rowland replied.

"Do they think he'll die?" Brewer asked.

"Reese said the paramedics were working on him, but he looked real bad, when they put him in the ambulance."

"Jesus! What a day!" Brewer said. "The Mayor's dead, Simmons was all over my ass, now Traxler. What's next?"

The Chief's Secretary buzzed him on the intercom again. "Pick up line two, Chief. Dispatch is on the line. It's an emergency!"

Goddamnit! What is it now? He thought as he put Rowland on hold and said. "Chief Brewer."

"Traxler has escaped, Chief!" Riley, the dispatcher said.

"Aw shit! That's all I need! I've got another call, hold on. He punched the other line and said. "You aren't going to believe this, Rowland! Traxler's escaped. I've got to let you go."

"Wait a minute, Chief! How did he escape?" Rowland asked.

"I don't know yet! Hold on, I'll find out." Brewer punched line two and asked. "What happened, Riley?"

"Traxler overpowered the paramedics and he's stolen their ambulance."

"Jesus Christ! Didn't they send a patrolman with him in the ambulance?" Brewer asked.

"I guess they didn't think they needed to, him being unconscious, and being a cop, Chief." Riley replied.

"He's a felon." Brewer barked. "He's not a cop anymore. Did you get someone on it?"

"I put out an all points, Chief." Riley replied.

"Let me know when you get him back in custody." Brewer punched line one and asked. "Are you still there, Rowland?"

"Yeah, what happened? How did he escape?"

"He overpowered the paramedic's and stole their ambulance. This is all I need, goddamnit! Get on it, Rowland! Find out where he lives, you know he'll go there first to get his car!"

"Right, Chief." Rowland said and hung up.

This is the shits! Brewer thought. *Now, I've got a bad cop roaming the streets and I know goddamned well he'll be trying to even the score with me.*

He called his wife and said. "Traxler's escaped! Lock all the doors, pull the blinds and get my automatic out of the nightstand. I'm sending a patrolman over to watch the house. Don't answer the door, even if they say they're a cop. I'm coming home right now. You'll know it's me when the garage door goes up!"

He hung up thinking about Traxler pointing his gun at him and threatening to kill him and thought. *He's probably crazy enough to try it again.*

He pressed the intercom button and said. "Call dispatch and tell them to send a cruiser over to my house. Tell them to do it right now, and tell them to give the patrolman a picture of Traxler. I'm going home. Call me if they catch Traxler."

He left his office and headed for the parking lot.

Another screw-up! He thought. *I've got to get as far away from this city as I can. I'm turning in my retirement papers tomorrow!*

THE CHIEF GETS A SURPRISE

CHIEF BREWER ROUNDED THE corner to his house and saw the patrol car sitting out in front. It didn't make any difference that he was the Chief of Police, he felt better with another cop watching the neighborhood.

He pulled slowly past the cruiser, waved to the patrolman inside, turned into his driveway and stopped. He got out of his car and went to see which officer was sitting in the cruiser. The officer inside stepped out and pointed his gun at Brewer.

"It's me, goddamnit!" Brewer barked. "Put your damn gun away!"

"Get back in your car, Chief!" The officer ordered.

"What the hell?" Brewer asked, and then saw it was Traxler, with the patrolman's hat and jacket on.

"Get back in your car!" Traxler ordered. "We're going for a ride."

Brewer got back in his car, as Traxler slid into the seat beside him, and said. "Get going!"

Brewer backed his car out of his driveway and headed back up the street. His wife pulled back the blind and saw his car driving away. She saw the cruiser still sitting out in front, thought her husband had forgotten something and would be back soon. She didn't give it a second thought and went back to watching TV.

Jean Simmons was back live, reporting from in front of the Police Station. She had just began reporting on Traxler's escape and the all points bulletin out for his capture.

I hope they find him soon. The Chief's wife thought as she went back and checked on the cruiser. Seeing it, and feeling the safety it provided, she went to start supper, thinking the Chief would be back soon.

"You can't get away with this, Traxler!" Brewer snarled.

"Shut up and turn on your radio!" Traxler hissed.

Brewer flipped on the regular radio in the car, and music started playing.

"Not that one, goddamnit! I want to listen to the police band!" Traxler snapped.

Brewer reached over to turn off the radio and Traxler yelled. "Wait! Hold on, don't turn it off!"

Jean Simmons had just come on the air and was being carried live on KQTV's affiliate radio station. She was reporting Traxler's escape story, from Police Headquarters.

"That's where we're going, Chief!" Traxler barked.

"Where?" Brewer asked.

"Police Headquarters! Put your emergency light on the roof, but don't turn on the siren and step on it!"Traxler ordered. He had a fixed look in his eyes, as he pointed his gun at Brewer.

"Where'd you get the gun, Traxler?" Brewer asked.

"Why don't you ask that rookie, you sent out to guard your house? That is, if you live long enough. Give me your gun, Chief…easy now… use your left hand." Traxler said.

"What did you do to him?" Brewer asked, as he handed Traxler his gun.

"He'll be okay, when he wakes up." Traxler said.

"You won't get away with this, Traxler! He'll call in the minute he does!" Brewer snapped back.

"He's not calling anybody!" Traxler retorted. "He's cuffed and gagged in the trunk. Now, drive and shut up!"

Brewer drove on, with his light flashing, picking up speed, weaving his way through traffic, as they neared the Police Station.

"You better think twice about what you're doing, Traxler! It's just getting worse for you!" Brewer said.

"I'll never see the inside of a jail again! You can damn sure bet on that! Pull up by the KQTV van." Traxler ordered.

The crowd stepped back and parted, as they saw the Chief's car arriving, with its light flashing.

"Here comes the Chief's car now." Jean said, still live on TV and Radio. "I'll see if I can get the Chief to comment on this latest problem, for the San Diego Police Department." She felt smug, seeing an opportunity to needle the Chief, wanting to see him squirm.

"I thought you were the Police Department's biggest problem, Jean!" Someone yelled from the crowd.

Jean cringed and shrugged it off, as the people started laughing. She was going to be on her best behavior this time. The station manager had warned her she was on shaky ground, before she went out on the assignment, but she was still going to stick some legitimate barbs in the Chief. She watched as the Chief's car pulled to a stop and the passenger door opened.

"Chief!" She yelled, as she walked toward his car thinking the Chief was getting out.

Traxler jumped out, and fired three shots into Jean. Her face contorted in surprise and pain, in full view of the camera as she fell dead to the ground, still clutching the microphone in her hand. The crowd started screaming and ran for cover.

Traxler turned toward Brewer and said. "You're next!"

Before he could fire, Brewer shot Traxler twice with his back up gun, he had pulled from his waistband.

Traxler slumped, looking at Brewer, with surprise in his eyes. Brewer shot him again, this time right between the eyes. Traxler fell to the street, dead.

Police were streaming out of the Police Station with guns in hand, and were running toward the Chief's car. With shaking hands, Brewer picked up his mic and called dispatch.

"I'm in front of the station! Traxler just shot Jean Simmons! I think she's dead, but you better get an ambulance anyway."

"What the hell happened out there, Chief?" Riley asked.

"Traxler was waiting for me when I got home. He forced me to drive him to the station and then he shot, Jean Simmons."

"Where is Traxler? Did he get away?" Riley asked.

"I killed him! He won't need an ambulance! Call the coroner and then send a couple cruisers to my house and tell them to free the officer that's locked in the truck of his cruiser, in front of my house."

"Jesus, Chief! Anything else?" Riley asked.

"Call my wife and tell her I'm okay and I'll be home soon, then tell Rowland to get out here, and drive me home. I'll fill out a report when I get home and send it back with Rowland."

Those watching TV, who saw Jean Simmons get gunned down, couldn't believe their eyes. The station returned immediately to the studio as Jean fell to the pavement. Other TV stations that were on the scene were still reporting live and kept looping the tape of the murder of Jean Simmons and then of her laying in a pool of blood, face down in the street.

There had been no love or respect for Jean, from other reporters or from other stations. Although it didn't seem proper, one station pointed out that she had went to her end, with her microphone still clutched firmly in her hand, trying to get the story.

Police quickly took charge and sent the camera crews back to a respectable distance and surrounded the area with crime scene tape. Brewer bent down and checked Traxler for a pulse and then checked Jean. He found none in either. He pointed to his gun laying on the ground and told a detective that Traxler had taken it from him and used it as the murder weapon. He handed his back up gun to the detective, telling him that he had used it to kill Traxler. Camera crews from all the major stations were still live, as Rowland drove up in a cruiser and Brewer got in. He told Rowland what had happened, and then said. "Take me home."

"Don't you want to get a new gun before we leave? Rowland asked.

"No. I'm putting in my retirement papers tomorrow."

J. L. Reynolds

DONNA'S HOUSE

VINCE WAS SITTING ON the couch getting ready to tell Donna what was troubling him, when she got back from the kitchen. They had been watching the TV while eating their hamburgers, not paying close attention. Jean Simmons came on live in front of Police Headquarters and Vince turned up the volume. She started off by reporting Traxler's escape.

"Get in here quick, Donna!" Vince yelled. "Traxler's escaped! They're reporting it live!"

They listened and watched as Jean went through the details of what had happened and was about to wrap it up, when she said. "Here comes the Chief's car now. I'll see if I can get his comment on this latest problem for the San Diego Police Department."

Vince and Donna heard the heckler yell at Jean and laughed along with the others who were in front of Police Headquarters.

Her new cameraman panned to the Chief's car as the passenger door opened and then back on Jean. She had a slight smile on her face as the camera caught her again.

"Chief!" She yelled and took a few steps toward his car. The next instant, Vince and Donna heard gunshots, from off camera, and saw Jean fall. The cameraman had instinctively followed Jean as she fell. More shots rang out an instant later and the screen went dark for a few seconds and then local programming came on.

"Jesus Christ! Did you see that?" Vince asked, changing channels with the remote. Another station was still carrying the scene live and was now focusing on the Chief's car as Chief Brewer stepped out.

"In a bizarre and horrendous turn of events, Jean Simmons has just been gunned down in a hail of bullets in front of Police Headquarters!" The reporter was flabbergasted and almost seemed panicked as he went on. "The gunman was also shot as he turned to fire on a police officer. Wait…my cameraman said the gunman arrived in the police car you are now seeing on your screen. The gunman apparently stepped from the police car as it arrived and shot Jean Simmons down at point blank range…hold on, I'm getting a further update."

Seconds later, he went on. "The police car the gunman arrived in has now been identified as belonging to Chief, Wayne Brewer. Chief Brewer is now being reported as the police officer that shot the unknown gunman, who had just shot Jean Simmons. Although witnesses say the unknown gunman was wearing police clothing, he has yet to be identified, but apparently, the gunman turned his gun on Chief Brewer intending to kill him next, but was himself killed by Chief Brewer, before he could fire his weapon. "

Vince and Donna continued to watch as the story was rehashed, time after time, learning Traxler had killed Jean Simmons after escaping custody earlier in the day, by commandeering an ambulance he had been riding in. No one had any explanation for why Traxler was in the ambulance, or why Chief Brewer and Traxler had arrived at Police Headquarters, where Traxler had killed Jean Simmons as she was reporting Traxler's escape, to a live TV audience. Finally seeing enough, they turned off the TV.

"Jesus Christ! What the hell is going on?" Vince asked. "Almost everyone who's had anything to do with me this time, is killing someone or being killed. Jean was following me today in her van and wanted an interview, now she's dead, and so is Traxler. The way it's going, everybody I have contact with in some way or another might be affected. It's like I've brought some kind of plague with me from 2009!"

"It can't be because of you! That doesn't make sense, Vince!" Donna said.

"Look at the people I've had contact with here, since I've come back." Vince replied. "The Epperson's, Woitasczyk, Traxler, the Mayor and now Jean Simmons. They've all been killed or died in some terrible way. I've been having dreams I can't explain since the Epperson's died. I wanted to talk to Woitasczyk about them. Now he's dead. Who's next? You, Jim, Dr. Leyland, or the Chief? Shit! I'm going crazy, Donna!"

Donna didn't know what to say. She was stunned. Vince was bent over holding his head saying. "What in the hell am I going to do?"

CHAPTER TWENTY-FIVE

THE CHIEF'S HOUSE

CHIEF BREWER'S WIFE WAS beside herself, waiting for her husband to come home. She had watched and re-watched the scene showing Jean Simmons being gunned down, after hearing Jean say the Chief was driving up. She had heard the second gunshots thinking the first had come from her husband's gun. She mistakenly thought her husband had finally had enough of Jean and had went back to gun her down. She knew full well, that it would be totally uncharacteristic of her husband to do anything like that, but despite knowing that, she waited anxiously, dreading she was going to hear her husband's name, given as the shooter.

When KQTV went to regular programming she switched channels and found one still covering what was now a murder scene. She held her breath fearing that any second they would name, Wayne Brewer, Chief of Police, as the shooter. Instead, she watched as the camera zoomed in and showed him bending down checking Jean for a pulse.

"It appears, that Lt. Traxler, a rogue police officer, was the gunman who shot and killed Jean Simmons, here on the Police Department steps. Details are not clear yet, but earlier today, the police department's spokesman revealed that Lt. Traxler had escaped custody shortly before he committed this heinous act of murder. Although not documented, it has been speculated that Lt. Traxler may have kidnapped, Chief Wayne

Brewer as he left his office for the day, and then forced him to drive back here to Police Headquarters, where Lt. Traxler, then shot and killed Jean Simmons, who was in fact, reporting on his escape."

"Oh my!" The Chief's wife said, as the reporter went on.

"There has been no reason or explanation given for Lt. Traxler's actions, but you will recall, it was he who placed Jean under arrest while she was covering another murder scene in El Cajon, a short while back. However, Jean was subsequently released and cleared of the charges, Lt. Traxler had arrested and jailed her for. Just recently, Lt. Traxler himself was arrested and jailed for assault with intent to kill, stemming from an incident in Chief Brewer's office, where he was being relieved of duty, relating to his inappropriate conduct a few days ago, when he closed the airport down in pursuit of a still unknown terrorist. He had taken this action without explanation to or knowledge of Chief Brewer or the Police Department. Apparently, Lt. Traxler, felt he had done no wrong and pulled his gun on the Chief Brewer when he was told by Chief Brewer that he was being suspended without pay until a hearing could be held on his behalf. The altercation led to his arrest and he was being held temporarily in the Police Department lockup, awaiting arraignment, on the assault charges. His preliminary hearing was scheduled for tomorrow, but it's now being reported that Lt. Traxler became ill while in custody and was being taken by ambulance to a local hospital for treatment, and somehow managed to overpower the ambulance attendants and commandeer their ambulance. Although we expect to know soon, we have not yet learned, how or why Lt. Traxler and Chief Brewer arrived at the police station in Chief Brewer's car. However, this tragic scene you see before you, is evidence of Lt. Traxler's last act, and unexplained rampage, before his own life ended."

The Chief's wife heard the garage door going up and rushed toward the door as he entered.

"Wayne! Are you all right? I saw the horrible murder on the television. Hold me." She said. "I want to feel you and know you're okay."

"I'm okay." He said and kissed her. "We're putting the house on the market tomorrow. I'm retiring."

"What? Retiring tomorrow? Selling the house? Why so soon?" She asked.

"I escaped death, by the blink of an eye, less than an hour ago." He replied. "If I hadn't had my backup gun, I would be dead. Traxler was going to shoot me after he shot Miss Simmons, but I got him first. I've had a bad feeling lately that something bad was going to happen. I was lucky when Traxler's clip fell out of his gun in my office. Tonight he told me it was my turn to die, before I shot him. I'm retiring tomorrow and don't try to talk me out of it. This job isn't worth getting killed over."

"Where are we going, and when will we leave?" She asked.

"We're moving to, Missouri, just west of St. Louis." He said. "I'll have to attend a hearing for shooting Traxler. I'll be suspended with pay until the board clears me."

"How long will that take?" She asked.

"A couple of weeks at the most. Call the movers in the morning. We can have them store everything until we find a place."

"Are you sure?" She asked. "We've lived here a long time. All our friends are here."

"I've never been surer about anything in my life." He answered.

"What do you want me to tell our friends when they ask why we're moving?" She asked.

"Tell them anything you want, but don't tell them what Davis has told me." He said. "They won't believe it for one thing and they'll think I'm crazy, for another."

"His story is hard to believe, dear, and it does sound crazy. No one moves to Missouri, from California. It would be the other way around." She replied.

"Tell them you're moving to Phoenix, if it's easier to explain. Once we're gone, they won't know where we are. I'll tell the department the same thing. Okay?" He asked.

"Okay." She said.

DONNA'S HOUSE

DONNA HAD SAT AND listened to Vince. He appeared to be a having a mental breakdown. She decided to take the tough approach with him.

"I'll tell you what you're going to do!" She said. "You're going ahead with your work at the lab and complete the job. You can't stop now. None of the deaths had anything to do with you. It's all a coincidence."

"But none of this happened the first time." Vince protested. "I didn't know any of the people the first time, who have gotten killed or murdered this time. I had never even heard of them and our paths never crossed then, like they have now. Whatever world I'm living in this time, is different. It's sinister compared to the first time. I led a humdrum, day in and day out life before, with no excitement except for a small earthquake now and then. People got killed and murdered, but I didn't know any of them. This time I've known or heard of all of them. Something evil is going on and I don't have any idea why it is, or why I'm connected to it in some way."

"Look, Vince." Donna said. "I don't think I'm living the same life I would have been either, but I don't know for sure. You said you learned I had joined the Air Force when you arrived at Area 51. I was thinking about doing just that, but I'm not thinking about it anymore. I haven't had any dreams about area 51 or anything else that happened in your description of the events in 2009 but I believe you, so does Jim and Dr. Leyland. You're not going to stop what you're doing, are you? Please don't tell me that."

"To tell you the truth, that's exactly what I've been thinking of doing. It might be better for everyone, including myself, if I leave and go back to Missouri. I can get a teaching assignment at the University of Missouri. I'm beginning to feel like it would be better to leave all of this earthquake and disaster shit behind. I can stay with my parents till I get set up. Will you go with me?" He asked.

"Of course I'd go with you." She replied. "At least I think I would. But, I won't go until we see this to an end here. If Beatty turns Dr. Leyland down, we can talk about it then. I'm not going anywhere till then. You have to finish your job here, Vince."

"I've been thinking about that, Donna. Let's just say the three of you go to Beatty with Dr. Leyland's Model and the new piece of equipment, which Dr. Leyland has already said she won't be receptive of, what good will it do?" Vince asked.

"Boy, you are down, aren't you? Is it because Dr. Leyland thinks you shouldn't go with us?" She asked.

"No, he's right, it's best that I don't go." Vince replied.

"What is it then?" She asked.

"Even if you explain how equipment will function with a satellite, if the government sends up a satellite, and Dr. Leyland explains his Model, trying to convince her to go along with the idea, what if she doesn't?" Vince asked.

"We have to try. You know that!" Donna said.

"I know we should, but I have a feeling I can't explain, that's telling me none of this is going to work out. Something inside of me is telling me to go back to Missouri."

"If it doesn't work out, I'll go with you." Donna said.

"Do you mean that?" Vince asked.

"Of course I mean that! None of us would be doing any of this if it weren't for you. You can't let Jim and Dr. Leyland down now. Jim stuck his neck out getting you the information you wanted and you've proved beyond a shadow of a doubt that what you've said, is going to happen. You're our leader whether you like it or not. Without you we might as well call it quits."

"Okay, I won't argue any more. I'll go back to work at the lab, but I still feel convinced, she'll turn us down." Vince said.

"Well we won't know if we don't try, will we?" Donna asked.

"No we wouldn't." Vince replied.

"If she turns us down, we can leave, but she may not turn us down. Have you thought of that?" She asked.

"Not really, but okay. Say she goes along with the idea and doesn't call Dr. Leyland an old fool, like she did the first time. She or someone will still have to convince the government. Bush is involved in a war he can't win. He isn't going to call for some new radical disaster avoidance plan to be put in place. He's too busy trying to frighten the world and the American citizens, with his divine war against terrorism, and in so doing, he's trying to justify the damn war." Vince said.

"I agree, but you still need to help us." She replied

"I said I will, but I know I'll be wasting my time. The government won't get involved until Lemming's in office, and that's not until 2008. By then it will be too late, just like the first time. I think the only reason all of this is happening to me, is to prepare me, so I won't be in San Diego when it does happen."

"Do you mean this is something, God wants you to do?" Donna asked.

"Hell no! I don't believe there is a God! That's what Bush said when he announced his plan for a war on terrorism, before he got elected. He said God told him he would defeat terrorism, but he damn sure hasn't done it has he? He's just made matters worse. No God is going to save this world from terrorism or the disaster, when it happens. It will end up, just as I said it did. The only hope I had was warning those that need to know, and make sure we're in Missouri when it does happen."

"Vince, don't do this to yourself!" Donna said, realizing Vince was beginning to sound paranoid.

"Look, Donna! I said I'd work on the project and I will, but we may as well be making preparations to leave at the same time, so we can be out of the way and safe when it happens. I can buy an old surplus helicopter and get the other things we'll need to be ready, when it happens."

Donna didn't want to believe what she was hearing from, Vince.

"Are you listening to yourself?" She asked. "Run away from it? Save yourself and a few others that believe you? Vince, you can't do that! I won't go with you if you do. You've got to help us and quit thinking about the future. We're here and this is now. It hasn't happened yet and you said yourself that it may never happen. You shouldn't even be thinking about leaving and moving to Missouri. You're acting as if you've been defeated and you haven't even tried to win. If you give up, you won't be able to live with yourself, and neither will I."

Donna could see the let down on Vince's face. She in essence had said she wasn't going with him if he kept thinking the way he was. She hoped she was getting through to him, but at the same time, thought she wasn't.

"I'm not going anyplace without you." Vince said. "But you have to understand, I'm no saint and I'm not a leader, but I don't believe for one minute that Sandra Beatty is going to go along with any of this. I was locked up for telling my story and told I had a grandiose projection of my own ego and imagination. You know she's heard about it, and she knows I work with Dr. Leyland. When he goes to her with the information, she's going to know where it came from, don't kid yourself for minute on that. I don't feel important and I don't want to be important. All I ever wanted to do was study geology and earthquakes, and where has it gotten me? I was locked up because no one believed me, and Sandra won't either."

"We believe you, Vince. I've told you that. I don't doubt for one second that what you say happened to you, did happen. I just wasn't there, even though you say I was. Sure, I had some oddball dreams, I did some oddball things in those dreams, and by that, I don't mean going to bed with you. That was the best part of the dreams. I want to go with you and be with you for the rest of my life, wherever you go or wherever that takes us, but we can't call it quits here, and skip out on everybody, just to save ourselves. Isn't that what you, disgustedly said, Lemming did?"

Vince's face lost the desolate appearance it had moments before. She could see he was thinking again.

"Yes, that's exactly what he did." Vince replied.

"You couldn't do that and you know it." She said.

"Okay, you're right, Donna. Say you do go with what we've got, which is just a small amount of evidence and a plan for a new way of detecting future events. The new equipment will look for the most part like the old equipment. All the changes are going to be inside. You won't be able to prove it will work, without a satellite to send the signals for it to receive. She won't take anyone's word for that." Vince said.

"I agree with you on that, but we still have to go." She replied.

"You can't go without a plan for a satellite to support the equipment. I know she's not going to buy any of it, if you don't have a plan and even if you did, it would just be another unproven theory of Dr. Leyland's." Vince said.

"Why did Lemming believe Dr. Leyland, when the others didn't?" Donna asked.

"I don't know, I never found out. I wish I'd asked him." He replied.

"It doesn't matter." Donna said. "You know you're right. Jim, I and Dr. Leyland believe you. Before you make any decisions you'll end up regretting, let's talk to Jim and Dr. Leyland in the morning. Let them hear what you're thinking, and then decide, which is the best path to take."

Vince sighed and said. "Okay."

"That's better." She said. "Come on, it's time for bed. We've had a long day."

POLICE DEPARTMENT...SAN DIEGO...ONE DAY LATER

CHIEF BREWER ARRIVED AT his office the next day, fully expecting to be put on suspension. His secretary gave him a message to call the Commissioner, which reaffirmed his expectations. *I might as well get it over with.* He thought, and dialed the Commissioner's office.

"Chief, I'm glad you called." The Commissioner said. "I wanted you to know that my office has reviewed the television footage. Get me your report and I'll recommend you were justified in your actions. There'll be no suspension."

"Thank you, sir. I'll bring a copy of the report to your office as soon as my secretary enters it into the system."

"Just send it over, Wayne." The Commissioner said. "There's no need to make a special trip."

"I'll be bringing my retirement papers for you to process, along with it." Brewer replied.

"Retirement? Jesus, Wayne! You just made Chief! Why do you want to go now?" The Commissioner asked. "You've done an excellent job."

"I've had a gun pointed at me two times in one week." Brewer replied. "I'm lucky I'm not dead. I want to get away. I'm going to Phoenix and retire there."

"Phoenix? It's hotter than hell there." The Commissioner said. "I'm staying right here when I retire. What's wrong with San Diego, Wayne?"

"Nothing's wrong with San Diego yet...I mean San Diego's fine, sir." Brewer said, correcting himself. "I just want a change of scenery."

"Suit yourself. You can stick that desert shit up a rattlesnake's ass, as far as I'm concerned. I'll need at least a month to choose your replacement, and the City Council will have to okay it. Can you give me that much time?" The Commissioner asked.

"Sure, I can wait a couple months if necessary. I'm putting my house up for sale. It might take that long anyway." Brewer replied.

"Do you have any suggestions for your replacement?" The commissioner asked and then said. "And don't tell me Captain Jennings. He isn't worth a shit!"

"Rowland, if he'll take it." Brewer answered.

"Rowland? He's a Sergeant." The Commissioner said. "There are too many officers above him. No one would be happy, if he was promoted over them."

"Maybe not, but he's the best man and Jennings isn't going anywhere with the Mayor dead." Brewer replied.

"Okay. I'll think about it." The Commissioner said. "I'll have to check his file. Get me your report."

"Yes sir." Brewer said, and hung up. He looked at the list of names, Vince had given him. In the coming days, he planned to use his influence to get as much information for Vince as he could. But for the time being, he had to prepare his resignation and arrange for his pension to be sent directly to his account with the Bank of America. He had already checked, they had banking facilities in Missouri also. He paged his secretary, and said. "Get Rowland in here I need to talk to him."

Ten minutes later, Rowland knocked on his office door, and stuck his head inside. "Come in, Rowland. Sit down." Brewer said.

"What's up, Chief?" Rowland asked.

"I'm retiring and I'm submitting your name to the Commissioner as my replacement." Brewer said.

"Me! Damn, Chief! I'm just a Sergeant." Rowland replied.

"You're the best officer the department has." Brewer said. "Take the damn job if he offers it to you. I'm not doing you any favors and you know it."

"What about Jennings? He thought he was getting the job, when you were appointed." Rowland said.

"Without the Mayor wiping his ass, he won't get shit. He's a Captain, only because of the Mayor. The commissioner won't even consider him. Remember, Traxler was one of his men, the stink won't die down from that shit for a long time." Brewer said.

"Jennings will raise hell and you know it." Rowland replied.

"Jennings won't say shit! Traxler got Jennings to sign for the wiretap at Dr. Leyland's office. He's up for a disciplinary hearing for that, I signed the papers." Brewer replied.

"I was thinking of retiring when you do, but what the hell. If I don't get chosen, I can still retire. Thanks, Chief." Rowland said.

"You're welcome. Now get out of here. I have work to do!"

UCSD SIESMOLOGY CENTER...SAN DIEGO

WHILE BREWER WAS, LOOKING over the list, Vince and Donna arrived at the lab. Dr. Leyland was already at work. Jim came in from the back room and greeted them. "Bankers hours, huh?" He asked.

"Vince had a rough evening last night." Donna said. "We need to have a meeting and go over some things."

"A little hard on him last night, were you?" Jim asked, with a smile.

"No I wasn't, smart ass!" Donna said. "We need to figure out what direction we're taking." Vince nodded in agreement.

"I thought we were going to Caltech and see Sandra Beatty. Is there something else we need to do first?" Jim asked.

"How about the new equipment? How far are you along on it?" Vince asked.

"I've got all the changes made and the board's installed. I finished it at home last night. Dr. Leyland said you could write a new program, Donna. When you're finished, I can test the equipment for bugs."

"Okay, I'll get on it. If it tests out okay, how will we know if it will really work without a satellite to download signals from?" Donna asked.

Dr. Leyland heard the conversation and joined the three. "Look at this." He said.

The three looked at a drawing and schematics Dr. Leyland had been working on. "It's a simple imaging, recording and transmitting device." Dr. Leyland said. "But it will work and it won't take long to build."

"How will that help, Dr. Leyland? It has to be in orbit, circling the Earth to collect and record information, doesn't it?" Donna asked.

"It's the principle we're after at this stage." Dr. Leyland replied. "In principle, it will work the same as one circling the Earth, that will of course, have far greater imaging, recording and transmitting power. Although this one will be limited in performance, it will still show my equipment works and that's all we need to do now."

"How will you simulate the signal as if it were coming from above the Earth." Vince asked.

"Oh that's easy." Dr. Leyland replied. "If I can't get the military to take it airborne, I'll hire a pilot with a private jet. All we really need is an aircraft that can reach, at least, forty thousand feet. In either case though, someone needs to ride along to make sure the settings remain constant. I will pre-set the signal but any jostling could get it out of adjustment. My plans for the final draft, would be one we can adjust remotely from Earth, after it's put in space."

Vince's enthusiasm returned with a meteoritic rise. "I'll go." He said. "I can fly a jet if you can't get the military to do it. Jim or Donna can go with me to adjust the transmitter if needed."

"I'll need to be in radio contact with the aircraft as it making the test run. The prototype might prove to be more touchy than the finished product." Dr. Leyland said.

"Is Sandra's office set up for radio communication?" Donna asked.

"Yes, it is, but none of what we're going to do was in my original plans. I was planning to develop the new equipment even if I had to finance it myself, but I wasn't planning to do so unless I was turned down by Caltech." Dr. Leyland replied.

"If this works as good as you think it will, they couldn't possibly turn you down now." Vince said.

"You may be right, but I hope others are there, when we take the equipment to her office." Dr. Leyland replied. "Knowing Sandra Beatty as I do, I fully expected to be turned down without the new equipment, but now it's all changed. She'll still think of me as an old fool, but she will listen when she finds out about the new equipment. When it works, she'll try to find some way to lay claim to the idea."

"Is she really that bad?" Donna asked.

"That bad and more." Dr. Leyland replied. "I regret not submitting my resume for the West Coast Coordinators position. It would be much easier now if I had. When Sandra was my assistant, she had a high opinion of herself. She rose up the ladder faster, than anybody before, or since. This office was just a stepping-stone for her. She had her sights set on the coordinators position when she arrived here. She wasn't really in line to take a position of that importance, she didn't have the experience or time in grade to have made a step like that."

"How did she manage to get it accomplished." Donna asked.

"She's connected very highly and very significantly, somewhere in this state or on the Federal level. In any case, it wasn't even a contest when I stepped aside. What really stuck in my crawl, was her arrogance and ego. She actually told me it was good thing I stepped aside and avoided the embarrassment of coming in second behind her. I'm not going to relish seeing her, because I know if we can't convince her one hundred percent, she'll turn us down. Her ego won't let her back something that might prove wrong or be a failure. She wouldn't want her name connected to it."

Vince had heard relatively the same story when he had talked with Dr. Leyland at Camp Davis after Dr. Leyland had been rescued from Scott Air Force Base. The story brought back memories of those harrowing days when they were struggling to stay alive. He knew none of the others could begin to imagine what they'd all gone though and also knew it wasn't going to be the same for any of them this time. Donna interrupted his thoughts.

"I'm going with you when you see Sandra. I won't let her roll over you or blow you off." She said to Dr. Leyland.

Vince's phone rang interrupting them, he picked up the phone, Chief Brewer was on the line.

"I've ran down some of the people on your list, Vince. General Morgan is one of the Chief's of Staff and next in line for the chairman's position. General Johnson had been Morgan's liaison officer for a quite while, but he's on some new assignment, it's classified."

"He's taken over at Area 51 as commanding officer." Vince said.

"How do you know that?" Brewer asked. "I couldn't get anything recent on him."

"He was the commanding officer at Area 51 when I was taken there." Vince replied.

"Oh yeah, in 2009, I forgot." Brewer replied. "I couldn't find anything on a General Lawson. The only thing I could come up with was a Colonel Lawson who was stationed at Nellis, until a month ago."

"He's also at Area 51. He's in charge of security there." Vince said.

"Captain Cooper dropped off the radar also, along with Lieutenant Randall and Sergeant Collins. The FBI agent told me General Clemmons is probably going to retire, if General Morgan gets the appointment to the chairman's position instead of him. Bush doesn't like Clemmons because he won't kiss ass. I'm still working on the two secret service agents. That's a tough nut to crack, but here's an interesting piece of news. Governor Lemming is going to be in town tomorrow for an impromptu West Coast Governor's meeting at the Hyatt, that our Governor, Randall Turner has set up. If you want to see Lemming, I can arrange it. I'm handling the security arrangements with the Highway Patrol and Sheriff's Office. I'll be in charge at the hotel. Do you want to see him?"

Vince thought about for a second and said. "Yes, maybe I can convince him to talk to Turner and put pressure on Sandra Beatty."

"Sandra Beatty? Who's she?" Brewer asked.

"She's the West Coast Coordinator for seismic activity." Vince said. "She works out of Caltech. Dr. Leyland's going to L.A. to see her soon. He's taking his new equipment and Model to present to her, but it's going to take someone with some influence to get her to listen to him with an open mind. Even then, I think it will be hard for him to get her to see things our way. Lemming might be just the person to do it. He eventually sets up the project after he's elected President in 2008, but the trouble with that is, 2008 will be too late."

"Jesus, Vince! Are you a betting man?" Brewer asked.

"No, why?"

"Hell! You know all about this stuff that's going to happen in 2008 and 2009. You could make a fortune in Vegas laying down bets on the presidential and governors races alone."

"I never thought of that." Vince replied. That's an interesting thought."

"I guess I could lay some bets down with the information you've told me and build me a nice nest egg too. I'm retiring in a couple months and I'm moving to Missouri like you said. The money would come in handy for setting up a new place there."

"Take them to the cleaners, Chief." Vince said and laughed.

"Could you give me your parents address and phone number, Vince? I'd like to look them up when I get there. Your dad might know of someplace for sale inside the diagram you gave me."

"No problem." Vince said. "Set up a meeting with Lemming for me tomorrow and I'll bring my parents information to you then."

"Okay. I'll get it arranged and I'll send Rowland with a car for you. You won't be able to get through security otherwise. Rowland will have a security badge for you to wear."

"Can you get one for Donna and Dr. Leyland?" Vince asked. "I'd like for them to come with me."

"No problem. May I ask you one favor?" Brewer asked.

"Sure." Vince replied.

"Get rid of the beard, the blonde hair and wear a suit. You look like a beach bum." Brewer said.

"Will do, Chief. Can Rowland pick us up at Donna's place?"

"Sure. Rowland can swing by there before he picks up Dr. Leyland."

"May I go to my house and pick up some clothes? When I left, I didn't take much with me." Vince asked.

"I don't see why not. Do you have a key?" Brewer asked.

"No I gave mine and the garage door opener to the Epperson's." Vince replied. "They weren't in the bag of things, Rowland gave me."

"They're probably in the crime scene evidence." Brewer said. "I'll get them and meet you at your house in an hour, if that's all right."

"That's fine. I'll see you there. I'll bet the place is a mess." Vince replied.

"No, it's not. The Epperson's personal effects are all gone. Someone from the family had them packed and shipped when they claimed the bodies. They hired a professional to clean up the mess and the carpet's been replaced." Brewer said.

"Would it be okay for me to put the house up for sale, then?" Vince asked.

"Sure, it yours, sell it if you want to. My wife's getting an agent to sell ours. Do you want me to have the agent call you?" Brewer asked.

"Have the agent call me at Donna's. Can you bring the addresses and contact information for the people you've located?" Vince asked.

"Yes. I'll see you in an hour." Brewer said.

Vince hung up and told Donna about the meeting with Lemming set for the next day and meeting Chief Brewer at his house.

"Let's get some hair color on the way." Donna said. "You can get a haircut, after we meet the Chief. I was liking your looks, but the Chief's right, you have to make a good impression."

VINCE'S HOUSE

VINCE AND DONNA MET Chief Brewer an hour later. Vince looked at the yard, It was getting overgrown, he'd forgotten to get a landscaper. He'd actually not even thought of his house, since he'd heard the Epperson's died there. Brewer unlocked the door and gave Vince the list and garage door opener and left. Upon entering the house, a strong chemical odor hit he and Donna's nostrils. The house was stuffy and the air conditioning wasn't on.

"Damn! This place smells terrible!" Vince said. "Let's get some windows open and get the air on."

All the rooms were empty, but clean. He checked the garage and found his furniture and effects neatly stored in one bay. The Epperson's had put his clothes in garment boxes, they had used to move their clothes in. He opened one of the boxes and smelled the clothes. The chemical smell hadn't penetrated the box. He selected two suits and the rest of the clothing to make up his attire in case he had to meet with Lemming more than one day.

Donna came out to the garage, joined him, and asked. "Are you planning to move back here?"

"No, I'm putting the place up for sale." He replied.

"Why don't you have your things moved to my place? You can store it in the garage till you decide what you want to do." She said.

Vince agreed. While they were loading his clothing in his car, his neighbor Larry saw him and yelled. "Hey! Who the hell are you? What do you think you're doing?"

"It's me, Larry!" Vince yelled back.

"Me, who?" Larry yelled back.

"What's going on?" Larry's wife asked, as she came to the door.

"Some asshole's stealing some shit out of Vince's house." Larry replied.

"Maybe you should call the police." His wife said.

"Hey! I'm calling the police!" Larry yelled at Vince.

Vince saw Larry's wife standing there with Larry and said. "Cindy, it's me, Vince!"

"He's a lying son-of-a-bitch!" Larry said. "Look, he has blonde hair!"

"Who are they?" Donna asked Vince.

"Larry and Cindy Williams." Vince replied.

"Mrs. Williams!" Donna called out.

"Yes, who are you?" She called back.

"I'm Donna Stevens. I work with Vince at UCSD. He's Dr. Davis, he's just dyed his hair and grown a beard."

"Is that you, Vince?" Larry yelled.

"It's me, Larry!" Vince yelled back.

"Well bite my ass! I would have never recognized you! Are you moving back in?" Larry asked as he and his wife walked over.

"No, I'm putting the place up for sale." Vince replied.

"No shit? Why are you doing that? I heard they cleared you of all that bullshit." Larry said.

"They did, but for now, I'm living with Miss Stevens." Vince replied.

"Good move!" Larry said, eyeing Donna. "Did you get married?" He asked.

"Not yet." Vince replied.

"That's none of your business, Larry!" His wife said.

"What are you doing home from work, Larry? Are you on vacation?" Vince asked.

"A permanent one!" His wife snapped. "They fired him for coming in drunk! I warned him, but would he listen to me? Oh, no! He had to keep drinking a twelve pack or more every night and two or three cases every weekend. I don't know what we're going to do. We can't afford this house now."

"It's just temporary! Don't make it sound so bad!" Larry retorted. "I'm going to sign up and take the cure, like my friend Rick Rhoads did. They let him come back and they'll take me back, after I'm cured."

"What did you say your friends name was?" Vince asked.

"Rick Rhoads. Why do you know him?" Larry asked.

Only in 2009. Vince thought, but he knew it couldn't be the same person. "Have you ever thought about moving?" Vince asked Larry.

"Where would we go? We've lived here all our lives." Cindy said.

"I would recommend moving to St. Louis. Houses are cheap there compared to here. You could probably buy a place and pay for it for what you get out of your house when you sell it." Vince said.

"They'll never give your job back to you and you know it! I don't give a damn if you do take the cure, it won't work. Rick's wife told me he's already back drinking. The only thing that's saved his ass so far, was going on the day shift." Cindy said to Larry.

"Maybe I could just taper off and get another job." Larry said.

"Taper off, my ass!" Cindy said. "Vince is right. We need to get away from here and start over."

"St. Louis? I hate the Rams!" Larry said, and then went on. "Wait a minute. The Epperson's were from St. Louis weren't they?" He asked Cindy.

"Yes, I believe Margaret did say they were from St. Louis. She told me there was going to be a disaster there, a big earthquake or something. That's why they moved here from St. Louis. Poor woman, they had her on all kinds of drugs. She had an appointment to see a psychiatrist at the Gifford Mental Center, but she went crazy and murdered her husband and then hanged herself. It was terrible." Cindy said.

"Hey, Bob said you went to the Midwest." Larry said to Vince. "Were you looking for the earthquake she was talking about, Vince? Did you find it?" Larry asked.

Vince was floored. He knew nothing about what Cindy had said regarding Mrs. Epperson, but it was all clear to him now. She was the one that Woitasczyk was supposed to see and treat. Woitasczyk had said a woman who had similar disaster problems was coming to see him, from the Midwest. What he was hearing was like a bad dream or nightmare that was coming true. It must have shown on his face.

"What's wrong, Vince? You look ill." Donna said.

"I'm all right, Donna." He replied and then said to Larry. "Yeah, I found it, Larry and I'm serious! There is going to be a big earthquake and it's going to start here in Southern California, but you've got some time. If you do decide to move, and I would recommend it, call me, I'll tell you where to move to in St. Louis."

"Jeez! You are serious, aren't you?" Larry asked.

"Yes, I am. We'll be moving there sooner or later ourselves." Vince said.

A car drove up in front of the house, a lady stepped out and said. "Dr. Davis?"

"I'm Davis." Vince replied.

"Hi, I'm Judy Rizzo with Century 21. Chief Brewer said I might catch you here. He said you're interested in selling your home. I'd like to help if I could. The market is very strong and most properties sell before they're advertised." She said, handing Vince her card.

"Sure, that's good. Here's the key, go in and take a look around, I'll be with you in a few minutes." Vince replied, and then said to Larry. "Here's your chance, Larry. You heard what she said. The market's strong. Have her put your place up too."

"Shit! I don't know. This is all kind of rushed." Larry replied.

"Do it, Larry!" His wife said.

"Hey, maybe I can get a job at Budweiser." Larry said.

"You'll do no such thing! Send her over when she though at your house, Vince." Cindy said.

"Hey, do you want a beer, Vince? All I've got is Old Milwaukee Light. That's all I could afford, since I was shit-canned." Larry said.

"No thanks, Larry. I've got to sign the papers on my house and then we have to get going." Vince said.

"Send your real estate lady to our house, when she's finished at your house." Cindy said.

Vince signed the papers and turned his key over to Judy Rizzo, who said goodbye and then went next door to the Williams house. Vince had one less worry on his mind, as he and Donna left for her house.

"What was bothering you back there?" Donna asked, as they drove.

"The Epperson's. I wish now, that I hadn't met them." Vince replied.

Donna figured that's what was bothering him. She dropped the subject, and said. "Don't forget to get a haircut."

They arrived at Donna's house forty-five minutes later. She dyed his freshly cut hair, back to a darker shade and he shaved off his beard. He tried his clothes on, wanting to be sure, he would present a professional look, when he talked to Lemming the next day. They both approved of his choice and appearance. Vince sat down at his laptop and started preparing a written presentation to take with him. He added a picture of the penny for good measure.

"Take the penny with you, Vince." Donna said. "He might doubt the picture, but he can't doubt the real thing."

After he finished the presentation, Vince read it over and then gave it to Donna to read.

"I don't have any trouble understanding what you've written." She said. "But you better make an extra copy to take to the meeting for Lemming. I think it would also be wise to take your laptop to show him Dr. Leyland's latest Model and calculations. The plans for the equipment will help too."

Vince agreed and called Dr. Leyland asking for the things he would need to take with him to the meeting.

"I'll have what you need ready." Dr. Leyland said. "But I've thought it over and I really don't feel up to going. I don't think I would be of much help anyway. I don't know Lemming and I doubt that Turner will attend. I've met Turner, I didn't care for him, but it would be better if you could convince him to be there."

"I still wish you were coming with me." Vince said.

"It's your experience and only you can tell it. I'll have my secretary draft a letter explaining that I concur with what you're saying and that I believe you." Leyland said.

"Thanks, Dr. Leyland. I'll be by later and pick up everything." Vince replied. He hung up and told Donna, Dr. Leyland wasn't going to the meeting, but he had given him an idea. "I'm going to call, Chief Brewer, and see if he can get Governor Turner to sit in on the meeting. I'm going to make an additional copy of the presentation , just in case."

"That's an excellent idea, but I've heard he's an asshole!" She said.

"Dr. Leyland told me he doesn't care for Turner." Vince replied. "He must be an asshole if Dr. Leyland doesn't like him."

"Why isn't Dr. Leyland coming?" Donna asked.

"He doesn't feel up to it. He's sending a letter saying he agrees with what I'm going to tell them." Vince replied.

"That will help. Dr. Leyland has a lot of clout." She said.

Vince made the additional copy, in hopes that Governor Turner would attend the meeting, but he wasn't getting his expectations up. If all he could do was, break the ice with Lemming that would be a good start. He called, Chief Brewer, and asked him to try and set up the meeting with both governors. Then they left for the lab to pick up the information from Dr. Leyland.

CHAPTER TWENTY-SIX

TROUBLE ON THE HOMEFRONT

CHIEF BREWER'S SECRETARY RECEIVED a call from Kenneth Coldfeldt, the Commander in charge of the U.S. Marshall's office in San Diego. He asked to speak with the Chief, who was busy setting up security for the governors meeting, scheduled for the next day.

"I'm sorry, Chief Brewer is not available at the moment, may I take a message?" She asked.

"Yes, please. Tell Chief Brewer to call my office, as soon as he returns." Coldfeldt said.

"May I ask what this would be in reference to?" She asked.

"It's in regard to the classified documents, Chief Brewer, turned over to my deputies. The matter is urgent. I'll have to speak with him personally." Coldfeldt replied.

"I'll see to it and make sure, Chief Brewer gets the message." She said.

"Wait a minute! Make sure, Chief Brewer, knows this is an urgent matter. I need to speak with him as soon as possible." Coldfeldt said.

"I've noted that information, sir. Is there anything else?" She asked.

"Does, Chief Brewer have a cell phone number where he can be reached?" Coldfeldt asked.

"I'm not allowed to give out personal information on the Chief or any member of the Police Department over the telephone." She replied.

"This is the U.S. Marshall's office, goddamnit!" Coldfeldt snarled.

"I'm sorry, sir, but I have my orders. Will there be anything else?" She asked.

"Is, Chief Brewer, in the building?" Coldfeldt asked.

"No, he has logged out for the day. Will there be anything else?" She asked.

"What's your name, lady?" Coldfeldt growled.

"I'll put your message on, Chief Brewer's desk, Commander." She said and hung up.

Coldfeldt was livid. "The bitch hung up on me!" He shouted.

"What do you want us to do?" Stewart asked.

"Get your asses over to Police Headquarters and find out where he is." Coldfeldt shouted.

"Jeez! You don't have to take it out on us!" Landreth said.

"When you find Brewer, find out who messed with those discs and arrest their ass!" Coldfeldt barked.

"Yes, sir. Anything else?" Landreth asked.

"Find out who that sterile bitch was, that I was talking to." Coldfeldt said.

"She's the Chief's secretary?" Stewart replied.

"Oh, is she now? I know that you, idiot! Get her name!" Coldfeldt bellowed.

"Her name is Billings." Landreth said.

"How do you know that? Have you been dating her?" Coldfeldt asked.

"It was on her nameplate on her desk." Landreth said.

"Well, get your asses over to the Brewer's office and tell, Ms. Sealed Lips to find Brewer or she's going to be arrested for obstruction of justice." Coldfeldt said.

"Jesus! She hasn't done anything, Commander." Landreth said.

"I knew it!" Coldfeldt spat out.

"Knew what, Commander?" Landreth asked.

"You've been dipping your wick in her, haven't you? You were warned about that. I told you to keep your dick in your pants!" Coldfeldt shouted.

"Jesus Christ, Commander! I haven't touched her! She's old and all wrinkled up!" Landreth replied.

"That didn't stop you the last time, did it?" Coldfeldt asked.

"That was different! I was drunk and she took advantage of me!" Landreth said.

"She was a Federal Witness and it was your job to protect her, not get drunk and screw her!" Coldfeldt retorted.

"I wouldn't have screwed her if I hadn't been drunk! She led me on for Christ's sake! She said she wanted it!" Landreth retorted.

"She said it was rape!" Coldfeldt barked.

"She didn't pursue it." Landreth shot back.

"Are you still porking her?" Coldfeldt asked.

"No! Hell no!" Landreth retorted.

"I better not find out you've been hosing the Chief's secretary, Landreth!"

"Why would you think I would screw her?" Landreth asked.

Coldfeldt turned to Stewart and asked. "Could you have told me what the Chief's secretary's name is?"

"No." Stewart replied.

"Why not?" Coldfeldt asked.

"I'm not interested in grandma pussy, like Landreth is." Stewart replied.

"Case closed!" Coldfeldt said and slammed his hand down on his desk.

Landreth started to protest, but, Coldfeldt interrupted him. "Get your asses over to the Chief's office and find out where he is."

"Yes, sir." Stewart replied.

"Get a warrant to search Brewer's office and the Cryptology department. If Brewer's secretary gives you any problems at all, arrest her!" Coldfeldt said.

"Yes, sir." They both said and left.

CHIEF BREWER'S OFFICE

THE CHIEF'S SECRETARY CALLED him and let him know that Coldfeldt had called.

"I know what he wants." Brewer said.

"What do you want me to tell him if he calls back?" She asked.

"Tell him I'm going down to Baja for the weekend. Tell him I won't be back till Monday. I've already booked the flight and made the arrangements." Brewer replied.

"You better tell me what this is all about." She said.

"I can't. The less you know, the better it is. He's going to be trouble though, I can tell you that." Brewer replied.

"I've got your retirement papers finished. You'll have to sign them before they can be processed." She said.

"I'll sign them Monday." Brewer replied. "The Hyatt has given me some rooms for police use, till the governor's conference is over. My wife is here with me and we'll be using one of them. I'll call you from time to time and touch base. Thanks for covering for me, Ms. Billings."

"That's my job, Chief." She replied.

Brewer hung up and called the Seismic Center and was speaking to, Vince. "We've got trouble." Brewer said. "The commander of the U.S. Marshall's Office wants to speak with me and you know what he wants."

"What are you going to do?" Vince asked.

"For now, I'm not going back to the office, I've taken a few days off. I'm at the Hyatt setting up security. The Hyatt's given me some rooms for police use. The wife and I are staying here till the conference is over, then we have reservations in Baja for the weekend. I'm not planning on being back in my office until Monday." Brewer replied.

"Did your secretary stall them off till then?" Vince asked.

"I just spoke to her and told her to tell them I'm in Baja for the weekend, in case he calls back." Brewer replied.

"He probably won't call back. He'll probably send Marshall's to your office with warrants, to search for copies of the discs." Vince said.

"How do you know that?" Brewer asked.

"Jim copied them before he messed them up. They probably have software that can detect tampering." Vince said.

"Do you think they called, Jim and he told them what I did?" Brewer asked.

"They couldn't have. They don't know anything about, Jim." Vince replied.

"Then how do you know they want to search my office?" Brewer asked.

"It's obvious. They're trying to find out who altered the discs." Vince replied.

"How do you know that? My secretary didn't ask what he wanted." Brewer said.

"What other reason would they have for calling your office? They already have the discs and they've found out they're altered. My guess is that they'll be at your office within an hour. Did you leave anything there they can tie to the discs?" Vince asked.

"Not to my knowledge. I removed the sticker that had the case number the discs were associated with." Brewer said.

"Which case was it? Was it mine?" Vince asked.

"No. They were associated with Woitasczyk's case. We recovered the discs from his office when it was searched. They weren't in your file, but Woitasczyk mentioned them in one of his tapes, after his session with you." Brewer replied.

"That's bad. Where are the tapes?" Vince asked.

"I think Forrester has them. His office had all the evidence against Woitasczyk. I got the discs from him." Brewer replied.

"Then they don't know about the tapes, but we're going to have to find a way out of this, Chief. Otherwise we're going to get bogged down in a bunch of red tape." Vince said.

"What do you want me to do?" Brewer asked.

"Does your secretary know about the discs?" Vince asked.

"No, I never told her about them, but she covered my ass by stalling those Marshall's, when they came to my office." Brewer replied.

"Then she does know something's up." Vince said.

"Yeah, but she doesn't know what." Brewer said.

"Call her and tell her you need her help at the Hyatt. Get her out of there before the Marshall's get there and get someone to cover for her." Vince said.

"Okay, I can do that." Brewer replied.

Who's handling your job while you're at the Hyatt?" Vince asked.

"No one. I'm right here in town if they need me." Brewer replied.

"You said you'd be in Baja for the weekend, who's taking over for you then?" Vince asked.

"I've already appointed, Rowland as acting Chief for the weekend. I've submitted his name for consideration as my replacement when I retire. I thought the experience would look good in his file." Brewer said.

"Can you move his appointment up and make it start today?" Vince asked.

"I'd have to call the commissioner." Brewer replied.

"Do it after you call your secretary. Get her out of there first, then get a replacement for her, then call the commissioner about Rowland, then call Rowland and tell him to go to your office and take over. You better get on it right away, you probably don't have much time." Vince said.

"Jesus Christ, Vince! Have you become a clairvoyant?" Brewer asked.

"I don't know what I am, Chief, but I know I don't want to get tangled up in this mess and I will if you don't get everything done as I said." Vince replied.

"Okay, I'll do as you say. What's on those discs that so important to go to all of this trouble to keep them from finding out?" Brewer asked.

"Too much for them or anyone to understand. If they got a chance to read the files, they won't know what to make of it. If they found out what's on them, they would probably classify the information as a conspiracy being planned for the future, and then go right to Clemmons and Lindsey for answers." Vince said.

"I'll take your word for that. I'm hanging up and calling my secretary." Brewer said.

"Put her up in one of the rooms at the Hyatt and tell her to lay low. My guess is they'll be coming to see you, at the Hyatt before this day is over."

"Jesus Christ, Vince! You're scaring me!" Brewer said.

"It will all work out. Just be busier than hell if they come to see you." Vince said.

"What do you think they're going to ask me if they do come?" Brewer asked.

"They're going to want the name of the person that altered the discs and the information that was on them." Vince said.

"What should I tell them? Should I act dumb?" Brewer asked.

"Lay it off on the technician in Cryptology. I'll lay odds that he's the one who called the U.S. Marshall's office."

"Jesus! How do you know that? I didn't tell you that, did I?" Brewer asked.

"No you didn't, but it would make sense. If they arrest him, let them sweat him for a while, since he's the one that called them."

"Goddamn! Where is this going to end?" Brewer asked.

"I don't know, but my guess is that it won't end there." Vince replied.

"Why not?" Brewer asked.

"They probably won't find the classified files they're looking for on his computer at Police Headquarters. If he copied them, he probably put the files on a pen drive. You're a policeman, where would you look next?" Vince asked.

"His home computer." Brewer replied.

"That's right. Maybe he'll have enough shit on his hard drive to get him arrested, but I hope he didn't copy the discs. I'll be shot down if he did and they find them." Vince replied.

"Okay, I've heard enough. I'll call you back later." Brewer hung up and called his secretary, putting the plan in motion. After making the rest of the calls, he called Vince back and said."It's done. What's next?"

"Nothing. Just wait for them in case they come." Vince replied.

"I don't know if I can carry this off, Vince. Are you sure about all of this?" Brewer asked.

"Jim wouldn't have left his prints on discs when he made the copies and altered the originals. The only prints that are going to be on the discs are yours and the technicians in Cryptology. Since he was eager to call the Feds, I'll bet he's also the leak at headquarters, you're looking for." Vince said.

"You might be right. I'll look into it when I get back from Baja. I've got to go, I'll be ready for them if they show up."

U.S. MARSHALL'S DESCEND

"WE'RE HERE TO SEE Chief Brewer, is he in?" Landreth asked the new girl behind the desk, while flashing his credentials.

"I'm sorry, Chief Brewer is not in." The girl replied.

"We have a Federal Warrant to search his office." Stewart said, producing the warrant.

"Oh, my!" The girl said and asked. "Has Chief Brewer done something wrong?"

"We're asking the questions." Landreth said and then asked. "Where's Ms. Billings?"

Stewart eyed him and shook his head and said. "Remember what, Coldfeldt, said."

"Get off my back, Stewart!" Landreth replied. "Where is she?" He asked the new girl.

"I'm not sure. I'm filling in for her until she returns. Sgt. Rowland is acting Chief, he's in Chief Brewer's office now. Would you like to speak to him and ask if he'll allow a search of the Chief's office." The girl asked.

"We don't need anyone's permission to search Brewer's office! This warrant gives us permission to do that! Come on, I'm going in." Stewart said.

"Wait, I'll announce you." The girl said.

Stewart paid no attention and brushed by her desk and opened the Chief's door and went in, followed by Landreth.

Rowland was going over the previous days reports and was startled by the sudden entrance of the two men. He jumped up, pulled out his service revolver and said. "Hold it right there!"

"Put the gun away, Sarge!" Stewart barked and flashed his credentials. "We're, Deputy U.S. Marshall's. This is a Federal Warrant to search Chief Brewer's office.

"What the hell for?" Rowland asked, putting his gun back in the holster.

"That's none of your business! Take a chair over there, while we do our job."

Stewart, slowly went through the paperwork on the Chief's desk and then rifled through the drawers. Landreth was going through the file cabinet as Rowland sat and watched. They were through in less than ten minutes, and had found nothing,

"What are you looking for? Maybe I can help you." Rowland said.

"I said it's none of your business. Where's Brewer?" Stewart asked.

"He's on vacation." Rowland replied.

"Where's he going?" Landreth asked.

"I don't know, he doesn't include me in the plans for his private life." Rowland replied.

"Don't get smart with me, buster!" Landreth said.

"Don't call me buster, deputy dog! You're not even dry behind the ears." Rowland shot back.

Before Landreth could reply, Stewart asked. "Has he left town yet?"

"No. He's setting up security for the governor's conference tomorrow and then he's leaving." Rowland replied.

"Where's the meeting?" Landreth asked.

"At the Hyatt." Rowland replied.

"The Hyatt, downtown?" Landreth asked.

"I don't believe there's another Hyatt in San Diego, big shot!" Rowland replied.

"Look, I can arrest you for obstruction of justice and have you in front of a Federal Judge, before you can blink your eyes." Landreth shot back.

"Go ahead, you're through searching aren't you?" Rowland asked.

"Come on, Landreth, we're through here. We need to get down to Cryptology." Stewart said.

"Where's Brewer's secretary?" Landreth asked.

"She's helping Chief Brewer at the Hyatt." Rowland replied.

"Hey, we need to check her desk, Landreth." Stewart said.

"I'm not through with you, Sarge. We'll be back." Landreth said and joined Stewart in the outer office.

"We're going to have to search your desk." Stewart said to the new girl.

"I'll get the file cabinet." Landreth said.

The girl got up and sat down on an office chair as Stewart rummaged through Ms. Billing's desk and found something. "Well lookie here." He said to Landreth.

"What have you got." Landreth asked.

"Brewer's retiring. His papers are all filled out." Stewart said.

"So what?" Landreth asked.

"How long has Chief Brewer been considering retirement?" Stewart asked the girl.

"I have no idea. I'm from the secretarial pool. I fill in where I'm needed." She replied.

Rowland entered the outer office and answered the question. "He's had a gun shoved in his face two times in the last week. He called it quits after that. I think he's going down to Baja this weekend and scout retirement places out."

"Let's get down to the Cryptology department." Stewart said.

"We can search that later. I want to go down to the Hyatt first." Landreth said.

"That can wait. We need to finish up here first." Stewart said.

"I said we're going to the Hyatt! We had orders to question the Chief." Landreth shot back.

"Coldfeldt didn't say anything about questioning the Chief! You just want to sniff out his secretary again, don't you?" Stewart asked.

"Lay off that shit, Stewart." Landreth retorted.

"Are you through here?" Rowland asked.

"Yes." Stewart replied. "Come on, Landreth, we'll go to Hyatt first. Does that make you happy, little boy?"

"I said, lay off the shit!" Landreth replied as they went out the door.

As the new girl returned to the desk and started straightening it up, Rowland looked at his watch. It was three-thirty.

"You can take the rest of the day off." Rowland said. "I'm closing the office early. I'm going down and help, Chief Brewer."

As she left, Rowland picked up the phone, called Brewer's cell, and said. "They're coming to you, just like Vince said they would."

"Jesus! This is getting scary." Brewer replied.

"They haven't checked Cryptology yet." Rowland said.

"Good. I'll set that part up." Brewer replied. "Come on down and bring a camera. I want you to get their photos, while I bait them."

Stewart and Landreth were on their way downtown, when Stewart said. "You've got to get some help with that grandma pussy fixation you've got."

"Mind your own business, Stewart!" Landreth shot back.

"Hey! I'm not shitting you! You should have seen your eyes light up when Sergeant, what's his name, said Brewer's secretary was downtown with Brewer."

"They did no such thing!" Landreth spat back.

"The hell you say! You looked like a kid with a new puppy!" Stewart replied.

"Get off my case, Stewart! You don't know shit!" Landreth retorted.

"Oh no? Then tell me why you didn't give that young secretary the time of day! You started drooling the minute you heard, what's her name, was downtown."

"Her name's Billings." Landreth said.

"I don't give a damn what her name is! You didn't even notice the new secretary, did you?" Stewart asked.

"Screw you, Stewart! I'm not on trial!" Landreth shouted.

"Well one thing's for sure! You either need some serious help or glasses, Landreth!"

"Go to hell, Stewart!" Landreth replied, as they pulled into the Hyatt parking garage.

Stewart saw, Chief Brewer, directing activity, and said. "There he is!"

"How do you know he's Brewer?" Landreth asked.

"Goddamn, Landreth! We talked to him remember?" Stewart asked.

"I forgot what he looked like." Landreth said.

"That's because you had your mind on his secretary! Coldfeldt was right! You are messed up!" Stewart shouted.

"I'm tired of this shit! I don't remember what he looks like, okay? Is that a crime?" Landreth retorted.

"Didn't you see the photo of Brewer and some old crow on his desk?" Stewart asked.

"No, I didn't! I was busy!" Landreth replied.

"How did you miss that, Landreth? The old crow was right up you alley!" Stewart quipped.

"I've had enough, Stewart!" Landreth warned.

"Okay, okay! Look, Landreth, he's got all those gold stars on his epaulets, like he's a general or something. That's Brewer." Stewart replied.

They pulled into an empty space and a young officer came up and said. "You can't park there. You're going to have to move."

"We'll park anywhere we want to!" Landreth snapped, flashing his credentials.

"That's Chief Brewer over there isn't it?" Stewart asked.

"Yes it is." The officer replied.

"We need to talk to him." Stewart said.

"Come with me." The officer said.

Stewart and Landreth didn't see Rowland pull into the garage, pull up short and then park, but Chief Brewer did. Rowland focused the telephoto lens on the camera and started shooting photos as they walked up to Brewer and started talking. Brewer gestured toward a bench that faced directly toward Rowland, and the three sat down.

"Chief, I want you to know that we have warrants and we've searched your office before we came down here to talk to you." Stewart said.

Brewer acted surprised and then offended and asked. "What in the hell were you searching my office for? I don't have anything to hide."

"Settle down, Chief! We didn't find what we were looking for." Landreth said.

"If you don't mind telling me, why was the warrant issued and what exactly did you think you'd find in my office?" Brewer asked in an affronted voice.

"Evidence that the discs you gave us had been tampered with." Stewart said.

"What in the hell are you talking about? I don't know anything about the discs being tampered with." Brewer said.

"They were tampered with by someone, that's for damn sure and that's a Federal Offense!" Stewart said.

"Not by me, goddamnit!" Brewer retorted.

"We don't suspect you of knowingly, doing anything wrong." Stewart said.

"What do you mean by that?" Brewer barked.

"Someone altered the discs." Stewart said and was then, interrupted by Brewer, who said. "You told me that! Get on with it, damnit! I'm busy! We've got a governor's conference here tomorrow. I'm responsible for security."

"Don't get a flap going, Chief!" Stewart said. "We're not here to arrest you!"

"Arrest me?" Brewer bellowed. "You punks better think twice before trying that. I'd have your asses on the ground begging for mercy before you knew what hit you!"

"Hold on, Chief! We just need your help!" Stewart said.

"With what?" He asked.

"There were several sets of prints on the discs and the jewel cases. Some were old and not as clear, but a couple of the fresh ones matched your prints." Stewart said.

"So, what are you getting at?" Brewer asked.

"One set of prints matched one of the boy's in the Cryptology lab." Stewart said.

"That was Lucas. He was given the job of decoding the passwords, by Captain Glazier." Brewer said.

"We know that." Landreth said.

"Well what's all the fuss about?" Brewer asked.

"The discs were altered and we're trying to find out who did it." Stewart said.

"It wasn't me!" Brewer replied.

"We know that too." Stewart said.

"Then why are you here bothering me?" Brewer asked.

"How well do you know Lucas?" Stewart asked.

"I don't know him at all. I've been intending to discipline him for calling you guys, but I haven't had the time, with this meeting coming up. That question would be better directed toward his commander, Captain Glazier." Brewer replied.

"We've already talked to, Glazier. He says the guys okay, but we haven't searched his desk or anything yet." Stewart replied.

"Okay, let me tell you what I've discovered." Brewer said, as the two deputies leaned in closer. "Some scuttlebutt's been circling on Lucas."

"What is it?" Stewart asked.

"I was questioned yesterday by, I.A. The guy has been leaking police information to the media." Brewer said.

"What kind of information?" Landreth asked.

"He's been giving out the names of victims and things like that, to a reporter named Jean Simmons."

"She's the one that got killed by one of your men, isn't she?" Landreth asked.

365

J. L. Reynolds

"That's correct." Brewer replied.

"Wait a minute!" Stewart said. "You were the one that shot her killer, weren't you?"

"I had no choice, he was going to kill me." Brewer replied.

"Is that why you're retiring?" Stewart asked.

"How did you know that? I haven't turned my papers in yet." Brewer said.

"We found the papers in your secretary's desk." Stewart replied.

"Where is your secretary?" Landreth asked.

"Shut up, Landreth!" Stewart said and then said. "Go on with your story, about Lucas, Chief.

"Some of his co-workers says he looks at porno sites on the internet at lunch time. Now I don't know that as a fact, it could just be jealous co-workers trying to stir up some shit and get his job." Brewer said.

"Bingo, it's him!" Stewart said to Landreth.

"What do you mean?" Brewer asked.

"Whoever altered the discs, put a bunch of porno on them and it was done sometime in the 24 hour period before and up to the time we picked them up at your office."

"I locked them in my desk after I picked them up from Cryptology. They weren't altered after I got them." Brewer said.

"He must have done it right before you picked them up." Stewart said.

"What are you going to do?" Brewer asked.

"We're going to search his desk and impound his computer. We already have the warrant to do that. If we don't find anything, we'll get a warrant to search his home, he has to be the one that did it." Stewart said.

"You have the discs. Why are you so interested in finding out who copied them?" Brewer asked.

"It's Federal Offense to copy and destroy classified documents. Our boss doesn't care as much about what was on the discs as he does for catching the bastard that copied them, but we'll get both when we catch whoever did it, and it sounds like Lucas is our man."Stewart said.

"How do you know the discs were copied?" Brewer asked.

"No matter what anyone does on a computer, it leaves a trail." Landreth said.

"I know that, but wouldn't that information be on the hard drive of Lucas's computer? You said you hadn't been to Cryptology yet. How do you know he made a copy?" Brewer said.

The two laughed and Stewart said. "In the Police Department's lab, you'd be right. What you guys have for equipment in Cryptology, is ancient history. We can tell if a discs been copied by examining the discs, themselves. We can even tell how many times it's been copied and approximately when it was copied by examining the deterioration of the imprint left when it was copied."

"I'll be damned! That's pretty impressive boys! Hey, I'm sorry if I was a little rough on you. When you've been around as long as I have, you'll get a little crotchety too." Brewer said and laughed.

"No problem, Chief. I'm sorry we had to go through your desk and things, but you know how it is. We were just doing our jobs."

"Sure, I understand, but there's one thing you haven't explained." Brewer said.

"What's that?" Landreth asked.

"Who did the other prints belong to?" Brewer asked.

"We can't tell you that." Stewart said.

"Why not?" Brewer asked.

"It's classified." Stewart replied.

"Oh, I see. Well it would have been nice to know who's fingerprints I touched. Was it the presidents?" Brewer asked with a, tell me look, on his face.

"No, it wasn't the president's fingerprints." Stewart said.

"Was I close?" Brewer asked with the same look on his face.

The two looked at each other and Landreth said. "They probably shook hands with the president."

"You can't leave me like this! I've got to know!" Brewer said.

"I'll tell you what, Chief." Landreth said. "Get your secretary to come down to the bar and have a few drinks and I'll tell you whose prints they were."

"Landreth, this is bullshit! Coldfeldt will have your ass! Don't you remember what he told you today?" Stewart asked.

"Hey, he isn't going to know shit, if you don't tell him." Landreth said.

"I'm warning you!" Stewart said.

Landreth put his arm around the Chief and said. "This here's the Chief of Police of San Diego, California, Stewart. Look at those gold stars on his epaulets and look at those service stripes on his sleeves. Do you think he's going to tell anyone if I tell him whose prints they were? Come on, do you really?"

"I might tell my grandkids, when they get older." Brewer said, and laughed.

"How old are they now?" Landreth asked.

"The boy's two and his sister is four." Brewer lied. He didn't have any children or grandchildren. He didn't have any relatives except on his wife's side and he didn't consider them as relatives.

"Can you get your secretary to come down?" Landreth asked.

"I think so, but she doesn't look anything like that woman that was in my office today." Brewer said.

"I know what she looks like, Chief. Her name is Billings, Ms. Billings. Is she married, Chief?" Landreth asked.

"No, she isn't married." Brewer replied.

"Good! Call her up and see if she'll meet us for drinks in the bar." Landreth said.

"What about it, Stewart?" Brewer asked.

"Go ahead and call her, Chief. Landreth likes old pussy. He didn't even notice the woman in your office today. Man, she sure had some nice tits and her ass was a knockout! She was table stuff!" Stewart said.

Brewer was laughing on the inside and could hardly keep a straight face. He dialed his secretary's number, when she answered, he said. "I need a favor from you."

"What is it, Chief?" She asked.

"I've got a couple boys down here, from the U.S. Marshall's Office. They want you to come down to the bar for a few drinks." He said.

"Is it those two assholes that were in the office?" She asked.

"The very same." He replied.

"Well screw them! One of them was slobbering all over my desk. I thought he was going to start humping it or me, before he left." She replied.

"This would be a special favor to me, Ms. Billings. It's important or I wouldn't ask you." He replied.

"All right, I'll be down, but if the stupid one starts drooling all over me again, I'll bust his nuts! I swear!" She said.

"Thank you, Ms. Billings." He folded his phone and said. "She's coming."

"Hot damn!" Landreth said and started running for the entrance.

"What were the names he said he'd tell me, Stewart?" Brewer asked.

"Okay, here's the deal. If this ever gets out, I'll be in deep shit, so I'm not going to tell you." Stewart said.

"That's bullshit, he made a deal." Brewer complained.

"Well, I'm not talking!" Stewart said as he scribbled some names on his note pad and then dropped the paper and said. "It looks like Landreth dropped the note he wrote for you. I'm going to have a drink, are you coming?"

Brewer bent down and picked up the note and saw the names of General John Clemmons and Secret Service Agent David Lindsey, both active in the service of the government, written on the note. *Damn! Just like, Vince said!* He thought.

"Are you coming?" Stewart yelled at Brewer.

"Yeah, sure, wait up! I have something to tell you." Brewer replied.

Stewart stopped and waited till Brewer caught up. "What is it." He asked.

"Ms. Billings is a Lesbian." Brewer said and laughed.

"No shit?" Stewart asked.

"I'm not shitting you!" Brewer replied. "She said she was going to bust his balls, if he drooled on her again."

"He will, I'll guarantee it! Hurry up! I don't want to miss the fun." Stewart said, and picked up the pace.

As they walked, Stewart said. "I don't know what, Landreth, sees in the old pussy, he chases. It can't be any good."

"Don't knock it, till you've tried it." Brewer replied.

Stewart looked at Brewer, and thought of the picture on the Chief's desk, but he didn't say a word.

J. L. Reynolds

IN THE BAR

"I SHOULDN'T BE DRINKING in uniform." Brewer said as they sat waiting at the bar.

"That's the advantage of wearing a suit." Stewart replied as he downed a drink.

Landreth was getting anxious, and asked. "Where is she, Chief?"

"Here she comes now." Brewer replied.

The three stood up as Ms. Billings joined them.

"I'm Orville Landreth." Landreth said, sticking out his hand.

"Is he Wilbur?" She asked, looking at Stewart.

"No, his name is Gregg." Landreth replied with a puzzled look on his face.

"It's a joke, Landreth! You know, Orville and Wilbur Wright." Stewart said.

"Who are they?" Landreth asked.

"Never mind, Landreth. Let's have a drink, what will you have, Ms. Billings?" Stewart asked.

"Hey, I'm buying her drinks!" Landreth said.

"Help yourself." Stewart replied.

"What will you have, Ms. Billings?" Landreth asked.

"Jack Black, straight up on the rocks, make it a double." She said.

"A man's drink. I like that!" Landreth said.

"I had to miss the Ellen DeGeneres show, to come down here." She said.

"She's a dyke! Why do you watch her show?" Landreth asked, and then went. "Whoooof!" As Ms. Billings brought her knee up and planted it, full force, into Landreth's groin. As he began to fall, now holding his groin, and wheezing in pain, Ms. Billings delivered a straight right to his jaw, assuring his complete collapse. He dropped like a sack of potatoes and fell between his stool and the brass foot rail.

"Ellen is a nice lady." Ms. Billings said to Landreth, although he didn't hear her. She picked up her drink and said. "When he wakes up, tell him I said thanks for the drink, and to watch his sexist remarks, next time. I'm going back to my room and watch the rest of Ellen."

"She's a woman of her word." Brewer said as Ms. Billings walked away.

"That ain't no shit!" Stewart said reaching down and pulling on Landreth's arm. "Come on you dumb shit. We've got to get back to Police Headquarters and finish the job."

Landreth couldn't speak yet. He was gasping for air and wheezing as his lungs refused to work.

"You're pitiful, man!" Stewart said. "Maybe that will get you over chasing older pussy. You can't handle it."

Stewart said goodbye to the Chief and was half dragging, a still unstable Landreth, away. As they reached the door, Landreth began to vomit. Stewart dropped him at the first retch, and Landreth fell face first, into his pool of vomit.

Brewer saw Rowland coming in the door, and stepping over Landreth. He motioned to Rowland who joined him at the bar. "Can I buy you one?" Brewer asked.

"We're on duty!" Rowland said.

"I'm the Chief, Rowland! I order you, to have a drink!" Brewer barked.

"Yes, sir, Chief, sir!" Rowland said and saluted.

"What'll it be?" Brewer asked as the bartender arrived.

"Tequila, with a lime and some salt." Rowland replied and then said. "Leave the worm in it!"

CHAPTER TWENTY-SEVEN

THE HYATT MEETING...SAN DIEGO

ROWLAND PICKED VINCE AND Donna up and gave them their security I.D.'s, and whisked them through traffic to the Hyatt. They entered the parking garage and pulled up to the entrance where Chief Brewer stood waiting.

"It's going to be tight, Vince." Brewer said. "I had to squeeze you in between the governors meeting and the press conference afterward. I don't know how much time you'll get, but Turner's going to be there too. Turner's aide asked what the meeting concerned."

"What did you tell him?" Vince asked.

"I told him you were representing the San Diego seismic activity office, and you had some evidence of new seismic activity that would affect Southern California. He also asked me if Sandra Beatty was going to be with you. I told him I didn't think so, but I didn't know. Who is she?" Brewer asked.

"She's the West Coast Coordinator of r seismic activity. She doesn't know about the information yet. I'm hoping to get Turner's help presenting the information to her at Caltech." Vince replied.

The three entered the hotel and Brewer escorted them through security and led them to a smaller meeting room down the hall from the main conference room and left them, saying. "It'll probably be an hour or so. I'll come back and tell you when they're on their way."

Vince and Donna sat down, and Vince removed the presentations from the folder, laying them on the table. He had brought his and Donna's laptops, with the older and newer Models Dr. Leyland had made, as well as printed sheets with the calculations each Model represented. Vince knew the Models weren't going to be easily understood by the two governors, but he hoped they would show the effort that had been made, as well as the sincerity and concern, that Dr. Leyland and he had for the future. They waited nervously as the time slowly passed.

Chief Brewer returned 45 minutes later with a security man from both of the governors' staffs. "Two minutes, Vince." He said.

The two security men stared at Vince and Donna dispassionately, until Lemming and Turner entered the room followed by two more security men and the Police Commissioner. Chief Brewer introduced Vince and Donna, then he and the Commissioner left.

"All right, Dr. Davis." Governor Turner said. "You've got ten minutes, let's hear what you have to say."

Vince started off by telling them he was the Assistant Director of the San Diego Seismic Center and that he was there representing that office. He drew their attention to the two laptops on the table and explained the difference between the graphs on each screen.

"As you can see, the two Models are different. The first represents seismic activity that existed several months ago. The second represents the current readings taken just a week ago. Both are showing data collected from the same area. The second one shows the increased activity that we are now seeing. These Models were made by Dr. Wilson Leyland, who is the director of my office."

The two governor's looked at the screens and Turner said. "This doesn't mean dick to me! You'd better get on with it!"

Vince was stunned by Turner's callousness, but said. "Since I'm limited on time, I think it would be better to go on with the rest of my presentation first. We can get back to the Models when I'm finished."

Lemming interrupted and asked. "Why am I involved?"

Vince had no choice but to answer his question, hoping to get back to the details, before they both got up and walked out. "I was hoping to explain that to you as we go on."

"Get on with it then!" Turner barked.

First, he told them about the new equipment that Dr. Leyland had designed, showing them the plans, saying it would be operational soon. He then went straight into his presentation, wanting to make the best use of the allocated ten minutes, as possible. Lemming became impatient and said. "I still don't see how this affects me. What you're talking about is a California concern."

"What I have to say will affect the entire West Coast, sir." Vince replied.

Donna looked at Vince and said. "Tell him."

Although not wanting to get to the subject at that point, Vince went on. "There will be huge a disaster that will begin in 2009. You will run for President in 2008 and be elected and will have to deal with the disaster. That's why you've been included."

Turner laughed loudly, and said. "Carter, you didn't tell me you're going to run for President. When did you make that decision?"

"I haven't yet, but you'd be the last one I'd tell, if I was running." Lemming retorted.

"If there's going to be a big disaster, why isn't Sandra Beatty here?" Turner asked Vince.

Vince started to answer, but Lemming stopped him. "How did you know I was planning to run for President? I haven't even mentioned it to my wife." Lemming said, not picking up on the part about being elected.

"Are you really going to run for president?" Turner asked.

"I've been thinking about it, but I haven't told anyone. How did you find out, Davis?" Lemming asked, looking at his security men with disdain.

"The answer is in my presentation, along with a lot of other information you should both read, or let me explain to you." Vince said.

"What about me?" Turner asked. "Where do I fit into all of this?"

"I need your help convincing Sandra Beatty to endorse Dr. Leyland's findings." Vince said.

"I know who Dr. Leyland is." Turner said. "Why are you here instead of him?"

Vince handed, Turner and Lemming a copy of Dr. Leyland's letter of endorsement, and went on. "Dr. Leyland is working on the design for a

The Continent Of St. Louis - The Search For Answers

transmitter to go along with the new receiver he has designed. Together, these two pieces of new equipment, will confirm his findings. He has asked me to be here in his place, and give both of you a copy of his letter of endorsement, for what I'm about to tell and show you. It is his hope that you will listen to my complete presentation, and implement my recommendations."

Turner was looking at the presentation and asked."What is all this garbage? I don't see Dr. Leyland's name anywhere!"

"My presentation is not about Dr. Leyland's findings. It covers the details of an experience I had, which confirms the seriousness of the findings in Dr. Leyland's calculations. All the details are in your presentations."

"I don't have time to go all the way through this." Turner said to Vince. "You better start doing some fast talking and get on with what you have to say. We're running out of time."

"It's as simple as this, Governor. If Sandra isn't convinced to adopt Dr. Leyland's findings, when he meets with her, the whole thing will be tabled until 2008, when Governor Lemming will be elected President."

"Elected President? What the hell are you talking about? He said he hasn't made a decision to run yet! This is bullshit!" Turner barked.

"Let him talk, Randy. Go on." Lemming said to Vince.

"I already know the stage is set for Sandra to turn down Dr. Leyland's findings at this time. I don't know why, but in most likelihood, she will. If she does the whole thing will be tabled until after you're elected president, and set the project up."

"Jesus Christ?" Turner barked. "He's talking as if he can see into the future!"

"Give him a chance, Randy! I want to hear more. Go on Dr. Davis." Lemming said.

Vince knew it was now or never, and said. "As I said, there's going to be a disastrous earthquake in 2009 that will start in California and destroy the World."

"Goddamnit Carter! This is bullshit! I know California could have a large earthquake at any time, but goddamn, that's what we have the seismic centers for! We're on top of things in California!" Turner blurted out.

"I know and I'm part of part of that group of individuals." Vince replied.

Not for long! Turner thought, but instead said. "I've heard enough! You're wasting our time! Do you expect us to believe what you're saying?"

"Let him finish, Randy!" Lemming said.

Turner started to object, but instead, he looked at his watch and said. "You've got five more minutes, Davis!"

"Thank you." Vince replied, and then said."Governor Lemming, you will eventually endorse Dr. Leyland's findings in 2008, and then have Dr. Leyland's new equipment built and put into use in a top secret Forecast Room at Area 51, with Dr. Leyland in charge and Miss Stevens here, as his assistant. The Government will have a satellite built that will circle the Earth, which will send seismic signals back from space, but if we wait till then, a plot will have already been put in place to sabotage the data that's being received."

"By who"? Lemming asked.

"John Clemmons. He will be your vice president, and he's going to screw the whole thing up and the world will be destroyed."

"This is horseshit! You're not referring to, General John Clemmons, are you?" Turner asked.

"Yes, Governor, I am." Vince replied.

"That's ridiculous! I know General Clemmons very well. He's seen that several lucrative military contracts have found their way into the hands of some of California's finer manufacturers. Are you saying the he and the military already knows about this, and they're keeping it a secret?" Turner asked.

"No, that's not what I'm saying. No one knows about this yet. That's why I'm here explaining it to the two of you." Vince replied.

"Then you don't have any proof of a government cover-up or conspiracy going on, with General Clemmons involved?" Turner asked.

"The cover-up and conspiracy won't begin until Governor Lemming is elected president." Vince replied.

I've got to tell Clemmons about this! Turner thought, but said."I don't believe you, Dr. Davis. This sounds like science fiction."

Before Vince could respond, Lemming interrupted, saying. "John Clemmons is a no good son of a bitch. He fought me tooth and nail over government contracts for Boeing. Why would I pick him for a running mate?"

"He will run against you in the primaries, but he won't get the nomination, you will. You'll choose Clemmons as your running mate for his government and military experience in D.C., but you'll make the mistake of giving him too much power and he'll abuse that power by exercising too much influence in your decisions."

"You're not buying this shit, are you?" Turner asked Lemming.

"I don't like Clemmons, I can tell you that, Randy. He was pissed and didn't give me the time of day, when Boeing got the new government contract I lobbied for. He ignored me when I was there, for the contract signing." Lemming complained.

"You're being a little more than critical on Clemmons, aren't you, Carter?" Turner asked.

"Hell no I'm not! He's a prick and a big one at that! I know he swings a lot of weight with congress, but how would he control me or interfere with my decisions, if I was elected president?" Lemming asked Vince.

Vince started to explain and Turner interrupted again. "Goddamnit, Carter! You're not buying into this bullshit, are you?" He groaned.

"I don't have the luxury of having the Director of West Coast Seismic Activity located in my state, Randy, but you do. I never hear a damn thing about an earthquake until it happens. I want to hear what he has to say! Go on, Dr. Davis."

"Wait a minute, Carter! If this was so important, Dr. Leyland should have been here, not Davis! Dr. Leyland's well respected in his field and I would have listened to him. Why would he send Davis in his place? Does he really know you're here, Davis, or are you just trying to get his job?" Turner snarled.

Vince was stung. The meeting wasn't going the way he thought it would. Turner had turned it into a confrontation.

"No, Governor Turner, I'm not trying to get his job!" Vince replied.

"If I remember correctly, he turned down the coordinator's job that Sandra Beatty was promoted to, didn't he?" Turner asked.

"Yes, he did, sir." Vince replied.

"If all of this was so important to him, he should have been here himself!" Turner barked.

"He hoped that you'd understand that he's busy in his lab right now, working on his satellite prototype. That's why he sent his letter of endorsement with me, to give to the both of you. Dr. Leyland is hoping to gain your support before he goes to Sandra Beatty's office and gives her a practical demonstration of the equipment's abilities."

"Hold on, goddamnit!" Turner barked. "Dr. Leyland is a seismologist, for Christ's sake! Explain to me, how he's magically turned into an electronic genius, and an inventor!"

"He has a Doctorate in Electrical Engineering as well as Geology. Most people don't know that." Vince replied.

"If he was here, I might have given him more respect than I'm giving you! He's credible, but he's getting old, and you are neither. What experience do you have? What is your background and where are your credentials?" Turner asked.

"I admit, I don't have the credentials or background, Dr. Leyland has. It was not my purpose or intent to supersede him, or even try to make you believe I'm in charge. I came here today with Dr. Leyland's knowledge and approval. It is he that discovered all of this, but he didn't know how far it would go, until I told him." Vince replied.

Turner remembered an article he had read in the L.A. Times recently and asked."Weren't you in the papers a while back, Davis?"

"Yes I was." Vince said.

"What was it about?" Lemming asked.

"He claimed he had a future world experience. Is all this bullshit you're putting out, what it was all about?" Turner asked.

"Yes, but it's not bullshit. It's all in my presentation." Vince replied.

"I think we've heard enough!" Turner said.

"Hold on a minute, Randall!" Lemming said to Turner. "Tell me more, Dr. Davis.

Vince was feeling the pressure Turner was putting on him, as well as the embarrassment he felt in his stinging ridicule. For a second, the whole disaster flashed back in his mind when Lemming had said '*Hold on a minute, Randall*' In an instant, his thoughts had gone back to Taum Sauk and Camp Davis, where Randall had tried to attack the camp and had failed. In retreat, Randall had killed the guard members that had accompanied him and set them on fire. He had seen Randall die in the fiery crash and explosions as his truck ran off the road. Now, Randall was back, haunting him in his dreams. The very mention of the name, Randall, had caused him to lose focus.

"Shit, Carter! Are you daffy?" Turner asked Lemming. "This is a bunch of horseshit! Davis was put in a mental institution for his claims. I read all about it."

"Is that true?" Lemming asked Vince.

"Is what true?" Vince asked snapping back to reality.

"Were you put in a mental institution for making these claims you're showing and telling us about?" Lemming asked.

"Yes, it's true, but that's been cleared up. It was a misunderstanding. I was injured in a fall and suffered a concussion. I wasn't thinking clearly." He replied.

"But you're thinking clearly now, is that it?" Turner asked pointedly.

"Yes I am." Vince replied.

"I'm not listening to anymore of his cockamamie horseshit, Carter! I'm leaving!" Turner said.

"Wait, don't leave yet!" Lemming said. "There was no way he could have known I was going to run for president. He said I will get elected. I want to hear more."

"Oh, shit! All right, but it's just a waste of time. Go on, Davis." Turner said.

Vince directed his first comment to Governor Turner. "You won't run for Governor in 2008. Lt. Governor Sullivan will run and be elected Governor. When the disaster starts in Southern California, Governor Sullivan will then be sent to Area 51 by the newly elected, President Lemming, and ask me to take over the helm of the Forecast Room at Area 51, which I will accept and then be appointed as the Director of Homeland Disaster."

"Well there's two piles of horseshit for you to step in, Carter!" Turner spat out. "There is no Office of Homeland Disaster, and a minute ago Davis said Dr. Leyland would be in charge, at the imaginary, Area 51! He's as full of shit as a Christmas goose, Carter! Don't listen to him! He was diagnosed with a mental problem! I'll bet Dr. Leyland doesn't even know he's here."

"I beg to differ with you, Governor Turner." Donna said and handed Turner her card. "I do all of the technical work at the lab for Dr. Leyland.

He knows we're both here and he did, in fact, authorize Dr. Davis to come in his place, and present this information to you."

Turner looked at her card and asked. "Do you believe what he's saying?"

"Yes, I do." She replied.

"Let him go on, Randy." Lemming said.

"Okay, get on with it, Davis! But I'm only humoring you for Governor Lemming's benefit. I don't believe a damn word, you've said." Turner snarled.

Vince went on, telling them about the Forecast Project that Lemming sat up in secrecy at Area 51, with Dr. Leyland in charge, in the beginning. Then he explained the sinister plot Clemmons had put in place, which kept the pertinent information of the impending disaster from reaching Lemming ears and the orders Clemmons gave to have Lemming killed, so he could take over the presidency. The burning of Washington D.C., and the White House, his, Donna's and other individuals parts in the thwarting of Clemmons and his confederates. Clemmons death at Lambert Field in St. Louis, which, as far as anyone knew, would be the only inhabited part left, of the United States.

Turner couldn't take any more, and said. "No wonder you were put in a mental institution! He's crazy, Carter! He's talking about things he says are going to happen in the future, like they've already happened! Why in the hell are you listening to this shit?" Turner asked.

"Have you got any proof of what you're saying, Dr. Davis?" Lemming asked.

Vince took the penny out of his pocket and slid it across the table to Lemming, and said. "I found this on the floor of the terminal at Lambert Field, the day John Clemmons died."

Jesus! Now he thinks Clemmons is dead! Turner thought, but said nothing.

Lemming picked the penny up and looked at it. His eyes bulged, as he said. "Look at it this, Randy! It's a 2009."

Turner looked at the penny and said. "So what if the date is 2009? It's probably a fake. He could have had it made. Were you there with him when he found this, Miss Stevens? Were you in 2009 also?" Turner asked.

380

"No sir, I wasn't, but I believe him. He knows too many things he couldn't possibly know, for me not to believe him. Dr. Leyland believes him also. Several people do. He's not making it up. He was there." Donna said.

"So what you're both saying, is that he was in 2009, and has came back to warn everybody, and this new equipment that you say you'll have, will prove it. Is that it?" Turner asked.

"Yes, sir, that's it, and he's not crazy." Donna said.

One of Lemming's staff members interrupted, and said."Sir, It's time for the press conference. Past time in fact."

"Screw them. They can wait." Lemming said. He handed the penny back to Vince and went on. "I can't say that I believe you, Dr. Davis. However, I have been concerned, considerably about earthquakes. We have some very bad faults along the Washington Coastline and what you've said regarding earthquakes makes sense. Can we go into this further, after the press conference? Can I persuade you to wait so we can discuss this further?"

"Yes, that will be fine." Vince replied.

"Shit, Carter! You're not going to listen to more of this horseshit are you?" Turner asked.

"Yes, I am." Lemming answered.

"Goddamnit, Carter! He said he went forward and backward in time! You know he's full of shit! The bastard's been in a mental hospital, for Christ's sake! Turner hissed.

"Maybe so, but explain to me, if you can, how he knows I was thinking of running for president." Lemming said.

"How the hell would I know?" Turner replied.

"The penny looks real to me. On that basis alone I want to hear the rest of his story." Lemming said.

"Suit yourself, but it's a waste of time and I've got more important things to think about. He's also full of shit saying I'm not running for re-election, because I am. Sullivan, is a lamebrain, and everyone knows it! Where in the hell would you get such a stupid idea, Davis?" Turner shouted.

Vince knew it was useless to try and explain anything further to Turner. His mind was made up. Realizing that, he asked. "Will you at least, talk to Sandra Beatty, Governor Turner? She's going to reject Dr.

Leyland's findings if you, or someone, doesn't convince her to listen with an open mind. She has no respect for Dr. Leyland."

"I'm not promising you anything. Sandra's in charge, and she's the best there is. She wouldn't be in her position if she wasn't, now would she?" Turner asked

"Sandra's in the directors' position, because someone wanted her there." Vince replied.

"Are you saying I made a mistake appointing her?" Turner asked.

"In so far as a person with an open mind and the experience to know when to listen, yes." Vince replied.

"Then you think Dr. Leyland would have been a better choice, because he's listening to you." Turner said.

"He had the most experience. He should have gotten the job under any circumstances." Vince replied.

"Dr. Leyland removed his name from consideration. It was his decision, not mine. All of this is moot subject. Sandra's the coordinator and I have full confidence in her abilities. I don't know anything about earthquakes and especially the one you're talking about." Turner said, with a scowl on his face.

"Neither does Sandra, and what bothers me the most, is she knew before she was appointed she would get the job. She thinks Dr. Leyland is an old fool and told him so. She won't hesitate to reject his plans, unless someone steps in." Vince said.

"It won't be me, and criticizing her capabilities won't change my mind! I don't doubt Sandra's capabilities in the least. It's you that I have serious doubts about." Turner replied.

"Could you at least ask her to listen when we take Dr. Leyland's findings and the new equipment to Caltech?" Vince asked.

"There's been no authorization or budget proposals that have went through my office for any new equipment. Who authorized purchasing the new equipment?"

"Dr. Leyland is building the equipment on his own, but Sandra's not going to listen to him unless she's told to do so." Vince replied.

"You don't know that without presenting the findings and new equipment to her. I suggest you do just that. Come on, Carter, we're late." Turner's presentation was still laying on the table, as he and Lemming, left for the press conference.

"Wait here, Dr. Davis. I'll be back." Lemming said as he left.

One of Lemming's staff members came back in and told Vince to make sure, he waited, saying Lemming would definitely be back after the press conference.

Chief Brewer came in as they left, and asked. "How'd it go, Vince?"

"Lemming's coming back, but Turner's not." Vince replied. "He said he didn't believe me and seemed upset that I would question Sandra Beatty's position and abilities. He appointed her and I'm sure he's going to let her know about our discussion. We'll know for sure when we get there."

"That's interesting." Brewer said. "One would think Turner would have been the one to want to know more, but it's a step in the right direction, just the same."

"Maybe, we'll see." Vince replied.

"Did you show them the discs?" Brewer asked.

"No, I haven't had time to go all the way through the files myself." Vince replied.

"Do you think it would have helped convince Turner, if you had?" Brewer asked.

"No, I don't think it would have and I don't want the U.S. Marshall's back on our trail." Vince said.

"They won't be back. They found everything you said they would and I got rid of the leak in my office." Brewer replied.

"I feel like Turner's an enemy now, rather than an ally." Vince said to Brewer. "He was almost angry when he left. If we can't get Sandra to go along, nothing will be done until Lemming's elected, and by then it will be too late. I won't accomplish anything, other than wasting my time, and that of the others involved, and everything will go down, as it did the first time. We all might as well pack our bags and move with you to St. Louis, and prepare ourselves for the inevitable."

Donna had sat listening the whole time and finally spoke. "Let's cross that bridge when we come to it. Sandra might listen and agree, Vince. It sounds very much like you're expecting her to reject the findings, but remember, because of you, we know more than Dr. Leyland did the first time. We have to go and give her an opportunity to see the new evidence and equipment, before you can admit defeat."

"You're right, Donna." Vince said. "But I have a bad feeling about, Turner. He may have been the one behind her rejecting Dr. Leyland, the first time. I may have made a mistake including him."

The three continued talking until Governor Lemming returned. He sat down and said. "Dr. Davis. I want you to go over your presentation step by step with me. I want to hear every detail, don't leave anything out."

Vince started with the very beginning, the morning of August 18th, 2009. He finished two hours later with him waking up the same morning in 2005, himself not believing what he had experienced. He showed Lemming his scar and the penny again and re-told him about Clemmons retiring from the Army and being his running mate. He emphasized the part about the plot and conspiracy Clemmons would be involved in, to take over the presidency.

"I guess I better not pick Clemmons for a running mate, if I run for president." Lemming said.

Vince acknowledged his statement and went on, explaining how he had ended up in the mental institution and escaped. He told of Donna's and Jim's dreams and his own, that had become bizarre of late. He ended his explanation with the names of the other principals who he was going to contact, and see if they had experienced similar dreams.

When Vince finished, Governor Lemming spoke. "I'm going to be quite honest with you, Dr. Davis. You're story is in itself, unbelievable. It does sound like something an insane person might conjure up in the mind, convince their self it's true, then try to get others to believe and go along with."

Vince felt himself anticipating the Governor's next words and was preparing himself for the let down he knew was coming and would soon feel.

"I can understand why you were placed in the mental institution." Lemming said, and hesitated.

He thinks I'm crazy! Vince thought, as Lemming went on.

"If I were a doctor, I probably would have done the same after hearing the story, but I'm not a doctor, and there's one thing I haven't told you, or anyone for that matter. I have been having bizarre dreams also. You hit the nail right on the head when you said I would run for president. In my dreams, I am the president, and I'm facing a disaster, and those around me are treacherous, and I lose control. I truly had not thought of running for president, and couldn't understand why I was dreaming that I was president. I haven't told anyone of my dreams and I imagine I might have wound up like you, if I had. Now you've told me your story and I know the reason why I had the dreams. I'm going to try and help you, but I don't think you're going to get any help from, Governor Turner. He thought I was crazy coming back to hear you out. I'm glad I did though, it eases my mind somewhat, and at least gives me a reason for having the dreams. It's still unbelievable, and something I'll will not share with others. Your story has also fueled my imagination, Dr. Davis. Perhaps I can run for president and win, but that's a decision I'll have to make later. Any help you might need in finding people, I'm sure I can help you with. I have some very good friends, in high places, on Capitol Hill."

Vince was flabbergasted. He was having a hard time believing his ears. He thought he might be dreaming again, but he knew he wasn't.

"You can count on me, Dr. Davis." Lemming went on. "However, the personal things I've told you here today, can't leave this room. Do you understand?"

"Yes, sir, I do." Vince replied.

"Good. Here's my card." Lemming said. "It has my home phone and cell phone number on it. I don't want those shared either. You understand?"

"Yes." Vince replied.

"I'm taking your presentation with me." Lemming said. "My staff member has recorded our conversation, so I can listen to it, and refer to the presentation when doing so. If I do decide to make a run at the presidency, at least I'll have a jump-start on some of the pitfalls that would accompany the office. If there isn't anything else I should hear or know, I'll be leaving."

They stood up and Lemming stuck out his hand and shook with Vince and said. " I want to thank you, Dr. Davis, let me hear from you soon."

"Tell him, Vince!" Donna said referring to the discs.

"I don't think it's the right time." Vince replied.

"The right time for what?" Lemming asked.

"I have some CD's that were found on the bodies of Vice President Clemmons and David Lindsey, the Secret Service Agent I told you about."

"What?" Lemming asked.

Vince pulled the CD's out of his briefcase and showed them to Lemming, and said. "Two of them belonged to Clemmons and the other one belonged to David Lindsey."

"Does the government know you have the CD's?" Lemming asked.

"No, but they were looking for them." Vince replied.

"How did the government find out about them?" Lemming asked.

"Let me explain the whole story." Vince said and went on. "I found them in my fatigue pocket when I returned from 2009. They were lost for a while when I was in Gifford. I told the doctor that was treating me that I had them at my house along with the penny, and lost them when I fell and struck my head. I learned later that the discs were found in my bathroom and recovered by a team the hospital sent out. They ended up in the doctor's office and were taken to Police Headquarters when he was arrested."

"How did they come into your hands?" Lemming asked.

"The discs required a password to view the files. No one knew the passwords so the files were never opened and the CD's ended up in Chief Brewer's office with other evidence. He had his Cryptology Department recover the passwords and gain access to the files." Vince said.

"What was in the files?" Lemming asked.

"I don't know for sure. I haven't had time to go through all of the files." Vince replied.

"Why not? If they have something on them, say, some proof of what you're claiming, wouldn't it have been better to have presented that proof?" Lemming asked.

"Yes it would have, but there wasn't time. Things got a little complicated when the technician that recovered the passwords, opened the discs, and found a warning saying the information in the files was classified government documents. He called the Feds and that's when the trouble began." Vince said.

"How did you end up with the discs, if the Feds knew about them? Didn't they want them?" Lemming asked.

The Continent Of St. Louis - The Search For Answers

"Oh, yeah, they wanted them all right and they got them. What they have now are the originals and these are copies that were made from the originals." Vince said.

"If the government knows what's on the discs, why aren't they backing you up or arresting you for having classified information?" Lemming asked.

"They don't know I have these discs." Vince replied.

"Jesus! Having them in your possession is a Federal Crime. It's worse than a felony. They could consider you a spy and execute you!" Lemming said.

"It's classified information from the future." Vince said. "None of it has anything to do with today's world with the exception of me learning how Clemmons was able to pull off the cover-up and conspiracy. If I can find out how he did it, I can try to find a way to avoid it." Vince said.

"If the world is coming to an end and everything you've told me is true, what can you do about it without government assistance?" Lemming asked.

"Not much, unless we can get approval to go ahead with the new equipment. The government would have to send a satellite up, we couldn't." Vince said.

"How could you expect any cooperation, even with the new equipment, if it can't actually be tested and proven?" Lemming asked.

"We've solved that problem. We're sending the data collector and transmitter up in a jet and have it collect information along the fault lines. We're going to run a test flight first, just to make sure everything is in order. Then we're going to make a final run, and hopefully have the new receiver in Sandra Beatty's office, to prove to her and everyone else, what's really going on under the Earth's crust." Vince said.

"Let's say the test is a success, and I hope it is. Will the results you collect enable the government to get on top of the disaster and stop it from happening?" Lemming asked.

"Nothing will stop it from happening, sir. The only thing we'll gain is valuable time to prepare. I know where and when it's going to happen, and I know what the results are going to be. If I can get the government on top of this now, we'll have almost four years to relocate some of the population and the government. The rest of the world would have to do the same." Vince said.

"There's no way to avoid it at all?" Lemming asked.

"No, we'll just have to get out of the way." Vince replied.

"Who knows you have the discs?" Lemming asked.

"Only the four of us working at the lab and Chief Brewer know I have the discs." Vince said.

"Do you believe him, Chief Brewer?" Lemming asked.

"Yes, I'm helping him locate some of the people he told you about." Brewer replied.

"I'll do what I can to help you, Dr. Davis, but I can't go to Washington with this. You know that don't you?" Lemming asked.

"I believe we'll be successful with the equipment and test runs. Maybe then, Governor Turner will be convinced, and if so, the two of you would be hard to ignore on a Federal level, with the facts and data, I could provide." Vince said.

"We'll see." Lemming said.

"Would you like a copy of the discs?" Vince asked.

"I couldn't accept them in good conscience." Lemming said. "I would be violating the laws of the United States to have them in my possession. I may or may never be the President of The United States, but I am the Governor of the state of Washington and intend to continue in that capacity. I can't give my opponents any cause to doubt my sincerity and duty to my office or our country. Therefore, this conversation never took place." He turned to his aide and said. "Give me the recording of this conversation." He then extended his hand and shook with Vince, and said. "Good luck in your endeavor. You've got my phone numbers, let me know if you're successful at Caltech."

CHAPTER TWENTY-EIGHT

ACTING CHIEF ROWLAND'S OFFICE

"WHEN'S THE CHIEF GETTING back?" Glazier asked Rowland.
"Not till Monday." Rowland replied.
"I need a new man to replace, Lucas." Glazier said.
"Who?" Rowland asked.
"Earl Lucas. He was the one I had to put on suspension. The Feds searched his home and found all kinds of espionage and bomb shit on his hard drive. He was working for somebody, but so far, they haven't found out who. That's his file on your desk. My bet is, that he'll lose his job and end up in jail, so I need a new man right away." Glazier replied.

Rowland knew about the technician's suspension. He had laid the paperwork aside for the Chief to handle when he got back. He hadn't looked at the paperwork and didn't know the man's name.

"Have you submitted a request?" Rowland asked.
"Not yet. The Chief has to approve a personnel request, before it's submitted." Glazier replied.
"I'll review his paperwork. If I find substantial reasons for his dismissal, I'll sign the request for you." Rowland replied.
"Shit, Rowland! You're a Sergeant! Don't let sitting behind that desk go to your head!" Glazier retorted.
"Have it your way. Anything else?" Rowland asked.

"Yeah, there is one thing." Glazier replied.

"What's that?" Rowland asked.

"Lucas printed out the files that were on one of the discs, the Fed's confiscated."

"Did you give the print-outs to the Feds?" Rowland asked.

"No. The Feds were gone when I found the print-outs." Glazier replied.

"I thought they searched the place." Rowland said.

"They did, but Lucas had put them in a mailer and gave it to the mail clerk to mail." Glazier replied.

"Who was he mailing the files to?" Rowland asked.

"Some guy named Lindsey, in Washington D.C. He didn't put enough postage on it and it came back." Glazier replied.

"What did he do that for? He knew they were classified files!" Rowland said.

"How the hell would I know that? Do you want them? I don't want them in my desk, if those Feds come back." Glazier said.

"Run them through the shredder." Rowland replied.

"You know damn well anyone can put shredded papers back together! I've seen that done on TV, so you know goddamned well the Feds can do it! They took all of the trash out of all the waste baskets and shredders with them." Glazier replied.

"Have you got the print-outs with you?" Rowland asked.

Glazier reached inside his jacket and pulled out a thick envelope wrapped in tissue, and handed it to Rowland.

"I made sure my prints aren't on the envelope. You better do the same. Look where it was going." Glazier said.

Rowland looked through the tissue and saw the addressees name and address. The addressees name was David Lindsey, Agent, c/o The White House, 1600 Pennsylvania Ave. NW., Washington D.C. 20500.

"Son-of-a-bitch!" Rowland said.

"Son-of-a-bitch is right! The hot potato's yours now." Glazier said and started to leave.

"Wait a minute, goddamnit! I want Lucas's personnel file in this office and I want it now!" Rowland barked.

"Get it yourself!" Glazier replied.

"I'm giving you a direct order, Captain Glazier! Get his file!" Rowland barked.

"I wouldn't have had to take this shit off of you two days ago, Rowland! I know you're the Chief's pet and that's why you're sitting there! You can kiss my ass!" Glazier shouted.

"You're out of line, Captain Glazier!" Rowland shouted back.

"You're not Chief and you're not getting the Chief's job when he retires! You better keep that in mind, Sergeant, when you're throwing your temporary weight around!" Glazier shouted.

"You're on report, Captain Glazier! You can explain your behavior to the Chief, when he gets back!" Rowland yelled.

"Wait a minute! You can't do that!" Glazier whined.

"Consider it done! You're dismissed, Captain Glazier! Get out of here!" Rowland ordered.

Glazier left mumbling under his breath and passed the new secretary on the way out and asked. "Where's Ms. Billings?"

"She injured her right hand, helping the Chief down at the Hyatt. I'll be here for a couple weeks in her place." She replied. Her intercom buzzed and she answered. "Yes, Chief."

"Get me the personnel file on Earl Lucas. He worked in Cryptology." Rowland said.

"I'll get it right away, Chief." She said.

Glazier was standing there, staring at her tits. The sweater she had on was low cut, showing ample cleavage. She looked up, caught him and asked. "Is there anything else I can help you with, Captain?"

He cleared his throat and said. "No. Uh…Thank you, I'll be going."

Five minutes later, Rowland had Lucas's personnel file on his desk. He was going through the background information and came to the list of relatives that the department required. There were no known felons in his family and he had passed the background check and had been hired. Although he wore a uniform similar to that of a San Diego Police Officer, he was in fact, not a regular San Diego Police Officer. He was hired by the technical department for his skills in cryptology, and was never trained in regular police work or carried a gun. Rowland saw that he had originally lived in Arlington, Virginia, and his parents and a half brother named David Lindsey still lived there. The backgrounds of each relative had been checked and it was noted that David was a Secret Service Agent. No address was listed for him, but Rowland already knew what it was. The address was on the envelope that had been returned. *1600 Pennsylvania Ave. N.W. Washington D.C. 20500.* Rowland thought looking at the envelope, he hadn't touched or opened, and wondered. *What were you up to, Lucas?*

He slid the envelope inside Lucas's personnel file and thought. *Maybe I should call the Chief.*

He got out his cell phone and hit speed dial. Chief Brewer answered on the second ring. "What's wrong, Rowland? I'm on vacation you know!" He said.

"I know. I'm sorry, but something's come up you should know about." Rowland said.

"It better be important! What is it?" Brewer asked.

"Earl Lucas may have been a plant." Rowland said.

"I know he was leaking information to the media, if that's what you mean." Brewer replied.

"The Feds found a bunch of espionage and bomb making, shit, on his home computer. The Feds arrested him and their holding him for questioning. Glazier suspended him till they charge him with something." Rowland said.

"I know that! Is that all you called me about?" Brewer asked.

"No, Chief. Glazier brought me a letter that Lucas mailed to his half-brother in Washington D.C." Rowland said.

"What was in it?" Brewer asked.

"I haven't personally looked, but Glazier said Lucas printed out the files on one of the discs. He said the print-outs are inside the envelope he gave me." Rowland replied.

"Jesus Christ! Why didn't you say so in the first place? Who did you say he was mailing them to?" Brewer asked.

"His half-brother, David Lindsey. He's a Secret Service Agent. Lucas sent the envelope to, The White House, at 1600 Pennsylvania Ave. N.W. Washington, D.C., zip code 20500. I checked his name against Lucas's personnel file. His half-brother is listed and he was an agent when Lucas, hired on."

The Chief flashed back to the sheet of paper he had picked up off the ground when Stewart had dropped it. David Lindsey was one of the names on it.

"How did, Glazier, get the letter?" Brewer asked.

"It was returned for more postage. It came back today and Glazier brought it to me. He said his prints aren't on it. He handed it to me inside of tissue paper." Rowland replied.

"Does anyone else know about this?" Brewer asked.

"I can't answer that, but Glazier was anxious to get rid of it. Those Feds scared him shitless." Rowland said.

"Okay, I'm coming back early. David Lindsey is one of the people Vince said was in on the cover-up and conspiracy before the disaster. I want you to take that envelope to Vince right now. Have him scan the contents and make copies of all of it and then bring back the originals and shred all of it." Brewer said.

"Will do, Chief." Rowland replied.

"Is that the only envelope, he sent?" Brewer asked.

"I don't know, Chief. I just got this one." Rowland replied.

"Call down to the mail room and see if Lucas mailed any other envelopes that day." Brewer said.

"What if he did?" Rowland asked.

"Check the log and find out who they were mailed to. I hope there weren't any others, but if there was, we'll probably have the Secret Service down on our asses next." Brewer said.

"I put Glazier on report." Rowland said.

"What for?" Brewer asked.

"He was insubordinate." Rowland said.

Brewer laughed and said. "Give 'em hell, Rowland!" I'll see you tomorrow."

"Tomorrow's Saturday, Chief. It's my day off!" Rowland complained.

"This was one of my days off, and you called me, didn't you?" Brewer asked.

"Yeah, but you're the real, Chief!" Rowland said.

"Not in Mexico, I'm not, I'll see you tomorrow." Brewer folded his phone, and said to his wife. "Pack up, we're going home."

J. L. Reynolds

THE WHITE HOUSE…WASHINGTON D.C.

"Here's a letter for you, Lindsey." The mail clerk said.
"Put it in my inbox. I'm busy, I'll look at it later." Lindsey replied.
"It's marked urgent." The clerk said.
"Well give it to me!" Lindsey said. He took it and looked at the front. It was from his half-brother in San Diego.
He better not be sending me any more of his worthless spy shit! He thought as he ran his letter opener across the top and pulled the contents out. The first page was written in hand and said.
'David, You better check this shit out! I printed these pages from a disc I cracked the password to access. When I got in, the disc was Secret Service classified information with your name on it, and contained secret files! I didn't have time to read the files, my boss was breathing down my neck most of the time. He told me to close the files and call the Feds when he went to lunch. I'll have to call them, but I thought you should know in case they come breathing down your neck because of a security leak. I couldn't copy the disc because it leaves a trail and they'd know I did it. If the disc wasn't yours, then someone's penetrated your hard drive with a back door worm and copied your files. The disc came down from upstairs. I don't know where the Police Department got it and I won't be able to find out. I was in a hurry to print the pages and get them to you, but there were too many pages to fit in one envelope. This is the first, the other envelope has more pages and they're mostly copies of your email correspondence. I mailed them the same day, so you should have both of them. I cracked a couple other CD's but they weren't yours. They belonged to some Army General, he was one of the Chiefs', but I didn't know who the guy was, so I didn't print the files on those discs. Nothing else going on here.'

Earl.

What the hell? Lindsey thought after reading the message. He looked up and saw the mail clerk leaving and called out to her. "Wait a minute, Miss! Do you have another letter for me?"
"No, sir. That's all there was." She replied.
"There's another one coming!" Lindsey said. "Make sure I get it as soon as it arrives!"

The Continent Of St. Louis - The Search For Answers

Lindsey looked at the second page and found scans that contained office memorandum's and replies with notes he'd written to himself. All of it was stamped classified. He couldn't remember writing them and didn't recognize some of the names in the headers of the correspondence. Other notes contained names of individuals he was running routine background checks on. He picked up some of his current correspondence and notes for comparison.

They match! Jesus Christ! I don't remember writing these or scanning them or putting them on a disc.

He saw a couple names he recognized, but those names were still on his current list. They were low risk individuals, who continually stayed on the list of people who were constantly protesting at presidential speeches and getting into scrapes with the law. He flipped through the pages and one stood out. It was an 'Action needed immediately' memorandum from the vice president's office, seeking information on a man named, Dr. Vince Davis.

Who the hell is he? Lindsey wondered and read on. Beside the name was a post it note in his handwriting that read. *Number one priority! John wants this info ASAP!*

"What the hell? What is this shit?" Lindsey said aloud.

He flipped the pages further and saw other names as well as Davis's with information he'd collected on each, such as email addresses, phone numbers and other contact details. On another page, toward the bottom, Davis's name appeared again. It was underlined and beside it, was written. *'All hell's broken loose! Lemming wants him now. Get him at all costs! Per JC*

Lindsey was floored, he had no idea what any of it meant. *Lemming's the Governor of the state of Washington. Jesus Christ! What is all this shit?* He wondered.

He knew who John and JC were. He had been John Clemmons liaison officer when he was in the Army. It was Clemmons who had pulled the strings that got him his Secret Service job. Although he still kept in touch with Clemmons, letting him know what was going on at the White House, he was too smart to make any reference to those contacts in writing, and was at a loss to explain what the notes were doing in his files. He looked around to see if anybody was watching him. Finding no one, he re-read his brother's cover letter closer and found the answer. *Jesus Christ! Earl had other discs that belonged to John Clemmons!*

He picked up the phone and dialed his brother's number. An answering machine came on that said he was either at work or out prowling around. The beep sounded and Lindsey left a message. "I got your letter! Call me back as soon as you get this message. I'll try you at the station."

He hung up and called the San Diego Police Department, identified himself and asked to talk to Earl Lucas.

"I'm sorry, sir. Mr. Lucas is not available at this time." The operator said.

"When will he be back?" Lindsey asked.

"That information is not available, sir." She replied.

"What do you mean, it's not available? I'm his brother for Christ's sake! I'm a Secret Service Agent!" Lindsey retorted.

"I'm sorry, sir. I don't have any further details. Is there anything else?" She asked.

"No." Lindsey said and slammed down the phone. He was instantly angry. He never knew why, but it was uncontrollable when it happened. He started slamming things around on his desk and in the process, the sheaf of papers his brother had sent him, went flying and fluttered to the floor. He kicked his wastebasket and sent it flying and felt the anger subsiding. He sighed, bent down, and started picking up the papers. He was arranging them back in numerical order when his eye caught a detail he hadn't noticed in his hurried examination of the pages. Underneath the note regarding Lemming wanting Davis, he'd written a smaller note that was smudged slightly. He drew the page closer and read the words and date. '18, August, 2009 – 0430 hours PST. Target recovered and delivered.'

"Jesus Christ!" Lindsey whispered as he flipped through the pages and found that all the notes and memorandum's had dates beginning in January, 2008, and continued through August, 2009. *This shit is fake! Someone's messing with me!*

He looked up expecting to see other agents laughing at him for falling for the joke, but no one was. *I'll get even with the bastards!* He thought as his anger welled up again.

He slipped the pages back in the envelope, logged out of the office, drove to F.B.I headquarters and requested a rush job for fingerprints on the papers.

An hour later, he got the results. Other than his own prints, the only other identifiable prints were his brother's and a thumbprint belonging to a, Captain Thomas Glazier, of the San Diego Police.

How can that be? Lindsey wondered, having felt that someone at the White House was pulling a joke on him, but now, it didn't appear they were.

As he left F.B.I headquarters, he decided to smoke out the persons responsible. His first step would be to talk to his brother and learn what he knew about the discs. He then intended to use his authority as a Secret Service Agent to find the source of the discs, where they now were and who had them. He looked down at the note the F.B.I technician had given him and thought. *Captain Glazier might have all the answers.*

As he drove back, he formed a plan to find out who was responsible. He went straight to his boss, William Bowles, when he returned and showed him the letter and contents. He gave an Oscar wining performance regarding his concerns, citing what appeared to a breech in White House Security, if the whole thing wasn't a prank being played by other agents.

"No one's playing any pranks on anyone that I know of and they better not be playing one on you!" Bowles replied.

"If it's not a prank, then it's a breech in security, and it must not have been in this office. I need to go to San Diego to get to the bottom of this. My brother said there were other discs that belonged to an Army General. We need to recover all of the discs and find out who penetrated classified, Secret Service and Army files!"

Bowles started to hand the documents back to him and then said. "I'll have the F.B.I. do a full run-up on all the pages. I'll have them do hair, fiber and fluid, since you've already had the prints run."

"I can take care of that." Lindsey said. "I'll have them make copies when their finished. We'll need extras for all the departments."

"Good thinking, Lindsey. Will you need any help handling this?" Bowles asked.

"I could use a couple men to help me when I go to San Diego. That's where the letter came from and that's where the discs will be. Some back-up would be handy, if I turn up a terrorist cell or something." Lindsey replied.

"Take Gray and Segar with you." Bowles said.

"The two new boys?" Lindsey questioned.

"They've got to get their feet wet sometime. When you get through at F.B.I, headquarters, go on over to Andrews and wait for a flight. I'll put the three of you on a priority waiting list." Bowles said.

"Have them meet me at Andrews. I've got to go by my house and pick up some things." Lindsey said.

He didn't like the idea of dragging two fledgling agents around with him, but he didn't have a choice and wasn't going to argue. He hadn't mentioned the dates on the documents, nor had he mentioned knowing the General his brother had referred to. No one but him and his brother knew it was John Clemmons. What was throwing him, was the memorandums from the Vice President's office, that weren't signed. *Cheney never sends me any memorandums!* He thought as he left the office.

He felt fortunate that his boss hadn't noticed the dates and then questioned the whole thing. He wouldn't be on his way to San Diego, if he had. *I would have noticed it. I'll have the stupid bastard's job someday!*

Lindsey headed straight for his house. He had no intentions of going back to F.B.I. headquarters before he left.

I'll do it when I get back, just to cover my ass! He thought as he imagined himself being rewarded with a promotion, when he found the responsible persons, and had them behind bars. While he was imagining himself being lauded by his boss and associates, it suddenly dawned on him he might be in over his head and he didn't want to lose his job. He thought it over and decided to make a call to the one person who had the power and authority to cover his ass in case something went wrong. He made a call to his former boss, John Clemmons and told him what was going on.

U.S. MARSHALL'S OFFICE...SAN DIEGO, CALIFORNIA

"GIVE IT UP, LUCAS! Who are you working for?" Coldfeldt snarled.

"I work for the San Diego, Police Department!" Lucas replied.

"Don't give me that shit! You might as well tell me who you're really working for! I'm going to find out sooner or later anyway." Coldfeldt barked.

"I told you who I work for!" Lucas snapped back.

"And you're lying to me, you prick! Why did you mess up those discs and where are the copies you made?" Coldfeldt snarled.

"I didn't do anything to those discs and I didn't make any copies!" Lucas retorted.

"Don't be a wise guy! You're the only one that had them. The discs were copied and then erased." Coldfeldt said.

"I didn't do it!" Lucas protested.

"Well who did then? Do you think you're smarter than the Federal Government?" Coldfeldt asked and then went on. "Well you're not! I can damn well, guarantee you that! That equipment of yours is stone age, compared to what we have. You copied the discs, erased the files from the originals and then put porno on them."

"It wasn't me!" Lucas whined.

"Look, we found porno sites on the hard drive of your PC at Police Headquarters, and the one you have at home. So quit denying it and tell the truth!" Coldfeldt growled.

Lucas didn't want to lose his job, although he felt it was already in jeopardy for printing the files out and sending them to his brother.

"I'll make a deal with you if you promise to help me keep my job." Lucas said.

"No deals and I'm not promising you shit! You don't really think you're going back to work for the Police Department after leaking all that information to the media, do you?" Coldfeldt asked.

"Who said I was leaking information?" Lucas asked.

"Look, we know you were leaking information. Chief Brewer knows all about it. Now get on with it and start telling the truth!" Coldfeldt retorted.

"This is way above your head, Coldfeldt!" Lucas countered.

"Don't get smart with me!" Coldfeldt barked.

"I'm not! You're going to get the Secret Service down on your ass!" Lucas replied.

"Quit your bullshitting and tell me why you messed those discs up!" Coldfeldt hissed.

"I didn't mess them up and I didn't copy or erase anything. All I did was print out the files on one of the discs because they belonged to my brother David. I mailed the copies to him in Washington, D.C. " Lucas said.

"What kind of shit are you trying to hand me?" Coldfeldt roared.

"It's the truth. My brother is a Secret Service Agent. He works at the White House. He's one of President Bush's personal bodyguards. He's not going to like it when he finds out you've been screwing me around!" Lucas replied with a tone of importance.

"Horseshit! That's what that is, it's horseshit!" Coldfeldt spat back.

"His phone number is in my address book. You've got it, call the number next to his name and see who answers." Lucas said.

"Get the book." Coldfeldt said to Landreth.

Landreth complained about having to do everything and slowly limped out and returned with the book. Coldfeldt dialed the number and the operator answered. "How may I direct your call?"

"Who is this?" Coldfeldt asked.

"How may I direct your call?" She asked again.

"I need to speak with, David Lindsey." Coldfeldt said.

"I'm sorry, sir, Agent Lindsey is out in the field. Would you like to leave a message?" She asked.

"You're damned right I do!" Coldfeldt snapped.

"What is the message, sir?" She asked.

"Tell him to call Deputy U.S. Marshall Coldfeldt. I'm the commander of the San Diego unit. My number's 888-555-6700."

"I'll make sure he gets the message, sir. Is there anything else?"

"When will he be back?" Coldfeldt asked.

"That information is not available, sir." She replied.

"Thanks." Coldfeldt said and hung up.

"See! I told you!" Lucas said with a smile on his face.

"This is what I see!" Coldfeldt snapped. "There's some shit going on here and I'm going to get to the bottom of it. Put him back in lock-up!"

"I told you the truth!" Lucas protested.

"Well we'll find out when your, so called brother calls back, won't we? Get him out of here, Landreth!"

"What do you want me to do, sir?" Stewart asked.

"Go over to Police Headquarters and get a copy of Lucas's personnel file." Coldfeldt said.

"I'll need a warrant." Stewart replied.

"Well stop standing around here with your thumb us your ass! Go get one!" Coldfeldt ordered.

"Yes sir."

CHAPTER TWENTY-NINE

CHIEF BREWER'S OFFICE

ROWLAND'S INTERCOM BUZZED AND he answered. "What is it?"

"A deputy from the U.S. Marshall's office is here, Chief. He has a warrant for Lucas's personnel file."

Shit! I wished I'd never agreed to be acting Chief! Rowland thought, but said. "Send him in."

Stewart walked in, and asked. "Where's the Chief?"

"In Baja. He won't be back till tomorrow. What can I do for you?" Rowland asked.

"Oh yeah, I forgot, the Chief told me that. I have a Federal Warrant for the personnel file of Earl Lucas. He worked down in Cryptology." Stewart said.

"I know where he worked!" Rowland said.

"Jeez! Are all of you city cops this touchy?" Stewart asked.

"Give me the warrant! I've got to send it to the legal department for verification, before I can release Lucas's records." Rowland said.

"What kind of horseshit is that? Chief Brewer didn't have to get our warrants for the discs and the search of Cryptology certified." Stewart protested.

"Well he's the real Chief, and he can do whatever he wants to. I'm just the acting Chief, till he gets back, and I'm covering my ass. If I do something illegal, Lucas could sue me, the Police Department and the City of San Diego. Take a chair outside and I'll get back to you." Rowland said.

"What is this shit?" Stewart yelled. "I'm a deputy U.S. Marshall! You can't mess with me and you can't question that warrant!"

"I'm not questioning it, and I'm not messing with you! It's called red tape, Stewart! I'm required to have it certified before I can release personal information on any employee. It's the law! Don't you Federal boys keep up with current legal bulletins?"

"Hey, wait a minute! You can't talk to me like that. I'll arrest your ass for interfering with a Federal Investigation, if you keep screwing with me!" Stewart yelled.

"You must be forgetting where you are, Stewart." Rowland said. "That badge you've got in your pocket is worth about ten cents here. I could have ten cops in here dragging your ass down to the tank, before you could blink your eyes. Now get out there and sit down!"

Stewart started to reply, but he knew he was getting in over his head and said. "I'll be in the outer office. Make it as fast as you can. Coldfeldt is going to be all over my ass if it takes too long."

"I'll call you back in the second I get the okay." Rowland said, but thought. *You'll have blisters on your ass by the time you leave here.*

Stewart thought about calling Coldfeldt and telling him of the delay, but thought better of it, knowing Coldfeldt would ream his ass. Instead, he started making small talk with the secretary. "Where's Ms. Billings?" He asked.

"She's off on medical. She injured her hand and can't use it on the keyboard. She'll be back in a week or so."

Stewart thought back to bar at the Hyatt and the right hand, Ms. Billings, had landed on Landreth's jaw. It was the cleanest, one punch knockout, he'd ever seen.

"It's her right hand isn't it?" Stewart asked.

"I don't know. I wasn't told." She replied.

Stewart couldn't understand what Landreth saw in the older women, but what he was seeing when the secretary bent over, revealing about fifty per cent of her breasts, was interesting him.

"Nice tit...day isn't it?" He said, fumbling on his words.

"Why yes it is." She replied.

"Are you married?" Stewart asked.

"Why, no I'm not. Why do you ask?"

"I've got some tickets to the Chargers game, Sunday. Would you like to go with me?" Stewart asked.

"I'd like that very much, Mr. Stewart. Football is my favorite sport and of course, the Chargers are my favorite team." She replied.

"It's a date then." He said, but thought. *Landreth's going to be pissed when finds out he isn't going.*

Stewart soon forgot his mission as they exchanged personal information and football stories. He was sitting across the edge of the secretary's desk chatting with her and looking down the front of her sweater at every opportunity. Two hours had passed, when Rowland finally walked out of his office, with a copy of Lucas's personnel file and handed it to Stewart.

"That didn't take long." He said to Rowland.

Rowland looked at the clock on the wall, rolled his eyes and thought. *Pussy will get a man's mind off of his job every time.*

Stewart thanked Rowland and said. "I'll call you later, Joyce." And left.

"How did he know which hand Ms. Billings injured?" The secretary asked Rowland.

"He must be good at sniffing things out." Rowland replied and went back in his office.

COMMANDER COLDFELDT'S OFFICE

"WHERE IN THE HELL have you been?" Coldfeldt asked Stewart.

"At Police Headquarters, getting Lucas's file." Stewart replied.

"What took so damn long?" Coldfeldt snapped.

"The regular Chief wasn't there. The acting Chief wasn't sure of himself and had to have the warrant certified before he could hand over Lucas's file. He had to cut through a lot of red tape. That's what took so long." Stewart replied.

"You've been gone three hours! It couldn't have taken that long! Have you been out drinking? Let me smell your breath!" Coldfeldt said and started sniffing close to Stewart's face. He didn't smell alcohol, but he did pick up a strong perfume scent and shouted. "You've been out chasing pussy, you son-of-a-bitch!"

"Honest, Boss! I haven't been out chasing pussy! I was in the Chief's office the whole time! Call him if you don't believe me!" Stewart pleaded.

"I'll just do that! Wait outside!" Coldfeldt barked, and dialed Brewer's number. The secretary had gone for the day and Rowland picked up the phone.

"This is Rowland." He said.

"This is Coldfeldt over at the U.S. Marshall's office. I was just checking up on one of my men. His name is Stewart."

"Stewart left a half hour ago." Rowland said.

"I know, he's here now. He said he had to wait over two hours because you had to cut through a lot of red tape, but I think he's been out chasing pussy." Coldfeldt said.

"What makes you think that?" Rowland asked.

"He reeks of cheap perfume. I think he got himself a hooker or a lap dancer, while he was gone." Coldfeldt said.

"I wondered why he smelled like that when he walked in my office." Rowland replied.

"That's what I thought! Thank you, Chief." Coldfeldt hung up and yelled. "Get your ass in here, Stewart!"

Stewart could tell by the tone of Coldfeldt's voice, that he was going to get an ass eating, he didn't deserve. He was thinking fast, trying to find a way to get back into Coldfeldt's good graces and came up with an idea. Coldfeldt's phone rang as Stewart walked in, he sat down and laid Lucas's personnel file on Coldfeldt's desk, with the two tickets he had to the Chargers game, laying on top of it. Stewart knew that Coldfeldt was a diehard Chargers fan, but he also knew that Coldfeldt was too cheap to buy season tickets. Coldfeldt noticed the tickets while he was talking and said. "I've got to go." He hung up and asked Stewart. "What's this?"

"I got a couple tickets to Sundays' game and I can't go. I thought maybe you could use them."

Coldfeldt scooped the tickets up and said. "Thanks Stewart. I really appreciate that. What were we talking about?"

"Lucas's file. There it is." Stewart said, pointing to it.

"Oh, yes. That's right. Thank you. That will be all."

Stewart left Coldfeldt's office breathing easier, but he had a new problem. As he walked down the hall, he was talking to himself and asking himself a question.

"What in the hell am I going to do now?" He mumbled.

He wasn't worried about telling Landreth he wouldn't be going to the game. He was worried about how he was going to tell his newfound cutie, they weren't going to the game.

"I'm screwed!" Were his next words.

MIRAMAR MARINE AIR BASE...SAN DIEGO

LINDSEY'S PLANE TOUCHED DOWN and taxied to a stop. The three of them deplaned and went to a waiting car and headed for San Diego Police Headquarters.

"How did your brother get mixed up in this?" Gray asked.

"I don't know, but I'm going to find out." Lindsey replied.

"What about the other guy?" Segar asked.

"You mean, Davis?" Lindsey asked.

"Yeah, his name seems familiar to me, what did he do?" Segar asked.

"Maybe nothing, I don't know, but I'll find out." Lindsey replied.

"Have you tried contacting him yet?" Gray asked.

"I tried his phone number. It's out of service, so I had the Highway Patrol go by and check his house. It's vacant and it's for sale." Lindsey replied.

"Where does he work?" Gray asked.

"He's a seismologist. He works at UCSD. We're going there after we get through at Police Headquarters."

CHIEF BREWER'S OFFICE

ROWLAND WAS READY TO call it a day and head home. He was walking toward the office door when the phone rang.

Shit! What now? He thought, picked up the phone and said. "Rowland."

"There are three Secret Service Agents from Washington here to see, Chief Brewer. I told them he's on vacation, but they won't take no for an answer. They want to speak with whoever's in charge."

"Have someone bring them up." He replied and thought. *What in the hell do they want?*

He pulled out his cell phone and dialed the Chief's number. Brewer answered and asked. "What is it this time, Rowland?"

"There's three Secret Service Agents from D.C., on their way up. What do you want me to do?" Rowland asked.

"Do you know what they want?" Brewer asked.

"No." Rowland replied.

"Lucas must have sent another letter. It couldn't be anything else." Brewer replied.

"What do you want me to do? They're going to be here any minute." Rowland said.

"Find out what they want, but don't give them any information. I'm at the airport. Our flight leaves in a half an hour. Tell them I'll be back in town tomorrow, and I'll talk to them then." Brewer said.

"I've had the U.S. Marshall's up my ass again today. Now this." Rowland said.

"What did the U.S. Marshall's want?" Brewer asked.

"Lucas's personnel file?" Rowland replied.

"Did you give it to them?" Brewer asked.

"I had to, he had a warrant." Rowland said.

"Shit! You should have called me!" Brewer said.

"You weren't very happy the last time, so I just winged it." Rowland said.

"I'll be glad when I retire." Brewer said.

"I'm going with you." Rowland replied.

There was a knock on the office door. An officer escorted the three agents in and said. "This is acting, Chief Rowland, gentlemen."

"I've got to go." Rowland said to Brewer.

"Call me back when they leave." Brewer said.

"What if you're in flight?" Rowland asked.

"I'm the Chief of Police of San Diego! I'll answer my phone, any damn time I want to." Brewer bellowed back, and hung up.

"Sit down, gentlemen. How may I help you?" Rowland asked.

"I'm Agent David Lindsey with the Secret Service. This is Agent Gray and Segar. I need to speak with Captain Glazier, but I was told he isn't in. You'll have to call him back in, and do it right away. This is a matter of extreme urgency!" Lindsey said.

"I'm sorry, I can't do that. Captain Glazier's been given disciplinary time off." Rowland replied, but thought. *Shit! Lucas did send another letter!*

"I don't think you understand, Sergeant! I want him called back in immediately!" Lindsey demanded.

"I'm sorry, but I can't do that. What's the problem? Maybe I can help you." Rowland said.

"How many police officers are on the San Diego Police Force?" Lindsey asked.

"I don't know, maybe a thousand or more. Why?" Rowland asked.

"I've never handled matters of this significance with a Sergeant. Aren't there any higher ranking officers on duty that I can take this matter up with?" Lindsey asked.

"Chief Brewer will be back Monday." Rowland lied.

"I can't wait till Monday! Find someone that has the authority to handle this matter, immediately!" Lindsey barked.

"What did you say your name was, sir? Rowland asked.

"My name is, David Lindsey. I'm a senior agent with the Secret Service and assistant to the head of White House security. Our office believes there's been a high-level security breech in the San Diego Police Department that affects White House security. I'm here to look into the matter. I'm requesting the full cooperation and resources of the San Diego Police Department, to complete this task. Where may we set up offices, so we can begin?" Lindsey asked.

"Well, sir, I'm just a lowly Sergeant and I can't help you. You'll have to come back Monday and talk to, Chief Brewer. He'll be here in his office from eight to five. I'm off the clock and I'm going home, I'll escort you out." Rowland said.

"Listen you son-of-a-bitch! You're not going anywhere till I say so!" Lindsey snarled.

"You don't have any say so, in that regard." Rowland replied.

"Who is your direct superior?" Lindsey demanded.

"Police Commissioner Barkley, until Chief Brewer gets back." Rowland replied.

"What's his number?" Lindsey asked, taking out his cell phone.

"I have no idea." Rowland replied.

"What do you know?" Lindsey snapped.

Rowland didn't answer the question, instead he asked a question he knew the answer to. "Are you from Washington?"

"You're goddamned right I am!" Lindsey snapped back.

"Then why haven't I received any requests for compliance, from your office?" Rowland asked.

"This is a matter of National Security! We don't waste our time asking for cooperation! We give the orders and you better damn well comply!" Lindsey snarled.

"Without a request for compliance, you'll need a warrant to do any snooping around here. Do you have a warrant?" Rowland asked.

"I don't need a warrant!" Lindsey hissed.

"There's nothing I can do for you until you get the warrant. I suggest you get one." Rowland said.

"Listen you tin horn, desk jockey! I not taking any more of your shit!" Lindsey roared, as his temper flared.

"Hold on, Lindsey!" Gray said. "Let's get the warrant and come back."

"Yeah." Segar said. "I want to go down and check out the beach."

"I don't need any advice from either of you pups!" Lindsey roared.

"Your boys are making sense, Lindsey. You better listen to them." Rowland said.

"I'm giving you a direct order, Sergeant! Find someone that can assist me with this investigation, or I'll place you under arrest!" Lindsey threatened.

"You need a warrant, Lindsey! I'm in charge until Chief Brewer gets back. You aren't getting anything, till you get one!" Rowland snapped back.

"That's it! Arrest him, Gray!" Lindsey barked.

"What for? He's just doing his job." Gray replied.

"Just do it, goddamnit!" Lindsey roared.

Rowland put his hand on his revolver and said. "You're not arresting me or anybody else, Lindsey! Get the warrant and I'll see to it you get the help you need!"

Lindsey lost control and made a lunge toward Rowland. Rowland stepped aside, pulled his revolver, and struck Lindsey on the back of the head with the barrel. Lindsey collapsed, bouncing off the desk and landing in a heap at Rowland's feet. Rowland looked at Gray and Segar and said. "Now, you two can leave peacefully or you're going into the tank, with him. Do I make myself clear?"

"No problem, Sarge! He was out of line and we apologize for his behavior. We'll find our own way out, come on Segar." Gray said as he and Segar left.

Rowland rolled Lindsey over, took his gun and said. "Get up!"

"You'll regret this!" Lindsey threatened, as he started getting up.

"Shut up! Put your hands on the desk and spread your legs." Rowland said.

Lindsey got up slowly. He was wobbly, but still filled with anger, and said. "You've just bought yourself a truck load of shit!"

Rowland patted Lindsey down, took his credentials, cuffed him, and said. "Come with me."

"I'll be out in ten minutes and then I'm coming after your ass!" Lindsey snarled.

"We'll see about that." Rowland replied. He walked Lindsey to the elevator, went down to the basement and led Lindsey to the booking desk.

"What do we have here?" Carl Reese, the booking Sergeant asked.

"Put him in the tank, Reese." Rowland said.

"What's the charge?" Sgt. Reese asked.

"He's not being charged yet, Carl. Chief Brewer said to hold him for investigation. He'll be back tomorrow." Rowland said.

"You said he wouldn't be back till Monday!" Lindsey shouted.

"Shut up and empty your pockets, mister." Sgt. Reese ordered.

"Empty them yourself. I'm cuffed!" Lindsey shot back.

"I'll help him." Rowland said, going through his pockets and laying the contents on the desk. Sgt. Reese listed the items and slipped them into a large envelope.

"Add these to it." Rowland said, handing Reese, Lindsey's gun, credentials and holster.

"Jesus!" Reese said, looking at Lindsey's credentials. "He's a Secret Service agent. What did he do?"

"Attempted assault. The Chief wants him held in the tank, till he gets back."

"No problem." Reese said, as he led Lindsey away.

"I need to call my office, goddamnit!" Lindsey screamed as they went down the corridor.

"No phone calls, and no visitors, Reese!" Rowland yelled.

"I'll take care of it, Rowland." Reese replied.

Lindsey continued screaming, citing rights violations and threatening Sgt. Reese, with reprisals. The door slammed shut and snuffed out Lindsey's voice, as he was taken the rest of the way, and locked in the tank.

When the door had closed, Rowland left and went back to the Chief's office to fill out the paperwork on Lindsey. It was then that he saw a folder on the floor that Lindsey had dropped. He picked it up and pulled the contents out and read the cover letter and then looked at printed out file pages.

"Shit! This is the second letter! I've got to call the Chief!" He said aloud. He pulled out his cell phone, hit speed dial and waited. A recorded message came on saying. "The Verizon customer you're trying to reach cannot be located."

Rowland folded his phone and looked at the papers trying to think of what to do. He knew the papers rightfully belonged in Lindsey's envelope, down in lockup. As he looked over the files, he hatched a plan.

MISSION BEACH...SAN DIEGO

AFTER CALLING IN AND talking to their boss, Gray and Segar were walking on the beach, watching the waves roll in.

"This wouldn't be a bad place to live." Segar said.

"What about the earthquakes?" Gray asked.

"I'm not worried about earthquakes. We have the worst fault there is in, Missouri." Segar said.

"I never heard of any earthquakes in Missouri." Gray replied. "My folks live in Highlandville and they never said anything about earthquakes."

"They never told you about the New Madrid Fault?" Segar asked.

"I guess not, what is it?" Gray asked.

"It's a giant fault zone that's located along the Mississippi River, close to New Madrid, Missouri. The fault runs for miles in several directions." Segar said.

"When was the last time they had an earthquake there?" Gray asked.

"The big ones happened in 1811 and 1812. They tore the shit out of the landscape. The Mississippi ran backwards, and the land that was thrust upward, formed waterfalls. The shockwaves were felt all the way to the East Coast. Some people thought the world was coming to an end, some say it might still, if the New Madrid Fault builds up and goes off, full force."

"Now that you mention it, It seems like I've heard about that before." Gary said and asked. "Where did you look up the information?"

Segar thought for a few seconds and finally said. "I don't remember looking it up. But it's clear as day in my mind, and I don't know why. I've been having a lot of strange thoughts in my head lately that I can't figure out. I guess being in San Diego and you mentioning earthquakes, brought it back."

"Yeah, me too. Remember that guy Lindsey said he was going to look for after he got finished at Police Headquarters?" Gray asked.

"Yeah, his name was Dr. Vince Davis." Segar replied.

"I know. I remember hearing that name before, but I can't remember where." Gray said.

"You want to hear something even stranger?" Segar asked.

"Yeah, shoot."

"I remember hearing that name in Washington D.C., but I can't remember when." Segar said.

"No shit! Then I'm not crazy. I must have heard it there also." Gray replied.

"What do you want to do?" Segar asked.

"Do you want to get some beers and shoot some pool?" Gray asked.

"Hell yes! Where can we find a place?" Segar replied.

"There's a place in Santee my mother told me about. She used to live in Santee. She said it's a dump called the Driftwood on Mission Gorge Road. They have karaoke every night." Gray said.

"Sounds good to me, let's go." Segar said.

"I want to ride the roller coaster first." Gray said.

"All right, I race you there. The loser pays for the ride. Say when!" Segar said.

"Go!" Gray yelled. The two of them took off in a foot race for the roller coaster, like two school kids.

"If you beat me, I'll pay for the beers." Gray said as he left Segar behind.

The fact that Lindsey was locked up, wasn't going to interfere in their plans. They had done all they could, by calling it in. Lindsey was in custody and there was nothing they could do except wait for further orders from their boss, who hadn't been happy when they had reported Lindsey's hostile behavior and resulting arrest, at San Diego Police Headquarters. They had been told to standby while their boss worked on getting Lindsey released.

As Gray and Segar headed to the Driftwood, they had no idea their boss hadn't been able to get Lindsey's release accomplished. It was early evening in San Diego, but due to the late hour on the East Coast, it had been impossible to get a Federal Judge in that jurisdiction to issue a warrant or a writ for Lindsey's release, since the matter didn't involve a threat or danger to the president. Their boss had contacted the Western District, before it had closed, in hopes of getting the warrant and writ from that office. The clerk had requested the name of the person to be served and supporting evidence for the writ, before he could go forward and ask the judge to issue the warrant. Gray had furnished Rowland's name, but he didn't have a copy of Lindsey's paperwork. He had agents search Lindsey's desk for copies of the paperwork that Lindsey had shown him, but nothing was found. He had then called F.B.I headquarters and learned that Lindsey had never returned with the papers for further processing. With no other choice, he called the clerk of the Western District and told him to forget about the warrant. Not knowing what else to do, he next called San Diego Police Headquarters.

J. L. Reynolds

A CALL FROM WASHINGTON...FRIDAY, 5 P.M.

EDWARDS WAS KILLING TIME, waiting to go home. He was looking at a Hustler Magazine at his desk, when his phone rang. He glanced at the clock and thought. *What now?* He picked up the phone and said. "This is Edwards."

"Hello. This is Secret Service agent, William Bowles, in Washington D.C."

"What can I do for you, Bowles?" Edwards asked.

"I believe you have one of my men in custody. I'd like to speak with him please. His name is, David Lindsey."

"I'm sorry, I can't help you with that. You've reached the detective unit." Edwards replied.

"Can you transfer me to the right person?" Bowles asked.

"I'm not a switchboard operator! I'm a goddamned detective! Call back and ask for, Chief Brewer. He's the man you want." Edwards replied.

"What would be the extension number for the Chief's office?" Bowles asked.

"Jesus! How the hell would I know, I never call him!" *And that's for damn sure!* Edwards thought and then said. "Just call back and ask for, Chief Brewer!"

Edwards slammed the telephone down and went back to looking at the centerfold in his Hustler Magazine.

Bowles finally got through to the Chief's office and Rowland answered, thinking it might be, Chief Brewer calling. "Chief's office, Rowland speaking."

"May I speak with, Chief Brewer? This is William Bowles, I am the head of White House security, and I'm calling from Washington D.C." Bowles said.

"You don't say!" Rowland replied, acting impressed.

"Yes, that's correct. May I speak with, Chief Brewer?" Bowles asked.

"I'm sorry, Chief Brewer's on vacation. He won't be back until Monday." Rowland replied, and then said. "I'm Sgt. Rowland. Is there anything I could do to help you?"

"Yes, there is, I need to speak with one of my agents. David Lindsey is his name. I've received a report that's he's been incarcerated and is being held in at your Police Station." Bowles said.

"Let's see…" Rowland said, shuffling through some papers on his desk and then said. "Oh yeah, here it is. Secret Service Agent, David Lindsey, you're right, he's being held for questioning."

"May I speak with, Agent Lindsey?" Bowles asked.

"Let's see…" Rowland said again and then said. "No, sir, I'm afraid not. The orders say no calls or visitors."

"How can that be? If he was arrested, he's entitled to a lawyer. My office will provide one." Bowles replied.

"Lindsey wasn't arrested. He's being held for questioning until Chief Brewer returns, therefore no calls or visitors. You know the rules." Rowland said.

"That's impossible!" Bowles argued. "He's a Secret Service Agent and he was doing his job. He was representing my office and had my authorization to investigate a classified matter."

"Is, Bush, here in San Diego?" Rowland asked.

"No, President Bush is here in the White House. Why do you ask?" Bowles replied.

"It's your guy's job to protect him, isn't it?" Rowland asked.

"Yes it is, and I'm proud to say, we do a good job." Bowles replied.

"Then I guess you have enough men to cover the job at the White House." Rowland replied.

"Of course we do! Can we get back to the subject of Agent Lindsey, please?" Bowles asked.

"Sure thing." Rowland said.

"What can be done from my end to get, Agent Lindsey, released? I'd like for him to finish his job there." Bowles said.

"Nothing." Rowland replied.

"That's absurd!" Bowles replied

"It may be absurd, but it's true. Lindsey isn't going to see the light of day, until Chief Brewer gets back." Rowland replied.

"Maybe you can help me with something else then." Bowles said.

"I will if I can. What is it?" Rowland asked.

"Agent Lindsey had some classified documents in his possession. I would like to be assured that those documents still remain in Agent Lindsey's possession." Bowels said.

"Were they the papers he had on him when he barged into Chief Brewer's office and assaulted the acting Chief?" Rowland asked.

"I didn't know he assaulted the acting Chief." Bowles lied and then said. "Yes, they may have been the papers. Were they classified?" He asked.

"There's no way to tell." Rowland replied.

"Why not? That would be easy to determine. They would be stamped classified." Bowles replied.

"Not now, they aren't." Rowland replied. "They burned up in the Chief's ashtray."

"Oh, Jesus! How did that happen?" Bowles asked

"They must have fallen out of his hand when he tried to assault the acting Chief. I guess nobody noticed and they burned up." Rowland replied.

"Did you save the ashes?" Bowles asked.

"Yes, we did that. They're in the envelope with the rest of his personal articles." Rowland replied

"Thank goodness! The F.B.I has techniques to examine the ashes and recover the data." Bowles said.

"Can they do dust?" Rowland asked.

"What do you mean?" Bowles asked.

"I'd say that ninety percent of the ashes are dust. Some of it got mixed up with the ashes in the ashtray, so some of it's probably cigar ashes, but there were a couple small pieces still intact. We saved them too." Rowland said.

"What did you say your name was?" Bowles asked. "I've been making notes and I must have missed that."

"Sgt. Rowland." He replied.

"Is there anyone at the station above your rank I can speak with, Sergeant?" Bowles asked.

"Not on Friday night. They've all gone home and so am I." Rowland said and hung up. He was smiling as he walked out and thought. *That was a hell of an idea! The Chief will be proud of me.*

He patted the pocket he had Lindsey's papers in, and thought. *Let them sift through that dust. They aren't going to find shit!*

CHIEF BREWER'S OFFICE...FRIDAY, 10 P.M.

"HERE'S THE PAPERS LINDSEY was carrying, Chief." Rowland said.

"Thanks for coming down, Rowland. I know you've had a long day." Brewer said.

"No problem. I got a little shuteye after reading those papers. Look at dates." Rowland said.

"Jesus Christ! They're all dated 2008 or 2009." Brewer replied.

"Yeah, and Davis's name is on several pages." Rowland said.

"Where? Which pages are you talking about?" Brewer asked.

Rowland pointed out the pages and Brewer read the information and said. "Damn! Did Lindsey say anything about, Vince?"

"Not a word. He didn't mention the files and he said nothing about Earl Lucas being his half brother. He wanted to talk to Glazier, but I gave Glazier a week off without pay, for insubordination." Rowland said.

"You'll make a good, Chief!" Brewer said and asked. "What did Lindsey say?"

"Not much of anything. All he was interested in was throwing his weight around, and demanding someone of higher authority to speak to. I pushed his button and he got belligerent. The bastard has a nasty temper." Rowland said.

"Who were the other two that were with, Lindsey?" Brewer asked.

"They were both agents, I know that much, but Lindsey was so busy running his mouth and trying to be important, I never had a chance to talk to them. They left when I cuffed Lindsey."

"Shit! I wished you'd have gotten their contact information. I'd like to talk to them and see how much Lindsey knows or has guessed." Brewer said.

"Lindsey's cell phone is in lockup. He called one of them Gray and the other Segar. Maybe you can find their contact numbers in the directory." Rowland said.

"How do you remember shit like that? I would have never been able to remember their names." Brewer said.

"Me neither, Chief. I had my recorder going for backup in case I needed it. Here's the tape."

"Good job, Rowland. I'll make sure the commissioner hears about the job you've done, while I was gone. That should add a few points to your ability to handle matters in a tough situation." Brewer said.

"I'm not taking the job, even if it's offered. I'm putting in my retirement, and going with you to Missouri." Rowland said.

"Not in the same damn car, you're not." Brewer replied.

Rowland laughed and said. "Good to have you back, Chief. Let's go down to lockup and check Lindsey's cell phone."

THE DRIFTWOOD...SANTEE CALIFORNIA...11 P.M.

GRAY'S CELL PHONE RANG and he answered it thinking it was the boss or Lindsey. "This is Gray."

"Hello, Gray. This is Chief Brewer of the San Diego Police Department. Is there any way I can speak with you and your partner tonight?"

"Hold on, Chief." Gray said. He looked at his watch and motioned for Segar to come over.

"Is that, Lindsey?" Segar asked.

"No. It's the Chief of Police. He wants to know if he can talk to us tonight." Gray replied.

"Is he releasing, Lindsey?" Segar asked.

"He didn't say. I'll ask him."... "Chief, have you released Lindsey?" Gray asked.

"No, I haven't. Your boss called here earlier and I need to talk to the two of you and get your side of the story. I know it's late, can I meet the two of you somewhere?" Brewer asked.

Gray relayed the message to Segar and the two agreed to meet with the Chief. "We're at the Driftwood in Santee. It's on Mission Gorge Road." Gray said.

"We'll be there in a half hour." Brewer replied.

Gray and Segar went back to shooting pool as a heavy set, dark haired girl took the karaoke stage and began singing, 'Love Will Lead You Back.'

"Damn! She's as good as, Taylor Dayne!" Segar said.

"Maybe better." Gray replied. The two listened as couples got up and began to dance.

"Look at that gray haired old fart with the beard and the parrot shirt on. He's got his hand on the blonde's ass." Segar said.

"She's smiling." Gray replied and they both laughed.

Chief Brewer and Rowland pulled into the parking lot of the Driftwood and went in. They were dressed in civilian clothes and no one paid any attention to them as they looked at the crowd, through the dense smoke.

"There they are." Rowland said pointing to the pool table area.

They walked over just as Gray scratched the 8 ball, shouting obscenities, and ending the game. Rowland began the conversation. "Hi, Gray." He said.

"Hi, Sgt. Rowland. This must be, Chief Brewer." Gray said. He finished his bottle of Corona and then asked. "Do you want a beer?"

"I could use one." Rowland replied.

"I'd rather we go outside and talk. It's too noisy in here." Brewer said.

"Shit, Chief! I'm a little dry." Rowland said.

"You can drink all you want to after we're through talking. Come on!" Brewer said.

The four walked outside, got in the Chief's car and he started the conversation. "Sgt. Rowland filled me in on the details of Lindsey's arrest. I have a tape recording of the conversation that went on just before Lindsey attacked Sgt. Rowland. I'd like for the two of you to listen to the tape and tell me if you agree with what went on." Brewer said.

"Sure, go ahead." Gray said.

Brewer played the tape and both agents confirmed what they heard.

"Thank you." Chief Brewer said and then asked. "What made Lindsey act the way he did?"

"We're both fairly new with the Secret Service. This was our first assignment with Lindsey, so we can't tell you what triggered his behavior, but we were warned that he's a hot head and used to getting his way." Gray said.

"What exactly was your assignment and what did it have to do with the San Diego Police Department?" Brewer asked.

"We weren't briefed on all the details, but Lindsey said someone from the San Diego Police Department mailed him a letter with printed out files that were classified Secret Service documents. Lindsey said they were scans of his notes and memorandums." Gray said.

"Did you see the files?" Brewer asked.

"Not all of them, but the ones we saw were Lindsey's and the envelope was sent from the San Diego Police Department." Segar said.

"We know who sent the letter. It was Lindsey's half brother. He worked in Cryptology and was given some discs we recovered in a case we were working on. At the time, we didn't know what was on the discs and we didn't realize that the technician who worked on the discs was Lindsey's half-brother." Brewer said.

"We heard about the discs. Part of our assignment was to impound the discs and take them back to Washington. Lindsey said someone must have penetrated the Secret Service's database and copied the files. Do you have the discs?" Gray asked.

"Not any longer. Someone called the U.S. Marshall's office and told them we had the discs. The Marshall's office sent two deputies to my office with a warrant and took custody of them." Brewer said.

"Lindsey didn't know that." Segar said.

"If Lindsey had given Sgt. Rowland the courtesy of an explanation instead of barging into my office and throwing his weight around, he would have found out that we didn't have the discs and that his half-brother had been arrested for tampering with the discs." Brewer said.

"Is Lindsey's half-brother in jail with him?" Gray asked.

"No, we didn't arrest him, the Marshall's did. They have him in custody." Brewer replied.

"Then what Lindsey did, was cause himself a lot of problems." Segar said.

"That's for damn sure!" Brewer said, and went on. "I'd be willing to release Lindsey, but I'll have to talk to your boss first. I don't like Secret Service Agents coming in my office and throwing their weight around."

"Have you got his number?" Segar asked.

"I've got it. Bowles is his name." Rowland said.

"Lindsey's his assistant in charge." Segar said.

"Look boys, the San Diego Police Department is out of this. The Marshall's office is handling it and Lindsey's half-brother won't be coming back to work for me. If your boss will agree to drop the investigation and put Lindsey in your custody, the three of you can leave town."

"Lindsey said he had one other lead in the San Diego area he was going to check into after he was through at Police Headquarters." Gray said.

"What was it?" Brewer asked.

"He was going to check up on some guy named, Davis." Segar said.

"Dr. Vince Davis." Gray added.

Brewer laughed and Rowland joined in.

"What are you laughing about?" Gray asked.

"Dr. Vince Davis was put in a mental hospital. It was in all the news, didn't you see it? It was on CNN." Brewer said.

"I remember that. That's where we heard his name!" Segar said.

"Why was Lindsey looking for Davis?" Brewer asked.

"Davis's name was on the notes. We both saw it." Segar said.

"Davis escaped from the mental hospital and one of my officers shut down the airport looking for him and caused a terrorist scare. That's probably why Davis's name was in his notes." Brewer said.

"I think Lindsey must have over-reacted." Rowland said.

"Do you have copies of Lindsey's files?" Brewer asked.

"No, Lindsey had them. We weren't given any copies." Segar said.

"Okay, here's the deal. I'll call your boss Monday morning, and if he agrees, I'll release Lindsey into your custody and you'll have to put Lindsey on the first flight out." Brewer said.

"We'd have to catch a hop out of Miramar. It might take a few hours." Segar said.

"The Secret Service makes you take MATS flights?" Rowland asked.

"Only when were on secondary assignments." Segar said.

"Your boss is going to have to authorize public transportation. I'm not going to have Lindsey in town one minute more than necessary!" Brewer said.

"I've got Bowles cell number, do you want to call him at home?" Gray asked.

"Jesus Christ! It's three in the morning on the East Coast." Brewer said.

"That's what he gets paid for, Chief. He's the boss." Gray replied.

Brewer thought about his vacation that had been cut short because he was the boss and said. "What's his number."

Brewer made the call and woke Bowles. Brewer told him the case was in the hands of the U.S. Marshalls and that the Marshall's office had the discs, as well as the individual responsible for tampering with the discs, who happened to be Lindsey's half-brother. Bowles was astonished to learn that Lindsey's half-brother was involved and assured Brewer that Lindsey would be reprimanded for his behavior, as well as for not revealing where he gotten the information and not giving all the details in the case. He agreed to the deal, apologized for Lindsey's behavior, and said he'd have his office fax new orders for Lindsey to the Police department, as well as having tickets ready at the counter for the trip back to Washington the next morning.

"Okay, boys. You heard what I told him and he agreed. You can pick Lindsey up at the station in the morning. Your boss said he'd have tickets for the three of you waiting at the ticket counter. I'm going home and get some rest. I'll see you boys in the morning. Let's go Rowland."

"I'm going to stay here and shoot some pool, if you don't mind." Rowland said.

"How are you going to get home?" Brewer asked.

"We'll give him a ride home, Chief." Segar said.

"Suit yourselves. But don't call me if the Sheriff arrests your asses for DUI." Brewer said.

"Come on, fresh meat!" Gray said to Rowland.

The three of them walked back into the Driftwood and cut their way through the smoke.

SAN DIEGO POLICE STATION...SATURDAY 8 A.M.

GRAY AND SEGAR WERE waiting with Brewer and Rowland as Lindsey was released from the tank. He was still in an angry mood when he was led to the desk. Reese handed him the envelope and said. "Check the contents and sign here."

Lindsey opened the envelope and poured the contents out on the counter, with a thud. He picked up his gun and credentials and Gray said. "I'll take your gun, Lindsey."

"What the hell for?" Lindsey asked.

"Read the orders from, Bowles." Gray said handing him the fax.

Lindsey read it and asked. "What kind of shit is this?"

"You've been relieved of duty. You're in our custody till we get back to Washington and turn you over to Bowles." Gray replied.

"This is bullshit!" Lindsey retorted.

"Come on, Lindsey. You've caused enough trouble here." Segar said.

"Where's my paperwork?" Lindsey asked.

"Right there." Rowland said pointing to a baggy full of ash dust."

"That's a bunch of ashes!" Lindsey shouted.

"You're right about that." Rowland replied. "Your papers fell in my ashtray when I slugged you. I found the ashes and a couple of burned ends when I went back to my office. I wouldn't have known they belonged to you if your folder had burned all the way up."

"The papers were evidence! I have an investigation to complete!" Lindsey snarled.

"The U.S. Marshall's are handling the case, Lindsey. They have the discs and your half-brother in custody. Bowles was pissed when he learned the letter came from you're half-brother and you hadn't told him." Brewer said.

"We're off the case, Lindsey." Segar said. "There's a police van waiting out in front to take us to the airport. Come on!"

"I'm not going anywhere till I find out about, Davis!" Lindsey shouted.

"Davis is in a mental institution. It was in the news, that's why Segar and I both remembered his name. He's crazy." Gray said.

Lindsey looked at them with a foolish look on his face and said. "Then, that's why his house is for sale and his telephone's been disconnected."

"I'm sure it is." Brewer replied.

"Okay, I'm going." Lindsey said, handing Gray his gun.

As the group walked to the front, Brewer said. "It's too bad about your papers. You have copies of them back in Washington, don't you?"

Lindsey didn't say a word and Brewer went on. "You can fax copies to the U.S. Marshall's office when you get back."

"I don't have any more copies. The Marshall's can get them from the discs." Lindsey replied, and then asked. "What about my brother?"

"I can't answer that, beyond saying, he won't be employed by the San Diego Police Department. He shouldn't have tampered with the discs." Brewer said.

"What do you mean?" Lindsey asked.

"He replaced your files with porno." Brewer replied.

"What about, John Clemmons files, that were on the other discs?" Lindsey asked.

"Your brother messed them up too. The Marshall's office told me that." Brewer said.

Lindsey knew he was in deep shit. Without the discs for evidence, even if he had printouts, they wouldn't prove anything. He knew he was screwed and said so. "Okay, Chief. I'm screwed, but my brother really didn't do anything wrong."

"How do you figure that?" Brewer asked.

"None of my notes or memorandums were credible evidence. That's why I came to San Diego." Lindsey said.

"Why weren't they?" Brewer asked.

"They were dated 2008 and 2009." Lindsey replied.

"Shit! This is 2005! Why would your boss send you out here if he knew that?" Brewer asked.

"He didn't notice the dates and I blew it all past him. I wanted the discs that belonged to Clemmons." Lindsey said.

"Why?" Brewer asked.

"I don't know. I thought they might be important. He's one of the Chief's of Staff."

"Did you tell him about it?" Brewer asked.

"No." Lindsey lied, and then said. "I was his liaison officer before I joined the Secret Service. He's not going to be happy, when he learns someone got into his database and copied his files." Lindsey said.

"Were his files from 2008 and 2009?" Brewer asked.

"I don't know, I never got to see them." Lindsey replied.

"Well no one else is going to see them either, so you might as well forget about the whole thing. I'll talk to the U.S. Marshall's office and tell them what you said. If they don't have any other evidence on your brother, they won't take him to trial." Brewer said.

"I caused all of this trouble for him, Chief. Would you consider taking him back if the Marshall's office releases him?" Lindsey asked.

"Not a chance, Lindsey! He was leaking information to the media on cases we were working on. He's through here." Brewer said.

Lindsey became apologetic and said. "I'm sorry for what my brother did, Chief. He's into spy and espionage shit, I know that, and sometimes he can't help himself. He probably thought he was doing the right thing sending me the files, but I don't have any idea why he replaced the files with porno. I also apologize for being such an asshole in your office, Rowland."

"Don't mention it. I've already forgot about it." Rowland lied.

Lindsey shook hands with Brewer and Rowland, and got in the van.

"We shouldn't hear any more out of him." Rowland said as the van's engine started up.

"We'll see." Brewer replied.

"How did you know Lucas was leaking information to the media?" Rowland asked.

"Vince thought he was, and he was right." Brewer replied.

"How did he know?" Rowland asked.

"I don't know, he just did." Brewer replied.

"If Lindsey had learned Vince, wasn't in Gifford, he would have caused a real stink." Rowland said.

"His boss will take care of him." Brewer replied. "I think he's going to be out of job, right along with his half-brother."

"What was on the discs that Lindsey said belonged to Clemmons?" Rowland asked.

"Proof of his evolvement in covering up the disaster." Brewer replied.

"Goddamn! This is like a paradox." Rowland said.

"It's worse. It's all true." Brewer replied and said. "I've got to call, Vince."

"I'm going home." Rowland said.

"Wait a minute! You're acting Chief, until Monday." Brewer said.

"With my authority as acting Chief, I called Jennings in to cover for me." Rowland said.

"Is he up there in my office?" Brewer asked.

"Yeah, he is." Rowland replied.

"Shit! I better not find Edwards and Harper up there!" Brewer said.

"They were both there looking at Hustler Magazines. Edwards had just cut a nasty fart when I left." Rowland said.

"Goddamnit! I'll have to have the place fumigated! Tell me you're kidding!" Brewer replied.

"I'm not shitting you, Chief! Jennings is up there with them. He thinks he's getting your job when you retire." Rowland said.

"Not if I have anything to say about it!" Brewer snarled.

"Jennings said Unroe has put in for Traxler's job. Are you going to give it to him?" Rowland asked.

"What do you think? Can he handle it?" Brewer asked.

"Yeah, he'd be better than Edwards or Harper, but they'll be pissed." Rowland said.

"Well screw them. I'll transfer Unroe to the Detective Unit if he wants the shitty job, but he's not getting a promotion. I'm going to move you over to the Detective Unit and bump you up to the Lieutenant's desk. If Jennings gets shit canned, I'll move you up to the Captain's desk." Brewer said.

"Jesus! That will stir up some shit!" Rowland replied, as they watched the police van round the corner and head for the airport.

"I hope that's the last we see of Lindsey." Brewer said.

"Me too. I'll see you Monday, Chief. I'm going home, I have a hangover." Rowland said as he walked toward his car.

THE RIDE TO THE LINDBERGH FIELD

LINDSEY WAS THINKING AS they made their way to the airport, he felt like a fool, but he was angry. *Those asshole's had no right to throw me in the tank.*

He smelled of his suit jacket sleeve. It smelled like urine, he took it off and threw it on the floor and said. "I'll get even with those bastard's for throwing me in the tank!"

"You aren't doing anything, Lindsey. You might not have a job when we get back." Gray said.

"Give me my gun!" Lindsey barked.

"You're not getting it!" Gray retorted.

"Look, goddamnit! That's an order! I'm your superior!" Lindsey snarled.

"Put your cuffs on him, Segar." Gray said.

Lindsey lost his temper and started struggling with Gray. Segar hit him over the head with his gun and Lindsey slumped over in his seat. Segar put his cuffs on Lindsey and said. "He won't be working for the Secret Service when we get back and tell Bowles what he just pulled." Segar said.

"Good riddance! Throw his jacket out the window, it smells like piss." Gray said.

"We can't do that! I'll get a plastic bag when we get to the airport." Segar replied.

A strange thought occurred to Gray and he said. "I just had a strange thought, Segar. It was like a premonition. It seemed like we were changing history."

"How? Segar asked.

"I don't know. It was like in that movie, Back to the Future." Gray replied.

"I saw that, what do you mean?" Segar asked.

"I saw Lindsey shaking hands with someone getting off of a military jet at Andrews. The next minute he was gone, and we were there, shaking hands with the guy."

"Who were we shaking hands with?" Segar asked.

"I don't know who it was, I'd never seen him before, but Lindsey just disappeared." Gray said.

"He'll be gone when we get back, I'd bet on that." Segar said.

"I had too many Corona's at the Driftwood last night." Gray said.

"Yeah, I've got a hangover." Segar replied.

"How much did you lose to Rowland?" Gray asked.

"Fifty bucks!" Segar replied.

"He got me for forty! He set us up. The bastard's a pool shark." Gray said.

"Yeah, but it was fun." Segar replied.

Lindsey started moaning and both of them said. "Shut up!"

CHAPTER THIRTY

MONDAY...UCSD SIESMOLOGY CENTER

VINCE, JIM, DONNA AND Dr. Leyland had assembled for an early morning meeting, but Vince's mind was miles away. Chief Brewer had called him on Saturday, after Lindsey had left Police Headquarters in the custody of the two agents who had came with him. Brewer had also told Vince the two agents names were Gray and Segar, saying he had crossed Lindsey's and their names off the list, Vince had given him. When Brewer told him their names, Vince had been stunned, and even more so, when Brewer told him that Lindsey was actually after the two discs that had belonged to Clemmons. He had told Vince not to worry about any of it, telling him he had the print-outs that Lindsey had brought with him and Lindsey was taking a bag of ashes back to D.C., with him. Brewer finished by saying, Lindsey had also intended to question him and find out what his connection to discs was, but that he had told Lindsey that he was in Gifford.

Vince was relieved somewhat knowing Lindsey had been removed from command, and was fairly certain he wouldn't be coming back to cause any more problems. He hadn't told the others about any of it. None of them knew who Lindsey was, he was out of the way now, and shouldn't cause any more concern, but he was thinking of the many ways that Lindsey could interfere in their plans, if he came back asking questions, and found out he wasn't in Gifford. *As it stands, Lindsey only came here because of the files his half-brother sent him. His half-brother would have never done that if I hadn't come back to 2005 with the discs. Even then, he still might not have come or known anything about the information on the discs if his half-brother didn't work in Cryptology at the Police Department. The coincidences in all of this are becoming mind-boggling. Lindsey was an enemy in 2009 and now he was here as an enemy in 2005. It's like a bad dream that won't stop.*

Vince had spent the day before going over Lindsey's disc and those of Clemmons. He found all of the things that Dr. Leyland had told him had happened, before he had joined with the government, and then went to Area 51 to set up the project. But there was no record of why it had taken so long to recruit Dr. Leyland or why he had been turned down or who had been behind the rejection. He had finally turned his laptop off and started thinking of what they needed to do to convince Sandra Beatty, but his mind drifted back to Lindsey and being prepared if he came back. He knew it was foolish to worry about things he had no control over, and things that hadn't made sense to him, but he did. *He's been in my dreams, but I didn't dream he was coming to San Diego.* He thought about finding Lindsey's crushed body at Lambert Field and remembered finding the discs and trying to open them on Lindsey's laptop. *If I had been able to open them at Lambert, and saw what was on them, I would have probably thrown them away and Lindsey would have never came to San Diego.*

He had no idea whether Lindsey had gotten copies of Clemmons files. They weren't among the papers he had brought with him, but his half-brother had mentioned them in his letter. *That's all I'll need, if Clemmons comes looking for me.* He thought and remembered his dreams with Clemmons watching as he was being executed. *Clemmons was dead! I killed him at Lambert Field, but he really isn't dead. This is 2005 and he'd be just as cunning and treacherous now as he was in 2009. I shouldn't have ever taken his discs, and why did they end up back here with me anyway? They really don't tell me anything I didn't know already. Maybe I'll quit dreaming about the bastard, since I know what was on his discs. The discs didn't help me find a way to keep Clemmons from doing what I know he'll do. Maybe I'll find the answer in a dream.*

He knew that dreams weren't forums for predicting the future, but that didn't help. He still had dreams and some of the things he was dreaming proved to be correct, but that still didn't explain why he dreamed it in the first place. His dreams, that were now nightmares, had gotten worse. He had lost the battle with his enemies long ago, but he wasn't dead. Instead, he was strapped down to a bed, like he had been at Gifford, he felt drugged, and was struggling to wake up. That dream had repeated itself over and over, but he had never been able to wake up, no matter how hard he tried. Every dream had seemed to be the same, he had always seen blurry, unrecognizable figures leaning over him, but in each dream, he had felt weaker, like his life was slipping away. The figures in his dreams would be talking to each other and he would try to speak back, but the words wouldn't come. He had felt more trapped in those dreams than he had at Gifford, where morning always came and he would wake up, locked in his room. The dreams he was having now felt real, but when he woke up from the dreams, he realized he was never in the situation, he had dreamed about.

When Chief Brewer told him about Lindsey, it was as if he already knew and he instantly had a feeling they wouldn't ever see Lindsey again, not even in 2009. He knew that was an absurd feeling, because he'd already met Lindsey in 2009. Lindsey was a key figure in the conspiracy and he had died at Lambert Field. Although he intended to put Lindsey out of his mind, since he was gone, he knew it would be hard to do. What bothered him most was, he couldn't help thinking of how Lindsey had shown up in 2005, as a belligerent enemy, when it had never happened the first time. *What if he does come back and I have to kill him? He was Clemmons right hand man in pulling off the assassination of Lemming. How will that affect the future if he's dead? Shit!*

He hadn't told Donna the full story about Lindsey or the Epperson connection, and wasn't intending to. He felt, more than responsible, for the Epperson's deaths, and was at a loss to understand, why it had happened. *This is driving me crazy!* He thought.

"Vince! Snap out of it!" Donna said

He jumped as he came back to reality and said. "Sorry, my thoughts were elsewhere."

"Well get them back here. We've got important things to discuss." She replied.

She was right. For now, there were more important things than what he'd been thinking about. He looked at the two new pieces of equipment that were ready and listened as Dr. Leyland was going over the features of the new equipment. He gave them each a printout of the equipments capabilities, probable causes of failures, and remedies for fixing them.

"When are we going to get to try out the equipment?" Jim asked.

"General, Lawrence Haskell is the base commander at Miramar. Lawrence is an old friend of mine, and has agreed to install the receiver and transmitter and do a test run in a T-38." Dr. Leyland said.

General Haskell? He was the Marine Chief of Staff when Jim and I were taken to Area 51, in 2009. Vince remembered, but asked. "What kind of aircraft is a T-38?"

"It's a two seat training aircraft the Marines use. I've pulled some strings and gotten clearance for you go along as an observer. A Marine Courier will be picking up the equipment shortly. I want you to go with him and supervise the installation of the equipment." Dr. Leyland said.

"Did they say how long it will take to get it installed?" Vince asked.

"An hour, at most." Dr. Leyland replied.

"When do we get to try a test run and see if it's working?" Vince asked.

"I've arranged for a test flight, this afternoon, but only if the transmitter is working properly."

"What's the flight plan for the test run?" Vince asked

"First, it will head east over the Imperial Valley, then north to L.A. and then you'll do a return leg down the coast to San Diego." Dr. Leyland replied.

"That sounds simple enough." Vince said.

"I know it does, but I want to make certain that everything's in working order before we meet with Sandra Beatty. I don't want any hitches when we're in her office. One mistake or malfunction would be enough for her to call the whole thing off." Dr. Leyland said.

"Have you set up the meeting yet?" Donna asked.

"Yes, you and Jim will be going with me. I've arranged a meeting in her office for tomorrow. Governor Turner's going to be there also. If we can convince him, we won't have any trouble with Sandra." Dr. Leyland said.

"He pretty much blew me off at the meeting." Vince said. "I'm going to call Lemming and see if he interested in coming. I don't think we can count on Turner to be on our side, without him."

"You should have made him take a copy of the discs." Donna said.

"It wouldn't have helped, if I had of convinced him to accept copies. There wasn't any information on Clemmons discs that pertained to Sandra rejecting Dr. Leyland's theories or why it took so long for the government to become involved." Vince replied.

"Then it's going to have to work the first time." Donna said.

"There won't be a second time, I can assure you of that." Dr. Leyland said. "If it doesn't work, I might as well retire. I have a bad feeling about all of this and I wasn't going to mention it, but I had a dream last night, it all went bad for me and Sandra Beatty was gloating and ridiculing me."

Vince and Donna looked at each other for an answer. They had all had crazy dreams, but they hadn't told Dr. Leyland.

"You're just on edge, Doctor." Donna said. "We've all been under a lot of stress lately. It will work out."

"I hope so." Dr. Leyland said. "I've formulated a final flight plan scheduled for tomorrow, when we're in Sandra's office. The run will start here in San Diego, going east to the Salton Sea area, as we're doing today. Then instead of simply flying to L.A. and coming back, the final run will go all the way north to the State of Washington, then turn back and follow the fault lines south over San Francisco, L.A., and ending back here in San Diego. I know it's short notice, but It would be better if Lemming can attend the meeting. His state is included in our final run and as you said, ultimately in jeopardy also."

They all agreed. Vince called Lemming's office, leaving a message, giving the details and location for the meeting. Shortly afterward, the courier arrived for the transmitter and everyone wished Vince good luck. Donna gave him a kiss, and Vince left with the courier.

MIRAMAR MARINE AIR BASE

ARRIVING AT THE BASE, Vince was issued a temporary I.D. at the base entrance, then the courier dropped him off at the hanger office where he was met by a mechanic. "Follow me." The mechanic said and they headed inside the hanger, where Vince got his first look at the T-38 that would be used for the test run.

The T-38 was a sleek looking aircraft, standing on its tricycle landing gear. It had swept back wings, located behind the cockpits, and looked very much like many other, later day fighter planes. The canopy was open, Vince walked up the gantry stairs and looked inside. Other than the stick and rudder pedals, nothing inside was anything like he'd seen before.

"Do you want to watch while we install the scanner and transmitter in the nose cone?" The mechanic asked from the foot of the stairs.

"Sure." Vince said as he went down to join them.

The mechanic carried the components to the front of the T-38 where another mechanic joined him. Vince watched as they effortlessly installed the scanner and transmitter into a specially prepared housing.

"Now we'll get the monitor installed in your cockpit. Your pilot should be here before long." The mechanic said.

Vince watched as they installed the monitor, finishing by snapping the wiring harness in place.

"It's ready for your test flight." The mechanic said, and stepped back. "You can check it out now."

Vince checked the equipments readiness with the remote Dr. Leyland had configured and found it working perfectly, and said. "Good job men, it's working perfectly. Thanks."

A Marine Captain climbed the gantry steps and introduced himself to Vince. "Dr. Davis, I'm George Cooper. I'll be your pilot for today's mission."

"Cooper?" Vince asked.

"Yeah, that's right." Cooper replied.

Captain Cooper looked nothing like the George Cooper he'd went through all of the struggle with in 2009, but he had the same mannerisms. They shook hands and Captain Cooper pointed to the monitor housing, and said. "You're going to be a little cramped for room in there, but you'll be okay. The mechanics modified an existing housing to fit the scanner, transmitter and monitor from Dr. Leyland's plans. We'll be using a DC converter to power all of it up. I understand you have experience in jet aircraft, Dr. Davis." Cooper said.

Vince thought of his flight from D.C. to Springfield, Missouri, and said. "Not fighter aircraft. I've flown multi-engine passenger aircraft only."

"It's all the same. Just a lot more engine and a lot more speed." Cooper replied.

Damn! That's almost the same thing George said to me when I took the controls of the Air Force passenger jet after we left, D.C. Vince thought, but said. "I think I can handle it."

"You're going to like the ride in this baby." Cooper said. "We're cleared to make a test run when you're ready. If you give me the go-ahead on the equipment installation, we can go inside and get suited up."

"It's working fine. Let's get suited up." Vince said.

As they walked to the ready room, Vince couldn't help noticing that this Cooper was the same height, build and walked just like George did.

"Were you ever in Astronaut training?" Vince asked Cooper.

"Yeah, I was. I washed out. The C.O. here at the base was responsible for that. " Cooper replied.

"Do you mean, General Haskell?" Vince asked.

"One and the same. He's an asshole! Do you know him?" Cooper asked.

"I've met him." Vince replied.

"We're you ever in the service?" Cooper asked.

"No, I wasn't." Vince replied.

"Where did you learn to fly?" Cooper asked.

"I took lessons when I was in college. I needed to fly places that commercial airlines didn't fly to." Vince replied.

"What other type of aircraft have you flown?" Cooper asked.

"I can fly a chopper." Vince said.

"No shit! So can I. Where did you learn to fly a chopper?" Cooper asked.

"I took lessons." Vince replied, knowing he couldn't tell Cooper who had taught him or when he'd learned.

They were suited up and ready. Vince called, Dr. Leyland and told him to power up the receiver. He tucked his cell phone in his suit and the two headed for the T-38. Until the flight was completed, they would be communicating by radio to the lab, for adjustments to the settings, if needed. With the small sensing scanner and transmitter in place in the aircraft's radar compartment, Vince would be able to see the readouts on the LCD monitor in the cockpit as he was recording and transmitting them to the lab. The flight crew checked all the items on the ready list and saw that Vince was buckled in properly. The crewman explained that Captain Cooper could activate the ejection seats for both of them, in the unlikely event, it became necessary. Vince felt good, but yet strange, in his Marine Airman's outfit. The helmet had seemed heavy at first but he had become used to it and was ready for a new experience. They were towed outside to the apron, where Cooper fired up the engines and lowered the canopy, saying. "Here we go."

As they taxied toward the main runway, Vince saw two other fighters ahead of them, heading in the same direction.

"What type aircraft are those ahead of us?" He asked Cooper.

"Those are F-18 Super Hornets." Cooper replied. "A couple of reserve boys are going along for the ride."

The two F-18's began their run to take off. Cooper fell in behind them, and followed them into the air. As they swung slightly southeast heading for the Imperial Valley, Cooper pulled up between to the two Hornets and accelerated past them in a burst of speed. Vince had never experienced the speed and maneuverability the T-38 exhibited. He was impressed and started thinking over the reasons why he hadn't he got into flying for a living. Cooper broke his thoughts, as his voice sounded in Vince's ear.

"I'm calling the lab, we'll be over the valley in fifteen minutes. You can turn on the scanner and transmitter any time to check for reception and transmission."

Vince watched the altimeter as they climbed through forty thousand feet, leveling off at forty five thousand. He flipped the switch and the LCD screen lighted up showing the information it was collecting, sending, and at the same time recording. He listened to Cooper as he talked to Dr. Leyland.

"How's your reception, Dr. Leyland?" Cooper asked.

"We're getting a perfect signal here, Captain Cooper." Dr. Leyland replied.

Vince could hear the excitement and enthusiasm from Jim and Donna in the background.

"Roger that, Dr. Leyland. I'm going up to our ceiling, as we approach the valley and turn north."

Vince watched as the altimeter rose to forty eight thousand feet. He had never been over forty three thousand feet, and only then, with George on the way to D.C.

"Where'd the Hornets go?" Vince asked Cooper.

"They're down below us." Cooper replied. "They can't reach this altitude. Look at your radar screen."

Vince looked and saw the images of the two fighters below. He looked at the airspeed indicator, they were moving at 560 knots. He looked down, everything below appeared to be in miniature. The mountains they were crossing over appeared as ripples. He saw the Mohave Desert just beyond the mountains, stretching for miles, as the Salton Sea came into sight. His mind was engrossed in the flight as they slipped effortlessly through the air. He had to keep reminding himself to keep watching the LCD for any sign of trouble. There was none, the scanner and transmitter were working perfectly.

"How are you liking the trip so far, Dr. Davis?" Cooper asked.

"Unbelievable, and you get paid for doing this?" Vince asked.

"Not enough." Cooper replied. They both laughed and Cooper banked to the left and headed north as they passed over the Salton Sea and followed the flight path Dr. Leyland had formulated.

"Want to get a feel of this baby, Dr. Davis?" Cooper asked.

"Sure, hell yes!" Vince replied. "Are you sure it's okay? You won't get in any trouble will you?" He asked.

"Not as long as you don't crash it. We'd both be in trouble then." They both laughed again and Cooper said. "Take the controls, Dr. Davis. I won't let anything go wrong."

Vince assumed control of the T-38. The nose dropped slightly as he did and he overcorrected. "Damn!" He muttered between his teeth as he brought the aircraft back into level flight.

"Good job, Dr. Davis. She's a little touchy isn't she?" Cooper asked.

"Yeah, I'd say so." Vince replied as the nose dipped down again and he brought it back up.

"You'll get used to it." Cooper said "The T-38 is one hell of a fine aircraft. Northrop knew what they were doing when they designed it. It's called a Talon, there's been two upgrades since they were first put into service. All branches of the military use them for training now. Except for the armament, they're as good as any 4th generation fighter and better than some. I was training in a T-38 when I was with NASA. Kick it in the ass and try a couple of maneuvers. You'll see what this baby can really do."

Vince shoved the throttle forward and felt a burst of speed that he had never experienced. As he watched the air speed indicator rise rapidly, Cooper came on and said.

"Pull the nose up and kick in the afterburners and hold on to your ass. We've got two thousand more feet to go to reach our ceiling." Cooper laughed as Vince complied.

The force of the G's now being generated were extreme. Vince felt like he was being pinned to the back of his seat. Feeling himself beginning to black out he asked Cooper to take over and then lost consciousness.

"How are you doing partner?" Cooper asked with no reply. He took it the rest of the way to their ceiling, leveled out and pulled the throttle back.

"How are you doing, Dr. Davis?" He asked again.

Vince was just coming around and said. "Not so good. I've never experienced G's like that."

"The G's will get to you, that's a fact. Just relax, the rest of the trip will be smooth." Cooper replied.

Vince felt sluggish and no longer in control. His eyesight was still a little fuzzy and he realized his body was not yet in good enough shape, to handle the extra stress, it had just been put through. Slowly he felt the blood returning to his brain and his mind cleared.

"I guess I wasn't ready for that." He said to Cooper.

Cooper flew the rest of the pattern and they landed back at Miramar, having completed a successful test of the equipment, but Vince wasn't as elated as he thought he should be.

After landing, he had spoken with Dr. Leyland and Donna, who were both extremely excited, that the test run, had been a complete success. They along with Jim, were leaving for Los Angeles with the new receiver, and the results of the test flight for their appointment with Sandra Beatty, but Vince was having second thoughts about not being able to go with them. He also didn't like the separation anxiety he was feeling. He was feeling alone and he didn't like it. He knew Sandra Beatty was going to be a tough nut to crack. He was almost sure, although he didn't know why, but he felt it would take a direct order from Turner, to get her to accept the proof Dr. Leyland would be able to show her the next day. If Sandra turned them down and Turner didn't give her a direct order to implement production of the new equipment, he was certain she wouldn't endorse anything, even if everything turned out perfect. From Dr. Leyland's description of her, he knew her ego and self-elevating personality would be hard to overcome. He was worried, there was no doubt, but so far everything had gone perfect and the test run had been a complete success, even though finding George Cooper as his pilot had been disconcerting.

Despite his trepidations, he had complete confidence in Donna. She had amazed him by her ability to fall into place, right along side of the others. She was a capable as any of them with the Model and Dr. Leyland's findings. He knew she would be just as much of a hard liner as Beatty, when push came to shove. Despite that fact, his second thoughts and doubts increased, the longer he thought about staying behind to make the final run. He felt something was wrong, but he couldn't put his finger on it, and found himself thinking.

A technician from the base could have flown in my place on the final run, with a small amount of training. The equipment functioned perfectly on the test run. There shouldn't be any problems tomorrow.

He knew what he was feeling was anxiety. He had significant misgivings about not going with them. He didn't know if was because of the apprehension he felt in regard to Sandra Beatty or was just simply the fact that he and Donna were apart. They had spent 35 days together in 2009 and were once again together in 2005. He had wanted to go with them to Los Angeles, but he hadn't said so. He had wanted to see and meet the infamous, Sandra Beatty. He almost thought of her now as a Black Widow, guarding her nest. Donna had convinced him to stay at the base and her reasoning was sound. They couldn't afford to have the final run go sour. All the chips were on the table and Donna wouldn't be swayed. He had agreed, but hadn't told her about blacking out during the test run. He now wondered if that was a mistake, he didn't want the test to fail because of him, but he wasn't feeling up to par. *I've got to do it.* He thought. *This may be our only chance.*

Cooper and he had both laughed about his experience as they walked through the hanger. Cooper had said it was normal for anyone who hadn't experienced that many G's. Vince felt better about it and was laughing with Cooper as they walked, but his legs weren't under him like they should have been. They were weak and rubbery and he was hiding it as much as possible not wanting to be scrubbed from the next day's mission.

As Cooper and Vince parted company, Cooper said. "I'll take it easy on you tomorrow, rookie."

They both laughed and Vince headed for his temporary quarters. As he walked in and shut the door behind him, he felt his legs weakening further. He was exhausted and thought he might need the next day to recover and thought. *Maybe we should have scheduled the final run for Wednesday, but it's too late now to change it. All the plans have been made.*

His weary mind was rambling, he couldn't remember the date. He'd lost track of time again. He looked at the calendar on the wall and saw the date. *Tomorrow will be the 23rd of September. The beginning of…Wait a minute! Today's the 22nd. That's the day in 2009 when we were sitting in front of the Arch discussing a name for our island.* He thought about how happy they had been, discussing their new home, and trying to choose a name for it. He wondered what was going on now in their world, not knowing if he was still there, or had just disappeared. He knew he would never know, but was thankful that he'd again developed the same kind of relationship he had with Donna in 2009. *Oh well, tomorrow night this will all be over and with any luck at all, I'll be holding Donna, while we congratulate each other for a successful mission.*

Despite his feelings of gratitude, he was still worried about completing the final run of the mission. He felt those worries and the force of the G's he had sustained, setting in. It overpowered his feeling of elation he had felt after the successful test, which he had shared with Donna on the phone. He felt hungry and knew he should eat something, but he couldn't muster the strength to go to the chow hall and get some food. He sat down on his bed and started unlacing his boots and began feeling woozy.

"Shit! I've got to lay down. Screw the boots." He said aloud.

He collapsed onto his bed, feeling the reality and weight of the day slipping away. He struggled to stay awake, but only momentarily, as sleep blanketed him and all awareness of his surroundings left.

Sometime while he lay there, he began dreaming and his subconscious mind began fighting the dream.

Not again! I've got to wake up! Coursed through his sleeping mind, over and over. Then he heard the voice of a woman calling out to him.

"Wake up, Vince!" The voice in the dream pleaded. "Wake up, it's me! Come back to me!"

The voice was familiar, but he couldn't make out the face of the person calling out to him. He thought for a second that it was his mother calling out to him, remembering he hadn't called his parents since he had escaped. As the dream went on, he realized he was lying in a bed that seemed to be in a clinic or hospital.

How did I get here? His weary mind asked as he tried, without success, to focus his eyes. He tried to lift his arms to rub his eyes, but he couldn't do it. His arms seemed pinned down as if a large weight was sitting on each. He tried again to focus his eyes. The room seemed familiar to him but he was confused and his senses seemed as weighted down, as his arms had been. He struggled in a delirious and useless effort to figure out where he was and then he remembered the final test run scheduled for the next day.

I have to get up. I have to make the flight. Everyone and everything is depending on it.

His eyes opened and for an instant. He thought he saw Donna's face and wondered how she had been able to get back from L.A. and be in his room. He wanted her to know he was all right and said. "I'll be okay. It must have been the G's I pulled."

Then the face turned to a blur as his strength ebbed. His lips moved slowly trying to form the words he was thinking.

Is that what's really wrong with me? Was it the G's? Were the words he meant to ask next, but couldn't, as his eyes closed.

Faintly, he heard the voice of a man in the background and thought he heard him say. "This will relax him."

The voice, although faint, was familiar. He slowly opened his eyes and as they fluttered, he saw the blurred figure of a man in a white coat approach his bed and lean over him, just as he had in all of the other dreams. Then all of his questions, concerns and thoughts left his mind, as he felt himself slipping away into total darkness.

"We don't want him to strain himself." The voice in the white coat said as Vince fell back.

"He was trying to talk." The woman's voice said.

"Yes, I heard. He said something about lying down, screwing the boots and something about the G's he pulled. Do you know what he was talking about?" The voice in the white coat asked.

"No, I don't." The woman answered.

"I don't either." The voice in the white coat replied.

"Does this mean he's getting better?" The woman asked.

"Perhaps, but we'll have to take this one step at a time. We don't want to jeopardize his chance of recovery by asking him questions right now. If he's going to recover from this, overtaxing his mind isn't going to help." The voice in the white coat replied.

"Thank you. I know you're doing your best for him." The woman said.

"Don't mention this to the others. We don't want to get their hopes up." The voice in the white coat said.

"I won't." The woman answered.

The words of the two dissipated as Vince heard a loud knocking sound and a voice calling his name. "Davis! Are you in there? I need to talk to you!"

"Shit!" Vince said as he slowly woke up and yelled. "Who is it?"

"Captain Cooper! I need to talk to you!"

"It's open! Come on in!" Vince yelled back.

Cooper walked in with a General at his side and said. "This is General Haskell, he's the C. O. here at the base, he needs to talk to you."

Vince's head was still fuzzy from the dream he'd been wakened from and said. "I'm glad you woke me up, I was having a stupid dream." He stood up and stuck out his hand, they shook and Vince said. "I'm glad to see you again, General, what's going on, Captain Cooper?"

"Have we met before?" Haskell asked.

"We met at meeting once." Vince replied, realizing he had made a mistake saying they had met.

"I don't seem to recall ever meeting you. Where was it?" Haskell asked.

"It's not important. Maybe I'm mistaken." Vince replied.

"I'm sure you are! I never forget a face. Let's get on with this." Haskell said.

"You better sit back down." Cooper said.

"Why?" Vince asked.

"We've got some bad news. I'll let General Haskell tell you. He's already told Dr. Leyland."

"What is it?" Vince asked, imagining the worst possible thing he could think of. "Did something happen to Miss Stevens?"

"No, she's fine." Cooper replied

"It's about the final flight." General Haskell said.

"What about it?" Vince asked, thinking Haskell knew about his blackout and was intending to scrub him. "I don't have to make the flight. I can train one of your pilots to monitor the equipment."

"I'm sorry, Dr. Davis, there isn't going to be another flight." General Haskell said.

"What? Why not?" Vince asked.

"I've received orders from Washington to call it off." Haskell replied.

"Why would they do that?" Vince asked.

"I'm afraid I don't have an answer for that." Haskell replied.

"Why not?" Vince asked.

"My orders were to call off the final flight, and I don't question orders from the Joint Chief's." Haskell replied.

Vince was astonished, but crushed at the same time. It must have shown on his face.

"I'm sorry, Davis." Cooper said. "I know how disappointed you must feel."

Vince was speechless. He just stood there thinking about the effort they had all put in, and now it had all been in vain.

"I'm going to have to ask you to leave the base." Haskell said. "I have a courier waiting to take you back to your office."

"What about our equipment?" Vince asked.

"I've already gone over that with Dr. Leyland." Haskell said.

Vince felt defeated, but it would only be temporarily. He was already making plans in his head. *All isn't lost, we can get by without the military. I have plenty of money. I can charter a plane that will do the job, even if it can't reach 50,000 feet.* He thought and said. "Well thanks for your help, even if we didn't get to finish the job. We've got plenty of time. We can charter a jet and install the equipment, and still make the final run."

"I'm afraid that's not going to be possible, Dr. Davis." Haskell said.

"Why not? Vince asked

"The State of California obtained a court order and has confiscated the equipment. Dr. Leyland already knows that." Haskell said.

"How could they do that? It was Dr. Leyland's equipment. He designed it." Vince said.

"Your correct only in one aspect, Dr. Davis. Dr. Leyland did design the equipment, but state funds and property was used in the manufacture of the equipment. Dr. Leyland is an employee of the state and his designs weren't copyrighted away from his office. It was all done on the job, therefore, California State Law dictates that any ideas or plans for use within or on state property, automatically belongs to the state. Dr. Leyland and I are old friends, I hated breaking the bad news to him. I'm afraid there's nothing more I can do for you except offer you a ride to your office."

CHAPTER THIRTY-ONE

FINDING OUT THE TRUTH

VINCE WAS IN A bad frame of mind, on the way back to the lab. He thought of calling Donna, to let her know he was on his way, but didn't. As the corporal pulled up in front of the lab, Donna and Jim were waiting for him. The looks on their faces mirrored, what he knew his face must have looked like. Vince broke the silence.

"General Haskell told me." He said.

"This isn't right, Vince! Why would they do this to us?" Donna asked.

"It's just a setback. We can go ahead on our own. Maybe Sandra Beatty will look at the Model and specification sheet anyway." Vince said.

"She's not going to listen to anyone now! She called Dr. Leyland earlier and told him we were all going to be fired! She was right, they gave us our letters when they arrived. None of us work here anymore, including Dr. Leyland!" Donna blurted out.

"She doesn't have the authority to fire any of us! Who does that bitch think she is?" Vince roared.

"She didn't do it, Governor Turner's the one that did it! Sandra was just gloating and rubbing it in on Dr. Leyland. The guard has your letter from the Governors' office. We've all been dismissed!" Donna said.

"Are they closing the lab?" Vince asked.

"No. Turner's not closing down this office. Sandra told Dr. Leyland that Turner's sending Willard down from Caltech to take over as director." Jim replied.

"What? Why would he do that? Willard doesn't know anything about what we've been doing." Vince said.

"It's pretty obvious, Turner doesn't care about what we were doing. He's cancelled our project and had all of the new equipment and records confiscated. Willard's going to be the boss now. It should all be in your letter." Jim said.

"Where's Dr. Leyland? I've got to talk to him about this." Vince said.

"He's gone. He said it all worked out just like it did in his dream, and wasn't going to wait for them to come and fire him. He left after General Haskell called. I think, General Haskell must have told him they were coming. He gave me his letter of resignation to give to them when they arrived." Jim replied.

"Did he say where he was going?" Vince asked.

"No, he didn't say much of anything, except that he had expected it, sooner or later." Jim replied.

"This is horseshit, Jim!" Vince barked.

"We know it is, Vince, but it's not over for Dr. Leyland. He may still be facing charges for misappropriating state funds and overstepping his authority." Donna said.

"What? They can't do that, can they?" Vince asked.

"I'm afraid so. Two of the agents left for Dr. Leyland's house. If they find him, he'll be arrested." Jim replied.

"Did you call him and tell him they were coming?" Vince asked.

"Yes, but he didn't answer. Where would he go? He has no family in the area." Donna replied.

"Someplace where no one can find him, but he'll go on with his work. I'll guarantee you that!" Vince said.

"How do you know that?" Jim asked.

"I'll tell you later, but if my guess is right, Dr. Leyland had already made plans and was ready for what's happening now. I'm going in and go to my office and get my personal items, then we can get out of here and go to Donna's house. We need to talk where no one can hear what we say." Vince replied.

"I think they've already cleaned out your office, Vince." Donna said.

"I'm going to look it over and make sure." He replied.

As Vince entered the door, a security guard stopped him and asked. "Where do you think you're going?"

"I want to check my office and get my personal things." Vince replied.

"Who are you?" The guard asked.

"Dr. Vince Davis, I'm the Assistant Director." Vince replied.

"I'm sorry, Dr. Davis, I can't let you do that. You've been dismissed. Here's your letter from the governor's office." The guard said.

Vince took the envelope from him, and said. "I just wanted to get my personal belongings."

"Your personal belongings are in that box." The guard replied, as he pointed to the box, and added. "You're going to have to leave now, and you'll have to give me your I.D. badge before you go."

Vince looked at the guard, with anger welling up inside. It must have shown on his face, causing the guard to warn him. "I know you're upset, Dr. Davis, but there's nothing more you can do here. I have my orders, you're going to have to leave. Don't force me to call the police."

"May I at least, check my desk and see if anything was overlooked?" Vince asked.

"I'm afraid not. I have my orders. Please go." The guard said.

"Why are we being treated like this?" Vince asked, as his angered increased. It seemed to him that nothing had gone right since he had awakened in his bed, and found himself back in 2005. Now they were being cast off like used condoms and there was nothing he could do about it. He felt like throttling the security guards' neck, but he knew none of it was his fault. Jim could hear what was being said, and saw the anger on Vince's face. He opened the door and said. "Come on, Vince. You better leave!"

"He's right. You better listen to him." The guard said.

Vince realized the uselessness of further argument and handed the guard his I.D. badge.

"If you know where Dr. Leyland is, you'd be wise to tell me." The guard said.

"I don't have any idea where he is." Vince replied.

"Okay, have it your way. We'll find him with or without your help. Let's go." The guard said as he opened the door.

The thought of slugging the guard entered Vince mind. The guard saw the look in his eyes and said. "I wouldn't, if I were you."

"Come on Vince!" Jim called out again, echoed by Donna.

"Okay, I'm coming." Vince said as he picked up his box and went outside.

As they walked down the sidewalk in silence, Jim looked back and saw the guard on a radio, and said. "The guard's radioing his boss and telling him we're gone."

"Have you ever seen him around here before?" Vince asked.

"No, we've never had any security guards, we didn't need them. Nobody was interested in what we were doing." Jim replied.

When they reached Jim's car, Vince got in back and opened his box. He saw his laptop at the bottom. The rest of his personal items were haphazardly thrown in on top. "My laptop and everything else is here, let's go." He said.

"They confiscated our laptops, they were state property." Jim replied.

"So is mine. That's odd." Vince said.

"Maybe they were hoping to get rid of you without a hassle." Donna said.

Vince's distrust of authority figures kicked in. He looked back and saw Willard standing with the guard at the door. "Something's not right." He said.

"What do you mean?" Donna asked.

"Willard's standing there with the guard, and he's got the radio now." Vince replied.

"Maybe he's just making sure we leave." Donna said.

"I don't think so. When we get to your house, I want to go through our boxes thoroughly." Vince said.

"What for, Vince? Donna and I looked at our stuff. It was all there except the laptops." Jim said.

"I've got an uneasy feeling. I've had a lot of them lately, and I don't know why, but I don't think they're through with me or either of you yet. I think they're going to try and keep tabs on us." Vince said.

"What for? We can't go on with our work or do anything on our own." Jim said.

"They're counting on that and because of that, my guess is they're hoping we'll try to find Dr. Leyland and lead them to him." Vince replied.

"We don't know where he is. Do you?" Donna asked.

"I've got a good guess, but before I tell you, I want to make sure they didn't put a wire or bug in our personal belongings. I'll look for it when we get to Donna's house." Vince winked as he replied to Donna, and handed her a note he had scribbled, which read. *Keep asking me where Dr. Leyland is and go along with what I say.*

INSIDE THE LAB

"DID YOU HEAR THAT? Davis is on to us." Willard said to the guard.

"Yeah. Turner said he was a smart cookie, but he won't find the bug. Davis will do our job for us just like Turner said. Keep listening." The guard replied.

Donna read the note, and said "Vince, if you know where Dr. Leyland is, I want to know! He was like a father to me and I'm worried about him!"

"I'd rather not say until we get to your house." Vince replied, and encouraged Donna to continue.

"You're being paranoid, Vince! They're not interested in us! Tell me!" She demanded.

"Oh, all right! He's probably down in Mexico by now. He had a close friend who worked in the seismology field down there. He'll probably join forces with him and continue his work."

"What's his name? We need to find him, Vince! He's in ill health, promise me you'll help me find him." Donna pleaded, going along with the ruse.

"I don't know his name, but he won't be hard to find, there aren't that many seismologists in Mexico. I'll take you down there in a couple days." Vince replied.

Willard's eyes lighted up when he heard what Vince had said. "That's what Turner wanted to know. Get in touch with him and tell him what we found out." He said to the guard.

"There's no hurry. You heard, Davis. He isn't going anywhere yet. I'm getting out of this goddamned uniform first." The guard said.

"Turner's probably not in his office anyway. If you can't get in touch with him, tomorrow's soon enough. Davis is probably too screwed up wondering what the hell's going on, to do anything anyway." Willard said.

"Did you work with, Davis?" The guard asked.

"No, I was assigned to the Caltech office. I never worked with him, why?" Willard asked.

"I just wondered. Turner said he's crazy and claims the World is coming to an end and was put in the nut house for a while for saying that." The guard replied.

"That's true, but what I don't understand is why Dr. Leyland went along with Davis. Look, where it got him, he'll be facing charges when they find him. I'm going to my hotel. I haven't got my stuff unpacked yet." Willard said and left.

As Willard left, the guard locked the door and pulled out his cell phone. He hit speed dial and Turner answered. "It's all taken care of. Leyland's somewhere down in Mexico, looking up a seismologist colleague he knows there."

"Did you get his colleague's name?" Turner asked.

"No, Davis doesn't know his name, but he said they'll be going to Mexico to find him in a couple days. We can follow them." The guard replied.

"We may not have to. Leyland probably drove down there. He wouldn't be stupid enough to fly. I'll have my agents find out what his license plate number is and have the Mexican Police pull him over and arrest him. Is Willard suspicious of anything?" Turner asked.

"No, he was too busy doing everything your boss wanted done. He didn't get to talk to Leyland or Davis." The guard replied.

"That's good. He's a real ass kisser, looking for the fast lane to the top. I picked the right man to do our dirty work, and you did a good job seeing that he did. The boss has an agent in town tying up some loose ends. When he's finished, the two of you can go to Mexico and bring Leyland back. I'll make sure the boss knows you did a good job. Call me tomorrow and I'll tell you where to find Leyland." Turner said and hung up.

DONNA'S HOUSE

"WHAT'S GOING ON, VINCE?" Donna asked as they went in her house.

Vince flipped open his note pad and wrote Donna another note, which read. *Turn on your TV and turn it up loud.*

As the sound reverberated through the room, Vince said. "Okay, let's keep our voices down. Firing us and Dr. Leyland wasn't a spur of the moment thing. Turner would have made sure everything was in place beforehand. That's why Willard's already there and he may have had someone follow us. They may be trying to listen to what we're saying, right now. They could already be anywhere on this block, or across the street, with a listening device. They might have planted one here in your house or at Jim's place, while you were gone. We have to be very careful of what we say and where we say it." Vince replied.

"I didn't see anyone following us." Jim said.

"We wouldn't know it if they did. They could be in any kind of car or van. It could be a commercial vehicle with some companies name on it, who knows." Vince replied.

"Why are you so suspicious?" Jim asked.

"The lab is state property. Why would Turner use a security guard to get rid of us, when he could have called in the Highway Patrol to do the job?" Vince asked.

"I never thought of that, but you're right. Why would he use a security guard?" Jim asked.

"They want Dr. Leyland, but they can't use law enforcement to find him. They're smart and I know what they're capable of, but Dr. Leyland doesn't. I'm sure they think we'll lead them to him, but we won't. If they haven't put surveillance on us yet, they will. If they don't, then they may have put a bug somewhere in our boxes. It could be a transponder or a transmitter or maybe both." Vince said.

"Is that why you said Dr. Leyland was going to Mexico and had us leave our boxes in the car?" Donna asked.

"Exactly. I put the bull about Dr. Leyland going to Mexico out, in case they put a bug in our boxes, or my laptop. They could have wired both of your cars too." Vince replied.

"Do you really think they would go to those lengths to find Dr. Leyland?" Jim asked.

"Yes I do. At the Hyatt meeting, I told Turner I was there on Dr. Leyland's behalf and that he endorsed what I was telling them. Turner read Dr. Leyland's letter of endorsement, so he probably thinks Dr. Leyland's the key to all of this." Vince replied.

"He should have known better." Jim said.

"Maybe so, but Turner left before I laid it all out to Lemming, so he didn't get the whole story. Turner was down on me from the start, especially since we hadn't run any of it past Sandra Beatty before asking for a meeting with him. He knew I had been locked up at Gifford, that's why he left. The first place I'm looking for a bug is in my laptop. I'm going to go get it and take it apart." Vince said.

"Wait, Vince! I didn't want to tell you this, but I have too." Donna said.

"Tell me." He replied.

"The guard said you were the reason we were fired and we'd be better off getting as far away from you as possible. He said that everyone knows you're crazy and everything you've been saying and having us do is wrong." Donna said.

"Well that cinches it! If he were just a guard, he wouldn't know anything about any of us or what we were doing, or care for that matter. I'm sure he's not really a guard and I'm also sure he was told to tell you that, hoping it would split us up. What did Willard say?" Vince asked.

"We didn't talk to him or see him, until we were leaving." Jim said.

"Who gave you your letters?" Vince asked.

"The two agents that went looking for Dr. Leyland." Jim replied.

"If Willard is the new director, that should have been his job, shouldn't it?" Vince asked.

"You're right, but he didn't give us our letters." Donna said.

"Okay, here's what we've got. Willard's a new guy, he hasn't been on the job for much over a year. No one would let him take over the director's job at the lab unless they thought they could use him and tell him what to do. He just doesn't have enough experience to handle the director's job." Vince replied.

"You're right. Willard attended the same college I did. He doesn't have much on the ball. I was surprised when they hired him. Him taking over as director is ridiculous." Jim said.

"He probably doesn't even know what's going on." Vince replied.

"What are we going to do next?" Donna asked.

"First we need to go through our boxes and look for the bug, but I'll bet my bottom dollar, it's somewhere in my laptop and I also bet that it's always active, whether the laptop's on or not. After I find the bug, I'm going to remove the hard drive and ship the rest of it by UPS to the seismic center in Mexico City. That will keep them busy for a while. They'll think I still have it and I'm going to meet up with Dr. Leyland." Vince replied.

"A bug in your laptop sounds paranoid, Vince." Jim said.

"Maybe so, but you have no idea what men like Turner are capable of. Especially if they owe tribute to someone for favors." Vince replied.

"Where do you really think Dr. Leyland is?" Donna asked.

"Where no one will look for him. His family owned a silver mine in Nevada and I know where it is and that's where he'll be. After we find him, I'm going to go to Las Vegas and sell the penny to that coin dealer for all I can get out of it." Vince said.

"Why?" Donna asked."

"I don't need it anymore, and without paychecks, we'll need the money." Vince replied.

"What will we need the money for? None of us will have any problems finding another job." Donna said.

"I'm not so sure of that. If Turner's being used to get rid of us, whoever is using him, will have him, blackball all of us. If they do, no one will hire us, at least not in the seismology field and especially not in California." Vince replied.

"I never thought of that. You're probably right. What will we do?" Donna asked.

"We don't need to work for now. My house should sell soon and we'll have that money to operate on. Remember, someone, somewhere wanted us shut down and they got the job done. Next, they're going to make sure Dr. Leyland can't start over. They'll freeze his funds first to try to smoke him out, and if they find him, they'll kill him and say he was resisting arrest on those trumped up charges. He'll be there at the mine, so we need to move fast and get him out of there before the authorities put two and two together. It's obvious they didn't think we were important enough to bother with, other than getting us out of the picture and using us to find Dr. Leyland. He's the one they're really after." Vince replied.

"He's a nice old man. Why would they want to cause him trouble?" Donna asked.

"My guess is, someone's afraid he'll contact another country with his evidence and get them to build his equipment. That's why Lemming made him head of the Forecast Project and set it up at Area 51. That way, no other country ever found out what Dr. Leyland knew. They'll kill him and then us, to keep it quiet. They might even try to get rid of Lemming too. He and Turner are the only ones that they know of, that knows about it." Vince replied.

"What about Chief Brewer? He knows." Donna said.

"Turner doesn't know he knows about it. Besides, he'll be gone before long anyway, but I'm going to call him and tell him what's happened and make plans to meet him in St. Louis. There's nothing more we can do here, in regard to the disaster. We'll have to wait and talk to Dr. Leyland and see what he's planning to do first." Vince replied.

"Then, you're saying it's the end of the line for us here." Jim said.

"Yes, unless either of you want to stay, but this is going to get sinister and I know it. None of us will be safe if we stay and they find Dr. Leyland before we do." Vince replied.

"I sure as hell don't want to be here when the disaster strikes. I'm going with you." Jim said.

"I am too. Are we going to Missouri, after you find Dr. Leyland?" Donna asked.

"That's what I'm planning on doing. After we find a safe place there, I have to do something, that can't include you or Jim." Vince replied.

"What?" Donna asked.

"Think about it. There's more to this than meets the eye. Someone ordered Turner to shut us down, and that someone must be Clemmons. He must have discovered what we were doing somehow and wanted to make sure we couldn't finish the job. I'm sure he's behind all of this, but I don't know how he found out what we were doing." Vince replied.

"So what if he is behind it? What can you do about it?" Donna asked.

"I've got to go to Washington, and kill Clemmons, before he has me or Dr. Leyland killed, and the two of you can't go with me. If I don't make sure he dies, it's all going to end up the same this time, as it did last time, and I can't let that happen." Vince replied.

"You can't stop the disaster by killing him, Vince!" Donna said.

"I know that, but the World will have a better chance, and it will be a safer place for all of us, without him in it. Do you still have my gun?"

VINCE'S HOUSE...EARLIER IN THE DAY

"I LIKE IT, I'LL buy it." The man said.

"Why that's wonderful, but you'll have agree to and sign the full disclosure agreement. There was a murder and suicide that occurred in the house recently. However, the house has been thoroughly cleaned, freshly painted and has new carpet throughout." Judy Rizzo replied.

"That won't be a problem." The man said.

"Would you like for me to look into financing for you, Mr. Lindsey? Fannie Mae and Freddy Mac have some wonderful rates." Judy said.

"No, this will be a cash deal." Lindsey replied.

"My! That's a lot of money." Judy said and asked. "What line of work are you in, Mr. Lindsey?"

"What difference does that make, if I have the cash?" Lindsey retorted.

"Why, none, of course. I'm sorry, if I offended you?" Judy said.

"No offense taken. I'm a private investigator. The less people know about me the better. I don't have to fill out any of that personal information to buy the house, do I?" He asked.

"Why, no of course not! You'll only have to sign the disclosure agreement, and then provide a letter from your bank showing proof of funds to cover the cost of the house and escrow fees. Other than that, there will be a small amount of paperwork required by San Diego County, which will be handled by the escrow company, who will close the property for you." Judy said.

"How long will that take?" Lindsey asked.

"Perhaps a month or more." Judy replied.

"Okay, no problem." Lindsey said and then asked. "This house used to belong to Vince Davis, the lunatic they have locked up in Gifford, didn't it?"

"Why yes, it still does." Judy replied and said. "But he's not locked up. That was all a mistake."

"A mistake? What in the hell are you talking about? The Chief of Police said he was in Gifford." Lindsey snapped.

"Well he was, but not anymore. That was all straightened out. I believe he's back working at UCSD. That's what is says in my records." Judy said.

"Are you sure?" Lindsey asked.

"Why yes, I am. Do you know him? He's a very nice man." Judy said.

"No, I don't know him, but I would like to talk to him. I'd like to ask him some questions about the house. Have you got his number?" Lindsey asked.

"Why yes, I do. I have his number in my book, but I'm not allowed to give it to you. I would be violating privacy laws and real estate ethics." Judy said.

"I see." Lindsey said, and then asked. "Would it be all right if I use the restroom?"

"Why certainly. It's going to be your house." She replied.

Lindsey went to the bathroom, pulled out his gun and screwed the silencer into the barrel. He went back to kitchen where Judy was organizing the paperwork for him to sign. "I'm almost ready." She said as he walked up.

Lindsey smiled and said. "You're finished!" He shot her once in the forehead, took the paperwork, went through her purse and found her cell phone and contact book. Then he looked down at her and said. "Thank you very much, Ms. Rizzo. You've been very helpful."

He flipped his cell phone open, and hit speed dial. When the call was answered, he said. "This is David Lindsey. I need to speak with General Clemmons."

"Certainly, Captain Lindsey, he's been expecting your call. How are things going, over at the White House?" She asked.

"You know I can't tell you." He replied, and was telling the truth. He'd resigned, rather than being fired.

"I was just joking." She said. "Here's General Clemmons."

Clemmons answered, and Lindsey said. "Call me back at 619-555-3216. Use a clean line."

Judy Rizzo's cell phone rang, he answered it and said. "It worked. I've got all of Davis's information. Davis isn't in the loony bin anymore, he's back working at UCSD. He'll be easy to get rid of now." Lindsey said.

"You can't do it yet. There's been a new development to things I didn't foresee. Davis is back at work, but he and his colleagues are going to be fired today." Clemmons replied.

"What? Who in the hell is doing that? I thought we were going to force Dr. Leyland to give us a demonstration of the equipment, and get all the information from him and then kill him! What the hell happened?" Lindsey asked.

"It's too late for that. Turner bungled his part up and didn't get on top of it fast enough. Leyland had been spending state money on the equipment without authorization. The state comptroller found out and issued orders to confiscate it. Turner didn't have any choice, he had to go along with the comptroller. The only way out of it was to have the equipment put in lock up and take Leyland into custody, but, there's a snag. Leyland found out what we were planning and he's disappeared. We can't operate the equipment without his know how, so we have to find him." Clemmons said.

"Jesus Christ, John! I killed this woman for nothing then!" Lindsey retorted.

"She was collateral damage, David. Cool down, you still have work to do." Clemmons said.

"How are you going to get the information you need with Leyland missing?" Lindsey asked.

"I've taken care of that. I forced Turner to appoint a guy from Caltech named Willard to the director's position in San Diego. He's already at the lab, and he's already faxed me all of Leyland's plans for the equipment, and the information he was going to take to Sandra Beatty. When we find Leyland, I want you bring him back to San Diego. Turner's arranged for a safe house to keep him in, until we get his equipment and get it set up. After my asset learns how to use it, you can get rid of Leyland. He won't be any use to us after that." Clemmons said.

"How much does Beatty know?" Lindsey asked.

"Not enough to make any difference. Turner kept her in the dark about the equipment and test flight, and she doesn't know anything about Leyland's Model or predictions. Turner said she laughed when she heard Leyland was getting fired. She's a cold bitch, but she'll do anything Turner tells her to do." Clemmons said.

"What about Davis and the other two?" Lindsey asked.

"After Davis leads you to Leyland and you've got him, you can get rid of the rest of them, if they're with Davis." Clemmons replied.

"Where is Davis?" Lindsey asked.

"Probably finding out he's been fired. My asset is at the lab right now posing as a security guard, but he's really an electronics engineer. He's planted a state of the art listening device and transponder in Davis's laptop. Since Davis was Leyland's right hand man, Leyland will be contacting Davis, when he does, you and my asset can go get him."

"Am I just another one of your assets, John?" Lindsey asked.

"You know better than that, goddamnit!" Clemmons retorted.

"What am I going to do about Ms. Rizzo? I rode over here with her." Lindsey said.

"Just wait there. I'll send a cleaner by right away. He'll make the place look like new and get rid of her body and car. You can go with him when he leaves." Clemmons said.

"Screw that! I'm not hanging around here any longer than I have to. I'll take her car." Lindsey replied.

"Make sure no one sees you when you leave. You better wait until it's dark, to be on the safe side." Clemmons said.

"Okay, I can do that. Anything else?" Lindsey asked.

"After you get Leyland to the safe house, I want you to get my discs and I don't care who you have to kill to get them for me!" Clemmons snarled.

"Brewer said all the files had been erased, and replaced with porno. Why do you want them?" Lindsey asked.

"I'm not talking about the discs Coldfeldt has!" Clemmons barked.

"What do you mean? My brother said the discs Coldfeldt has, are the only discs there are." Lindsey replied.

"Well, he's wrong! I've got copies of your brother's interrogation tapes. Coldfeldt said they discovered the discs had been copied." Clemmons said.

"By who? My brother said he knew they'd find out if he copied them, that's why he sent me print-outs of mine." Lindsey said.

"I know, but someone copied the discs, and it wasn't your brother. Coldfeldt didn't find any traces of them on your brother's computer at Police Headquarters, or at home. That means someone else did it, and you're going to find out who." Clemmons said.

"Where do I start?" Lindsey asked.

"Well, you damn sure can't go back to Police Headquarters asking questions, after that fiasco you pulled there! Pin your brother down, find out who had the discs before and after he had them!" Clemmons barked.

"He's in jail. I can't go to see him, and start asking questions." Lindsey replied.

"I pulled some strings. Your brother's been released. Find out what he knows and get everyone's name that had anything to do with the discs." Clemmons said.

"Okay, I can do that." Lindsey replied.

"You're going to have to get rid of him, after he gives you the information. You know that, don't you?" Clemmons asked.

"Jesus, John! Do we have to kill him?" Lindsey asked.

"I don't care who you have to kill! Just do it! He knows too much and there's too much at stake! He's got to go, and it has to look like an accident." Clemmons said.

"That's pretty cold, John! He is my half-brother, for Christ's sake!" Lindsey complained.

"Be that as it may, when you get the names, his usefulness to us is over. When you get it done, and have the discs, I'll guarantee you'll be head of White House Security, when I'm elected president." Clemmons said.

"Okay, I'll do it." Lindsey replied.

"You better make damn sure you get rid of Leyland and Davis! I've had to guarantee one of my supporters the contract to build Leyland's new equipment, when Bush is out of office, and I'm not going to get the Chairman's seat with the Chiefs'. Bush is going to give it to Morgan." Clemmons said.

"Will that hurt us?" Lindsey asked.

"It won't help, that's for damn sure, but I made a deal with Morgan a month or so ago. He's promoting Lawson to Brigadier General, and sending him to Area 51 as head of security, in exchange for me agreeing to send General Johnson there as C.O." Clemmons said.

"I don't know anything about General Johnson, but Lawson's a prick! You better watch your ass around him. He's gathered a lot of intelligence on a lot of people. I already know he's blackmailed the C.O., at Nellis." Lindsey said.

"That's exactly why I want him at Area 51. His information will come in handy, when the time comes." Clemmons replied.

"You're calling the shots." Lindsey said.

"You're damn right I am, and I don't want you leaving a trail! Who's number was it I just called?" Clemmons asked.

"The nice real estate lady's, that's laying on the floor." Lindsey said.

"Get rid of it! I don't want any traces to my office found on it, or anything else, so you damn well better get me that disc to guarantee it. Do you understand me?" Clemmons hissed.

"Perfectly, John. Goodbye." Lindsey said, as he unplugged his recorder from the phone, and slipped it in his pocket. Ignoring what Clemmons had told him about waiting until dark, he walked out the door with Judy Rizzo's keys, got in her car, started it and drove away. As he rounded the corner, the first of two things happened, he had no way of knowing about.

I'll teach him to question me! He wouldn't make a pimple on an asset's ass! Clemmons thought as he attached Lindsey's name, current motel location and room number, to a text message and sent it to his best hit man. The message simply said; one week. Clemmons smiled as his message cleared his screen.

Next, Cindy Williams was looking out her window and saw Lindsey drive away in Judy Rizzo's car. She remembered seeing them arrive together and thought it odd that he was alone.

"A man just drove away in Judy Rizzo's car." Cindy said to Larry.

"So, what?" Larry asked.

"He came with her when they arrived." Cindy replied.

"Jesus Christ! You're beginning to sound like a busy body, minding other people's business! You shouldn't have taken over as neighborhood watch captain. It's going to your head!" Larry retorted.

"It is not! Judy called me earlier and said she had an appointment to show Vince's house. Then she was coming over here and give us our copies of our papers, before she left. Now he's left in her car and she's nowhere in sight." Cindy replied.

"Maybe she's still over at Vince's." Larry said.

"I'd better go see. Come with me, Larry." She replied.

"Do I have to?" Larry asked.

"Yes!"

TO BE CONTINUED.

Made in United States
Orlando, FL
27 November 2021